WHITE PURGATOR

❧*❧

Book 5 of the

Kestrel Harper Saga

❧*❧

Tamara Brigham

Cover Design by:

Published by:
Tamara Brigham
PO Box 151
Clearlake, CA 95422

Printed and bound in the United States of America

First Edition

ISBN # 978-1-7336708-8-3

≈*≪

~For Richard~
for your support, encouragement,
and inspiration

≈*≪

❧Chapter 1❧

The blackness of Lake Eladhán's vast depths and the narrow churning river that wound from it towards the Eastern Sea stretched below the northwestern wall of the great Elyri city of Clarys, gradually eroding its foundations despite centuries of effort to shore up the stones and build the ramparts down into the cold waters of the primordial lake. In coming centuries, the edges would inevitably give way to collapse, bringing much of the northern quadrant of the city down with it. Would it, Kavan mused, be as devastating as imminent events had the capacity to be, not just for Elyriá, but also for Enesfel, the Lachlan dynasty, and the Faith itself?

The embracing white stone arms at the center of the Faith offered no comfort or answers. They offered nothing but silence.

"sai móh, bhydáni?" asked the third nameless, faceless gdhededhá to have found him here since his arrival, someone who noticed him in this isolated place and thought it wise to investigate and make sure he was neither lost nor up to mischief.

"naim, gdhededhá. áti nyrráhn náir," Kavan murmured without looking at the speaker, taken aback by the title of address.

At this closer distance, Kavan's identity was obvious, even to those who did not know him, but what title he should go by, if any,

❧❧

was not. He listened to the rustle of clothing that indicated a bow and an agreeable, "chóbhael," before the speaker left him alone again.

The things Kavan needed were not things the gdhededhá could provide.

The Teren election of Claide as the leader of the Faith in Enesfel had not yet resulted in the bloodbath Kavan feared, but it was still early, Claide's rule still in its infancy. A mere few weeks was hardly enough to gauge the path of days to come. The election had but recently come to pass and Claide, shortly thereafter, had departed Rhidam for unspecified business in the kingdom's southern cities. Some of that business had been official, as reported by Sir Gabersdon to the Crown, visits to the southern Sees, closed-door meetings with city officials that Balint was neither invited, nor allowed, to attend.

No such meetings, however, had occurred in Nelori. Claide had avoided all interactions with anyone of import within the sphere of the Duke's ruling influence.

The devastating Rhidam blaze that devoured a swath of the northern end of the city had resulted in the significant loss of property, life, and income. It also led to the discovery of a cache of corpses who had, it appeared, been sacrificed in the name of anti-Elyri sentiment. Following the gdhededhá's election and subsequent departure from Rhidam, it was bloodbath enough for Kavan. He was confident he had cleansed the ancient temple of the creeping, insidious roots of darkness grown deep and spread throughout the lands, but he did not know what the result of his efforts would be. He could not excise malevolence from the hearts of men nor erase the prejudices they harbored, no matter how he wished he could.

If it is possible, he prayed again as he stared at the gently lapping water from atop the white stone wall, hoping that k'Ádhá or Dhágdhuán or Kóráhm would reply, *show me the path that I might cleanse peoples' hearts too.*

Perhaps, as Ártur often reminded him, the hearts of humanity were not his responsibility, but that did not prevent Kavan from wishing there was more he could do, something he could change or influence. Nor did it dispel the belief that prayer was the first necessary step to attaining peace. Kóráhm had written that change begins in the heart of one man. The Faith held that tenant to be true. Though Kavan knew he was not the only one desiring change, nor the only one striving for it, it did not dampen the need to strive towards a more desirable world for those he loved than the one in which they lived.

He arrived in Clarys too late for the desired audience with k'gdhededhá Dórímyr, but the man's aide, Hwensen, promised to escort him into the prelate's presence at the earliest hour possible the next day. Kavan hated the waiting, hated being away from his newly acquired family, but he dared not risk missing this summons, early or late, should Hwensen gain him audience at an unexpected hour.

It was arranging for his new family that had kept Kavan away from Clarys longer than he liked. Wanting Sóbhán to have every advantage, including those Kavan had never experienced, he arranged for the boy to study with the other village children beneath the tutelage of the village bhydáni and gdhededhá. Despite Tíbhyan's prior decision to cease full-time teaching, he agreed to spend a few hours each day with Sóbhán, and both Bhen and Aleski agreed to the nimble-fingered boy's apprenticeship so that he could experience the harp-making trade and decide if it was a path he wished to pursue. Sóbhán's dexterous fingers, frequently carving on bits of wood scavenged from the hearth or on his outdoor forays, seemed best put to good use, and Kavan hoped his uncle would be less disappointed in his failure to take up his father's trade if he provided a child to learn it in his stead. Sóbhán had yet to spend time in the workshop, however, thus time would tell how well suited to it, how interested, he might be.

❧❀❧

One day a week, Sóbhán would return to Rhidam with Ártur to continue the education he received with Gaelán. Likewise, a single day each week, Gaelán would come to Bhryell to train with Tíbhyan. Kavan believed the arrangement would benefit both young men. The more sources of knowledge each had access to, the better educated he believed they would be, and in these unsettling times, the choice was better than isolating them from their friendship.

Tíbhyan was grateful for Kavan's brief, early morning visit, his return to Bhryell, and for the explanation of the great power eruption felt on the night of the chapel's cleansing. He accepted Kavan's apology for not coming sooner, understanding that duty came first and that Kavan would always return if he could. There was concord between them, a relationship no one else could boast having with the bard, and now that Kavan would be living in Bhryell, both men hoped to see one another on a more regular basis. Whether Kavan had more to learn from the sage was moot. He had much to teach, to share, and Tíbhyan was excited for the chance to remain as he had been…the most learned bhydáni in Elyriá. The likelihood that Kavan would exceed him, might already have done so, was never considered or discussed.

The woman Syl brought to the house mid-morning, once the sun brought with it their first day as a family, came none too soon, as it seemed to Kavan that Dhóri wanted only to eat. With her own child to feed, even if Chethá was close to weaning, and duties of her own to attend, Syl could not provide for the demands of a child barely two months old. Nuryé, a contemporary of Aleski and Bhen, had given birth to a daughter less than three weeks previous, only to lose her young husband in a lumbering accident a week later. With no living family and few skills with which to support herself and a child, Nuryé elected to pursue the first means of income she could think of. Another local family had paid her to nurse their child while the mother recovered from illness, but the opportunity to serve

Kavan on a longer, more permanent basis, caring for child and home, meant a secure income. In exchange for sharing the housework and childcare duties with Zelenka, the position also offered a room and meals for herself and her child.

Kavan did not view her as a servant, only as the helper he desperately needed, and thankfully, Nuryé displayed none of the fear, none of the staring awe, of the White Bard that many in Bhryell continued to exhibit. Between the two women and Wortham, Kavan had no doubts his home would be well maintained when duties such as this one in Clarys, and the duty still to come, kept him apart.

Those arrangements, and the visit with Tíbhyan, meant that Kavan was unable to be free of Bhryell until the dinner hour passed, too late to expect Dórímyr to accommodate him. It had been, however, early enough to leave Bhryell and avoid his cousin's return from Rhidam and the questions the healer would invariably ask.

How, Kavan wondered again, could he explain fathering a child when his sole memory of intimacy with Orynn existed only as a dream about a woman he had not then met, a dream while asleep at the foot of St. Kóráhm's shrine? A dream should not have produced a child...two children if those who had brought Dhóri to him were truthful...and yet somehow it had.

What was Orynn, he mused, that such a thing could happen? How could she send one child into his care and deny him access to the other without warning? Had there been any choice for her? Would the other, destined to assume her place as k'ílshwythnec, ever cross his path?

With Orynn dead, never to be seen, heard, or touched again except through the product of their union, did what she was matter?

Kavan had loved her, loved her still, and would love this precious gift just as deeply. That was enough. Wortham accepted the child's existence as a simple fact. That simplicity, however, would be less acceptable to Ártur.

❧ ❧

Here on this wall, the warmth of day gradually leeched from his body as darkness passed, but his skin was beginning to prick with it again, speaking of the return of the sun before his senses detected the city's reawakening. He had not intended to spend his night here, staring in meditation. He had wanted to visit the náós, to determine if the ancient negativity of Coryllien's evil remained or if cleansing the underground chapel had meant a cleansing in Clarys as well.

There was too much traffic within the náós now, the Faithful and those on business with the gdhededhá passing through her doors in a growing river of movement, and Kavan, not knowing what he would find within those walls, chose to wait until evening to visit the altar, if the chance arose for him to do so. The sounds of the day, the coming of winter crisp in the air, and some sense that this was an important place to be, kept him on the wall when part of him would rather return to Bhryell.

Yet he would accomplish nothing productive where he stood. With his heart longing for family, he pressed his hand over the crystal, the half-moon pendant, and Kílyn cross he wore always around his neck, and decided to return to the labyrinth halls at the center of his Faith. There had to be news by now. He needed this audience with Dórímyr. He needed to go home.

☙*☙

"k'gdhededhá…it is an honor to have you in Rhidam."

It took every diplomatic skill Diona had learned from her father, from Kavan, from her brother and uncle, for the newly appointed Queen to greet the paunchy, sagging prelate with poise and calm she did not feel. The cold sharpness of his eyes belied the non-threatening appearance of his aging body, and though Diona was not particularly religious, it was difficult not to believe, when looking into the man's face, that he could condemn a person's soul just by deciding to do so.

☙6☙

Kavan had promised to prevent this visit if he could, had promised to be present if he could not talk the Elyri k'gdhededhá out of this seemingly foolish act. That had been a few short days ago, however, when the prelate first sent word of a visit in three weeks' time, barely enough time for Kavan to settle in Bhryell, and surely not enough time to have had an audience with the prelate. If he had done so, his effort had seemingly failed, and there was no sign of the bard as gdhededhá Tusánt and his novice-guards escorted the Elyri prelate into the Great Hall where the Queen anxiously waited. Prince Harcourt, newly returned from Hatu with two ships of lumber and men for rebuilding the city, waited beside his wife, with Prince Owain and Princess Asta behind them, each hoping to temper her nervousness. None of them had seen Ártur today, to ask if Kavan had traveled to Clarys as intended, a question Diona had not considered until the prelate's premature arrival was announced.

No one had expected Dórímyr to follow through on his promise to come, not after countless years refusing to set foot outside of Elyriá. She wondered if it had taken his messenger three weeks to reach Rhidam, if that was why Dórímyr's arrival followed so hard upon the heels of his announcement, or if the prelate had intentionally misled them to catch them ill-prepared.

But he was here now, in all of his dour, ill-humored regalness. There was no choice but to make the best of the situation and provide him with whatever he had come for.

The ancient man huffed, a sound that might have been in arrogance or might have been a product of being out of breath as his face was red as though from overexertion after trekking across the city. Such briskness and haste were understandable, whether prompted by Tusánt or the k'gdhededhá, for no Elyri wanted to be on the streets, alone or in the company of others, any longer than necessary. The rumors about Enesfel that Dórímyr may have heard in

Clarys were likely the worst of them, and they were likely all, or mostly, accurate.

"Where is the King?"

The Queen's first impulse was to bristle at the question, but because it was likely that the news of her brother's death had not yet reached Clarys, she struggled not to take offense. "My brother," she replied with a touch of pain that she made no effort to hide, "was murdered..." She paused for a quick internal debate before adding, "...during an assassination attempt on Lord Cliáth."

Prince Espen side-eyed her, and then Prince Owain, but quickly regained his neutral mien, confident that the prelate, in his focus on Diona, had not noticed the questioning glance. Of course, Dórímyr knew Kavan. There were few men or women of import in the Five Sovereignties who did not know the White Bard's name, and this man, Diona knew, had met the bard face to face at least once.

Espen, however, questioned the wisdom of equating the bard with King Hagan's death.

Conflicting sentiments darted across the ancient man's face but she could not interpret them as she had hoped. Diona wished again for Kavan's gift of reading thoughts, emotions, and body language. It would have been beneficial. Was Dórímyr appalled, pleased, or guilty over an attack on one of his people...this one man in particular...that prior action taken against Claide might have been able to circumvent?

When he finally bowed, realizing that this woman was not the wife of the king but rather Queen in her own right, a Lachlan by birth, and that snubbing her would be ill-advised, Dórímyr said, "I mourn your loss, Your Majesty. I am sorry to hear it."

His tone gave away no emotion nor any of the thoughts behind it. He might as well be talking about the air.

Knowing that women held secular power in Elyriá, she did not interpret his comments as biased but rather misinformed. They had

❧❧❧

no reason to dislike one another aside from race and a lifetime of tensions that had kept him from doing what many saw as his duty to the Teren Faithful. However, neither of those differences mattered to Diona, and so long as the prelate respected her, she was determined to likewise respect him. "Thank you, k'dedhá. It was a shock to us all, but the kingdom remains strong." Enesfel had survived worse tragedies over the centuries; unless she failed as Queen, she believed Enesfel's survival remained secure.

"gdhededhá Tusánt informs me k'gdhededhá Claide is not in Rhidam?"

She blinked, surprised by news she had not heard, and shot a quick questioning glance at Rhidam's sole Elyri dedhá, who nodded with a hint of frustration. She swallowed. "If he says it is so, then it must be. I have not seen or spoken to k'gdhededhá Claide since the night before last…when he informed me of your impending arrival."

"Perhaps he is visiting parishioners or making arrangements for your arrival," offered Prince Owain from his position behind and to the side of her.

"Perhaps, Chamberlain Lachlan," she said warmly by way of introduction. Tusánt had introduced both her and Espen to the prelate, but not Owain or Asta, both of whom were equally content to remain unidentified in the background as observers to the unexpected, momentous occurrence of Dórímyr's long overdue visit.

Dórímyr snorted again as if that was an obvious statement but did not address his too-early arrival, saying instead, "I have little time, I fear…I must return to Clarys before nightfall. I hope his return is prompt. If Your Majesty can spare time to join the gdhededhásur and me in discussion…"

"I suggested we conduct our business in the keep," Tusánt spoke again, "as there are few rooms in the náós which do not leak rain or which are not open in some way to the cold."

"I hope repairs are underway…"

❧ ❦

This time, it was Tusánt whose face darkened with indignation. There was evidence of labor around the náós, craftsmen at work in the early dawn hour of Dórímyr's arrival. A large portion of the goods sent by the King of Hatu were delivered to the náós for the work, stacked beneath makeshift shelters to keep the materials dry. The work on the roof, in the hopes of keeping the worst of the winter weather from damaging the interior, was progressing quickly. But it was not, as Tusánt pointed out, complete enough for a meeting with the man he and others in Enesfel considered to be the true appointed leader of their Faith despite Claide's election and the decision made to operate separately from the establishment in Clarys.

"We expect to have the most critical repairs complete before the worst of the rains begins."

"Not all? It does not appear…"

"There are numerous people without homes, without businesses. We must care for their immediate needs as well, k'gdhededhá," the Queen said, trying to hide her disdain for the implications the man seemed to make. "Surely you agree that the needs of the Faithful must be tended to. The gdhededhá are feeding them, the náós sheltering them, but that cannot continue indefinitely."

Again, Dórímyr snorted with a hint of distaste. "True, it cannot."

Behind the prelate, Tusánt's indignation became an expression of indignity and embarrassment. It was bad enough that Claide spoke often to Rhidam's flock about the Elyri Faith leadership's apathy towards Teren and their welfare. To have Dórímyr appear to confirm that very thing…for the soldiers and servants around the room would undoubtedly spread those words like compost across Rhidam…was a recipe for disaster. Tusánt did not believe it to be a widespread opinion in Elyriá, but all it took was for the k'gdhededhá to claim it to make it appear otherwise. Tusánt was heartsick and disgusted.

Dórímyr continued without apparent notice or care for his own words. "Certainly; that will suffice. Please, invite those gdhededhá who wish to join us..." he looked at the Queen, "that is, if you permit and accept their attendance here within these walls..."

The Queen, duty-bound to be accommodating, even if it meant tolerating Claide's presence in the keep, nodded. "Invite any who wish to attend to the State Room in one hour, dedhá Tusant. Let us hear," her gaze returned to Dórímyr with an expression that sweetly but sternly challenged his mien of condescension, "what k'gdhededhá Dórímyr is here to discuss."

She hoped one hour would allow Owain and Asta enough time to find Ártur and for the healer to in turn find Kavan. Diona did not look forward to a meeting with the prelate without the bard present to keep the peace.

⮞*⮜

Hwensen, wringing his hands in frustration, met Kavan at the desk where he normally worked outside the door of k'gdhededhá Dórímyr's chamber. His expression was pale, flustered, and Kavan was certain, frightened. "I should not be here...but I promised..."

Alert to the cold shock forming in his stomach, Kavan frowned. "What has happened?" A different aide told him of the k'gdhededhá's illness the evening before, allowing the opportunity to partake in a quick morning repast and a long period of prayer and reflection in the náós gardens. When another aide came, presenting Hwensen's summons to a private room in an unfamiliar part of the compound, Kavan went to him quickly, hoping for the desired audience at last.

The prelate, to Kavan's knowledge, had not been seriously unwell in years, and had not allowed previous minor ailments to keep him from his duties. That the man had taken to bed the night before, asking not to be disturbed, and remained there this morning, complaining, it was rumored, of fever, of pains in his chest and tremors in his hands, was not a fortuitous sign. Hwensen had begged his superior to see a healer, but Dórímyr refused, claiming he would be well soon enough and promising that, if he did not feel improved by evening, he would accept a healer's attention at that time.

That evening hour was drawing nearer.

Illness of the heart could be tricky for Elyri; it was the most common cause, outside of plague or childbirth...or murder in some other kingdom...of Elyri death. From Hwensen's demeanor, Kavan feared that Dórímyr's condition had worsened. "How is he?"

"I don't know." It pained the aide to say it. Before Kavan could ask further questions, he continued, "I went to see him at noon, as he requested...but he was not there."

"Not there?" A cold wave of shivers rushed over Kavan's skin.

"Not there...and not...as far as can be determined...here." He gestured to the empty corridor around them that led back into the Halls of the Faith before his hands returned to their nervous twisting and wringing. "We have searched...the guards and I...and are prepared to send a party throughout Clarys...in case he has become delirious and wandered away...but I fear he is not in Clarys."

"How could he not be...?"

The most obvious answer was that Dórímyr had felt that ancient pull that Elyri experienced at the end of their days, to disappear into the wilds and not return. Yet it would be difficult for a man of Dórímyr's position to have left these ancient halls without anyone noticing...unless he had used a Gate.

But as cold as that thought made Kavan, Hwensen's reply made him colder still. "Your cousin, ílMairós MacLyr, was here..."

Kavan's fists balled in frustration, knowing without words what Hwensen had not yet said, and he barely swallowed the howl of fury that clawed at his throat. He should have heeded the gnawing in his gut, the quiet voice that had cast doubts on the old man's suspiciously timed claim to illness. Yet there had been no rational reason to suspect that the k'gdhededhá would dare to go to Rhidam alone and unprotected without notice. If anything, a feigned illness would have been an excuse not to make the journey. Such a solitary trip by any Elyri was risky; for a man of Dórímyr's social standing, it was suicide...and not in keeping with the prelate's well-established overly cautious character.

"Alone?" The answer was obvious, but Kavan wanted to hear it, to use those moments as time to think this situation through.

Thankful he did not have to spell out what, in all likelihood, his superior had done, Hwensen replied, "It appears that way, for none of the staff are absent or have failed to report for their duties. You knew he was...?"

"A letter in his hand was delivered to k'gdhededhá Claide a few nights past, which he, in turn, presented to the Queen on my last night in Rhidam. He claimed intent to visit Rhidam in three weeks' time. Given the conditions in Enesfel, I came to talk him out of this ill-timed folly. After so long refusing to...if I had known he intended to act this quickly..."

Perhaps the message was delivered to Claide long before that night and Claide had been negligent in sharing it, or had chosen not to. What Kavan had read on the parchment, however, had not suggested that, had suggested instead a more recent writing. The letter was presented to the Queen the day it arrived in Claide's hands, within the same hour. There was no justification to suspect Dórímyr would travel to Enesfel so soon after sending it.

No, Kavan thought bitterly, wondering who had delivered it, if none in Clarys knew of his whereabouts. No, it was Kavan's arrival in Clarys that forced Dórímyr's hand, forced him to act sooner than intended, before Kavan could attempt to talk him out of his visit. The bard did not understand the man's motives, but looking back, he felt he would have been justified to heed his own instincts. He should have entered the k'gdhededhá's chambers during the night and confronted him, in person, in a dream, in any way he could, before the man could act. That he had failed to do so made this change in action as much Kavan's fault as Dórímyr's...but how could he have anticipated this without some form of direct intervention of the Sight, by Kóráhm, by anyone at all?

"I should have waited in his..."

Hwensen nodded vigorously in agreement, for no one but Kavan and Kyne Mórne had the slightest chance, he believed, of learning the truth about the prelate's unusual choices or talking him out of action. Kavan, however, aborted the thought as abruptly as he began to say it. If Dórímyr had not yet returned to Clarys, Kavan had a fair chance of confronting him in Rhidam if he left now, before circumstances changed again. Before it was too late.

"Are there k'rylag?" Kavan already knew there were several here, by logical deduction and the traces of power emanating from each that he could feel when he passed them. Revealing that knowledge to anyone, including Hwensen, was an unnecessary risk.

"Yes...there are..." Hwensen's blue eyes widened to almost painful proportions and his wringing hands squeezed tight. "There is one in his chambers."

The ancient traveling constructs had been in place as far back as Elyri memory stretched, and some, Kavan had learned, were far older than that. Although the art of their creation had been lost to history, or perhaps was taught to only a select few, it was reasonable that there would be one strategically placed for the k'gdhededhá's use. No Elyri would believe that such a placement would make the prelate vulnerable, as no Elyri would dare attack the leader of their Faith. Because he would require one for Faith business, it would be logical to have one conveniently located...or for the first k'gdhededhá to have constructed his chambers where a Gate already existed. From Hwensen's reaction, Kavan suspected Dórímyr rarely, if ever, used that Gate. In Kavan's experience of the man, he suspected Dórímyr's use of his Elyri talents was rarer still. Why, Kavan beseeched the silent holy voices, had the man deemed this a good time to use both power and Gate?

He followed the redhead through the maze of corridors, up staircases and through guarded arches, to the private level that housed the k'gdhededhá and a select few others who served him in private capacities. Hwensen's rooms were here, and Kavan imagined there were empty chambers for guests, for family members, and, it was rumored, the occasional mistresses the gdhededhá were not supposed to have but sometimes did. Chastity and celibacy were requirements put into practice for all gdhededhá in the early days of the Faith, in the belief that Dhágdhuán had never married and that it was good for gdhededhá to be likewise unencumbered to focus on lives of servitude. Kavan admired the custom of gdhededhá being unwed in order to devote themselves to their calling, being faithful to the tenants they had sworn to uphold. With the injury of his hands and the journey made to Gorbesh and back, Kavan now questioned how realistic many of those rules and expectations were. Had the founder of their Faith been celibate? Had he married? What if everything Kavan had been raised to believe was based on nothing more than the choices of other, fallible, men and women who themselves may not have upheld such customs?

Thinking about such matters made him sick at heart when he had more important matters at hand, and thus he pushed the thoughts into the recesses of his psyche and entered the k'gdhededhá's rooms behind Hwensen.

He did not know what he expected to see. Sheer austerity, perhaps, or opulent clutter accumulated over the nearly two centuries the man had held this post, but the room looked little different than any other religious person's chambers might. The furnishings were those fitting for a man of status, the art tasteful and largely spiritual in nature, some older works, some newer. Books, scrolls, and pieces of parchment, blank or written upon, were scattered on nearly every flat surface with the expected vials of ink and an assortment of writing quills. An open cabinet contained a variety of carafes, and the remnants of a meal, likely the previous evening's dinner, was still spread on a corner table. Nothing bore a trace or hint of a man in a rush to act, and though Kavan glanced at the open pages nearest him, nothing there suggested haste. To his eye, it seemed nothing more than a gdhededhá's preparation for a weekly Gathering lesson, or the study of holy texts, pages marked with parchment, ribbon, or cloth, one bearing a peculiar symbol Kavan recognized but could not immediately place. Given time to study the pages in detail, he might be able to decipher some clue as to why the man had chosen this out of character path, why he had acted hastily.

Or he would find nothing, and time spent in a possibly wasted investigation was something Kavan could not afford.

As in many ancient dwellings, the k'rylag was not in a closet, not hidden in a shadowed corner, but was placed in the open, on the balcony, in sight of anyone who might be looking. Kavan followed the energy signature in the room, through the opened balcony doors that made the room too cold for anyone to find comfortable without using Elyri power to keep warm, until he found it. There was no evidence to explain or suggest Dórímyr's choice.

From the balcony, which stretched around three sides of the great tower room to view north, east, and west, Kavan could see in the distance the place where he had spent the night on Clarys' northwestern wall. It was a significant distance, far enough that even if a person was noticed there, they would not be easily recognizable, but perhaps the white of his hair had given his identity away or else some other Elyri sense had alerted Dórímyr to the proximity of one he perceived as a threat. Perhaps one of those individuals who had spoken to Kavan during his hours there had reported his position to the prelate. It might explain Dórímyr's rush to action, but that rush, and the imagined need to disguise it, led Kavan to wonder what the man was hiding.

"Pray that I find him...that it is not too late," Kavan muttered, as much to Hwensen as to any holy powers that might be listening.

"I shall," Hwensen said with a nod to the already empty air. It was the only time in his life he had witnessed the use of a Gate.

One moment Kavan was there; the next he was gone.

Hwensen stared at the vacant balcony long after Kavan vanished.

k'gdhededhá Dórímyr was not in Hes á Redh Náós when Kavan stepped into it, although there was a trace of him there, lingering power within the Purification chamber, in the wood, that suggested the prelate had touched the walls to steady his balance or regain his bearings after a journey he was not accustomed to making. The náós was dark; candles refused to stay lit in the drafty room as air and rain drove icy fingers through the damaged roof. The floor, the benches, and the altar were still littered with debris, dust, wood shavings, and small pools of rainwater, but not as much as Kavan expected to see. A day's work had left this here, and if, Kavan judged by looking above, the crews were allowed another two or three weeks of decent weather, they would have the damaged roofing, the windows, and doors, covered enough to keep the building weather-tight for the winter. Painting, repair of the glasswork currently patched over with waxed canvas, and any reworking of a more decorative nature, would wait until spring. A functioning, usable náós was the best anyone could ask for as winter arrived.

There were people asleep on the benches and floor, those without homes who had not yet found beds in a warmer, more secure shelter or had not chosen to leave Rhidam. At least here, they were out of the worst of the weather, a blessing most would not find fault with, even those who might believe their damaged or destroyed homes should already be repaired or rebuilt. Kavan extended his senses, seeking the man he hoped to locate. But Dórímyr was not here, nor in the thóres. Most of the gdhededhá were abed for the night or in their chambers in prayer, but Tusánt, Rankin, and Claide were not within the náós walls. Kavan hoped that they, and Dórímyr, were at the castle with the Queen. Choosing to forgo the risk of crossing Rhidam on foot in the dark, Kavan reentered the k'rylag and arrived quickly in the upper oratory, the one Gate he knew he had unlimited access to. There were others Gates, some on the ground floor in closer reach to where the people he sought would most likely be, but he did not want to risk easy discovery. Not when his efforts to instill order in Enesfel could be damaged by a single, misplaced action.

Heads bobbed as he passed soldiers and servants on his way to the Great Hall. No one was within, but the lanterns were lit and beginning to sputter as their fuel supply neared its end. Far to the rear of the Hall, through the door leading into the State Room, voices were heard, three matching the individual identities he could detect. The Queen, her husband, and Prince Owain. Perplexed, Kavan closed his eyes and reached out his senses again. Dórímyr had been here, the remaining traces of him were recent but not fresh. He was not on this level of the keep nor any other within Kavan's reach.

Where, he wondered in a moment of frustrated panic, had the prelate gone?

"Lord Cliáth." The Inquisitor Princess studied him with concern, her gaze that of a much older woman despite her youth, but there was no threat in it as he had once felt in Diona at this age. She must have been speaking to him as his senses had searched the keep and he had not heard her voice or her approach. "You are looking for k'gdhededhá Dórímyr? He has already left..."

Had he said the man's name aloud or was the prelate's visit the most likely excuse to bring Kavan here, the reason easily deduced by someone of Asta's perceptive attention.

"When?" Kavan scowled and glanced around the Hall. Had the prelate taken one of the other palace Gates directly to Clarys? What of Claide, Tusánt, and Rankin? Had they gone with him?

"I would say fifteen minutes," the princess replied, "with Edward, Saul, dedhá Tusánt, and several Lachlan guards..."

"They went...through town?" The thought of that danger filled his spirit with fear and for a moment he could not breathe. Flashes of the things that could go wrong, attempts on the k'gdhededhá's life, abduction and torture of the sort Jermyn had suffered...not flashes of Sight but those of fears logical to expect in Rhidam now.

"Most of them, yes...most much earlier. k'dedhá Claide was not here. dedhá Tusánt said he is away, although he did not know where he's gone or when he will return. The consensus is he's visiting parishioners, but that should not keep him out so late into the night..." Asta shrugged, "I suspect he is in Rhidam still; he could not have traveled far on such short notice. I have people looking. Wherever he is, I will find him."

That Claide and Dórímyr had not yet met meant there had been no chance for a clash between them. That was a relief, as Kavan feared the outcome of such a meeting. The disadvantage, however, was that the prelate had not gained firsthand experience of the sort of man Claide was, what the prelate had condemned Enesfel, and those within her borders, to suffer by his refusal to conduct the appointment of a Teren k'gdhededhá.

Asta continued in a quieter voice. "He met with as many dedhá who would come to the keep, with Diona, Espen, and Uncle Owain. He heard opinions on Claide from each of us, except for Tusánt who refused to speak against him."

A wise choice. The Elyri gdhededhá was already in a precarious position. He was beloved by most in Rhidam, except for a few disgruntled voices and the one man who could destroy his career, perhaps his life, if he chose, particularly since Claide was striving to usurp the ultimate power with the Faith outside of Elyriá.

"He said little, mostly asked questions, took notes, and promised to consider everything we shared in making his decision."

Kavan scowled. What was there to decide? The election had already been held. The only decisions, and actions, the prelate might be able to make now would be to claim an illegal appointment of office or, as had happened at other times in Faith history, the stripping of a gdhededhá from their post due to significant complaints from the people they served. It had been done when an individual was no longer physically or mentally competent for the post but refused to leave it. Rarer still, a gdhededhá could be accused of immoral or unacceptable behavior resulting in their removal. There was little proof of immoral behavior from Claide, however, beyond misspoken words, ill-timed and awkward deeds, and the suspicions of many within and without the Lachlan court. Was suspicion enough to qualify him for dismissal? Could Dórímyr demand a reading? Would he? Would Claide consent to it if Dórímyr commanded, or would he refuse and spark further violence for an unwanted arm of interference come too late?

If Dórímyr intervened now, what was the likelihood of a backlash from Enesfel's people about Elyri interference where it was not wanted?

"Apologize to the Queen for me, please, Asta. I regret I was not here when he arrived…but he came without word to anyone in Clarys, and I was unable to speak with him in time. If there are consequences to his visit, send word at once. Ártur can reach me if necessary…and I shall return if I am needed."

"Aye, my lord…I shall…and I will tell you what I learn of k'dedhá Claide."

For a time, however, Kavan would be beyond her reach, as this newest predicament placed upon him another urgent need, but he did not speak of it to Asta. She, more than anyone, would understand the concealment of some duties, but this was something Kavan was not going to speak of until it was done. Whatever Dórímyr's intentions were for this secretive summit, removing the holy relics to somewhere more secure was more imperative than ever. Kavan did not want to risk them falling into enemy hands, whoever that enemy was, and undoing the sacrifices he had made on Enesfel's behalf.

⮞*⮜

Sounds in the night brought Wortham to the room where Kavan leaned over the tall rocking cradle fashioned of silver iron and red oak, his arms resting on the well-sanded sides as he stroked the infant's cheek with delicate, hesitant fingers. Nuryé was downstairs, tending to her crying child so that the noise did not wake Dhóri as it had Wortham. When the captain stopped beside his friend, the bard unexpectedly leaned against him as though weak and weary and Wortham, not wanting to dissuade him as he took comfort and strength, did nothing more than smile faintly as he watched the child sleep. Such moments of expressed need from Kavan were rare, making Wortham wonder what had happened, what had kept the bard away longer than intended, what the results of that time away had been. But he did not ask. Kavan would tell him when, if, he wanted him to know.

"I must go to Gorbesh," the Elyri finally said quietly, the words aggrieved and strained.

Wortham nodded. "To return the Chalice. Aye." He knew that duty was still to be fulfilled; the objects on the nightstand to Kavan's left suggested that he felt the time to return them had come. What Wortham also knew was that returning to those lands would bring back the memories of Orynn…would mean facing whomever Kavan had met within the Gorbesh monastery who had affected him so deeply. There was a twinge of jealousy, but it was an emotion easily brushed aside. Kavan would return to him. He always did. Wherever his journeys took him, Wortham trusted him to return.

"I will guard him with my life, Kavan, you have my word. Both of them." He watched Kavan smooth down Dhóri's dark hair, kiss the tiny forehead, and then step away from the cradle. "Zelenka, Nuryé, and I...whether duty draws you away for a day, a week, a month...you need not fear for their welfare."

"I know, Wortham...and I thank you for it." It was the sole reassurance that would allow Kavan to leave come morning, for being away from the boys, despite their newness in his life, was a difficult thing to imagine. Here, in this place, with these people, Kavan had found family, and duty to something higher than himself was the only thing that could pull him away.

❧Chapter 2❧

Unsure of the welcome he would receive, Kavan chose the k'rylag that deposited him in the fields outside of Gorbesh rather than using the one which would have brought him directly into the monastery. He had been instructed to return the Chalice and staff crown when his work was finished, but that did not mean he was free to come and go there as he chose…no matter how friendly the residents had been. And he could not be certain the work he had been directed, prophesied, to undertake, was complete. What he had done had been an awesome, excruciating ordeal, but that suffering, the eradication of the evil festering there, did not guarantee his duty was ended.

A sheltered conclave such as this could not be expected to amicably receive those appearing unexpectedly in their midst. Some might bid him welcome, but Kavan would not risk angering Qol.

The sky held the faintest hint of grey in the east, too early for the rosy orange of dawn, too early for villagers to be in the field. By the time Kavan traversed the ten-mile stretch of mountain road to reach the ancient structure, the sun would have crested the mountains. He did not mind the trek, nor the weight of the items in his arms; after the chill of Bhryell, the warmer weather in this arid land eased the stiffness in his body. He needed that additional comfort, for his heart pounded with anxious nervousness at the thought of being amongst those people, of seeing Myreth one more time. Perhaps he should have announced his coming, but he believed that Qol, at least, had expected him since the night of the cleansing. If anyone had experienced the power of that night, as Tíbhyan had, Qol and Myreth undoubtedly had. They should be awaiting his return.

There was no expectation of adventure as he followed the westward path away from the rising sun, striving to still his thoughts, his center, in preparation for what came next. What he was not prepared to see, however, was the gates of the monastery thrown wide with no visible trace of activity save for the scatter of chickens and goats that lingered in the courtyard and spilled through the opening onto the parched pathway outside of the gates. He scowled and scanned the walls.

He had feared that fire had ravaged the ancient place after what the Sight had shown him, but there was no sign of an attack, no hint of burning. No hint of danger. But he could feel in his center, in the prick of the powered air on his skin, that something was different. Not wrong but different than when he had been here before. There were no attendants or sentries, no one in the courtyard tending the animals. There was a single older man seated at the well, water jug at his side, who lifted his pinched face as Kavan approached and nodded once before scattering the last of his grain for the pecking fowl and rose in greeting.

Perhaps he should recognize the man, but his wizened features were nameless to Kavan.

"Welcome, Lord Cliáth. You are expected. Please…follow me."

Expected on this day, Kavan wondered as he did as the man requested? Had the man kept watch since the cleansing with the sole purpose of greeting him or had he been sent to greet him this morning? Instead of inquiring, he asked, "Where are the others?"

His escort balanced the full water jug on his hip and, after crossing the hot packed clay courtyard, opened the wooden dining room door to allow Kavan to pass into the building's cooler interior. The handle slipped from his hand and the wood collided with the rock wall behind it, sending a reverberating clatter through the halls, a sound of emptiness and abandon that made Kavan shiver. "Many are gone. This is what remains."

There were less than two dozen individuals seated around the old wooden tables, mostly older men and women plus a few who would have found travel difficult with the young infants they tended. They shared their meal as before, from platters of flatbread, cornmeal moistened with goat's milk, eggs, and a roasted, pulpy red vegetable Kavan did not recognize. The faces he most hoped to see were not among those here, creating a tightening of anxiety in his chest. "Gone? Where have they…what of Valesce…Qol…?" Myreth.

Before that third name crossed his lips, a name he was reluctant to utter for fear that speaking it would be as painful as the possibility of his dark twin's absence, one of the men he mentioned emerged from the corridor on the other side of the room, cleared his throat, and said, "Welcome, Lord Cliáth…the Prelate is waiting."

Praise be, Kavan thought, that Valesce and Qol were still here. It seemed likely then that Myreth was here too.

There was no offer of a meal today, the sparse collection on which the residents dined suggested there was little left for them in this place. Had trade with Gorbesh suffered? Had the town endured a lean harvest…or worse? Kavan had not bothered to discover how the village fared when he arrived and now he wished he had. The elderly Valesce made no offer to take the reliquary, reluctant, it seemed, to touch it, and Kavan did not speak or ask questions. Valesce had not been prone to answering questions before, preferring to leave the exchange of words to Myreth and Qol, and if, by some painful twist of fate, some harm had befallen Myreth, Valesce had likely been instructed to leave the telling of the tale to Qol.

The power in the ancient man's chamber felt diminished, faded as if the source of it was somnolent and worn and draining slowly into the air. Qol hunched at the window, his already slight figure appearing smaller, frailer, and though he turned on his stool in greeting, he did not rise as Valesce allowed Kavan into the room. His frailty disturbed Kavan, for he had not considered that even the phae k'kairá, if that was what this man was, might also be subject to the whims of mortality.

"All things pass," the old one chuckled, his voice strong despite his physical weakness. "Or at least...most things do. Some..." His words trailed off as he glanced at the brightening eastern sky. "Some die...some are worn to dust...some become other...some merely cease to be when their purpose is met...or when memory of them or belief in them ceases."

Blinking away unexpected tears, Kavan murmured, "And which, may I ask, causes you to suffer, my lord?"

Qol summoned him closer, bid him put the reliquary on the table, and then took the bard's hands in his bony ones. There was a flash in Kavan's mind's eye as power discharged between them, the sensation of time standing still, and when Qol released him with a gentle squeeze, Kavan was certain he had received more power in that contact than Qol had taken from him. "Why do you believe I suffer?"

"I thought...?"

Qol smiled weakly. "There comes a time when letting go is the best decision. I have done what I needed to do and the time draws near to give back to the universe the energy which has sustained me...so that some other might use it."

Giving back the energy. Was that what Qol had just done with him? Was that all that death was? What, then, was a man's soul?

Energy only, or something more? Kavan rubbed between his eyes to ease the sudden throbbing that began there. Knowing now, from that brief contact, that Myreth was not here, he asked, "Who shall carry on your work? Who shall lead if you…?"

Qol shook his head. "The time has come for them to pass into the world…to live amongst others as in ages past. Some will linger here, I know…rebuild what once was…a great center of learning and Faith, not shut off from life but rather part of it. Valesce will stay with them; it is already decided. They will find their way without me." With a wistful expression and a tone of regret, he continued, "I dare say it was pride that kept me believing I would remain needed here…or someone like me…but the doors opened with your visit…" He shrugged. "As you have seen, many have already left."

"Myreth?" Kavan knew the man had been grooming the raven-haired siren to replace him, to lead the people of this place into the future. But Kavan had been able to see Myreth's dissatisfaction with that plan for his life; he had been a man trained for the past, expected to be a light for the future, a dichotomy that could not be reconciled, particularly after Kavan's arrival exposed him to a taste of an outside world beyond his imagination. "Did he leave as well or has he…?"

Again, Qol sighed. Whatever his shortsighted, stubborn failings, he loved Myreth as a son. Losing him remained painful. "He was in full health when he left…the morning after…the cleansing ritual." His hand passed over the wooden chest without touching it, hesitating as if he might open it, and then dropped into his lap. "I believe he intends to find you…despite being told that you would come here if he would wait." He smiled ruefully. "He knows nothing of the vastness of the world. Your visit to our sanctuary instilled in him an unusual lack of patience. When you succeeded…I knew…and the moment word was given…he was gone. I think he believed he could find you before you returned. He has no concept of the vastness of the world beyond these walls."

Repentant to have been the chance cause of disruption in these peoples' lives, Kavan bowed his head. "It was never my intent to..."

"To fulfill prophecy? Fulfill destiny? No...I do not imagine it was. You owe no apology for the path you were chosen to walk. Things happen as they must. My time here has passed, it is as it should be...but there is one more thing I must ask you to do for me...for all of us..."

The words 'all of us' sounded more inclusive than merely those who lived within these walls, or who had lived here in the past, and Kavan shivered, a feeling that clawed into his core with icy fingers. It was likely, some tiny flicker within said, that those words included Elyri, Teren, k'kairá alike, and perhaps others as well. He had given much of himself already, faced death for the souls of others; what else did he have to offer except the life he had not yet been required to surrender?

Despite the inherent fear of that final sacrifice being asked of him, he murmured, "What must I do? You have only to ask."

The ancient man took Kavan's hand again, this time sparking a stronger exchange of power and another frozen moment. A heavy ache built at the back of Kavan's skull and behind his eyes, a sensation that made his vision blur as if he had spent too much time reading beneath too little light. He was tempted to withdraw his hand as if that would help, but Qol's grip was as iron bindings and Kavan suspected he could not break free if he tried.

"With our halls open to the world, and my dispersal from it soon to come, there will no longer be anyone to protect the holy relics. Those items, and others hidden within these halls, cannot remain here...and there is no one else with the power to hide them, guard them...see them hidden away from those who should never have use of them." Kavan opened his mouth to protest, but Qol continued. "For a time, while in your care, I admit I could barely feel their presence, their power...which tells me you have such a place, a means to protect them where they cannot be accidentally discovered. Put them there…along with those Valesce will give you…ward them if you can…shield them from the detection of those seeking power. When that is done…" A long breath escaped him but the words stopped, and Kavan understood what would have come next without Qol saying it. "Do this for me…for us…and we will be content. And when you see Myreth…" Not if. He squeezed Kavan's hand as if sealing those words in a promise, a gentle touch followed by a release as if he was set free. "Give him my blessing for a long, happy life…and give him my undying devotion."

Understanding that he was dismissed, though he had not verbally agreed to the commands made of him, Kavan rose slowly, looking away from Qol to the reliquary he had brought with him before lifting it once more from the table. "I shall tell him," he promised. The warm power of the objects within hummed between his hands.

"One more thing. In the items Valesce will have for you…there are things that may not be opened until the time comes for their return to the world. One of them is a gift that we ask you to guard with diligence, for it is a gift precious beyond measure."

"I require no gift, my lord, from you or anyone. What I did, what I do now, has never been for seeking gratitude…"

"This is not that sort of gift; you will understand when you see it." For the first time, Qol forced himself to his feet and embraced the bard awkwardly around the reliquary he carried. The man's form felt feather-light, like a bird's body quivering against him, and his voice, when it came, rang with a bell-like hollowness that chimed as though from a far distant hill. "Long life and happiness, Kavan. May k'Ádhá always be at your back, Dhágdhuán always before you, and Kóráhm always at your side."

His blessing felt particularly powerful and poignant as Kavan withdrew and backed from the room, knowing that he would never see this wondrous man again. There were questions he wanted to be answered: what would become of the man when he passed, what sort of afterlife did he believe in, how did he feel about what lay before him. But that knowledge felt too personal to inquire about and this was not the time to seek intimate things. The two maintained eye contact until Kavan was in the corridor with Valesce and the door closed between them.

Though Qol had hinted that he would remain until the relics were safely bestowed in a protected resting place, Kavan felt a warm gush of air, of spirit and power, and believed with certainty that, if he were to open the door now, he would find no one behind it.

Valesce brought with him an awkward collection of packs and bundles and a leather satchel slung over his shoulder. He carried all of it in silence as he led Kavan to the Gate. Several other items waited within the circle of power, an assortment almost more than one man could easily carry. Though Kavan longed to eat and share once more with these people, longed to linger in these halls, set foot in the chapel and drink of the spiritual power that filled these walls, for now, as Valesce helped adjust the bags, boxes, and tubes for the bard to carry, he would not have the chance. Kavan's being here was as much a melancholy reminder for these people of the life they had lived for generations as it was a reminder for Kavan of Myreth's absence. With Myreth and Qol no longer here, his business in this place was over, that song finished, that circle rounded to completion.

"If you see Myreth...if he comes back..."

"I will tell him you were here; of course." Valesce bowed and drew the satchel from around his shoulders, entrusting it to Kavan's care at last. "There are, we believe, no more than two of these. This is the original, left to us...and we are in agreement, after prayer and reflection, that you should have it. If it remains here, it may be forever abandoned...lost to time...but we know you will value and cherish it as we have these many long centuries."

Kavan shifted uncomfortably, the load awkwardly stacked, tucked beneath his arms, into the waistband of his trousers. How, he wondered, was he supposed to walk with such a burden?

What was in that satchel that came with the charge of extra care?

From far away, the noon bell peeled, the sound bouncing and echoing through the empty stone corridors. Kavan had not thought much time had passed in Qol's company, had not realized that within that room, time had been lost. In those physical touches of shared Power, perhaps, for their verbal exchange had taken very little time. "I have duties; they will expect me," Valesce said, stepping away. "We have much to do...to prepare..."

"Prepare?"

The older man shook his head. "Go, my lord...and when you pray each night, remember us to your záryph...that they will be with us, guide us, and protect us from the changes ahead."

"I will...and thank you..."

Valesce bowed again without speaking and made his retreat.

Curious about what he carried, what objects of power and history he was entrusted with, Kavan waited until he was alone to struggle against the host of conflicting power sources to connect to his destination. He murmured farewell to the empty room and let the power pull him away from this brilliant cornerstone of memory.

The Gorbesh field was abuzz with workers now harvesting the fresh crop of grain, perhaps the last, perhaps the first of the year, Kavan did not know. Not wanting to frighten them should they see him suddenly materialize before them, he wasted no time in connecting to the brightest Gate he could find, leaving no more than an eye-blink of an image for any observant worker to notice...and to question afterward whether what they had seen was real.

The speed of such a rapid transport, compounded by the abundance of power objects he carried, left him dizzy and disoriented, leaning against the walls of the narrow, confining stone chamber in which he stood. A loud nearby noise, a crashing of falling lumber he guessed, brought him lurching out of what he discovered was the Purification chamber in the largely unused náós in the city of Kílyn. The location surprised him, as did the brightness of the pull that brought him here, as this Gate was unfamiliar. But it made sense that power and spirit would lead him here, to the place of Kóráhm's martyrdom, after the cleansing of Rhidam's chapel, after his time in Clarys, after Gorbesh.

Nothing around him appeared freshly fallen, but visible signs of decay were everywhere, a sight for which he grieved. Kóráhm deserved better.

That notion turned Kavan's thoughts to the shrine on the hilltop not far away, and beyond to the distant monastery he had constructed in the man's honor. That was not a place commemorating Kóráhm's martyrdom, as the Hatu shrine had been built for, but rather a place to celebrate his life. The place with passages and chambers where Kavan knew these relics must rest, for no one except him and Khwílen Kesábhá knew how to traverse the tunnels and mazes that led to it. Their existence had not been Kavan's reason for choosing that site for the monastery, but finding those alcoves and hidden places had proven to be a blessing. They were ideal for protecting relics and texts that should not be out in the world.

Listening to the silence of the day, this náós removed from the thickest traffic by the hillock on which it stood, Kavan decided he would travel from Kílyn to Alberni, to St. Kóráhm's, to deposit these treasures before returning to Bhryell. Once home there would be time enough to puzzle out what, if anything, he could do to unravel the tangled mess he suspected Dórímyr's visit had left in Rhidam.

Now, a tribute needed to be paid to the man who had helped him during the most trying ordeals of his life. The man on whose behalf that chapel was cleansed. Perhaps Kóráhm had been unable to directly assist him that night, but one incident missed out of so many others was hardly a fault and did not undermine the gratitude, devotion, and love Kavan felt.

A steady, mild wind blew from the west, tugging Kavan's hair in front of his eyes as he trudged with his load of treasures up the worn path from the náós to the top of the sacred hill. With the weather cooling, with no holy days pending and it being mid-week, there were but three others at the shrine when he arrived, a trio of ailing men seeking healing. They ignored Kavan as he ignored them, and if any recognized the white of his skin or hair they did not react or comment. They were intent on prayer and penance, a relief as he stopped at the foot of the shrine and lay his burden down. Few dared draw near enough to touch the stone, to kneel on the ground christened with the Saint's blood. For Kavan, particularly now that he had shed his own blood on the Saint's behalf, a man who was his kin, this felt to be the most sacred place he could be.

With the holy and historical relics surrounding him, kept close so that he could protect them as he prayed and communed with the silence of the day, the hours crept by without his awareness. He dared not sleep, but as the sun sank behind him and the others left in favor of warmer shelter, he made no effort to move. He feared sleeping here, for it had been in this place that he had somehow fathered two children, without any physical act or knowledge of having done it.

"That will not happen again, átaelás mai, I promise you." The reassuring warmth of the Saint's company announced him before he spoke, and his voice prompted Kavan to open his eyes. The presence of power and calm, even the audible proof of his voice, did not guarantee the Saint's physical manifestation but Kavan was thankful that Kóráhm was here; it was the first time he had seen the Heretic-Saint since before the cleansing and seeing him brought relief.

"You knew?"

Kóráhm sat as near to him as the collection of relics would allow, his appearance more windswept than the evening breeze should have caused. "Afterward, yes. It was partially why she chose to journey with you...to help you find your way to redemption so that her...so that the others would find you a worthy ancestor for her successor."

"She should have asked me," Kavan retorted with a pout, although he knew why she had not. Even at the time of their parting, Kavan would not have been comfortable taking their relationship further, not without a wedding she could not give, that he had not felt ready for. Though he loved her, he could not say with certainty that marriage was what he wanted. Her people, whoever they were, were different from his, held different standards, and perhaps she, like Qol, had felt her time was ending, that she had done what was required and reached the time of passing the mantle of title and power to another. Despite the nervous twinge in his stomach that accompanied the fleeting thought of having been taken advantage of, he knew she had loved him in the fashion she had been able. She had proven that by aiding him, guiding him, sending him a son when she had not been required to. The boy could have been raised elsewhere, by anyone, and Kavan would never have known.

"And you could have said no," Kóráhm chuckled. "You probably would have."

Kavan's frown deepened, though he understood that Kóráhm's words were in jest, because he knew them to be true.

"Qol has given you the tome."

"Tome?" Kavan glanced at the unopened leather satchel on his lap. Curious again now that Kóráhm had drawn attention to it, he untied the straps with a flutter of anticipation and removed from within one of the oldest leather-bound manuscripts he had ever seen. There were no markings on the cover to identify the contents or its author, and the book itself was held securely closed with locked metal clasps. There was no visible key, but he hoped there would be one within the other packs he carried, for he was desperate to open it. What he read in the leather as his fingers brushed across it made him stare at Kóráhm in astonishment.

"Your third...?

Kóráhm laid his hand over Kavan's, where it rested on the leather and the clasps that prevented him from prying it open. "Do not read it, átaelás mai."

"Do not...?"

With a forlorn sigh, the Saint leaned forward and pressed his forehead to Kavan's. His patron seemed to struggle with things he wanted to share but could not. What the auburn-haired man did end up saying was, "In time...perhaps. But..." In that position, he stared into the younger Elyri's green eyes. "Your heart is pure, no matter how you judge yourself. Your intentions are those of a good man, an honest and just man. If you follow where your heart leads you...you will find your path, your own truths. Do not let my words lead you...and do not let them come between us."

There was fear in the Saint's voice, fear that brought Kavan's hand up to press to Kóráhm's face as he tangled his fingers in the auburn hair. "Nothing could ever do that, lásánai. It did once...but never again. But my heart...my soul..." He shuddered at the memory of his last meeting with Dórímyr, the accusation of heresy leveled and his reaction to it, as well as his own unintentional words that had spawned that allegation. He wondered if Kóráhm knew what he had said. "They are not as pure as you believe."

"Challenging long-accepted truths, believing otherwise, is not impurity, Kavan. It takes strength and courage to look beyond the comfortable to find what is true. Do not be afraid to follow that path. Do not fear the charges of others. Test your convictions, seek what is right and good...and in time you will read my words with the clarity to see them in the spirit they were written."

Though Kóráhm's words made sense, and he understood what the Saint was telling him, Kavan was confused and disheartened to be forbidden the one volume of writing he had spent a lifetime searching for. "How will I...?"

"You will know." Kóráhm pressed his lips to Kavan's forehead and got to his feet. "The same way you always know." Be it by Sight or by instinct, Kavan had an undeniable knack for knowing, even when he doubted that gift. "Do as you always do...lead yourself, read, listen, learn...fill the world with music...and you will know."

Kavan bowed his head, humbled and embarrassed, and waited as the presence faded. It was frustrating to be denied the opportunity to read the coveted Third Volume of the Articles of Saint Kóráhm, the book most condemned by the Faith, the one that had been, he had believed, utterly destroyed by the Faith's effort to erase the memory of Kóráhm's words from the annals of its history. Their efforts failed to erase the Saint from the memories of the Faithful, however, for the Heretic-Saint continued to be revered throughout the Sovereignties. Those pockets of reverence and the book in Kavan's hands, and another copy stored safely somewhere only Valesce might know of, proved that the keepers of the Faith had failed.

Would these words ever come to light, he wondered as he fell into prayer with one arm clutching the book to his chest? Would they be read, heard, and accepted by the Faithful?

The only question Kavan could answer was that this book, like the relics, would be safest in Alberni. No one, not even Ártur, must know of its existence. Not until Kavan could discern whether Kóráhm's fear of sharing them, and the Faith's fear of the same, was well-founded.

∾*∾

The Queen fingered the small scroll, a poem scribed and delivered anonymously at breakfast that had been carried tucked into her bodice ever since. She was not an admirer of poetry, was ill-adept at interpreting the metaphors often used in those rhythmic bits of wording, thus she did not have a good sense of what someone was trying to convey. For it was undoubtedly a message, not a random poem from an admirer, nor any sort of literary work to be enjoyed as a treasured morsel of entertainment.

She had shared it with two people thus far, her Inquisitor-cousin Asta…in the hopes that the message had come from Caol or one of the young woman's contacts…and then with Ártur, as she hoped that he could read something from the small scrap of parchment beneath the words. Not for the first time of late had clues, or evidence, come to them blocked from Elyri reading. According to the healer, such a feat required a handler to wear gloves to leave no trace, or for many others to have handled the item before it reached an Elyri reader. Kavan might be able to learn more, but after two nights of the bard's absence from Bhyrell, leaving no word as to his location except the instruction for Wortham to tell no one where he had gone, the healer was beginning to worry. Kavan had been in Clarys the first night of his absence, that much Ártur knew, but he had not been there this past night, and as far as he could determine to tell the Queen, there was no indication of when he might return.

Without Kavan, the Queen was forced to rely more on her own judgment than she believed her father had ever done.

Wrath burns
When the kid stands
Beneath the grey sky
Of a faithless heart.

She read the four-line poem once more and shook her head as the door to her private chamber opened. There was one person who had permission to enter without notice, and she smiled wanly as he closed the door.

"Something troubles you?" There had been no discussion about what troubled Diona before his journey to Hatu, what had kept them from consummating their marriage. Upon his return to Rhidam, she had simply welcomed him there as if her fear did not exist, although there were moments still when he saw it in her eyes. He wanted her to speak, share her concerns, but in typical Lachlan fashion, she pushed those qualms aside and charged ahead with life. He wondered if he would ever know what frightened her. Seeing her uneasy expression, he hoped she was on the verge of sharing at least one of her concerns.

Instead of speaking deeper thoughts, she handed Espen the small scroll with a trembling hand. "Does this mean anything to you?"

Though disappointed, he accepted that she was at least sharing this much with him. He read the poem once, then read it twice more, his expression more perplexed each time. "Should it?"

Diona grunted in frustration. "It means something to someone, else it would not have been sent to me. But by Ethenae…I have no idea what it is intended to say. Asta has copied it, is investigating in the hopes that it is some obscure Association code from her father…but in truth, I do not believe it is. Nor is it the whimsical poem of a suitor or admirer. This is something else…something important…something I need to understand."

"An admirer or suitor?" He chuckled, admitting that neither would give him cause for jealousy.

"You know it is not."

Espen smiled. "I know. It better not be." He put one hand low on her back and drew her to him. "In the meantime, if you cannot decipher it without further clues…there is something you can do."

She looked at him quizzically, a tingle of expectation, brought on by his proximity, coursing through her. Their relationship came easier now that she had struggled past her fears of intimacy and what might result from it. She was comfortable with him in a way she had not been before, and no longer afraid of the excitement he inspired.

He kissed her mouth, but she could tell in that action that his thoughts were not turned in the direction she first assumed. "There is an envoy of nine Elyri," he explained, "young ones I would say, from Bhryell, in the courtyard…"

"Healers?"

"I think not. Traders I believe…with three drays of food, clothing, and goods…for those who lost everything in the fire."

Three Elyri wagons crossing Enesfel without incident, or at least safely enough to arrive unscathed in Rhidam, was the brightest news the Queen had heard in weeks…save for Kavan's return and the healing of his hands…for it meant, she hoped, that Enesfel was recovering its balance, as Kavan had predicted it would.

"By all means," she exclaimed, "let us give them a warm reception…a meal and rooms if they require it. Let us show them that Rhidam is not a place to be feared…that all are welcome here." For as long as Diona Lachlan ruled on Enesfel's throne, Elyri would be welcome, whether k'gdhededhá Claide wanted them to be or not.

❧Chapter 3❧

Unaware that anyone knew of his day-long absence, of the stir he had caused amongst the religious in Clarys, Dórímyr returned to his chamber long after the sun had set, when the majority of the gdhededhá, servants, and guards were abed. Everything appeared as he had left it, even the partially eaten breakfast tray was still on his table. He attributed that to a room left undisturbed as he requested, as he set down the items he carried and bolted his door to keep others out. The thought of being left unattended for that long, however, made him wonder how long he could lay seriously ill, or dead, before anyone came looking.

Wearily, he undressed and bathed with a cloth in the ever-present washbasin kept prepared at his bedside. That water, and the cloth beside it, was fresh and clean, meaning that someone had entered, but as nothing else had been touched, he presumed that someone had been Hwensen. So his absence had been noted. He scowled. He was going to have to think of an excuse for being out of his room, something plausible and realistic as Hwensen had undoubtedly initiated a manhunt when he was found absent. He was tired of the never-ending responsibility and wished it would stop, wished it would be taken from his shoulders. He had been doing this for too long. It was time for a change.

He was forced to admit, as he lay in the dark, that before visiting Rhidam, he had not believed the reports of the deteriorating state of the Faith in Enesfel. He had thought it surely a hysteria fostered by the violence to which the Teren kingdoms were prone. Yes, he knew there had undoubtedly been Elyri deaths; it was a risk Elyri took when traveling into Teren lands and he felt little sympathy for those who made such foolish journeys. But now he had heard too many reports while in Rhidam, from nobility, gdhededhá, servants and common folk alike, regarding the conditions of violence and the sort of man Claide was, for him to ignore such business any longer.

Though the evidence of violence was undeniable, however, Dórímyr felt he did not have enough evidence to make a fair judgment on the man who had been, as far as he could tell, legitimately, elected to his post. He had yet to speak to Claide in person, thus how could he judge? Stern, pious, religious men were often loathed. In truth, he could not think of a single case of it beyond public opinion of himself, or he was increasingly aware of the unrest spreading through Elyriá as the people questioned his beliefs, his actions, proving them unpopular ones.

But popularity was not Dórímyr's concern and he believed Claide likewise did not care about such things. Both men did care, in his view, about the Faith, the tradition and the letter of law. Though he was less verbal about personal views and attitudes, Dórímyr believed that his people did not belong outside of Elyriá and should practice none of their inherent gifts…or at best practice a limited few of them in only the direst or most extraordinary conditions.

In that, the truth of it was, the two men, Elyri and Teren, were more alike than different. It was for that reason, as he glanced over the collection of gifts bestowed on him by the gdhededhá of Rhidam, and the Faithful of that city, Dórímyr decided not to act, not to return to Rhidam, and not to give the matter a second more of thought. The Teren Faithful he would leave to Claide…and to Tusánt if the man thought he was capable of leading them. If the faith split, then k'Ádhá's will be done. Dórímyr was tired of the unrest. The violence in Enesfel would be sorted by the hands of the Queen and perhaps, he thought smugly, this would be enough to teach the Elyri people that they belonged nowhere except Elyriá.

☙*☙

By the hour when the sun's first rays peeped over the eastern horizon, Kavan was stiff and, because he had been focused on other things...prayer, Kóráhm's words, the artifacts in his care, and the occasionally present yet fleeting sense of Orynn's distant presence, cold into his bones. It made rising and walking difficult as he forced warmth into his blood, into his limbs to will them to cooperate. No one else was at the shrine at this hour, others having less conviction, or, he thought with amusement, more sense, than to stay in the cold, kneeling for so many hours. The time spent was worth the chill and stiffness, however, for his mind and spirit were calm. He was ready to return to Enesfel, to Alberni, and perhaps, briefly, to Rhidam before returning to Bhryell. He wanted to see the boys, wanted to see Wortham. He wanted to be home.

At the bottom of the hillock, as he reached it and paused to stretch his grumbling muscles, a trail of oxen driven wagons approaching from the south on the north road greeted him. The man at the lead, a thick, squat fellow with a tangled mass of wild blonde hair, spoke to the fellow driving the wagon, jumped from the worn wooden seat, and sauntered purposefully towards Kavan.

"My lord," he said, his gravelly accent marking him as a man from the far north coast of Cordash. "I knew I would find you here."

"I...have we met, sir?" Kavan believed he had a good memory for names and faces, but the majority of his last year was a blur. What he did recall was wrapped in layers of self-loathing, anger, and depression. He had been too inwardly focused to remember most of those who had crossed his path.

"No," the man laughed jovially. "I would remember a man like you...even if you did not remember me." He offered his broad hand. "Fendel Geli...most call me Fen."

Around the awkward load he carried, Kavan accepted the gesture. "Kavan Cliáth."

"Harpmaker? Or...?" His head cocked sideways as he took a step backward, his infectious grin widening. "The White Bard. My apologies...your clothing is..." He released Kavan's hand and continued, "I did not recognize you in the dream, but I should have."

"Dream?" Use to seeing events and people in his dreams, it surprised Kavan that someone should have likewise seen him in one.

"I dreamt of a white-haired fellow at the foot of Kóráhm's shrine who'd need this...and pay a fair price too." He gestured towards the wagons that had now caught up with him and stopped on the road behind his cart. "Supplies for mortar and bricks...pegs and nails and shingles...they were all I could trade for at my last stop, and I've been fretting over what use I could have for such things...where I could sell them. Do you have use for such materials, my lord?"

Momentarily speechless, Kavan stared at the wagons, mentally calculating what those supplies might be worth. Finally, he said, "I do not myself...but if you take your goods to Rhidam, to the Queen...such items are sorely needed there. Give her my name; tell her I sent you...that should assure a more than equitable price. And if not..." He did not know the state of the Crown's purse, though he knew King Arlan had run at a significant surplus for much of his reign. "If they cannot pay you what is owed, I will see to it that you are properly compensated."

This man's face, his stance, and handshake and the sense of him gained in that moment of contact told Kavan that, however roguish he might be, Fen Geli was an honest, good-hearted man who would not cheat either the Crown or him for the sake of a profit.

"Aye, I shall, my lord. Would you care to journey with us? I could use a spot of intelligent company." The man driving the lead wagon growled in amicable annoyance, and Fen laughed.

The idea was tempting, but Kavan declined. "I have duties to tend…but I suspect we shall see each other again." He would swear to it if asked, though he had no proof to support that certainty.

"Well, if you change your mind, I'm sure you can find me on the road. G'day to you…and pleasant travels." Fen climbed onto the wagon with an agility that did not match his build, smiled and gave a salute before urging his team on. Kavan watched, curious as to why Fen, who seemed younger than the Queen but older than Hagan, seemed familiar…and why he believed they would meet again.

❧*❧

Johan Alty, better known to some as Caol Dugan, uncle to the Queen, listened to the conversations around him with gnawing concern. The night the fire had erupted in Rhidam, he had been in the city on a reconnaissance mission for Layton, who had suffered a fall during a previous night's raid on a farm for supplies. Caol felt disgusted for robbing the poor, but it was for the greater good, to find the leader of the Corylliens and put a halt to a more dangerous threat. And surely, he argued, theft was better than murder. He kept the names of the families and individuals his compatriots wronged in a secret journal, to see that the Crown, or someone, compensated the families accordingly when Enesfel, at last, knew peace.

He could have left the firefighting to others, but Rhidam was his home, and despite how the late king had viewed his activities and associates, Caol wanted what was best for the city and its citizens. In the chaos of people combatting the flames, running into his daughter had been unexpected. Of course, she would have found a way to help; Asta was not the sort of woman to wait helplessly on the sidelines, letting others do the work if she could find some way to be useful. Having watched her progress, her successes as Enesfel's interim inquisitor, from afar, Caol was proud of her, of what she was becoming, even as he worried about her welfare when he was powerless to protect her. Being unable to be her father, to shield and direct her when she needed guidance, he trusted her to be careful…and trusted that Ártur would be nearby to take care of his little girl.

Most of the Elyri he knew had left Rhidam, had left Enesfel to protect the kingdom's future. All except the healer, gdhededhá Tusánt, and the Cáners. Even Kavan had gone, something that troubled Caol deeply. Were matters so hopeless that the bard felt he must leave? Since no one in the keep, other than Ártur, knew of the infant in Kavan's care, Caol had yet to learn of it. Word of Tayte's exile, however, had reached Caol, which seemed a reasonable cause for the Elyri chamberlain to resign…both for his sons, his wife, and his family name, and Caol grieved for his friend that the violence in Enesfel had come to this. To have one's child turn against them had to be difficult to bear. But what, Caol mused as he stared through the tiny slit of a window into the maze of lengthening shadows of Rhidam's streets, had motivated Kavan's decision?

What concerned the rabble gathered with him was the collection of new Elyri ensconced within the castle fortifications. They were merchants, Caol reasoned, altruistic individuals wanting to aid the city's devastated population. As much as it irritated his alternate persona of Alty to have more Elyri in Rhidam, near the Lachlans, the merchants were no threat. Others in the room contended that the extra aid was not needed or wanted, that no one in Rhidam should accept aid from Elyri out of principle…in spite of the gratitude and relief expressed by the city when the wagons had rolled through

Rhidam. The city needed as much aid as could be procured, but some of those in the room, it seemed, would sooner do without than accept Elyri assistance.

As the men debated whether to confiscate the clothes and food and destroy it, to attack those who accepted and used such aid, or perhaps attempt to attack the Elyri, Caol rubbed his temples and hid his thoughts behind closed lids. Without leadership, this ragtag collection of what remained of the Corylliens…some thirty men with perhaps another dozen not in attendance…was spiraling out of control. Layton's condition was gradually worsening, the blood poisoning of his improperly tended injury eating through his body. If he died, the Corylliens would become a riot looking to erupt or else would collapse into such disarray that they would be quickly caught and put down. While that would not be a bad thing, it would leave the Crown without Anri Heward in chains, and as long as that man remained to recruit others to his cause, the violence would never end.

These men refused to listen to Caol, some because they viewed him as the newcomer, some because they felt they knew how best to proceed, some because they did not trust him, and others because they coveted the right-hand status he had worked hard to obtain from Layton. Layton either could not or would not appoint someone to lead in his stead and continued to act as if he was capable of guiding the group he had led since their formation. Caol hoped Layton's inaction would prompt Heward to step up to lead them. It would prove dangerous, both to the citizens of Rhidam and to Caol, but it would put a man to the name that he could then relay to his daughter and the Queen to allow the final arrests to be made and the Coryllien threat to be put down. Then Caol could go home to his daughter, see his granddaughter for the first time, go back to being himself, whether Inquisitor or not.

Catching the tail end of someone's suggestion from beneath his private thoughts, Caol straightened on his stool and stared at the speaker in disbelief. "That is madness! That would be suicide. Even if some of us could get inside…"

"There are places along the wall we could…"

"…get yourselves killed…"

"Alty," someone barked, a big man who fancied himself a leader because of his size, a man who often used it to muscle his point of view onto others. "We can do this. If you don't want to help, butt out…but don't tell us what we can do. All it takes is planning…"

And a huge amount of luck, Caol thought with a scowl, slouching on the stool before getting to his feet and leaving the room. He did not want to be part of this folly. Someone followed, he could hear footsteps behind him, but when they seemed satisfied that he was leaving and not sneaking off to cause trouble, the footsteps returned to the room to participate in the planning. Caol, utilizing every skill the Association had taught him, circled around, found a place of concealment, and absorbed the finalized details of the 'plan' the gaggle came up with. He might have left them to it, as it was a plan likely to get some, or all, of them captured or killed. But it was also, if they succeeded even in part, a plan that could result in the slaughter of innocents, and for that reason, Caol listened and made plans of his own. Succeed or fail, the risk to his cover was worth the need to subvert the horror he overheard.

"Lord Cliáth…we were not expecting you."

The fidgety man who ran his home and lands had served as steward since Prince Muir and King Arlan bestowed the Alberni dukedom on Kavan. He was nearing the age where he would be ineffectual in many of his duties, losing his sight at a steady rate, but he had three sons to aid him, men Kavan had known and trusted for most of their lives. For now, the bard relied on Martin Darys' sharp mind to manage the estate for the foreseeable future. The oldest son would one day take his father's place while the youngest two retained their current positions, an arrangement they were all amenable to. The family received substantial income from the properties they managed, significant freedoms in their daily lives, and the trust of the duke that benefited them in ways beyond financial gain and parcels of land.

The Darys were gradually becoming landholders of means in their own right, an outcome Kavan was happy to contribute to in exchange for the loyalty they showed.

"I know, Mister Dary…it is an unexpected deviation. I have business at the náos and wished to see how you are, how the estate is fairing, while I am in Alberni."

The old man nodded, his wispy white hair flopping as his head bobbed. He had known that the time would come when his employer no longer felt safe in Enesfel, when he would be forced to leave the Alberni estate in his steward's hands. Life had been good for the Darys here, and he and his family would do everything in their power to protect their home, and their duke, wherever he chose to reside. But Martin had not expected to see Kavan so soon after his departure for Bhryell.

"You know they are good, my lord…"

"And you know you can reach me by…"

"The dedhá, yes…" Martin frowned. "Are you expecting trouble, my lord? Should we be concerned?"

Kavan smiled softly. "Expect, no…do not take my visit as a bad omen. As matters shift and settle in Enesfel, trouble is a possibility we cannot overlook, but I do not foresee trouble for your family."

Martin closed his hands around Kavan's. "Praise be for that…but we are ready for it should it come. The men Captain Delamo trained have been training others…should any troublemakers wander here, we will deal with them without fail."

His protectiveness eased some of Kavan's worries, though not those for the Darys themselves. "Please inform Tulda and Ninette that I will join your family for dinner. I will tend my business at St. Kóráhm's and return before evening."

The request from a lord, to share his meal with the staff, would sound odd to many others. Kavan, however, often dined with his staff when in Alberni; it was a normal request and Martin bowed and retreated to obey. For Martin, his wife and sons…who were wed with children of their own who also assisted in the estate's upkeep…and his daughter married to the captain of the Alberni Guard, such meals made for a full table. One additional place at the table made little difference in preparation.

The short stroll from the manor, his packs now reorganized to make carrying easier, allowed Kavan to enjoy the encroaching winter's air and greet some of the people whose lives his estate protected. Men and women welcomed him, children smiled, waved, or came to touch him, and at the chellé gate, visitors parted to allow him unobstructed entrance. It was a warmer, more satisfying greeting than he received in Bhryell, or anywhere, proving once more that Alberni was more his home than anywhere else in the Sovereignties. Someday, perhaps, he would spend more time here. Perhaps when Enesfel settled into peace he would bring the boys to Alberni and make this their home. It was a thought, he mused as he waved to the people beyond the closing gates, worthy of consideration.

The gdhededhá of St. Kóráhm's bowed, smiled, or gave quiet welcome as well, with few prone to exuberant greetings. He was grateful for it. Whatever they thought of his particular interpretations of Faith, interpretations he was willing to discuss with these men and women whenever they wished, no one ever challenged him with hostility. None called him heretic and none spoke of the miracles that had, in days passed, been delivered through his hands. Here he was no different from them, a man seeking truth and tranquility. Only his position as the patron who provided the funds and inspiration for their home, set him apart.

No one stopped him or offered to assist with his burden as he made his way to the door kept locked with both a physical key and an Elyri key he had taught only one other person to use. The physical keys, flat notched discs with a stylized K upon them, fit in the palm of a man's hand; Kavan and gdhededhá Kesábhá each had one of two he had created. Kavan kept his in the estate house in a location known to no one else, though he was beginning to rethink that location as well as the need for an additional key. Should a hostile force overrun his manor or the chellé, how would he get to it?

Fortunately, he thought as he palmed the disc into the corresponding indentation on the wall and channeled energy through it to snap and unbind the mechanisms that kept the door sealed, there was another way in as well, a way only he knew. He had shown no one the Gate here, had not even told Khwílen about it. Some day he might share that knowledge too, but not yet.

The corridor behind the engraved stone panel that disguised the door was a gradually sloping path down into the earth, with unlit lanterns on the walls positioned about twenty feet apart or at any point where the path twisted, turned, or branched off. None held candles or oil or any trace of a flammable substance when Kavan discovered them, causing him to wonder how old this labyrinth and its unending cavern were. He guessed it had been built within the same span of years as the tunnels below the Lachlan keep, some time long before the structures above them were put into place. The above-ground buildings were likely built to protect what was below.

Having been here many times since his discovery, Kavan knew which narrowing forks in the path to take. He needed no light for the trek as he had memorized the layout and could follow the glow of power that radiated from far ahead with his eyes closed. With only the sounds of his footsteps, his heartbeat, and his breathing to echo back to his ears; he was far enough beneath the ground that the peeling of the náós bells did not reach here. It was an isolating sensation, the silence, the cold air, the darkness. Anyone afraid of such things would go mad before reaching the end.

Eventually, he stopped, turned to his left, and stooped into a crawlspace easily missed the first time he was here. The items he carried made the fit too tight to pass; he put the items on the smooth worn rock before him and pushed them along as he crawled. Experience told him how far he had to travel before tumbling the six or more feet to the ground beneath the lip of the passage, the goods he had brought with him dropping out first. The familiar sound of crumbling bone, the remains of those who either had failed on their quest to come here or had, perhaps, been left to die a maddening death, echoed in the cavern.

There were no frightening ghosts, however, no spirits of ill-intent, no dark energies to block his progress. He had cleared a path to avoid landing on and breaking what could have been sacred remains, but the recent earthquake, felt as far away as Bhryell, had disturbed the bones and scattered some in his way. Fortunately, there had been no damage to the Alberni estate, or the town, and none, as far as he knew, to St. Kóráhm's. He wondered if Kóráhm had been here to protect this place dedicated in his name and the people who served him since he had been unable to be with Kavan the night of that cleansing.

Unscathed and clearheaded, Kavan got to his feet, retrieved his fallen collection, found the wall and tunnel behind him with his hand, and centered his back to it. He needed no light to know there was a chasm running across the cavern ahead, splitting the room in two, a chasm too wide for any man to jump without a running start…and there was not enough room on either side to permit that. What a light source would reveal would be no visible means of crossing the nearly eight-foot gorge. No doubt, there were bones at the bottom of it as well, broken and mangled from the unexpected drop or failed attempts to leap the distance.

The chasm he had crossed when in search of k'ílshwythnec had hinted how to maneuver such a challenge, and cautious exploration had revealed where the unmarked, unseen bridge was. Half a step to his right, a deep breath to brace his faith, and a short prayer that the trembling earth had not displaced the path, and he took three long, quick steps forward…

…onto solid ground over the chasm. His breath gushed out in relief that nothing had changed and he continued forward unhindered. The bridge was wide enough to cross normally, but even faith would not allow him anything faster than short cautious steps. Faith did not, he believed, necessitate foolish risk or preclude prudence. By using the same measured steps each time, he knew when he was safely across. After laying the packs at his feet, he opened his palm and his handlight dispelled the darkness.

Built over the face of the wall ahead, extending across the three faces of this side of the chasm, was thick iron grating and sets of gilded doors that protected the openings in the stone behind them. The shelves carved into the rock were empty when Kavan discovered them but, suspecting that they had once housed holy relics and manuscripts, he cleaned them of dust, consecrated them again for the purpose he intended, and brought many of St. Kóráhm's rarest texts to store here. The room was dry and cool, protected from the elements, thus he did not fear mold or rot. This far beneath the surface, in a stone cavern he believed no one, not even the worms could access, he was confident that anything stored here, including the Articles of Kóráhm the Faith had banned, would be safe. This was where the Coryllien daggers were kept, where he had stored the Chalice and staff pieces before, and per Qol's request, it was where he put those precious items now. If this place had shielded their power so that Qol was unable to easily feel them, it was the most secure place for them, and for the things Qol and Valesce had entrusted to him, to be stored.

Unbinding the tangle of power threads he used to secure the doors, a complicated process for anyone else but easy for him, Kavan centered the reliquary in one nook, the staff pieces in another, and the broken dagger hilt beside the still intact daggers in a third. Other objects, boxed or bound in protective canvas, still uninvestigated as he had not had time or opportunity to study them, were likewise given shelter. Lastly, from the satchel over his shoulder, the book he longed to read but had been discouraged from, was brought into the air. Even without Qol's and Kóráhm's warnings, he had no key to unlock the clasp and he did not have the heart to break such an ancient, treasured piece of history. It had been locked for a reason, perhaps by Kóráhm, perhaps by Qol, and despite Kavan's disappointment, locked it would stay.

After wrapping the book in the cloth that had absorbed his blood during the cleansing, crimson-brown now instead of the white it had been, Kavan stepped back and closed the grated doors, relocked them with woven threads of power, and stared with a sigh and his fingers curled around the metal. With the cleansing behind him and the relics safely bestowed, Qol, his centuries of knowledge and wisdom, would be lost to the world…if indeed he had not departed it already…with Myreth lost to his own journey, and Orynn likewise gone, a chapter of Kavan's life was closed. There was no use in looking back, in reliving pain, in chasing the shadows of memory that were forever beyond his reach.

Backing up two steps, Kavan felt for the energy beneath his feet, the energy of the k'rylag he knew was there. He could have Gated in; he had before. But today, perhaps because of the earthquake, or at least the cleansing, he had felt the need to walk the path, to carry the Chalice of Llyr those final steps towards its resting place. Facing the challenges of the path in the dark had felt necessary. And now it was done. It was time to share a meal with his people and return to Bhryell where others worried for him in their waiting.

☙*☙

Throughout the day he fretted, doing as the Queen asked, with the help of Sir Gabersdon. He showed the young Bhryell emissaries around the castle grounds, explaining the history of Elyri in the Lachlan court and Rhidam, and explaining the toll the great fire had taken so that they would know how their donations would be used. It was a task much better suited to his cousin, but Kavan was not here. Kavan was not anywhere that Ártur could find him although he had tried. He grumbled about it to Wortham, swearing that if his cousin had not returned by nightfall he was going to search regardless of the risk, even though he had no idea where to begin. Knowing he could do no such thing, however, made for a meaningless threat, making the healer fret more, and with the young ones from Bhryell here, due to return home themselves later this night after the feast the Queen had planned, he would not be returning home until late as it was. Syl made an exception for his lateness tonight because she knew many of those youngsters who had taken supplies to Rhidam and felt it was important that Ártur remained with them as a show of good faith.

The feast was set, tables brought into the courtyard as had been occasionally done during King Arlan's reign, to take advantage of the unseasonably warm evening and the night's full moon. Winter was nipping hard at the heels of summer, but this break in the chill had come at a fortuitous time.

As crews of soldiers and townspeople came and went far into the night and early in the morning, distributing materials and assisting in the rebuilding efforts, the gates to the keep were often open, the palace guard tripled accordingly to protect the Queen and her staff. They kept watch as a semi-circle of tables was erected near to the main doors of the castle, allowing the Queen and her guests an easy escape as necessary, placed far enough from the gates and walls to be safe from potential threats.

Or so everyone, including General Agis who had organized the placement, believed. Her guests were seated about her, engaged in merry conversation, relaxed and feeling welcome and safe in this haven where violence was absent. When a group of twelve workmen came through the gates, leading the horses and wagons the Elyri had brought with them back from the center of town where the supplies had been offloaded, there was no visible cause for concern. The men stopped, fussed with the animals and their riggings for several minutes as if waiting for someone to direct them to where the animals and carts would be kept for the night, but the palace staff was busy with their guests, and those sentries visible around them appeared to have duties other than aiding the wagoneers.

There was no interest in them or cause for concern until, with the sudden cry of "For Coryllien!" the twelve stepped away from the horses and wagons, weapons drawn, and opened their attack on the Queen's guests, a war waged with bows, slingshots, and rocks. More projectiles rained from the walls, and as soldiers, unprepared for such a brazen effort, scrambled into action, and servants threw themselves either on top of guests to protect them or pushed others through the open doors of the castle, another nearly dozen men burst through the open main gates with spears, clubs, and battered swords.

The screaming chaos and the glow of flame were detectable from outside the castle when Caol reached the scene. Heartsick, he listened and watched as soldiers from the nearest worksites in Rhidam rushed past to subdue the attackers within the courtyard. He was too late. The warning he had sent to the Queen appeared not to have arrived in time. He wanted to help, to protect his daughter, his niece, his friends, but as he carried only a knife, his efforts would be of little use. Nor could he risk being recognized, risk blowing his undercover status with the Corylliens. He could but pray as he watched, reevaluate the logic of his efforts and position, and hope that at least one of those attackers fled past him so that he might slit them open like the treasonous wretches they were.

Queen Diona was pushed, along with others, through the front doors and instructed by Chancellor McGranis to take refuge upstairs. Perhaps she should have gone up with her guests, but with Espen and Owain barring the doorway and Balint swinging his sword in the melee to prevent anyone from getting near the doors, she felt confident that no attackers would breach the castle. The shouts and clash of metal were short-lived, save for the cries of men throwing water on the burning tables where she and her guests had been dining moments before. Ártur stayed at her side, as did Physician Talis, both men knowing there would be injured in the courtyard and both willing to do what they could to protect the woman between them.

It was those injured that concerned the Queen.

"Clear," General Agis called from the middle of the courtyard, blood-spattered, towering in the midst of groaning, writhing bodies that he had happily butchered. They had made him look the fool, and he was in no mood to be merciful. Some of his men were injured, but none fatally, he presumed, unless they died of complications should the healers not get to them in time. A great number of the attackers, eighteen in total, had been slaughtered, another eight captured and currently held with their backs against the gatehouse, some bleeding, some disoriented, but each conscious enough to take stock of the chaos they had caused and to suffer the consequences of their actions with full awareness. In front of the castle doors lay a tangle of bodies, twisted and entwined, men and women who had tried unsuccessfully to reach safety or had stayed to protect others. Serving staff, pages, ladies in waiting, and Elyri, six of the nine, all of who had not been lucky enough to make it to safety or who had been struck in the initial attack.

It was into that tangle that Ártur and Rouvyn waded, heedless of the blood as they sought anyone, Teren or Elyri, who clung to life. One of those Elyri thought dead still lived, and three Teren, including the young page Peter, and thanks to the healers' quick work, the four would survive. The rest, fifteen individuals in total, succumbed to their injuries before aid reached them, and Asta, who picked her way through the bodies examining everything with an eye too calloused for a woman her age, sought clues as to who these attackers had been. The one clue, the shout that had precipitated the attack, still rang in her ears, and she prayed, as she turned to the bodies of the attackers, that her father was not among them...and that the lack of warning of this assault did not mean that harm had befallen him.

She already knew he was not one of the living held under the General's watchful guard.

"This is an outrage!" the Queen bellowed, stomping behind Asta, trusting her cousin to make sure her path was safe. "How dare they attack in my home!" She knew from the dead around the burned, demolished tables, that she had not been the target, that the Elyri she had welcomed had been the objective of the attack, but an assault on any within her walls, in her care, was an attack on the Crown in her view, and it was sheer luck that she had not been injured or killed.

Claide would have liked that, no doubt.

"Not many escaped us," the General growled. "Lord Gabersdon and Justice Corbin are in pursuit of those who were on the wall...three by our count...and I do not think any made it out through the gates."

"I want each of them flogged...in the square...tomorrow." She could not look at them, afraid that Caol could be there and that she could be condemning her uncle to suffering and death. "I want the pillory set...and each of them left there under guard." At least, she thought, until she came up with some other more humiliating torture and torment for them. Straightforward execution was too good for traitors such as these, and after months of civil unrest, of actions against Enesfel, against her family, friends, and staff, the newly anointed Queen had seen enough. If people viewed whatever punishments she devised as cruelly excessive, at least for such treasonous cases against the Crown and kingdom, then perhaps the whole of Enesfel would think twice before crossing her.

"Diona…"

She shot her husband a perturbed look. If he wished to discuss this with her, she would hear him in private, but she would not tolerate debate or disagreement before her soldiers and the prisoners.

Instead of disagreeing, however, Espen said, "Perhaps they should be read first…while they are fit to be read?"

"I don't care what they know! They are Corylliens; that is enough." Of course, she cared, and she would have berated her brother for missing such an opportunity, but in the passion of this moment, she was not considering that. "They could have killed any one of us! I will not put any of them," she pointed at Ártur, "through the hell of knowing the filth in those minds."

Looking at the healer, trying to calm the tense, reediness in her voice, she continued, "Ártur, go to your people…settle them…offer my regrets and any compensation they think fitting. I will be with them presently." k'Ádhá knew how she could make up for this, to those left alive, to the families left in Bhryell, to the High Mother who had chosen to honor her…and whom Diona had failed. What would the woman think of her now?

"Your Majesty," Ártur said in agreement with a bow. Despite her words, he too believed those men should be read, that any information they could offer would be valuable, and from Princess Asta's expression, the young Inquisitor felt likewise. But it was not their choice to make…unless, Ártur thought morosely, Kavan was in Bhryell when he returned with this grim tale. Kavan would come. Kavan would read them without regret. Kavan would learn the truth.

The Queen, despite her silence, as the dead were gathered…the Elyri and her fallen servants taken into the Great Hall for care…was hoping for the same thing.

She needed Kavan more than ever.

❧Chapter 4❦

A sharp pounding on his door, that Caol first believed to be in his head, brought him awake before dawn, eliciting a groan as he rolled on his sagging cot, rubbed his eyes, and tried to swallow the bitter metallic taste of cheap ale that lingered in his mouth. The night of binge drinking following the horror at the castle had given him little more than a headache and a nauseous feeling in the pit of his stomach...and a wavering conviction that perhaps it was time to drop the undercover work and return to the castle where he belonged.

How many months had it been? He barely remembered. He felt no closer to discovering the whereabouts of Heward, no closer to removing the leader of the Corylliens or ridding Enesfel of the violent scourge. By his reckoning, the core of the Corylliens had nearly depleted itself with this one act of supreme folly. What he assessed to be between thirty or forty members was now reduced by over half. Twenty-seven dead, or on the verge of death...one at his hands when the man leaping from the wall crossed paths with Caol in the alley through which he fled. It left Caol, Layton, Heward, and perhaps a dozen other individuals scattered about Rhidam, some of whom were, he knew, being hunted for their involvement in last night's debacle. Maybe there were more elsewhere in Enesfel, but in Rhidam, the movement was nearly ground out.

He suspected he should get away from Rhidam, far from the manhunt in case one of the others, especially the mountain of a man who fancied himself the leader in Layton's absence, chose to throw his name out as a participant…or worse, the instigator. Instead, Caol had gotten frustratingly drunk and now the pounding on his door which brought him lurching upright fast enough to unsettle his stomach, brought with it a panic that perhaps he had not acted swiftly enough in leaving Rhidam. One other person knew he rented this room, to his knowledge, but finding out he was here would not be impossible.

"Alty! Layton wants to see you!"

Caol rubbed his eyes and grumbled. If the man was going to blame him, Caol was tempted to slip his knife between the man's ribs and be done with this nonsense. Perhaps that was what he should have done sooner. With few to do his bidding, and no one to lead and control the Corylliens, Heward might be forced to the surface to start again. That might bring him into Caol's sights and mean a swift end to this game.

Perhaps he should stick to his cover a little longer.

As he staggered to his feet, to the window to peer outside in search of possible royal guards circling the building, he wondered through the fog in his aching head why he had not gotten rid of Layton long ago. He could see no one outside that looked suspicious, thus when the irritated shout of "Alty!" came again, accompanied by more banging, he barked, "Wait a minute!"

If these men were here for his arrest, they would have broken down the door instead of allowing him time or opportunity to escape through the window.

Nearly an hour later, Caol was in the grimy back room of a tanner's shop facing the ruddy-faced, sweaty, puffy, almost unrecognizable man who had brought him into the Corylliens. He was seated, his lower body covered with a filthy blanket that, when he shifted on his straw bedding, seemed stuck to what Caol imagined to be pussy, discolored flesh. Evidence of infection boiled off his skin, permeated the air with its stench; it took all of Caol's willpower not to cover his mouth and nose against it. He was surprised the man was still alive.

"I know...I know..." Layton coughed over the rim of a bottle of strong spirits. As much pain as the man was likely in, Caol imagined he was using the alcohol both to dull the worst of it and, possibly as a tool to finish the job the infection had not yet done. "Damned leg...wish it would fall off already."

Both knew that was not likely. When the leg went, Layton was going with it.

"Cover your nose if you want...I won't blame you." Layton gestured to an unsteady looking chair, but Caol did not accept.

"You want to see me?" There was little point in wasted conversation when the man might have mere minutes before the poison in his blood claimed his life.

"Nasty business that...last night..."

"I told Birl not to do it...they were determined," Caol said with a shrug and no accusation in his tone. The truth did not need added emotion to make it truer. His eyes took in the details of the room instead of meeting those of the dying man.

Layton bobbed his head, more of a side-to-side movement than a forward to back motion. "Should've seen it coming...but he barely listens to me under the best of times."

"Me either."

"Well...they'll listen to you now." Caol eyed him skeptically, finally looking at the man's bloated, discolored face. "Gotta leave someone in charge...since it's obvious I won't be back to it soon enough to make a difference. Talked to Anri; he agrees. We're putting you in charge."

Caol choked. Layton had met Heward face to face. Caol did not know if he should be intrigued or furious. "Me?"

Undaunted, Layton continued. "Planning, recruiting...especially recruiting...it's yours..."

"I'm no recruiter!"

"Have to be. Work's not done...and Birl ruined everything. We need more soldiers if we're going to get rid of..."

"Haven't we? I mean...yes...we had some come to deliver supplies to those hurt by the fires...but they would have gone...and the healer and his apprentice are the only Elyri in Rhidam. Levonne will deal with the other one...but the rest have departed..."

"Not finished until they're all dead...or gone from Enesfel...and they're no longer welcome here by anyone..."

"Can't control what people think..."

"We can try. We must try or else they'll come back here, invade...infest our land with their..."

Thankfully, he began to cough, which kept him from uttering words that Caol felt would likely have sparked a violent reaction. Layton began to drink again, and Caol tried his protest a second time. "I don't know anyone...I'm not a recruiter..."

"You'll learn. Keep your ears and eyes open for those with similar opinions...or who can be easily swayed and manipulated. He'll help you get started..."

Caol swallowed hard, hoping it appeared more a reaction of nervousness than of anticipation. "He? Heward?"

"He's off on business...not sure how long...but when he's back..." There was more coughing, more drinking, before Layton continued. "Right now, he wants us to lay low, get out of Rhidam, until this blows over, the hunt dies down and the Crown's wrath is sated. A couple of weeks...a month. That should do."

That much, at least, Caol had already been considering, though now he was thinking it would be wise to stay close and learn what was happening within the castle, how many more, if any, arrests had been made during the night, what the arrested men's fate would be. If he left Rhidam, Heward might choose someone else to put in charge of the killing, the looting, the destruction of property. Or perhaps, Caol thought wryly as he took leave of the dying man, this would be the ideal opportunity to fill the organization with double agents, meet Heward, and spring a trap for him from the inside. Yes. Perhaps that was what he would do.

As soon as last night faded into memory and he got back into town.

❧*❧

It was later than intended when Kavan broke away from Alberni with a heavy heart and a cold knot in his stomach that had, as far as he could determine, nothing to do with the Darys, Alberni, or his family in Bhryell. There had been an on and off tickle, a smell of blood, the faint echo of shouting within his skull, the weight of death around his neck, and a constant flutter of nausea that suggested the Sight was toying with him. But there was nothing tangible, nothing recognizable or obvious beyond the sense of death, thus there was nothing he could identify or address. By the time he left his estate after thanking his staff again for their dedication and respectful steadfastness, he took to flight in the hopes that it would clear his head of the unpleasant shadows. The effort worked to a degree, for by the time the sun began to rise and he climbed the steps of his porch, he felt nothing but a dull, unsettled pit of worry in his belly.

"Kavan!"

With the sun barely over the horizon, Kavan expected no one to call his name, to seek him out this early, particularly his cousin. The man's tone of voice made him turn with both alarm and fear. "What?" Something had happened. Someone, during his absence, had been injured...or worse, had died. His stomach knotted, a sensation that choked him of air.

Ignoring Kavan's dislike of physical affection, Ártur embraced him with relief. "Where in k'Ádhá's name have you been? It's been days...I've been looking for you..."

The bard gingerly extricated himself from his cousin's embrace. "I had duties to attend; there was no cause for..."

"You could have told..."

"Wortham knew where I..."

"You did not tell me!" He knew he was sulking like a petulant child, but Ártur had always been jealous over Kavan's loyalties and both men knew that was unlikely to change. The healer also knew it was largely his own doing, born from the months of distance erected between them before the death of King Donal. If he had not cut Kavan out of his life then, Ártur was convinced this distance would never have sprung up between them.

"Come...to the náos..."

"To the...?"

"There were nine of them," Ártur began to explain, "from Bhryell...they took aid to Rhidam..."

The chill in Kavan's blood grew stronger. All of Bhryell had known of those nine who had taken it upon themselves, with the hard-won support of their elders, to deliver food, clothing, and other goods to Rhidam. It had been Khwílen Kesábhá's visit to Bhryell, and Bhen's ongoing reports after each visit to Rhidam, which swayed the people of Bhryell to take the risk, to allow their children, their brothers, and sisters, to take the risk. How would they feel if disaster had befallen those they loved for an act of pure generosity?

"How many?" he eventually whispered as they approached the náos and the healer opened the door. Five bodies lay on tables at the front of the room, their four friends gathered near them, with others, parents and family, attending as well. Faces lifted to see who had come, but as quickly turned away and Kavan felt, or imagined he did, the blame aimed at him. It surprised him, for he had nothing to do with either this event or their decision to give freely of their time, their goods, or their lives.

"How…?"

"Corylliens stormed the courtyard where we were dining with the Queen," one young man murmured. Those four living, at least, aimed no visible blame or anger at Kavan. They had known what they were risking. It made the losses no easier, but at least they knew that the fault was with the Corylliens, not Kavan.

"Killed many of the serving staff as well," Ártur said quietly. "But at least most were killed or captured. The Queen is to decide their fate today. I offered to read them, but she declined…"

That news made Kavan scowl, and Ártur could see, in the tightening of his cousin's jaw, that the revelation had produced the desired effect. Kavan would go to Rhidam; he would read them and he would learn the truth.

The same young man who had spoken before grunted, "Of what use is reading? They admitted to being Corylliens. Their actions were plain enough…"

"They might have information about their leaders…and if those men are caught, it will be easier to end…" the healer argued.

"But not k'dedhá Claide's sway," said one of the older Elyri, a woman Kavan knew to be the mother of one of the murdered youths.

"That is true," Kavan reluctantly admitted, wondering how she knew of Claide's suspected involvement with the Corylliens in Enesfel. "But there are those striving to remove his influence…and the situation is improving…"

"This is improving?" She pointed at the dead.

Before the woman could verbally attack Kavan or accuse him of some hand in her son's death, Ártur, regretting having brought his cousin into this swirl of hostility, interjected, "This is the first time in weeks…" The looks thrown at him confirmed the faint voice in the healer's head that said his words were little consolation to those who had lost loved ones. Emotions were too high for rationality to win. Nor would words of comfort, reminders of bravery and sacrifice for the cause of peace, words meant to honor the hearts and lives of these young people, be of any good.

"I am heartily sorry for the losses you have suffered…but I honor their courage and compassion." It was all Kavan could think of to say, as weak and ineffectual as those words were.

"There will be no more foolish endeavors from Bhryell." People turned heads or bodies towards the five women to enter the náos, traveling hard upon the heels of dedhá Bhílári who looked as stricken and ill as Kavan felt. The woman who spoke, one of Bhryell's bhydáni who had served on the lómesté for much of the last sixty years, glanced at Kavan with disdain. She had been well-loved and well-respected, someone even bhydáni Tíbhyan admired, but the look of stubborn defiance on the four young faces as she reached the tables suggested that her popularity had waned during the time Kavan had been away. "We have lost too many…"

"You cannot prevent us from doing what is right, what is good…what we think…"

The elderly woman narrowed her gaze at the young man who spoke. "The lómesté refuses to condone…"

The young man, whose name Kavan had yet to learn, threw back his shoulders and continued to speak. Whether he had been the initial organizer of the donation efforts or was merely the one chosen to be the spokesperson, he was not shy nor afraid to confront authority. "We do not need your permission. There are people there…hungry, cold, lost people…who need help. We did what Dhágdhuán would have done...what Saint Kóráhm or any of the saints would have done..." He met Kavan's gaze with a nod.

"Do not mention that name!" someone barked.

"They are not our..." started the bhydáni.

"They are not Elyri...but they are people...and they deserve as much aid as would be given any town in Elyriá where fire had destroyed homes, businesses, lives. We bring honor to our families...to Bhryell...by our acts of kindness. If you cannot see..."

"What we see," the old woman sniffed with a haughty tilt of her head, "is a generation corrupted by blasphemy and heresy." Her cold gaze shot towards Kavan, and even a number of the parents of the deceased looked at him. Hearing that word, that accusation, hurled at him for the second time in so short a span of days, made Kavan ill. What was worse, being branded a Saint or branded a heretic?

"There is no blasphemy or heresy in aiding the downtrodden, the needy," Kavan managed to say with a faint touch of ice in his voice. As a child, he had respected, even idolized, the lómesté, the bhydáni, but over the years, learning what sort of people some of them were and growing to better understand the workings of the world, he had lost his fear of them. Let them accuse him. They had no authority to make charges of heresy stick, and Kavan would not allow them to condemn the others for the failings they perceived in him. "It is the teaching of the Faith; they should be commended for..."

"Deaths?" the old woman sneered. "We need no more martyrs to Bhryell's name. There have been enough of those." And too many saints; she did not say the words, but Kavan heard them as clearly as if she had spoken them aloud. If she considered him a saint, he wondered, why the disdain? Or did the disdain in the word indicate she refused to acknowledge those claims and thought them foolish? He was no saint, not in his own eyes, but he could not deny that many others used the reality of miracles as a basis for that title.

"We are not martyrs," the young man huffed. "We want to help."

"If you, if anyone, goes to Enesfel, it will be without our blessing, without our authorization, without our aid or support."

"So be it," said the lone surviving girl of the group of nine. The young men with her nodded and voiced their agreement. The deaths of their friends, too many of them, had been a painful blow, but they made the choice not to let that loss define or defeat them.

Members of the lómesté looked at one another, murmured behind raised hands as their leader stared down the spokesman. Nearby, Bhílári wrung his hands, listening but not voicing an opinion. He supported the relief efforts, for these young people were doing more than he dared to try, but he was not a man strong enough of heart to confront the authority of the lómesté. He was having a difficult enough time finding the courage to side with gdhededhá Kesábhá against the wrongs he knew the father of their Faith condoned against the people of Elyriá. He might not like the lómesté's stance, but at least they were trying to protect their own kind.

Finally, without another word to the survivors, to the families of the fallen, to the gdhededhá or to Kavan and his cousin, the lómesté stalked out of the náós. Kavan realized that others around him believed the five council members thought this matter insignificant and not worth their time since the survivors refused to heed their advice. They expressed no regrets, nor remorse to the families of the dead, gave no blessings or gestures of kindness, and everyone, even those who had lost kin, were united in their cause.

The spokesman of the four approached Kavan, his steps sure and confident even if his offered hand was not. "Tell us their deaths mean something. Tell us we did not act in vain."

Kavan searched his face, his eyes, for some clue as to why he felt he should know him as he clasped the offered hand. "Not in vain," he promised, his other hand cupping that clasped one. "Your generosity, the risk you took, will be remembered, and in the end, your selflessness will help gain the support we need outside of

Elyriá." They were not simply words of comfort. He believed them to be true. "What you have done will be spoken of…remembered throughout the Sovereignties…and it will make a difference."

Perhaps not immediately, but that difference would come.

Others in the room, parents and survivors alike, even gdhededhá Bhílári, came to him, touched him, shook his hands and spoke their thanks for any blessings he could leave to the children who lived and those who had died. Something had changed, a turnaround in attitude in Kavan's favor, and in those touches, the words of those who coaxed him with their bodies towards the dead so that he might lay his hands on them as well, Kavan felt the first honest traces of welcome in his hometown that he had ever felt. It shook him more deeply than the usual disdain would and he began to quake, his breathing coming too fast, until Ártur, sensing what he feared would be a breakdown, pulled Kavan out of the throng and out of the náós into the brightening village streets.

Thankfully, no one followed.

"I shouldn't have…" the healer started, but Kavan shook his head, cutting off his apology. This was not the welcome of people expecting miracles; this was not the underhanded welcome of those wishing him ill. This was the honest welcome of his peers, Elyri citizens of Bhryell, that Kavan had always hoped for.

"No…just let me…" He needed to think, to clear his head. "I need to go to Rhidam…to know what has happened…"

"But the Gate…?" Getting to it with this many people inside would be impossible if Kavan wanted to avoid them or keep his destination hidden.

"There are others." Flight to find one would do him good, one of the surest means, beyond music, to bring him back to himself. Flying to Rhidam, of course, would take too long, but there were many Gates within traveling distance he could reach, even the one in his home if he did not mind the delay of family.

Ártur nodded reluctantly. "Fly then…and tell the Queen I shall be there shortly…if you see her." He would have to face those within, answer their questions, but it was a duty the Queen was already aware of, having sent Ártur here with the survivors and the dead. He was surprised that she had not insisted on coming to Bhryell, but her focus was, as it should be, on her prisoners, the families of the dead palace staff, and on what those in the keep suspected would be the consequences of the attack. By now, Ártur imagined word had reached k'gdhededhá Claide, and he was not looking forward to whatever came of the inevitable meeting between the k'gdhededhá and the Queen.

With a slight nod, Kavan made no effort to hide or shelter his change, but with no one around to see, he was able to assume the familiar white kestrel shape within seconds, with Ártur as his sole witness. Breath stolen by the swift rush of power Kavan absorbed and expended to make so fast a change, the healer watched him lift into the sky. When he was alone, the bird no longer in sight, he returned to the others in the náós, where his duties as healer, his Faith, and his employer, required him to be.

Kavan's flight, circling Bhryell for nearly an hour rather than seeking another Gate as intended, brought him back to the náós after the living had gone home, and his cousin had, he believed, returned to Rhidam. Likely, the healer would fret and worry about where Kavan had gone. Assuming the guilty captives in Rhidam were alive when he reached them, Kavan would need a clear head and a focused store of power to read so many. His flight had given him both, and when he stepped into the streets of Rhidam from the emptiness of Hes á Redh, he believed he was prepared for what those vile men might reveal of the atrocities they had committed.

The quiet in the náós and the streets nearest the Gathering Hall was but a provisional bandage stretched over what festered beneath.

The few people he met gave little more than a passing glance, rather like in the days before this anti-Elyri violence had erupted. Kavan might have believed this to be the start of normalcy, if not for the pulsing in the distance, echoing in his head. He could hear shouting, booing, hissing, and, as he drew nearer and listened more carefully, there was the sound of stones bouncing off wood. A crowd had gathered before the keep, some passersby who stopped for a curious glimpse, some the sort who relished the suffering of others, some who believed that these men, the nine Kavan eventually caught sight of through gaps in the throng, deserved any manner of punishment their Queen bestowed. Soldiers stood nearby, under the command of Balint Gabersdon, to keep the onlookers in line and prevent misguided attempts to either set the men free or kill them before the Queen commanded.

Each of the nine trapped with neck and wrists in the pillory, legs shackled to the stocks and spread awkwardly apart, had been flogged with a scourge, multiple stinging strips of leather and rope tipped with bone or stone or metal to bruise, bite, and rip into flesh. Weeping red gashes spread across bare torsos, front and back, down over buttocks and legs, leaving the fabric of their trousers torn and bloody, and, in some instances, barely hanging on the body of the owner. Cracked lips proved the onset of dehydration and, from the cuts and bruises on their faces and shorn skulls, the assault of the crowd had been going on for some time. Small children scurried about, scooping up stones to bring back to the crowd for throwing again. The nine looked miserable, too far gone into pain to throw taunts at their abusers. Kavan was sickened by the amount of blood, but he felt no remorse. Attacking the Queen's guests, in her castle, was a suicidal choice, and none of the men deserved leniency. They would suffer at the hands of the community, but he doubted they would die here. The Queen would have a different end in store, and he was thankful he would not likely be here to witness it. Deserved or not, he had no desire to witness their executions.

The hail of rocks ceased when he reached the first man in the line, the people curious about what the White Bard intended to do. His reputation was of forgiveness and mercy, but he could feel, in the emotions roiling beneath the crowd's exterior, that more than a few hoped he would take the matter in hand and kill the nine…either out of revenge or compassion. The idea, he admitted as he laid his hand on the head of that first man, was a tempting one. He could kill each cleanly and easily with no more than a thought or a touch and no one would know what he had done. But he chose not to. The Queen would have her due. His purpose here was to glean information.

He was aware of the guards' side-eyeing him, of Balint watching him with unabashed interest, as he stepped from one prisoner to another, touching each, skimming their thoughts with well-practiced ease for details the Crown might be able to use against Claide, the Coryllien organization, or both. From one he gleaned a woman's voice, a whispery, nasal tone in an accent he could not place, a voice that gave him a chill he could not shake even after breaking contact with the fellow. Perhaps she was of no import, but Kavan believed he had met her before…or that he would meet her in the future.

It was a meeting he did not look forward to.

He learned nothing else of significance except for a few names of men who had escaped, or who someone hoped had escaped, or the names of children, family, parents, or friends. He spoke those names as he learned them, and Balint made sure to record each one in the hopes they would lead to arrests of others involved in the massacre. From each, Kavan learned the name of the one they had followed on their last fateful night of freedom. Not the name of Layton, as expected, not Heward, and not, as he feared, Caol. Thankfully, Caol's name and face were not among the identities Kavan captured.

The one they identified as the leader of the raid was the name Kavan saved for last, and he paused before the big, shaggy man staring at him with no surprise when the man stared back with open defiance. From the damage to both sides of his face, caused by stones and scourge, Kavan doubted the fellow had heard anything Kavan said, doubted he knew, or believed, that a simple touch could reveal anything of import. Many had heard tell of Elyri reading thoughts through touch, but few believed, when faced with the possibility, that it could work. Most Teren stubbornly insisted they had the skill or strength of will to keep an Elyri out of their thoughts. Kavan had encountered the phenomenon many times.

Despite his confidence, or perhaps because the exhibition was false bravado, the man whipped his head from side to side to avoid Kavan's touch. Lowering his mental shields had not been necessary with the others, but the need for haste with this obstinate man made doing so the surest means of gathering thoughts quickly. Unlike with the other eight, this would be a more jarring experience for both of them but it would not take long.

Braced for the jolt, Kavan grasped one of the man's trapped hands, a less direct point of contact than his face or head, yet a point unable to be easily yanked away. It was Kavan who broke free first, stumbling back when one tiny morsel of information slammed through him with enough force to choke him and steal his breath.

Sir Gabersdon, still following behind, began, "Lord Cliáth…"

Kavan did not hear him. He took several staggering steps backward, aware that the captive was staring at him with a smirk of triumph in thinking he had somehow hurt the Elyri or at least kept his thoughts hidden. But that was not it at all.

He had to get there…had to reach the man in time, he thought, trying to shake off the horror. He could not allow this to happen, no matter what his personal feelings were. k'Ádhá help them if he could not reach Clarys before it was too late.

ᴂChapter 5ᴂ

The large bay gelding, a horse better suited for the rigors of combat than pleasure riding or long-distance travel, skittered as the white-skinned man broke free of the crowd and ran past without noticing the animal was there. The blonde man on the horse, and his contingent of bodyguards and trailing wagon train of building materials, stone and tools, drew up short when he motioned for them to stop. The crowd, noting the arrival of someone of bearing and import, ignored both bard and the captives in the pillories in favor of this lord who came bearing much-needed supplies. The attention made the rider nervous, but since the guards at the gates failed to recognize him when he announced he had come with a delivery for Lord Owain Lachlan, he felt more at ease. They did not ask his identity, but nor did they allow him to pass, leading to speculation as to what the men in the pillories had done.

If he had been at home, those nine might have done nothing more than stumbled drunkenly across the road in his brother's path.

He could have introduced himself, and thought perhaps he should have, but no one asked, and with the tense air surrounding the group on this side of the drawbridge and moat, he felt that arrest would have been more likely than a nobleman's welcome. He decided against raising unnecessary suspicion and wait for his cousin to come to him.

Eventually, the portcullis drew back and Owain, accompanied by a collection of soldiers, stalked across the bridge over the glassy moat. He did not recognize the visitor's clothing, as Prince Kjell had chosen to wear neither a badge of rank nor identifying article of attire, but Owain recognized the man's bearing in his saddle and a grin spread across his face.

"This is a surprise," he said warmly, offering his hand, and then an embrace, when Kjell dismounted to greet him.

"Indeed. I was not certain I could twist my brother's thinking to allow such an endeavor...but it is done and I have brought what supplies he thought he could spare...and some I offer myself."

Owain took stock of the trail of wagons and the oxen, mules, and horses used to pull them. It was an impressive assortment, donated mostly, he suspected, by Kjell. "We will have to send our gratitude." To do anything less would be unforgivable, but being indebted to the Nethite King was not going to be an easy thing to shoulder. "Come...you are welcome here...but your men will be watched closely, I'm afraid. It is unavoidable."

"And understandable...they're Nethites." He tugged his horse's reins and followed Owain across the wooden bridge. "What is the meaning of...?" His head cocked towards the pillories, where the prisoners' reprieve from the derision of the crowd was short-lived.

"Corylliens," muttered Owain. "They made the mistake of attacking the Queen and her Elyri guests..."

"Lord Cliáth?"

Owain glanced sideways but continued walking. Bard and prince had met briefly, but Kavan often made a deep impression at first meeting, whether for good or ill. It pleased Owain that it seemed Kavan's impression on this particular de Corrmick had been a positive one. "He is not here...is no longer in Rhidam, I'm afraid."

"No longer...?" He was disappointed, but Owain's admission suggested that the man who had fled past him had been here unbeknownst to his cousin.

"After events of late...many of those killed by the men out front were Elyri who had brought aid...he deemed it safer to be elsewhere until the atmosphere settles. The only Elyri in Rhidam are the Court healers and gdhededhá Tusánt. We hope as things improve...after our capture of this many...the violence will cease and allow him and others to feel welcome again. Time will tell."

Kjell nodded. Such politics were tricky. Any law made would have its detractors, and it was impossible to force people to believe something by command alone. "If there is anything I can do...anything I can offer...you will let me know?"

Stable hands came for the horses and soldiers directed the wagons out of the main path of egress, while Chancellor McGranis, injured during the attack on the Queen but still pushing to work, took inventory of what had been delivered. Determining where such supplies could best be put to use had become part of his duties, something he took more seriously after k'gdhededhá Dórímyr's unexpected visit. Not because he took the old prelate's criticism about the lack of progress on the náós to heart, but because he wanted to show him, and everyone else, that his primary interest was making sure the residents of Rhidam had homes. There was no way everything could be complete by the time the storms came, the overcast sky this day already threatened rain, but crews would build as long as they were able, throughout the winter if possible, and into the spring and summer until the work was complete. The massacre had distracted his focus, shifted manpower away from the restoration work, but he was not going to allow it to stop.

"Uncle, I was told..." The Queen, along with Princess Asta, came through the castle doors with the monarch's increased retinue of soldiers and attendants, but she stopped when she saw the man at

Owain's side. While she did not recognize him, it was obvious to her that he and Owain were related, and that meant one thing.

A de Corrmick was in Rhidam.

"Your Majesty," Owain said, hoping to smooth over any awkwardness or hostility this meeting could generate, "I present Prince Kjell de Corrmick. Cousin…Her Royal Majesty Queen Diona…and Princess Asta."

The prince's gaze, which lingered a little too long, he felt, on the princess, shifted quickly to the Queen with that introduction. The princess was too young for him, and the odds were, she was already betrothed. It did not stop him from admiring the striking intelligence of her eyes however. He took the Queen's hand to kiss her knuckles, a gesture he was told was expected in Enesfel though it was not practiced in Neth. "At last, we meet," he said with a smile. "I have come with donations for the rebuilding efforts…from myself and from Merkar."

"King Merkar?" Diona stammered, not believing what she heard.

Kjell smirked and straightened. "It is difficult to believe, I know…and took some convincing to arrange…but I assure you it comes with my sincerest hopes it will be put to good use."

"Then it is to you I owe gratitude…and not your brother?"

"More or less…"

If he was capable of convincing the Nethite king to send materials to the despised middle kingdom, to the royal family who had cost him nearly a third of his realm, then this was a shrewd man to court as an ally…and to watch carefully as a suspected spy.

Fortunately, none of the Nethites were in earshot, occupied as they were with the unloading and distribution of materials from the wagons. Likely, thought Owain, Merkar had instructed them to leave Kjell unguarded in the hopes that harm would befall him. Even Glucke would have pushed to give Kjell as much leeway as possible in the hopes that the prince could gain the Lachlans' trust, enabling him to gather intelligence that might later be used against Enesfel.

"Regardless of my brother's expectations, I am here strictly to learn how best you and I might work together, Your Highness. I meant what I said to Owain; an alliance between us would be beneficial to both. How better to meet you than under an official guise of ambassador sanctioned by the King?"

Diona chuckled, finding his smile and mirth infectious. "How better indeed. Will you join me in the State Room, Prince Kjell, where we can discuss this new relationship?" She wanted to invite Asta, her chancellor, and her general into the meeting but decided that would be too much too soon. Until she and Kjell had a basis for mutual trust, until they had some plan for the future, or at least a sense of what the other wanted, it was best to deal with him with only Owain present as guardian, advisor, and, if necessary, mediator. Cooperation had to begin somewhere, and they both respected Owain. Kjell was entrusting her enough to come here; it was up to her to take a step in proving that faith well earned, and learning to trust him as well.

ॐ*ॐ

Attaching to the group of Nethite wagons awaiting entrance to the castle was an easier feat than Caol anticipated. The most difficult thing was avoiding the men in the pillories, men he was associated with, men who could identify him as a Coryllien and put him in the precarious position of needing to defend himself or blowing his cover. Having found the hair dying too much of an inconvenience to maintain, he had opted to shave his head and the much greater amount of time he spent outdoors had darkened his skin, meaning he might not be easily recognizable to anyone but his daughter and niece. He snagged a Nethite hat and cloak from one of the wagons without notice; it kept the Corylliens from recognizing him as the wagons waited to enter and be unloaded. He eyed the blonde leader of the caravan as the man spoke first to Owain and then to the Queen, a man, he guessed from similarities to Owain, who was a de Corrmick. Caol was curious, but his curiosity would remain temporarily unrequited. He had something else he needed to do.

His focus was primarily on his daughter, his reason for risking the keep today. He needed to reach her, to speak with her, and not through Marta or some other go-between. Caol had heard several disconcerting rumors and the best way to confirm them was to travel, a journey that might take several weeks if he could not find a faster means. He was hoping, with Kavan no longer in Rhidam, that Ártur would consent to be that form of faster transport. However this journey went forward, he needed to see Asta first. There were things he needed to say…in case he did not return.

He peeled off from the wagoneers as they discussed the dispensation of goods with the Chancellor and the Queen escorted their leader into the castle. Asta lingered in the courtyard, not invited to join them, but seeking instead her own source of information from these visitors. The presence of a large group of Nethites this deep in Enesfel warranted investigation, even if they had come with Prince de Corrmick. Caol chose those moments of indecision and reflection to approach her, his hat pulled low over his eyes, the cloak high enough around his neck to avoid recognition. With his best Nethite accent, something he had gleaned from Owain over the years, though far from authentic, he asked, "A word, my lady?"

The princess was aware of the man passing her, as she had been of each stranger in the courtyard, but as he carried a pack over his shoulder, she thought him to be one of those unloading the wagons and paid him no more attention than she paid the others. Surprised that he spoke to her, she started and asked, "Pardon?"

He stopped.

"A word, in private, if I may." Realizing she was about to refuse him, despite her curiosity, he looked over his shoulder and tilted the brim of his hat enough to meet her gaze. Her mouth popped open into an O, but a familiar look on his weather-browned face made her snap it shut.

"This way, sir," she stammered, her voice a squeak as he set his burden on the ground. The best places for privacy during most hours of the day were the three oratories as they were rarely used by anyone except Kavan, and sometimes Gaelán and Ártur. The healers were involved in lessons at this hour, and Kavan was not in Rhidam. The oratories on the first two levels were used less than the one on the third floor that Kavan had made his personal space, thus to avoid too many corridors and increasing chances of meeting someone, she headed for the first-floor oratory, her heart jumping in her chest.

As soon as the door closed, she threw her arms around the man who was no stranger and held him tightly, not speaking for words failed to form beneath the emotion choking her. It was reassuring to have him here, have him near, to have his hand in her hair, to smell the scent of him that was the same beneath unfamiliar clothing. Caol kissed the top of her head, likewise strangled with emotion, but he had little time to waste and forced his voice to work.

"You are taller."

"Nearly as tall as Diona," she agreed in a rough whisper. "Are you coming home?"

He drew back, shaking his head. "Not yet. The Coryliens are down to barely a dozen...and our leader's on his last leg...they're making me the recruiter...the leader...or they will be soon."

"Leader?" It took little thought to know the difficulties that would present, as her father would be expected to plan and execute anti-Elyri activities. "How will you...?"

"I don't know." He sat on the nearest pew and pulled her down beside him, wanting to protect her from his predicament, but the impulse to duty and the understanding of what she would need to know to perform her duties gave him no choice. "I have a few weeks to devise a plan...before I'm due to meet Heward." He tried to muster a smile at his daughter's excitement, but he did not feel as enthusiastic about that meeting as she was. It would mean a face to the name that was more than a drawing, a step nearer the end, but the danger involved in that meeting was high. "Do not speak of it yet...I need a plan first."

"I will speak to no one, I swear it."

"I know." Clasping her hands, he kissed them both, a gesture of longing and regret for forcing her into this position, denying her a father and pushing her into a world of obligation that many her age were not prepared for. "You are doing well, Asta. I am proud of you."

She blushed without looking away. His praise meant more to her than success.

"What I need from you, however, why I have come, is a favor."

"Anything, Father. I will bring you anything, find anything, hide you if you..."

"I need you to bring Ártur to me here."

Her expression shifted abruptly from girlish to serious. "Are you ill?" It was the most logical reason to request a healer though she saw no trace of ailment or injury.

Caol chuckled and kissed her nose, something he had not done since she had been a small girl. "I am well, Asta; do not fret. But I must go somewhere...and it will take too long to travel there on horseback. I do not know how long I will be away...perhaps a week or two...likely no longer." Not, he thought, if he was due to meet Heward at that time. Given what he needed to investigate, the trip might prove to be futile. "I must go...while the trail is hot..."

"To Elyriá?"

He stared at her.

"Wace intended to travel there, but I begged him to wait until after the executions." The bounty hunter, who had remained in Rhidam since King Hagan's murder and Kavan's arrest, knew nothing of Gates, and Asta thought it wisest not to mention them. His skills would be useful in the days leading up to, and following, the executions, and he agreed to stay as long as necessary out of respect for the Elyri who had been the primary targets of the raiders. Whether he stayed at Asta's insistence or the Queen's, Caol did not know, and he admitted finding it disconcerting that his daughter might be able to sway the bounty hunter when Caol could not.

"He spoke of rumors around k'gdhededhá Dórímyr...and intended to go before the k'dedhá came to Rhidam. He's told me little, that threats have been made that he thought it best to root out. I tried to get a message to you but have been unable to find Marta..."

"She is helping her family after the fire; I am certain she will reach out to you soon. Please...Asta...bring Ártur."

If Elotti had heard rumors similar to those Caol had heard, and thought them worth investigating, though less important, it seemed, than the state of affairs in Rhidam, than Caol wagered he was not alone in his concerns. Should Ártur agree to take him to Clarys, Caol could attend to matters the bounty hunter could not...and perhaps avert a catastrophe if the rumors bore any truth.

Rising, nodding, trying not to frown at losing her father again, she embraced his neck, kissed his ear and cheek, and disappeared without a word, not even a farewell. She understood duty, understood haste; as much as she hated them both at this moment, she would do what her father needed her to do.

Caol saw it and felt another flash of pride in his daughter's spirit and determination. He wondered, alone in the dark chapel, if her mother, wherever the woman's soul resided, was proud of their daughter as well.

≈*≪

Prince Kjell knew two truths from experience that left him less surprised with Queen Diona's choices than her subjects were. Women, on average, were kinder, gentler, more empathetic and understanding than men. Perhaps it was a product of their creation; perhaps it was a product of the force that placed them in the position of bearing and rearing children. He had, at various times in his life, felt certain that the Sovereignties would be better off if each was ruled by a woman. Elyriá had known only peace within her borders as far back as known history showed. Enesfel gaining a queen, the first female ruler on the Teren mainland in centuries, would bode well for peace and stability if she could draw the kingdom out of its quagmire. He might be wrong, but he steadfastly chose to believe it.

The other truth he was sure of was that a woman crossed could be the most ruthless, deadliest, most vicious thing alive. Here was a woman who had seen her brother murdered in the name of hatred, and had witnessed those in the castle attacked not by an army but by a few dozen ruffians who ought to have known better. Execution was the inevitable end for her prisoners. Everyone knew it.

Unlike Sovereignties who did not employ Elyri interrogators, torture was neither necessary nor practiced in Rhidam. The public flogging and time spent in the pillory as a lesson in humiliation had done its work, but it was time to end it. Another three men were captured during the day, thanks to information gleaned from an unnamed source. A total of twelve men now faced the wrath of a woman, a queen, with the strength and will to prove to all the lands that she would not be trifled with. Diona might be a woman, but she was neither squeamish nor a coward.

Six of them, chosen randomly, were loosed from the pillories, stripped, and bound securely to large spoked wheels, arms and legs spread painfully wide, flayed flesh pressed against roughened wood treated with animal fat. The wheels were rolled to where each of the six main roads came into Rhidam. As they traveled, the men were struck with clubs, rods, staffs or heavy maces, breaking limbs, crushing ribs, but not enough breakage to cause immediate death. The cracking of bones was barely heard over the roar of the crowds, people who followed and continued to throw stones and rotten food at the condemned for the crimes they had wrought on the Lachlan House. When the road heads were reached, the wheels were hoisted up on tall poles so that their spoked surfaces were out of reach of any man on foot or horseback. The poles were braced to prevent falling, and guards were posted to keep anyone from pitying the men by bringing them down...or killing them prematurely. Naked, the convicts were left to the elements, the cold, the sun, the carrion-eaters, and insects, as well as the ravages of hunger and thirst. It would be a painful, lingering death on display where everyone could witness the fate of those who angered and defied the new queen.

Kjell did not know what fate was chosen for the remaining six, although by the late hour in which the sentencing of the first six was carried out he expected the final deaths would fall the following morning. Long into the night, the sounds of building before the castle gates were heard as a makeshift platform was erected with materials intended for use in the rebuilding of Rhidam. The last the prince had seen the Queen, her bitter remarks about the waste of materials and extortions to the staff to build the platform in a manner that would allow the materials to be reused afterward were cut short by the arrival of a stranger seeking an audience with her. Everyone except Prince Espen had retired for the night by then, each curious about what horrific end the last six men would meet.

By daybreak, the platform was complete and a crowd had already begun to gather.

"Are you sure this is wise?" Owain asked, not because he doubted Diona's judgment, but because he worried about the reaction of the townsfolk if they learned of the horror she was about to unleash on the guilty. There appeared nothing unusual about the chopping block and heavy ax that rested nearby, nothing that suggested this beheading would be different from any other. It was the fate most often awarded traitors to the Crown.

But within the castle walls, amongst the Queen's advisors, the rumor was that this would not be an ordinary execution. An even smaller number knew the truth.

These executions would be conducted by an Elyri…and the six men brought to the platform, from the looks of terror on their faces, had heard that detail too.

"They believe Elyri to be a peaceful race incapable of…"

"Save for Duke Cáner…you forget that, Uncle," she murmured with a dark smile.

"What could possess an Elyri to want to…?"

Gaelán silenced him with a cutting glance. "What Elyri would not want to avenge what has been done to our people? Perhaps he's lost family, friends…" Gaelán's father had killed many in retaliation for the lives men such as these had taken. This man, whom Gaelán had neither seen nor met, might have similar cause for revenge. Or his outrage spread over the whole of Elyri lost, and Teren too, to cover the unnecessary violence that had gone on too long. He might have had enough of all of it. "If I was not a healer…"

Asta's hand pressed over his where it rested on his knee, her fingers curling and entwining through his. The tenderness of her action ended the red-faced tirade before it began; he swallowed several gulps of air and stared at their joined hands.

"He needs no reason," the Queen said, catching sight of the executioner at last. Tall, broad at the shoulder and thicker of body than most Elyri, his hair a deep, coppery red, the man did not smile, showed no glee in the responsibility he had been allowed to assume. He was Elyri, yes, but not entirely, for last night he had sported a thick, well-kept beard that indicated he carried Teren blood. This morning, he was clean-shaven, dressed in a traditional executioner's black robe but without his head and face covered as was the custom. Few wanted others to know they executed men for a living, but this man cared only that those about to die knew what he was.

He picked up the executioner's blade with one hand, a feat of strength not many could make, and ran the thumb of his other hand along the edge. It was sharp enough to draw a crimson bead which, in full sight of the condemned, he spread along the side of the blade as if christening it...tainting it with Elyri blood. The captives blanched, and those nearest to the platform, kept back by the presence of Lachlan soldiers, saw both the blood and the reaction. The men may have been willing to christen their consciences, their hands, their souls with Elyri blood but such blood on the blade which would end their lives was as unwanted as poison.

The charges were read against each man as they were dragged to the block, charges that brought booing, hissing, and derisive shouts from the audience. Balint had agreed to oversee the prisoners before returning to Nelori to tend important matters at home. k'gdhededhá Claide, returned from his travels, heard the final confessions of each before they placed their necks on the block. He undoubtedly noticed, as did the Queen and her court, that public support was swaying to favor the persecuted Elyri, or at least to favor their anointed Queen and her position. The Corylliens had taken their aggression and anti-Elyri violence too far by attacking the monarch inside the keep, and with the tensions high and uneasy as the consequences of the great fire, continued to settle, it seemed the people in Rhidam wanted nothing less than tranquility and security.

The ax fell with repeated precision. One criminal, one blow. No missed marks, no necessary follow-up strikes, death with a single swing. With each subsequent death, k'gdhededhá Claide scowled deeper and he looked as if he would be sick. Diona tilted her head, smiling smugly. Claide's suffering made this day worth the horror.

The last man, the one deemed the leader, struggled against his bonds as he was dragged forward, his bravado lost now that he faced a man who, days ago, he would have tried to kill. His knees buckled and he fell across the block. Claide, shaken by the unexpected fall, opened his mouth to speak, to ask for another confession or offer absolution as the herald with the scroll of charges began to read.

The redhead did not wait for either Claide or the herald. The big man on the block twisted to one side, facing the headsman as he attempted to wiggle out of the blood of his cohorts. He had no time to gasp, to stand, as the blade fell. His awkward position resulted in a sloppy cut, the first, leaving him alive in searing agony with the blade in his shoulder, long enough to gurgle curses before the ax was yanked free and fell again. It ended his life but, the executioner hoped, not his suffering.

The redhead was not the only one who hoped whatever afterlife the man found was one of suffering and torment.

"k'Ádhá damn you for denying…" k'gdhededhá Claide began to splutter, the roar of the approving crowd keeping his word from reaching royal ears, although the Queen could guess, by the prelate's furious expression, what he was saying. The condemned had already had the chance for confession, to atone in words before k'Ádhá, and thus she felt Claide had no just cause for outrage.

"Believe me," muttered the executioner, "he already has."

The ax fell to the platform with a thud before the redhead jumped from the platform where the bodies and heads were being gathered for display. People were already vying for the lumber of the stage, the chance to use both the precious commodity as well as to boast having a part of this historic day…bloody or not…that many could not pass up. Diona rose, the promise of payment on her mind, but she knew payment was not what her executioner desired. He had some other score to settle, some debt the dead had now paid, in part or in full. Whatever it was, Diona hoped that his service to her and Rhidam, in the name of armistice, brought the man peace and might even bring him back to her service.

The Lachlans could use a fearless man of such steel and strength.

❧*❦

He could have gated directly into k'gdhededhá Dórímyr's room, but Kavan saw little logic in raising the man's ire in that fashion. Since their last encounter, since the word heresy erupted between them, Kavan had felt an unsettled rumble in his core, a fear of something looming on the horizon that he did not want to think about or examine too closely. Pushing the most influential man in the Faith towards an unfavorable mood made little sense when, at the moment, Kavan's concern was saving the man's life. He knew of other Gates within the Faith's largest seat of worship, ones rarely used, and it was into one of those he arrived, heart hammering as he paused long enough to gain his bearings. He was on the same level as the holy man's quarters, in the chamber of some other member of the man's staff, someone who did not know this passage existed in the wardrobe of his rooms. Kavan stepped into the corridor, looked left and right towards the guarded double doors at the far end of the hall, and headed towards them with long, hasty strides.

"Announce me," he said while he was still many yards away.

"Halt," both guards charged simultaneously, stepping closer together to block passage, their bladed poles crossed to add further discouragement.

"It is imperative I see the k'gdhededhá at once…"

"Stay where you are!" The poles came down, their metal blades aimed at the approaching man. It made no difference if they recognized him. They had a duty they intended to fulfill. Violence in

Elyriá was a rare thing, they had little reason to think Kavan wished the k'gdhededhá harm, but his behavior was not that of a friend and the guards were, for once, confronted with a duty of import.

Kavan had a duty as well, a duty to his conscience, his faith, Elyriá, and Enesfel, to the people and the establishment of Faith across the Sovereignties. He could feel nothing beyond the barred doors, nothing except a flickering life force muted, he believed, by the density of the stone and the wooden doors. With little effort or thought, he touched the minds of each guard without breaking stride. They crumbled to the floor in a deep slumber, the clatter of their dropped weapons echoing down the corridor behind Kavan. Someone, somewhere, would have heard the commands to halt, heard the echo of the metal on stone as the weapons fell. Those others would be here soon, but as Kavan used a blast of power to break the doors' mechanism and push them open before reaching them, he believed he would have enough time to see what lay beyond, enough time to warn the k'gdhededhá of what was to come.

There was no time for warnings. The ancient holy father lay twitching, collapsed before the choking, smoky fire on his hearth, a scent Kavan recognized as Diwi mixed with something more, something that caused him to instinctively draw his tunic up to cover his mouth and nose. Kavan knelt beside the prelate, lifting his head and shoulders onto his lap, heedless of the blood that seeped from Dórímyr's ears, the corners of his eyes, from between his lips.

A wine glass lay tipped nearby, its contents spilled on the Hatuish rug, the glass chipped, the thumb on the man's outstretched hand cut and bleeding. Wine...not serbháló. Though no healer, Kavan tried to staunch the blood flow from the man's hand with his own but it was a wasted effort, and as the old man coughed, he sprayed blood on first one hand used to cover his mouth and then the other. Kavan tried to aid him upright to ease his breathing but it did not help. He could feel it in the man's aura, the gnawing burn of

Orec eating through the prelate's body. Dórímyr's eyes were open, though his vision was becoming increasingly unfocused. When he saw Kavan, his pupils dilated and his bloody mouth twisted into something between a grimace of pain and a disconcerting, almost wicked grin. The spasms in his body increased, as though he would escape the grasp of the man who held him, a man whose hand he squeezed tight with his good one in an effort, it seemed to share some dying thought.

He could not.

"You are not alone." Kavan could summon a healer, but it was too late for that. If there was Orec in the man's blood, nothing short of divine intervention would save him, and though Kavan kept his bloody hands on the withering body he held, trying to direct the poison away from the prelate's brain and heart, he felt no surge of power, no divine inspiration or interaction that could reverse the damage already done.

It appeared to take great effort when one old hand eventually came up to Kavan's face, flexing and trembling as it drew closer, until five bloody fingers raked down Kavan's cheek, pulling the fabric over his mouth and nose away. Running footsteps charged through the open doors, but Kavan ignored them.

"You..." Dórímyr choked, making one final effort to reach Kavan's mind. The feeling of malevolence and defeat that Kavan felt in the k'gdhededhá's expression and body seemed stronger in that short utterance, in that brief contact Kavan allowed. But then the prelate's body stiffened and the contact was lost when collapse came, his arm flopping back onto the floor, splattering blood droplets across the stone when it hit.

⋙Chapter 6⋘

"K'gdhededhá!" Hwensen's voice pierced the silence as the aide dashed in, intending to reach the man's side. The guards caught his arms and held him back, not wanting the scene disturbed as two others pulled Kavan away, allowing the lifeless body on his lap to slide to the floor.

Stunned, Kavan stared at the man who had taunted and haunted him since his childhood. Twice now, men of import had died bloodily in his arms, but that was less disturbing than the fragmented, disjointed flurry of images, words, and emotions that had bombarded him in Dórímyr's final touch. Arcane symbols, places he had never seen, words and phrases whispered or screamed in High Elyri that were too quiet or too loud to discern, powerful mixed emotions and a dragging sense of weariness, all too fleeting to latch onto in the early moments after the man's life faded from his eyes.

His life might be gone but his last conscious thoughts remained, crammed into Kavan's mind for reasons Kavan failed to comprehend. He had no doubt the man had intended to push thoughts into Kavan's head, that he had not expected to counter such strong resistance within the bard's mind. Few had an inkling of how formidable Kavan's gifts were. When Kavan allowed the images in, it had unsettled Dórímyr, startled him with the abruptness of the change of heart, and had, Kavan sensed, angered and frightened him, coloring the other impressions left for the bard to sift through and make sense of later. The underlying core of the man's message, however, was chilling. In those final few ragged breaths, the prelate had been content to relinquish his life...even welcomed the end though he had not, Kavan trusted, been the one to do this to himself.

There was a healer present now, a man Kavan had not heard enter as he tried to clear his head of the webby maze occupying it. He blinked, looked at Hwensen whom he realized had spoken to him, and blinked again. The man's lips moved, and though Kavan did not hear the words due to the rush of pounding blood in his ears and the faintness coming over him, he made out the question.

"Orec..." he murmured, the sole word that allowed itself to form on his tongue. He did not know if Hwensen or any of the others knew what Orec was. The guards continued to hold him though he did not struggle or attempt to be free. Eyes turned towards him, proof that no one knew that word, or what it meant, but the healer's word was readily understood by each of them.

"Poison."

The gazes passed back and forth between the healer and Kavan, some gaping with suspicion, others with surprise. Hwensen was arguing with the stunned healer, at least Kavan presumed he was since he could not hear the words, something about poisons not producing this much blood from a cut finger or from the ears, nose, and mouth. The smoke in the room had dissipated, though Kavan could still smell the tang of it. He shook his head, hoping it would clear his hearing, panic setting in as he tried to discover what had robbed him of that particular sense, but before he could give in to the panic, the guards were dragging him from the room.

Hwensen's hand brushed over Kavan's long enough for the aide to reassure him, but Kavan already knew what would be next. Another allegation of murder. Innocent or not, he was developing a reputation, suspicion he suspected that would haunt him forever. He was beginning to understand how such stories had come to follow Kóráhm, or other men, long after they left life behind.

❧*❧

The Queen, Prince Espen, Prince Kjell, and a few dozen guards and retainers remained at the execution site as the bodies of the deceased were collected. The heads were to be mounted on tall poles and displayed before the gatehouse so that the residents of Rhidam and any visitors to the city and castle would see them and know the fate of traitors, know that this Lachlan monarch would not be easily overcome. Beside her, Ártur looked faint and ill but he had insisted on attending this particular execution on behalf of any Elyri who were now, or had been, or whoever would be, in Enesfel. They deserved to be safe. He fidgeted now, however, the execution done and there being no need for him to watch the disposition of the dead. He glanced repeatedly at Asta, as if waiting for something from her, or sharing some secret with her, or perhaps it was his cousin he was carefully watching, as Gaelán's pale face had long since gone flat and emotionless and, even when Asta squeezed his hand or spoke to him, he failed to respond. That was cause for concern.

"Denyan, Avner, Waljan…escort Princess Asta and the healers inside," the Queen ordered. The healer looked relieved. Asta showed no inclination towards protest, for once not demanding to watch the bloody undertaking to its conclusion. She pulled Gaelán by the hand, and with Ártur nudging him from the other side, the younger healer shuffled along where they led.

Prince Kjell watched but did not speak until the healers and youngest Lachlan were beyond hearing. It had been difficult to miss Princess Asta's interest in the proceeding and he was hopeful for the chance to speak with her, to learn what matter of princess in Enesfel could stomach such a bloodbath. de Corrmick women tended towards extreme squeamishness in his experience. He had seen none of that in the Lachlan women. "Are such executions uncommon?" he finally asked. In Neth, one rarely heard tell of executions in Enesfel and it had been easy to believe the kingdom weak. It was equally likely, however, that such stories were suppressed to present the people of Enesfel as soft and feeble to the Nethite royal family and the subjects they controlled.

"Executions of this scale, yes," Diona replied, smoothing her hands over the fabric on her lap. "Until recently, there has rarely been a need."

"And hopefully," muttered Owain, having lost his taste for such bloodletting long ago, "there will be no further need in the future."

The Queen nodded her agreement as the thud of the first head onto a spike washed over the gradually diminishing crowd in the square. "If the assessments, the reports, are accurate, this Coryllien debacle should soon be behind us, allowing full focus on rebuilding, reparations, and recovery."

Curious about who the Queen thought she must make reparations to, Kjell said, "If I can be of assistance, do not hesitate to ask. Owain knows how to reach me...and I will do my utmost to communicate as best I may. I have resources..." And if he could convince his brother that continuing aid would keep Enesfel off-balance, lead the Lachlans to believe there was friendly intent instead of a ploy to gain trust that could be used against them, Kjell knew he could offer significantly more. It would be a dangerous game, but Kjell believed he had the cunning to succeed. There was, as far as he was concerned, no risk to Enesfel.

"We shall continue to discuss this, Prince Kjell." A crack of thunder shook the air behind clouds that had threatened Rhidam throughout the morning and were poised to unleash their burden.

"But," she smiled, neither the executions nor the impending rain dampening her spirits, "we shall talk over mulled cider if you wish."

"I do." It would be more agreeable than remaining in the cold rain, and the pleasant burn of warm alcohol would help erase the sounds, the smells, the tastes of death in the air. Kjell had not shown it, had not spoken of it, but he hated such brutality as much as the healers. If he had his way, Neth, too, would come to benefit from peace and the freedom from violence that Enesfel now strived for.

❧*❧

"Here…Gaelán…lie down…"

Asta helped the healer get the younger man out of his cold clothing and beneath the warmth of the down bedding while servants stoked the fire to make the room pleasant for the dazed novice healer. When Ártur insisted on witnessing the executions, Gaelán insisted on watching as well. Unlike the older healer, however, who was familiar with the bloodshed of war and had seen numerous past executions, Gaelán had not been prepared for what he witnessed and was paying the price for his inexperience. Asta felt bad for him, for such a gentle soul to have been subjected, even by choice, to that particularly grisly end of life.

"May I stay with him?" Physician Talis was not at court this day, and she knew her father was still waiting for Ártur who had been unable to provide the man with transport to Clarys before the executions and was due to take him now. With Gaelán's father no longer in Rhidam and Sóbhán in Elyriá, Asta was the only friend Gaelán had, and his welfare was a responsibility Asta took to heart.

"Yes…do." Ártur brushed the young man's hair from his face with a frown. He intended to bring Kavan here long enough for his cousin to get through to Gaelán, reach into his thoughts, draw away the horror and reassure him that he was safe. Ártur could try, but from experience, he knew Kavan's touch was more effective for soothing fear and agitation and that Gaelán, connected to Kavan in some inexplicable way, would respond best to the bard's presence. "I will return soon. He will be well; do not fear for that."

Asta nodded. "I know." Gaelán was sick in spirit, scared, disgusted and shocked, but not physically harmed. He needed time and reassurance. The first was not Asta's to give, but she would offer as much of the second as he needed. "I won't leave him."

The door closed, and after several minutes staring at the person she felt closest to, she slipped off her boots and her damp trousers and tunic, and crawled beneath the blankets to curl up beside him in her underclothes. Often as children, when one or the other of them had been afraid in the night, they had crawled into each other's beds, particularly when their parents were unavailable, and often even when they were. It was a familiar gesture of comfort, to snuggle close, to hug him, close her eyes, and pretend that nothing in the world could find them here, could touch them, pretend that they were safe as long as they stayed together, as long as they had each other.

෨⊷*⊷෨

As prisons went, this was not a bad one. An unused room somewhere in the heart of the religious complex with a narrow bed, a chair and desk with a water pitcher and basin, a water closet behind a foldable screen, and nothing more. Likely one of several rooms used by the religious for solitary retreat. Two guards stood within, two without, and his hands were left bound, as though there was no plan to hold him here long, as if they could prevent his escape if he desired it. They had no concept of what he was capable of, no idea that he could be free of the ropes and the room and their guardianship whenever he wished, but he saw no reason to compound the situation with an effort that would make him appear guilty of a crime he had not committed.

Kavan had no intention of taking this guilt upon himself as he had done with Hagan's death. He felt no guilt for Dórímyr's passing, as he had done all he could to prevent it. This time, he would defend his innocence, maintain it, prove it. He had nothing to hide. If necessary, he would escape and find the killer himself, for that individual, whoever it was, was a threat to Enesfel as well. If Claide's hand was in this death, as Kavan believed it had been in Hagan's and Jermyn's, that man had to be stopped at any cost.

He chose to wait in this dim room, lit only by the glow of some external source beyond the small, high window, until he was summoned to testify, to be read by those who could verify his innocence. He would sit on the bed, bound hands between his knees, listen, and wait.

He would pray that, in the end, the guilty would get their due.

✺*✺

Reaching the náós and waiting undisturbed was an easy thing, as most of the townsfolk gathered to witness the executions of a significant portion of the Coryllien organization. Caol chose not to bear witness to that, as much as he was relieved to have it happen. He could not risk being seen by those about to die, identified and possibly killed, or to have his cover blown by any Lachlan staff or family member who might recognize him despite his altered appearance. He had deemed it unwise to remain in the castle, once Asta brought word that the executions were about to commence and that the healer was to attend and was unable to offer transport until it was over. The longer Caol remained in the castle, the higher the risk of discovery. Here in Hes á Redh, a kneeling man in prayer, perhaps for the souls of the soon to be deceased, perhaps for their victims, or perhaps for reasons of his own, was merely another praying man. He made sure the healer knew where to find him, and waited.

And waited.

The executioner's ax could not be heard from this distance, but the roar of the crowd at each bloody ending marked the passage of time. When the count exceeded the number he had known were captured, an additional three deaths added, Caol fidgeted and struggled to remain calm. That left him with how many? Less than a dozen Coryllien agents? Would that draw Heward out sooner? If so, Caol had to act fast, had to get to Clarys and prevent a murder before it was too late then return to Rhidam in time, he hoped, to bring the last of the Corylliens down. It might not put an end to k'gdhededhá Claide's actions, but it would cut off the most virulent source of violence. What more could be asked of a single man?

Footsteps came and went across the stone floor, dedhá and Faithful going about their day in an effort to ignore what was happening elsewhere. Caol paid attention to any that came down the aisle nearest him, noting as each drew nearer that they did not belong to the healer and did not seem threatening. That impression of innocence changed, however, when footsteps stopped at the end of the bench, hesitated, and were followed by the creak of wood as the person sat near to where Caol knelt. Nerves and attention heightened, Caol did not look up, continued to pretend to be at prayer, waiting in case the stranger was to act.

Perhaps Heward had found him.

"You are seeking passage to Clarys."

The matter-of-factness of the statement brought Caol's head up, to stare at the copper-haired man who had settled beside him. His shoulders were broader than Bhríd's and Caol wagered him to be taller as well, but he was Elyri, at least partially so since the trace of razor burn along his jawline spoke of Teren in his blood. Dark blue eyes with a trace of lavender studied him, not in an intimidating way but merely as a man awaiting an answer he already knew to a question he had asked anyhow.

When Caol did not answer, he added. "I will take you there…if you wish…though I suspect it is too late."

"How do you…?"

The redhead shook his head, looking away towards the altar. Caol noticed the traces of blood on his hands, the splatter on his boots, and guessed that he had attended the executions.

"In a manner of speaking, I…"

"Stop it," Caol hissed. He knew from time with Kavan that there were Elyri who could read thoughts without needing to touch their subject; Kavan was one of them. At least Kavan chose not to pry and rarely spoke of the secret thoughts he learned.

The stranger shrugged with a frown. "Apologies," he murmured, his tone sad and sincere as he got to his feet. "I have things to do. If you want me to take you to Clarys…"

"I do not know you. And I have…"

"Healer MacLyr is delayed. I give you my word I will not…"

"I do not know what your word is worth."

The stranger chuckled, drew a dagger from his waist, an act that made Caol tense, and handed it over, handle end first. "You have my permission to take my life if I do anything more than promised."

Eyes still narrowed, Caol continued to stare, taking the dagger but not immediately moving. Time was getting away from him, and instinct told him that the healer was late. With the crowd likely still gathered before the keep, at least many of them, it might be some time before Ártur was able to escape to make it to the náos. Perhaps he should not trust this man…but something about him…the shape of his face, the outstretched hand that still beckoned, the tone of voice that sounded marginally familiar though it logically could not be, elicited trust, and Caol eventually nodded.

"Take me to Clarys," he agreed. If this was a mistake, he doubted he would live long enough to regret it.

꒰*꒱

Hwensen wrung his hands as he waited in the anteroom for Kavan to be brought in. It had taken hours of effort, and the calling in of decades' worth of favors to make the arrangements, but he trusted it was the right thing to do. He believed it; he had faith in the White Bard even if others did not. But in his semi-political position within the Faith, he was painfully aware that, should his faith be misplaced, it was his job, his reputation, perhaps even his soul or life that were on the line. Awareness of everything he risked losing made him anxious. Worse still was the impending avalanche threatening to overtake the Faith establishment as accusations, facts, and centuries of practice, custom, and secrets were opened to the world.

Whatever gdhededhá Khwílen intended in his campaign against the prelate, Hwensen doubted he had anticipated this.

When the ecclesiastical guards brought Kavan into the aide's small chamber, Hwensen was struck by how small and unimposing the bard appeared. Any other time Hwensen had seen him, he had considered Kavan to be a commanding figure, but not today. At the tall end of average for their race, slender yet not as thin as many Elyri the aide knew, his hair long and as straight as the gentle waves would allow in the style many Elyri men and women wore. The coloration of hair and skin and the intensity of his green eyes, however, set him apart at a glance. His hands were bound, though Hwensen believed he could be free of the ropes if he chose, and he stood quietly between the guards, head slightly bowed, making no effort to be free. Most guilty men would have sought escape, if not in action then in their stance and the set of their shoulders. Kavan, however, did not.

"Leave us," Hwensen said, his tone as rough as his nerves.

"He will…"

Snapping with irritation, his voice crackling beneath his agitation, Hwensen said, "I have my orders." He waved the scroll he carried under the men's noses to show them the High Mother's regal crest but nothing more. These were soldiers of the Faith, but they would not disobey the commands of the Kyne. They bowed and retreated into the corridor, stopping outside the doors that Hwensen then closed to afford Kavan as much privacy as possible.

"My apologies, Lord Cliáth," he said quietly as he hastily untied the bard's hands. "We do not have much time…but it is imperative I speak with you…before others come…"

"Others?" Kavan rubbed his wrists where the rope had chafed. He had expected to be taken to some manner of tribunal, to someone who would read him and tell him what was being done to find Dórímyr's killer. Being brought before the k'gdhededhá's aide, left alone with him, raised more questions then it answered.

Hwensen did not immediately reply but gestured to the empty chair as he began to pace. Kavan eyed it but chose not to sit.

"The room has been searched." Kavan would already assume that, as it was the logical thing to do at the start of any investigation, but telling him seemed an adequate place to begin. "It was awash with poisons…" Hwensen shook his head and swallowed to steady his voice. "They will not tell me anything…not what killed him…not what they found. There is too much secrecy already…"

"Understandably…"

"Yes…understandably." This was too delicate of a matter to make a rush to judgment or to hastily make the matter public. Someone had to control the situation, but neither Kavan nor Hwensen knew who that someone was. "But it is secrecy that reeks of deception…and I am hoping…as is the Kyne…that you can…"

"I am under arrest…"

"By the Tribunal, yes…but this…" He offered a scroll, crumpled in the middle where he had held it too tightly in his nervous fist.

"This is from the Kyne. As long as you carry it with you, you are free from prosecution…for now…in order to learn the truth."

With a trembling hand, Kavan accepted the document, recognizing the wax seal and braided tri-colored cord of red, gold and silver, and choosing not to break it to read the contents. Whatever it said, he elected to believe that the woman would keep her word and that Hwensen was not intentionally misleading him. There was no deception he could read through the parchment, only a sincere desire for the truth and a steadfast belief in Kavan's innocence, belief that had nothing to do with evidence only his long history of honesty and righteousness. What he also recognized in the aide's tone was that even the High Mother might not be able to protect him indefinitely, not when it came to matters of the Faith.

"You know nothing at all?"

Hwensen shook his head. "Very little…that he was poisoned, yes…but you already know that. I heard tell of poison in the wine…of something he had inhaled as well as something which entered through the cut on his finger…but no one will speak to me directly…and they will not make a report to the Kyne until there is something more to report then speculation. I need to know the truth."

The bard looked at him quizzically and Hwensen stopped pacing, feeling the weight of that stare as if it was the anchor that secured him in the troubled storm of his mind.

He frowned. "Something is not right. He had been missing, gone to Rhidam, and no one else knew he had returned. Now this. No one had access…except me…and you…and I know that neither of us has done this." He offered his shaking hands, making no effort to steady them. "Please, read me. I insist. Prove to us both that I am innocent of this crime. I wanted this insanity of callous inequity to stop, but I could not have done such a thing as murder a man…for any reason."

Despite their mutual trepidation, the invitation was accepted, less because Kavan doubted Hwensen's words then because doing it would relieve the aide's mind and perhaps bolster his own. Though he hoped to find some clue, Kavan saw nothing within the other man's thoughts and memories to suggest Hwensen could be capable of poisoning the k'gdhededhá or that he knew who had. What Kavan did see puzzled him, tiny fragments of memories that clicked into place with the snatches he had gleaned from Dórímyr in the moments before his death. But what, Kavan wondered, did it mean?

There was one more thing, however, something that caused Kavan's face to turn grey. A truth that did not shock him with its possibility and yet did so with its truth. "He was going to…"

Hwensen shuffled awkwardly and looked away as Kavan released his hands, marveling that he had felt nothing in that momentary contact save for the touch of the bard's hands. He knew what Kavan referred to, and though it should not surprise him that Kavan latched onto that bit of information, it did. "He was going to try. The proposal had been drawn up to present to the lómesté in two months' time. But no one…I assure you…there has been no talk to support such a measure. There have been no actions taken…nothing you have done would sway the others…"

"He had my words…"

"One incident of verbalization is not enough to condemn a man of unorthodoxy," Hwensen assured him, suggesting that he knew of the words Kavan had spoken to the prelate that had led to the charge of heresy. "That would require a repeated pattern of dissent, which you have never displayed." He noted the flicker of shadow that crossed Kavan's face, the hint suggesting there was much about the White Bard that Hwensen and the Faith authorities in Clarys did not know, but he chose to ignore it and continue. "Incidents from childhood hardly matter. No one expects a child to understand matters of deep faith…asking questions is natural for children."

"Perhaps," Kavan sighed. If any of these people in the halls surrounding him knew of the Articles he possessed, of the details in the miracles and the dissenting questions that dragged on Kavan's mind day and night, they likely would have cause to proceed with heresy charges.

It was a good thing he had not yet read Kóráhm's Third Volume of Articles.

"If anything, there is too much proof to the contrary to label you a heretic. A man cannot be as blessed as you and be a…"

"Kóráhm."

Hwensen opened his mouth to speak, took a deep breath, and then closed it. Yes, there was the Heretic-Saint, the contentious man the leaders of the Faithful continued to disagree on. Not familiar with Kóráhm's teachings himself, not knowing how closely some of Kavan's own beliefs came to mirroring those questionable assertions, Hwensen could not make any direct comparisons. But he knew what he had heard about Kavan, and he knew what he saw and felt in the man before him now.

No man's faith, Hwensen was sure, had ever been stronger.

Changing the topic slightly, he continued, "I destroyed the document before anyone could see it…but should they learn of it…of his intentions and accusations, it would shadow you with motive for his death…and that is something Kyne Mórne will be able to protect you from. Here."

He withdrew a chain from around his neck and placed the small silver key that hung from it into the bard's hand. "This will unlock his balcony door…though the inside bolt will need to be lifted. It is dark, no one will see you…and I have the Kyne's protection when the guards find you gone. See what you can find, what you can learn. I do not believe anything has been removed from his chambers. Come to me after; tell me everything. If there is a murderer within these walls, I must know who it is. I must know who they are protecting, what they are hiding."

Uncertain who 'they' were, Kavan promised, "I will tell you," as he slipped the key into his pocket. "If I flee…" He wanted to avoid the appearance of guilt by escaping, but Kyne's word, her permitted release, would have to suffice to undercut any perceived guilt.

"Trust her, my lord."

He wanted to. On a quest for truth, Kavan would have no choice but to trust the High Mother of all Elyri. "My family?"

Hwensen nodded. His years as aide to the highest religious authority in the lands had given him much practice in anticipating the needs of those he served. "It is already being taken care of. Do not go to them, stay with them, but trust they are being protected from accusation and harm. Please, Lord Cliáth; find the k'gdhededhá's killer before another is appointed, before anyone else dies."

The bard frowned and nodded. After Jermyn's assassination, and now Dórímyr's, fear of further murders was understandable. Kavan needed to return to Bhryell long enough to speak to Wortham, to alert him to the situation, but he would not stay there. For the time being, not endangering his family was the most important step he could take. He would find a way to do both, and he would find the killer if he had to search each of the Sovereignties and beyond to do it.

☙*❧

Asta opened her eyes, roused from her unanticipated nap by the sensation of a nose and lips running through the hair at the top of her head and gentle hands kneading across her shoulders. Without thinking, she sleepily tilted her face to look into Gaelán's haunted eyes. Neither moved, neither spoke, until the mouth that had been kissing her hair lowered to catch her lips instead. She whimpered softly at the unexpected kiss and wiggled her body higher, closer to his, to kiss him more fully. His hands, hands that healed and soothed, found the skin at the small of her back as she shifted and both shivered. Thought, logic, and reason fled them. This was where she was supposed to be. She had known it all of her life. Gaelán had known it too. There was no struggle with conscience or morality. Gaelán Cáner was the one; in that moment, he was hers and she was his in a way they knew no one else would ever be.

Kavan knelt in one of the prayer stations in the grand náós, a dangerous place to be with a swarm of gdhededhá, ecclesiastical guards, and Faithful wandering in and out of the ancient structure. Word of Dórímyr's death would not yet have been made public, for the abruptness of it, the unexpectedness and the mystery surrounding it would raise questions no one was prepared to answer. Elyri could die; sickness could claim them and sometimes did. But as the prelate had not been known to be ill, a violent death would be assumed and anyone who had heard Khwílen Kesábhá's words on the lips of travelers in and out of Clarys, would have the possibility of murder playing in their minds. That suspicion would be accurate, though the burden of it was not something the Elyri people needed to shoulder until the truth was known.

He listened as footfalls stopped to his right, his body tensed in case he needed to fight or flee, but a sideways glance revealed an older woman who paused to lean against the pew to catch her breath before continuing towards the front. He had hidden who he was, a long, hooded grey cloak and gloves shielded him from prying eyes so that the guards who passed paid him no mind. Hiding in plain sight, it seemed, was the best choice, though he would not remain here long. He wanted to pray, to seek guidance and comfort, but it was too dangerous to stay.

As Hwensen indicated, there had been a multitude of poison sources in the k'gdhededhá's room, too many to have come from a single individual, any that could have killed him without the use of the others. The open wine bottle, a gift, Kavan learned in the touch of it, which had come to Dórímyr through gdhededhá Tusánt, carried enough poison to kill quickly if an entire glass was consumed. But surely Tusánt would never have done such a thing as poison the prelate with a wine that most Elyri would not consume. Kavan had known Tusánt too long, knew his heart and his loyalties, or at least he believed he did. Elryi were not known to drink wine, as a very small amount could kill them. An Elyri's metabolism was not designed for the consumption of alcohol, though there were a few who were unaffected by it or knew how to imbibe without risking death. A bottle of wine was an odd gift for the dedhá to give to Dórímyr, and it was equally odd to find that the man had consumed at least a single swallow of the sweet red liquid.

The smell in the room that Kavan noted on first entry, the remnants of Diwi in the smoke, could not, in itself, have poisoned Dórímyr, though anyone unfamiliar with the substance might believe it to be a toxin. It was not an aromatic used in Elyriá, was not something often available this far north of Hatu; how the prelate had known of it, how he had obtained it, was a mystery. It had been added to the fire, a handful tossed onto the flames, Kavan guessed, as some of the yellowish powder was strewn across the stones of the hearth and dusted on the floor as if it had been squeezed out between clenched fingers. Dórímyr's body was no longer in the room and Kavan was not willing to risk finding it, to examine the man himself, but he knew there would be traces of Diwi on the prelate's hands...particularly the hand with the bleeding finger. The Diwi would not kill him, but something else in the smoke could have, something bitter and, Kavan thought, marginally recognizable.

On the table, next to the opened bottle, an octagonal porcelain chest lay open, gilded with gold, finely polished bits of wood. and tiny fragments of gemstones in an elaborate decorative pattern. There were coins within, ancient coins from across the realms, a smattering of costly gems, and small pebbles and trinkets that Kavan suspected were purported holy relics. A gift to the Elyri prelate by k'gdhededhá Claide and the people of Enesfel.

Kavan could hear the Teren's words, his nasal voice, when he touched the box. "…a gift from the Faithful…" the hawkish man had said. Pressing his hand into the collection of coins and objects revealed a variety of givers, men and women from across the realm, men and women who in no way could have time to send these objects as gifts in the short duration of Dórímyr's unannounced visit, and could not possibly have all been in Rhidam on that same day. This had been a gift accumulated for some time, possibly years, since the first time the k'gdhededhá promised to come to Enesfel but had failed to do so. This gift had waited through the breaking of each promised visit for the right day, growing in size and content until the opportunity to give it finally presented itself.

Because Claide had not been present in Rhidam that day, it had been Valgis who delivered the gift into Dórímyr's hands. Neither gdhededhá, however, had left the impression of poison on it, although Kavan was keenly aware of a sense of urgency left by the recently elected Teren k'gdhededhá, a sense of importance, desperation, and a more sinister emotion that Kavan could not immediately name. It made little sense for the man to have felt such a need to deliver money and relics into the hands of a man, an institution, he despised, unless, Kavan thought grimly, he had known of the box's lethal secret.

There were too many other impressions on the chest, too many exchanges of hands, for Kavan to determine where, or when, the poison was applied and by whom. A collection of faces and names pushed through his thoughts in that touch, merchants, lords, peasants, and gdhededhá, some with gifts of innocence and reverence, others with motives in their giving…as if they too had known something that no more than a select few had been privileged to learn about.

Like a threat to the Elyri k'gdhededhá.

Kavan brought his fingers to his nose to sniff them and frowned. Having come in contact with it before, having seen its work and nearly dying from his brush with it, Kavan recognized the scent of Orec and quickly closed the chest. The contents had been doused with it. It was a miracle Kavan had survived his previous exposure; Ártur believed he had some natural immunity but Kavan did not want to take another chance. There were no cuts on his skin, no way, he hoped, for the poison to enter his system if he washed his hands of it. But he did not know if contact alone could be deadly.

Without Ártur to draw the faces he saw, Kavan could not easily trace any of those paths. The tangled web in his head left him with no clear direction to investigate. The Orec must have been added recently to prevent others from being exposed, but it was less lethal to Teren, and it was not something commonly found north of Hatu. What Kavan had brought with him from the southern lands had been consumed in the cleansing ritual in the chapel below the Lachlan keep, and no one but Wortham had known what substances he had used. The poison within this box had come into Rhidam from some other source, someone who knew what it was, knew its uses.

Perhaps knew its connections to Dawid Coryllien.

But why? The Teren Faith leaders were already discussing secession from the Elyri establishment. k'gdhededhá Dórímyr's death would hardly influence that process, at least not in any way that Kavan could see. He doubted the man's death would have any influence beyond Elyriá's borders unless some sort of fanatical zealot was elected to take his place in Clarys.

Was that it, he wondered. Did someone know who the likely candidates for succession were? Was someone hoping to sway the vote, either in favor of the Elyri or the Teren, or in some other direction? Frowning, Kavan glanced over the man's partially eaten breakfast of lamb and bread with a dark orange fruit spread and the open book beside it, a treatise on Faith heresies. That research, Kavan believed, was connected to the efforts to declare him a heretic, nothing more. He decided the best place to begin was to uncover which gdhededhá would be eyed for the holy seat. Perhaps he would uncover a motive that would lead him back to Claide. He felt certain that man was connected to Dórímyr's death.

He had to figure out how.

The náós was beginning to fill for evening services when Kavan retreated, intending to avoid the press of people who might identify him and expose him to capture. He had to find secure shelter for the night and decide how to get word to Wortham about what his future entailed. The captain would not be happy, would want to travel beside him, but he would understand why he could not. Kavan's need for him this time was not as traveling companion but as a cornerstone for the family he would leave in Bhryell. Perhaps Hwensen, gdhededhá Bhílári, and Khwílen Kesábhá could direct Kavan towards the most likely candidates for nomination.

Without the time to study Dórímyr's room more, or the chance to examine the man's body, it was the best place for Kavan to begin.

Though deposited into the streets of Clarys and directed by the red-headed stranger to a Teren-friendly inn, Caol was on his own, a slightly daunting thing given that there were, to his knowledge, no members of the Association in Elyriá to turn to, no underground criminal element from which to glean information or resources, no one he knew or could trust. With no city map or idea where to start, Caol was left to wander, memorizing streets and landmarks, learning his way around as well as making mental notes of details that might, at some point, be useful, working his way towards the massive complex of white stone he had been told was the seat of the Faith.

He did not know what he expected to find or what he expected this náós to be like, but this sort of grandeur was not what he had imagined. Graceful spires, like a woman's fingers reaching into the sky, colored glass of vermillion, emerald, sapphire, and sunlight yellow, and polished metals both silver and gold that gleamed and glistened as it caught the fading rays of sunset, buildings of brick and stone, some naturally colored, some painted searing white. There were similarities between this náós and Hes á Redh, even similarities between it and the Lachlan palace that spoke of a shared history, how Elyri had once lived and ruled in Enesfel as was often told, how they had built great monuments meant to survive the ravages of time before the Elyri were driven from the land. Most traces of Elyri history in Teren lands had been torn down in the early days of the Persecution, leaving remnants of great structures to be later added to and disguised by the blockier Teren architectural forms. The result was a collection of homes and landmarks rebuilt as a mixture of types, a combined heritage that most Teren chose to forget.

The houses and shops along the spacious, airy stone-paved streets appeared clean, pastel shades of pinks, yellows, oranges, and white. There was no sign of the destitute or crippled, no suggestion of poverty though he knew from conversations with Kavan and Bhríd that there was certainly a line between the wealthiest in Elyriá and those of lesser means. Such lines were not visible to Caol, and without being able to read Elyri lettering, he had no idea what the signs above shops said, or how to find anything he wanted. The glimpses in windows were his only clues, but even that was of little use for finding his way.

Eyes set on those spires, wondering as he approached how he was to enter and announce a threat to the highest-ranking man of Faith in the lands without being deemed mad, he rounded a corner and plowed directly into a man coming from the other direction. "Apologies," he said earnestly, using the Trade tongue, hoping the other would understand. It was not until he locked eyes with the man, however, that he blinked in surprise and squawked, "Lord

Cliáth!" The bard, equally surprised to find Caol in the streets of Clarys, pressed his fingers to his lips, caught the man's arm, and pulled him into the nearest alcove. "What are you doing here?"

"I should ask the same of you," Kavan murmured, scanning with eyes and other senses for anyone nearby who might be a detriment to him. "How did you...?"

"Found a fellow to bring me...don't know his name; never seen him before...but I'd wager he's not full Elyri." He wrapped his hand around Kavan's wrist and the image slid easily between them. The face was not one that Kavan knew, but there was something about his features that told Kavan he should know him. "Tried to get to Ártur, but he was detained."

"Detained?"

Caol shook his head to belay Kavan's worries. "Coryllien execution this morning. Didn't stay to watch, but I wager it was a damn bloody mess. Asta told me they used an Elyri executioner."

Kavan's face lost what little color his white flesh showed. It seemed an unlikely scenario that any Elyri should seek out such a violent act but there was no reason to disbelieve Asta. Perhaps Bhríd had been encouraged to undertake the duty, or had offered to do it, as the man certainly had the strength, and currently, the anger, to take such action. Generally, however, the ex-chamberlain was a peaceful man. If it had been Bhríd, Asta would have said so, and thus Kavan refused to believe it until he could speak to his kinsman.

With people beginning to notice them in the alcove, Kavan tugged Caol back onto the street. "I need somewhere safe to..."

"I've got a room lined up...couldn't tell you the name of it, or how to get back there, but there's a golden sun on the threshold..."

"I know the place." It would do. It would be a haven for a few hours at least, but beyond that, Kavan was uncertain of his future.

"What's wrong?" Caol frowned. He had heard the bard's mention of safety but had thought Kavan had meant a safe place for

Caol. With Elyriá's reputation for peacefulness, he could not imagine being unsafe here. Kavan's demeanor suggested it was his own safety he was concerned for, not Caol's.

Steps long and purposeful, Kavan strode through the streets as if on urgent business and Caol struggled to keep up. "What makes you think...?"

"I know a fugitive when I see one," Caol scoffed beneath his breath, not about to say those words more loudly in case his hunch was accurate.

Kavan did not speak until they were ensconced in Caol's rented room. There was a single narrow bed, a cushioned chair near the window, and a table on which a water basin and oil lamp rested. He drew off his cloak, hung it over one of the bedposts, and hesitated there for several moments, his hands tightly gripping the wooden post. "k'gdhededhá Dórímyr has been murdered."

"k'Ádhá's teeth," Caol swore, not hiding his anger or frustration and not caring if Kavan took offense at his swearing. The threat against that man had been his reason for coming to Elyriá, but he had not expected the attempt to come this soon. "When? How? Where?"

"In his chambers...this morning...I was with him when he..." Kavan looked down at his clothing, and Caol noted the dried blood on the man's tunic for the first time. No one else had, only because Kavan's cloak had hidden the evidence. Eyes wide, he waited for the bard to explain. "Poison...a variety of them...multiple sources though I cannot be certain. But I am confident that Orec was the actual cause of death."

"The Coryllien poison." Most would not know what that poison was called, but a member of the Association, whose background was entangled with the legendary Coryllien daggers, was likely to know more about it than most.

"There was a decorative chest...a reliquary...the locking flange was sharpened...laced with it...as was the contents. He was given drugged wine…which he drank…there was poison in the hearth smoke…the walls reeked of it as if something had been in the air for a long time, possibly months…killing him slowly. I would not be surprised if his meal was poisoned, though I did not sample it, but I am confident that Orec was the most recently contacted agent. I suspect that, when combined with the other substances in his already compromised body, it killed quickly."

Frowning, Caol dropped onto the edge of the bed and steepled his fingers under his chin, his elbows resting on his knees. Then his hands separated and he began to drum on the other bedpost. "It sounds like more than one person wanted him out of the way."

"I think so as well. The difficulty will be in determining who was behind each attempt, who was behind the agent that killed him. The k'phóredhet believe I am to blame…arrested me…" He noted Caol's puzzled expression and corrected himself. "The ecclesiastical tribunal. They have not tried me…have not read me…and Kyne Mórne has given me opportunity to clear my name, find the killer. If, when…I am properly questioned, they will see that I am not at fault." He did not think, however, that would be enough to clear him. "Their healers, their readers, may trace the poisons to their sources, if they bother to try, and they should learn what little there is to gain from the room as I have. The wine was a gift from gdhededhá Tusánt…but a gift to him before he passed it on. I suspect the intent was to kill Tusánt, but unless we can find the source of that wine, the giver, I dare say Tusánt will be accused as I have been."

"Surely if it was a gift to him, no one could accuse him of…"

Kavan sighed and drew off the bloody tunic, suddenly sickened by the stain. "No crime of this magnitude has been committed in Elyriá in centuries. The last k'gdhededhá to be killed was during the Persecution. The possibility for overreaction, for unwarranted accusations and an attempt to punish anyone…rather than no one…is a possibility in Elyriá just as in Enesfel. Teren are not the only ones subject to hysteria at such times. Tusánt might escape prosecution, if he remains in Rhidam, but I cannot guarantee that…particularly if Claide sees it as a way to turn against and be rid of him."

"Hence your flight…before they officially accuse and condemn you." Having been in that position before, when Kavan freed him to offer the chance to clear his name and find the kidnapped children, Caol knew how Kavan must feel.

"Kyne will do what she can on my behalf; it is her hand that gained my freedom, grants me protection while I seek answers. She seems to believe I am capable of finding them…"

"If anyone can, you can," Caol said emphatically.

Kavan's head bowed. "Perhaps. I am determined to try. There are other details that do not connect…"

"Claide trying to kill him connects." Caol rubbed the back of his neck. "That's why I'm here. Word on the street in Rhidam…at least my parts of the street…is that he never left Rhidam when k'dedhá was there, despite the claims. That there had been a plan in place to keep the two from meeting…a plan involving the k'dedhá's death…and that death had been sent back to Elyriá with him. I tried to track down what sort of death, who planned it, how it would be done, but there was not enough time to dig deeper. I came here hoping to get to him, warn him, stop any attempt before it came…and Asta told me Elotti intended to come as well, having heard much the same. He could not make it quickly enough on foot or by horse, and Asta needs him there…" He frowned again at the uncomfortable thought of an alliance between his daughter and the infamous bounty hunter. "…thus he did not leave Rhidam. I thought death would be attempted by an assassin from the rumors I'd heard, not poison, but poison makes the most sense, I suppose…unless he brought a Teren back with him."

"Or the intended assassin was not Teren."

Fingers stopped drumming. "You think the killer could be Elyri?" That would be unexpected.

"It is possible." With the unrest Khwílen was stirring, anything had become possible, although an Elyri assassin was a sickening thought. "The reliquary was given by Valgis...who received it from Claide with the instructions to give it to Dórímyr. Its contents, coins, gems, trinkets and religious relics, were added by an assortment of donors...over several years...passed between parishes, too many hands have touched it, held it; it is nearly impossible to tell when the poison was applied...but I suspect it was not added until delivery was imminent."

"Nearly?"

"Ártur could sketch the faces if given the chance, so each could be found and examined, assuming they live. But the most accurate way to get that evidence would involve touching the flange."

"And exposing someone to the poison."

He had heard of Kavan's brush with a poison that incapacitated him for nearly a month but he did not know what poison that had been, nor did Asta. As Orec was deadly to Teren and Elyri alike, there was no reason to think Kavan's experience had been with Orec...or to think he had somehow survived it. No matter the poison, Kavan's near-death experience was cause enough for his reluctance to take that risk or to expose anyone else to it.

Kavan nodded. "It may come to that...but if I can get a message to Ártur, I can give him the faces I saw; perhaps they would provide some clues."

"Questioning so many without Claide knowing would be tricky, but it's possible, I suppose. I could pass a message to Ártur through Asta. But none of those would likely be Elyri agents..."

"I know. If his food was poisoned, however," Kavan continued, "if his meditation incense or candles or firewood were treated with a toxin, those things were done here. And I think he knew..." He shuddered and looked out the window.

"That he was being poisoned?"

"That he was dying. In those last moments, in his thoughts, he did not seem surprised...and did not seem surprised to see me." His frowning silhouette was framed by the darkening sky. "I think he was pleased that I might be accused of his death."

"Why would he...?"

"We had a history...and not a pleasant one. I challenged him in ways he did not appreciate. He may have seen me as a threat...to the Faith and to him."

"You?" Caol snorted, finding that difficult to believe. Other than the gdhededhá, he could think of no man more faithful than Kavan. The bard chose not to elaborate, however, and Caol knew better than to push for details. "So...what do we do?"

"Find out who in Elyriá might have wished him dead...and try to determine if anyone in Enesfel other than Claide may have wished the same thing...if Claide could have been involved."

"Not sure who has the more daunting task." Most people in Enesfel simply did not care enough about k'gdhededhá Dórímyr to have considered, or plotted, his death, but of those who might have, they would be smart enough to hide their tracks. Caol imagined it would be much the same in Elyriá, except that he expected the Elyri prelate was given more consideration, and more love and admiration, among his people. "I'll have to put Asta on it; I have to lie low for a while." He shrugged at Kavan's quizzical expression. "A lot of questions...a lot of hunting going on after that foolish attack on the keep. There're few Corylliens left; I find myself about to be placed in charge...of the planning, the execution, the recruiting. Layton's dying, probably dead already...perhaps a dozen of us left and no one else fit to manage them. I'm tempted to turn the others in and be done with it, but I'm to meet with Heward in a few weeks and I can't see dropping out before that happens."

"Possibly our best chance to capture him," Kavan agreed.

"Or at least learn more about him. When I know who he is…something more than a sketch…putting an end to the Corylliens will follow. After the executions, it makes sense for the few of us left to keep low…and if I'm away from Rhidam, as Heward suggests we be, no one will expect me to carry out Coryllien mayhem. Vandalism is one thing, but Rhidam has seen too much fire and death. I can't stomach causing more."

"Then we find ways to work together." He offered Caol his hand, a rare gesture of friendship from a man who did not normally seek physical contact. "It is fortunate you have come here."

"Fortunate I ran into you, you mean." The handshake was accepted. "I hope you're right." He did not know how he could help Kavan in this unfamiliar land, without the Association to assist him, but he was willing to try. He owed Kavan for rescuing his son long ago, and he owed Enesfel his life. This was time enough for repayment of both.

⸘Chapter 7⸘

The best place, the safest place, to meet those he needed to speak with was the village náós, a place of sanctuary far removed from the family he needed to protect. Unlike most times he traveled through this k'rylag, gdhededhá Bhílári was present tonight, alone on the front bench, shoulders stooped as he stared at the figure on the wall with a pensive, absent expression. He did not turn, did not notice Kavan's arrival until the bard stopped beside him in the dark. Kavan waited, not wanting to disturb his reverie, but when moments passed without acknowledgment, he cleared his throat.

"gdhededhá...I require your help."

Bhílári looked up, startled as much by the words as by Kavan's presence there. In the years he had known Kavan, he could count on one hand the number of times the bard had made any requests from him. If he sought help, some grave matter of import was at hand.

"Ask." He did not feel as close, as bound to the White Bard as some, having watched Kavan grow in power from childhood and feeling uncomfortable, inferior, in the face of it. But his belief in the man's holiness had not waned. Wavered at times, as events stretched the limits of what his rational mind could grasp and understand, but it had never ceased.

"Ártur is on his way; I must speak with him." Kavan had sought his cousin's mind across the miles the moment he had decided to leave Caol asleep in the rented room and come to Bhryell on his own. Though the healer was annoyed at being roused from sleep, that annoyance would not last. "First," he stepped back as Bhílári rose. "I need you to inquire of your friends, other gdhededhá you know...I need to know who amongst you is likely to seek nomination, or be nominated, for the position of k'gdhededhá in Clarys."

"You mean if Dórímyr were to..."

"He is dead."

Bhílári sank onto the bench, stunned.

"I was there when it...when he...was poisoned. This morning." Kavan swallowed the cascade of emotions the memories brought, his hand on the edge of the bench-gripping tightly. "Official word has not been made...may not be made until they find the killer...but the selection process will begin soon after, I suspect. I need to know who might seek his position...who might gain by his death."

"You think one of us has...?"

"Possibly. Someone has done this...in Clarys, in his chambers, and I mean to find out who." It was unlikely any Teren could have gotten into the prelate's chambers, and without Bhílári knowing about Dórímyr's trip to Rhidam, an Elyri murderer was the most logical. "I cannot...I must act silently...avoid attention...and no one must ever know I have been here. I am suspect because I was there in his last moments. Please, you must tell no one what I have revealed, protect my family..."

"Protect us from what?"

Ártur staggered up the aisle, dressed in his healer's cloak but untroubled by the chill. Behind him, holding the door, Wortham wore only a thin pair of trousers as if he had forgotten to dress in his haste. It was the healer who demanded answers, but the same questions and deeper worry were etched onto the captain's face.

"The k'phóredhet…the guard…"

"Why?" Ártur's eyes narrowed, not in anger but in suspicion. "What have you done?"

Ignoring his cousin's accusations, Kavan accepted the clutching of Wortham's hands and drew strength from the man's steadfastness. "I will not be able to be seen in Bhryell for some time…no one must know I have come. I will not risk your lives while the inquisition is made into Dórímyr's murder." He hurried on to cut off Ártur's questions. "They suspect me because I was there when he died, and until the truth is found, I will likely remain their target. I will not come home…will not endanger the children…and ask that you protect them, Wortham, until I can. Be a father to them…until I can be here myself. Speak well of me, do not let them doubt me…"

"Neither will think ill of you," Wortham promised gravely. "Is there nothing more I can do?" The thought of being indefinitely parted from his dearest friend was not a pleasant one, but a duty such as he had been charged with outweighed his disappointment.

"You will know when…if…there is."

"Is this why you needed these?" Ártur gestured to the satchel of drawing supplies Kavan had asked him to bring. He had dozens of questions, but Kavan seemed ill-inclined to answer them, particularly after Ártur's ill-expressed accusations. If his presence in Bhryell endangered his family, then he was right not to remain here any longer than necessary.

"There are suspects you must draw…that must be taken to Asta, to Wace if he can be found…to the Queen…"

"Teren suspects?" choked Bhílári. Having suspects so soon was not a surprise, as murders in Elyriá were rare and the dead would normally be read to determine the cause, to seek the murderer in their final memories. Crimes of this magnitude were rarer still. The prelate had not been read by others, it seemed, if Kavan was believed to be the killer. Kavan had been with the man in his last moments. If there were any other suspects to be had in the k'gdhededhá's memory, Kavan would know them.

If there was a Teren suspect in Clarys, how could such a person have gained access to the prelate to kill him in his bed-chamber?

Kavan continued without a direct answer. "I have other duties tonight, while this news has yet to break…so I must force all of them on you at once."

Ártur grimaced but nodded and offered his hands. Forcing information into a person's head could be as painful as drawing it out could be. It was not always the case, but there was a chance he would suffer because of it, but he could not refuse this request if it meant protecting Kavan from another accusation of murder. Instead of taking Ártur's hands, however, Kavan put one hand on each side of the man's head, closed his eyes, and within moments was pulling away. Ártur blinked. He had felt nothing, no transfer of energy, no force of power dumped upon him, yet his head felt abruptly full to bursting with dozens of faces demanding attention.

"They will fade as you draw them," Kavan promised, kissing the man's forehead before releasing him. Ártur wondered how that could be true, but rather than ask, he sat at once and began to draw.

"I must go. If you learn anything you think I should know, Wortham, hear anything, bring it to gdhededhá Bhílári." Feeling the dedhá's surprised distress, Kavan added, "or I can get information through you, sínréc…if you are open to it. But do not put yourselves in danger for my sake…any of you. This is too important…and I will not imperil your lives or souls for it."

"You put us in no peril we would not gladly take for you," Wortham assured him. "For the boys…I will be vigilant."

"Thank you." He embraced Wortham tightly, feeling there was much more he should say but failing to find the words. Instead, he stepped away, nodded to Bhílári and his cousin, and retreated to the Gate. He could not linger, could not wait. The men had their duties, and he had his, and dalliance damned them all. He needed to return to Clarys before Caol awoke, before dawn, so that they could begin their work. He prayed it would not be long before an answer was found and his name was cleared. He missed the boys already.

❧*❧

It was a risk going to the castle, even at this late hour, though not as much of a risk as visiting Tusánt in the náós had been. The Elyri gdhededhá was horror-stricken to learn that the bottle of wine given Dórímyr had been poisoned, that it might have contributed to the prelate's death. Having served in Clarys in his earliest days, having served the prelate briefly, he knew the older man imbibed occasionally, something Kavan had not been aware of. Since Tusánt, like the majority of Elyri, did not consume alcohol, and he had deemed the bottle safe enough to pass on to the other man as a token of esteem. It explained Dórímyr's willingness to imbibe without questioning the gift.

Tusánt knew nothing about who had delivered it to him, except that it had come to him three or four months prior in a basket of tokens and gifts. Such baskets as tributes of gratitude were often given to gdhededhá by congregation members they aided, and on this occasion, baskets had been left for each of the gdhededhá, with embroidered ribbons bearing a brass tag with the names of the intended recipient. gdhededhá Hazen had found them on the náós doorstep and delivered them, but Hazen was not the guilty party. Kavan had gleaned from that bottle that the person who placed it into the basket for delivery had neither opened the bottle nor delivered the baskets themselves. The shadowy, faint image of a face that Kavan could put with the bottle, an image faded with time, a hand testing the cork to be certain the bottle was sealed, was their single lead and Kavan assured Tusánt that Ártur was already working on putting that face to paper for identification. If that person could be found, then at least they might be able to clear Tusánt of any part in Dórímyr's death.

As Bhílári had been, Tusánt was sworn to secrecy with this unfortunate news. Should word of Dórímyr's death reach Claide, it might tip his hand, make him wary of being watched too soon. Kavan hoped that, as long as Claide believed Dórímyr was alive, that he was no suspect, he might make a mistake and reveal himself, if indeed he was guilty. Kavan had nothing more than suspicion now, a hunch based on clues accumulated over time, but there was nothing solid he could present to the Queen that would lead to an arrest.

He warned Tusánt to stay out of Elyriá, an unnecessary warning since the gdhededhá had no intention or reason to go there. Despite the threats to his life, Rhidam was home, and the people had begun to accept him as never before. Believing Kavan's words, that he had been a single vote away from the position Claide held, Tusánt was biding his time for the day when he might be granted that position on his own merit. Barring murder or disease, he would outlive Claide by centuries. If he waited long enough, he might be able to lead Enesfel's Faithful into a new era of tolerance.

There was no reason to return to the land of his birth where he had no living family to anchor him.

Kavan waited in the upper oratory of the Lachlan keep, not kneeling in his favored place as he longed to do, but rather standing at the altar, his hands spread flat upon it, his head hanging low. Gone from Rhidam barely a week and already he missed this room. It was a room like any other, some might argue, but so many hours he had spent here since the night Arlan had become king, so many prayers and songs and miracles blossomed here, moments forever etched in his memory and in the cracks, crevices, and pores of the stones with which the room was built. He ached for respite, for an end to chaos, for a time of music and reflection and calm, for the comforting presence of Kóráhm whom it felt he had not seen in far too long though mere days had passed since they had been together at the site of the man's martyrdom.

The door behind him opened slowly, his guest hesitant as if uncertain why she had come. It was not Kóráhm, of course, but rather the young woman he had come to the castle specifically to see. "Lord Cliáth...did my father send you?" Hoping he had found some other way to Elyriá since he had not been at Hes á Redh when Ártur had gone for him, Asta came to the bard's side. It seemed she had grown taller during that short week away,

"No...though I have seen him and can assure you he is well. How are things here?"

Asta shrugged and stared at the image of Dhágdhuán before them. She appreciated news of her father but wished they could speak more of him instead of rushing into business. "The Corylliens have been executed but I would not recommend walking around Rhidam unless you wish to see what remains of them."

Kavan scowled. Such a display of the executed was not unusual; Arlan had displayed his share of the vilest criminals he had punished, and it was well within the right and scope of her office for the Queen to make such a display, but the bard had not imagined that Diona would be capable of it. Perhaps, if Kavan had been in Rhidam at the time, a different decision would have been made.

Or perhaps Kavan would have been forced to endure it as he had with the Queen's father.

"Your father said they were executed by an Elyri?"

"I don't know his name; he did not give it to us. I don't know if he's still in Rhidam, if he's from here...but I can look for him if you wish to meet him."

"Tell him I do...if you find him."

"When." She grinned. If the man was in Rhidam or any of the immediately surrounding territories, she would find him, unless he was Association too and did not wish to be found.

Kavan nodded. "Ártur will bring sketches to you in the morning…people from across Enesfel. They will need to be found and questioned, if you can."

"About what?" When Kavan did not immediately respond, she said, "I won't know what to ask if I do not know what crime they are suspected of."

Though he scowled, disliking revealing this one bit of news to many others, Asta was right. She could not help if she did not know what she was looking for. "Involvement with Claide…attempting to poison gdhededhá Tusánt…killing k'gdhededhá Dórímyr…"

"Killing?" Asta did not know the ancient prelate, had only met him briefly during his too-short visit to Rhidam just days ago, but she knew of the animosity some in the Teren church felt towards him for his refusal, in the years since Arlan had claimed the throne and brought the Faith back to Rhidam, to visit what had become the center of the Teren Faithful. Year after year he had promised. Year after year, he had failed to come. It was little wonder he was ill thought of, but hated enough to be murdered? That seemed bizarre, even to her…unless the murder somehow connected back to Claide.

"There is a reliquary…its locking flange poisoned with Orec, filled with coins and gifts from many sources, also laced with poison. It was given to Claide, who in turn left it for Valgis to give to Dórímyr. Ártur will bring evidence of those connected to it."

That meant Claide had not likely left Rhidam before the prelate's arrival, but afterward. If he had left the city at all. Asta nodded. "You want to know who added the poison…and whether Claide was involved. Is this why my father journeyed to Clarys? Did he know?"

"To try to stop a rumored murder. One of his sources indicated that Claide had not left Rhidam, that there was a plan to keep the two k'dedhá from meeting…a plan involving Dórímyr's death. Whatever details are in Rhidam to discover, your father will be unable to investigate them for some time and has asked you to do so."

Her eyes lit though her expression remained tense. "I will, of course. And these sketches? What of them?" She could oversee both investigations simultaneously, but she could not leave Rhidam, and short of sending royal forces to the far reaches of Enesfel to bring each suspect to her for questioning, reaching them would be difficult.

"Perhaps this would be an ideal assignment for Wace if he is still in Rhidam." According to Caol, the bounty hunter had been here not many days ago, but that did not mean he was still.

"He is; if he will agree, I know he will get results," Asta concurred. With the man's ruthless reputation and deep connections, few would want to cross paths or tempers with him. Whether working in an official capacity for the Queen or not, he was the best chance Asta had to spread her reach across the kingdom. Tracking people was what Elotti did, what he did well. The difference this time would be that, as yet, the guilty individual, or more than one individual, did not have faces or names.

"Discuss this with no one but the Queen; there has been no official declaration of Dórímyr's death, thus the news cannot be made public without it. If you learn anything, get word to Ártur and he will get it to me. As there is a chance the killer is someone else…not Teren…your father and I will investigate in Clarys…and I promise if we learn anything that might benefit you, I will get the details to you promptly."

Asta reached for his hand and covered it with her smaller one. "Promise me my father will be safe, and I shall be content with that."

"He will be as safe as I can make him, that much I promise." Without knowing what manner of men they would face as they dug into the workings of the Faith and those opponents to peace, it was not possible to promise anything more.

❧Chapter 8❧

"I don't know who the fellow is," Chancellor McGranis said, awkward and uncomfortable with disrupting the Queen at breakfast despite knowing that duty sometimes required such things. He was well-versed in the ways of court, had lived most of his life in the castle, but his personality rarely lent itself to anything more than reservation and politeness. "He said that Duke Cliáth directed him here…he has building supplies he wishes to sell."

The mention of the bard's name was enough to prick the Queen's interest, coupled with the mention of sorely needed building supplies. It brought her to her feet, her hand extending to her husband. "Let us see what the Duke has sent," she said with a smile.

There were men, some of the dress and coloring of men from the south, some wearing fashion that suggested northern Cordash, milling around a collection of nine wagons and talking amongst themselves while casting wary, irritable glances at the circle of soldiers around them. Prince Kjell was talking to another blonde, a man shorter and broader than he was, wearing a patchwork cloak of reds, yellows, and greens. They were laughing, which the Queen interpreted as a positive omen.

"Queen Diona," the shorter man said with a flourished bow and a charming smile. "Fen Geli, at your service."

"Mr. Geli. Welcome to Rhidam. My chancellor informs me you have brought building materials from Lord Cliáth?"

"Not from the Duke, but aye. Not my usual wares, but it was all I could procure this trip. I met the Duke on the road; told me you had use for them." Traveling into Rhidam through charred streets that had yet to be rebuilt had made that need obvious, and judging by the soldiers around them, it was reasonable to guess that some violent trouble had led to that fire. Fen was a worldly man, astute enough to note those details and connect them. He was surprised the Queen had come forth to greet him, rather than setting some underling to the duty, but perhaps, he thought with a happy flutter in his belly, his mention of the White Bard had gained him the honor. "I could seek buyers elsewhere but circumstances directed me here and I think you need them more than anyone else. Is the Duke here, perchance?"

"No." She did not know that he had been in the keep last the night, as Princess Asta had yet to be seen. Nor did she know how the man could have crossed paths with Kavan. "He is in Elyriá. Do not fret, Mr. Geli, my chancellor will see you well paid for your wares. Will you have more soon?"

"I…perhaps…" It was an unexpected request, but a partnership that might prove profitable. "With the onset of the storms, journeying might be difficult, but I will endeavor to bring what I can."

Diona nodded. "Aye, the storms will delay more than travel." The reconstruction efforts would suffer, but there was work within buildings that could be accomplished, thus she did not expect it to cease completely. "I ensure payment for whatever you can provide. Lord Chancellor…see to Mr. Geli's wares and his needs."

Geli suddenly seemed to only half hear what she said, distracted by the young woman emerging from the palace. The sudden influx of men interested in Princess Asta had not gone unnoticed, and the Queen realized she would soon have to discuss suitors and the future with the blossoming young woman.

"Mr. Geli...Princess Asta..."

"A Dugan, aye?" he asked with a smile and regal bow.

"I am," Asta replied, taken aback by the notice.

Fen bowed again. "Our families have done business for generations; I know your kin, your brother in Durham, as I know Prince de Corrmick here..."

"You know Wilred?"

"You do get around, don't you, Mr. Geli." The Queen offered her hand again. She did not miss the undercurrent to the words "done business," but Diona kept that observation to herself. If this man had Association ties, no matter how tenuous, it was wisest, she believed, to stay out of it. If the man was a contact Asta could utilize, the Queen trusted that her cousin would do so.

"Traders do meet the most fascinating people," he agreed with an evasive smile.

"Well then...Asta, if you would kindly assist Lord McGranis in tending to Mr. Geli and his associates..."

"Aye, Your Majesty." Flannery bowed and began the inventory of unloading the wagon's contents, while Asta hooked her arm through Mr. Geli's and escorted him into the keep where they could discuss money and other details in private. She wanted to learn about her brother's business...and discover what else, beyond commodities trading, Fen Geli had to offer.

~*~

Gaelán's trembling fingers pressed the wax seal tight to close the letter against prying eyes, put the scroll into the leather tube, and quickly turned it over to the waiting messenger before he had a change of heart about sending it. Would his father be disappointed in him, he wondered? His mother? His heart, however, told him that this was the right thing to do, as did his upbringing within the Faith. That did not mean, however, that his parents would be pleased.

Through the morning room's window, he watched a collection of wagons being unloaded as his messenger's horse galloped through the front gate and saw Asta arm in arm with someone he did not know, had never seen. Family friend, he wondered, contact of her father's…or something else? The young healer growled, wished momentarily that he could call his messenger back, but instead he held his breath, closed his eyes, and counted as he slowly let it out. It was Asta being Asta, he reminded himself, a friendly, outgoing young woman well-schooled in duty and gregarious to a fault. He was used to seeing it, but he was not yet used to liking it. Particularly not this morning. Such momentary flashes of jealousy, however, would not make him change his mind, and thus sending that messenger was the right thing to do. His father would advise him, and everything, in the end, would be made right.

❧*❦

The ghostly image of a ship, a tall ship of Cordashian make, yet bearing no crest and traveling with a single light at her prow, punctured the cold lifting fog as early dawn gave way to mid-morning. The sighting brought Prince Muir to the parapet with men around him, armed and ready to protect their tiny island outpost from a threat they did not understand. What they did believe, as the three ships commissioned by the Prime Magistrate bore down on the interloper and chased her out to sea without a skirmish, was that these unmarked ships, some of which had dared to attack them, were a prelude to an invasion of the main island, but it was unclear who was doing the invading.

Not Enesfel or Elyriá. Relations between the sovereign island nation and Elyriá were positive, as neither had a desire for conflict. And since the intermarriages between the Prime Magistrate's family and the Lachlans of Enesfel, relations between those two lands had improved and restrictions between them had loosened to the point where trade volumes were increasing. The Council had recently lifted its centuries-old ban on involving themselves in foreign affairs to send two supply ships to the beleaguered city of Rhidam. There was little building material to spare on the islands, but there was fish, silk, wine, pearls, and a smattering of other natural gemstones. Such provisions could provide the Lachlans with collateral to trade elsewhere to purchase materials they could immediately use.

Hatu then? Neth or Cordash?

With the Enesfel Queen wed to a Hatu prince, it seemed unlikely the often unstable southern kingdom would take such a risk and the ships never came from the south. North. Always north. While Neth was known for being unpredictable and volatile, there had never been any cause for them to choose violence against the peaceful islands. There was not enough wealth or resources on the islands, most of its residents believed, to warrant an invasion from Neth, Cordash, or anyone else. The ships that had approached thus far were a conglomeration built in each of the other kingdoms, save for Elyriá. None bore flags or other identifiers to indicate their origin. The consensus, amongst men not paranoid enough to believe the whole of the Five Sovereignties was united against Káliel, was that some private entity or organization had hired, stolen, or purchased the ships for use and that their interest in Pháne was an interest in the outpost in which the prince now ruled, an interest in resources they did not, or could not, trade for.

If pirates or brigands controlled the islands, they controlled the Bay of Phállá. That might be cause enough for invasion. And if Neth could not strike out at Cordash and Enesfel by land, then perhaps they believed doing so by sea would be to their advantage.

But it was speculation. Until they captured a ship and its crew to ask questions, they could not know what the purpose of these skirmishes was.

Muir was tempted, as he counted his ships easing back to their moorings, to let these persistent fellows see for themselves that what they sought, the cavern where his half-brother had been robbed of life, no longer existed. If any treasure remained inside, it had been buried the day Kavan pulled the empty room in upon itself. Exploration of the island after that earthquake had revealed a bowl-like depression on the eastern side where the sea made an effort, with every high tide, to claim a treacherous new cove. If anything of that cavern remained, it was filled with rock and seawater and there was nothing else on Pháne, besides this man-made structure and a small collection of weather-twisted trees, worth fighting for.

"Keep vigilant," Muir called to his men. With fog still clinging to the gently rolling sea, that ship could have drawn far enough out to see them while remaining unseen, still be near enough to pose a threat. They might return, and Muir was determined they would not be caught unaware.

❧*❧

"Did you get everything accomplished you intended?"

Kavan had been in the rented room for some time, watching the morning brighten through the window without getting too close to it, as Caol continued to sleep, snoring softly until he shifted from his back onto his side. He might have been asleep, but Kavan was not surprised Caol knew he had been out.

"Ártur will deliver the sketches to Asta," he replied without looking at Caol, "and she will enlist Wace to find those individuals. He will do it for me." The bounty hunter had no loyalty to Enesfel, no loyalty to the Queen, but he did feel loyalty to Kavan. "I have the names of four gdhededhá in Clarys who are viable candidates for the vacancy…and three elsewhere in Elyriá. There will be more, men nominated by their parishes or other regional gdhededhá, but these seven give us a place to begin."

Caol pushed up to sit and leaned his back against the headboard. "How do we…I mean…we can't start asking questions if we don't want word of his death to get out?"

"I cannot…but perhaps you can." He turned in his seat to face Caol. He had visited his one inside ally before returning to this room and had already formulated what he believed to be a workable plan. "I have a contact, Dórímyr's personal aide, who will be able to get you inside, briefly at least, as a scribe. The gdhededhásur will meet multiple times to discuss reports of Dórímyr's failing health, the official explanation for his absences and neglect of duty. They will begin to take sides, draw into factions in preparation for the day an election is inevitable. The election system in Elyriá makes it difficult for those not already in Clarys to be elected; those already here are our most likely suspects. I may be able to gain access to their chambers, investigate…but I should still rule out the others…" Just because the Clarys gdhededhá were the most likely suspects, dismissing others simply because they lived elsewhere in Elyriá could prove to be a costly mistake.

"While I take notes of politics undercover." Though he scowled, Caol nodded in acceptance of the proposed action. "I can't go dressed like this, and I don't speak, write, or understand Elyri…"

A gesture towards the dresser revealed the simple green and gold robe worn by the Order of St. Kóráhm. "Most of the Order's adherents are Teren," he explained. "As a novice, a lack of language skills should not be suspect. If they do conduct business in Elyri, rather than Trade as they most often do, I will get the details of the meeting from you when we meet next. You should, at least, be able to judge physical actions, body language, tones of voice, and mood."

"I can do that." Elyri were not easy to read, at least Kavan was not, but Caol would do his best and hope that others were not so similar to the bard in that respect. Out of bed, he paused at the wall mirror long enough to examine his features and wash his weathered face in the water basin before dressing. Kavan chose not to watch. "We meet here this evening…and decide what to do next?"

He did not need to look to know there was a nod of agreement.

❧*❧

The Queen was accustomed to seeing the bounty hunter coming and going from the castle. The man, true to his word, assisted Asta in identifying Coryllien sympathizers, general troublemakers prone to using any source of chaos to their advantage and, as of this morning, two more Coryllien members who, having witnessed the execution of many they had associated with, eagerly gave up what they knew of the remaining members, news that both Asta and Diona hoped would lead to further arrests and the end of the Corylliens. Their report of another three dozen individuals did not correspond with what they had learned from the executed prisoners, but Justice Corbin was already on the trail, set to bring in each mentioned name for questioning. Perhaps the names given were innocents, individuals these two held grudges against. The two Elotti brought in were detained in the dungeon until the truthfulness of their statements was tested. Their lives might, if they were lucky, be spared by the Crown in exchange for information, but no one envied the position of men proven to be traitors to a cause. If they lived to be released, there was no guarantee they would continue to survive in Rhidam.

"Is he off to aid Justice Corbin?"

"No," Asta murmured. Her queen-cousin respected her knowledge, trusted her, but she preferred to be kept abreast of what was happening, wanting no secrets between them. This morning, however, there had been no chance to speak with her about the news

Kavan had shared, nor time to show the sketches and names that Ártur provided to fuel Wace's quest. If she had waited, the bounty hunter might have gone on to some other duty and it might have been hours or days before Asta saw him next. "He is seeking some people Lord Cliáth wants questioned."

"Lord Cli…?"

"Was here last night…briefly." Asta managed a quick visual scan for anyone who might overhear their conversation before continuing. "He and Healer MacLyr have provided a collection of suspects in the murder of k'gdhededhá Dórímyr."

Asta had sworn to tell no one else. The Queen, however, deserved to know the truth.

"When did this…? Murder?"

Nodding once, Asta continued. "Yesterday morning. Lord Cliáth prohibits us from making the news public, as it has not been announced in Clarys …and the scandal it could cause, us knowing before anyone in Elyriá, is not worth consideration. There is a chance, he believes, that one or more of these people he seeks can implicate k'gdhededhá Claide in the prelate's death." That was news she knew her cousin would be pleased to hear, news that might take the sting out of not being told of Kavan's visit.

"By Ethenae, I pray it is so. I swear…any witnesses brought before the Crown this time, any who suspect Claide of a single word of slander or act of sedition, will receive every protection we can offer. Does he believe…?"

The younger woman shrugged. "You know Lord Cliáth…he dislikes speculation. He hinted there were suspects in Clarys that he and father are investigating.

"Uncle is…?"

A slight tremor crept across the Inquisitor's mouth but her face otherwise showed no emotion. "In Clarys with Lord Cliáth. He cannot investigate this here, of course, so Elotti and I shall."

Embracing Asta warmly, the Queen murmured, "I wish you every success." They had no other blood kin in Rhidam; they needed each other. The Queen had promised to never abandon any witnesses the way she felt her brother had done. Together she and Asta would bring Enesfel back to the greatness her father had intended. They would prove that they did not need to be men to make it happen.

᠀*᠀

Caol remained where Hwensen placed him, two scrolls spread on the dais, scribbling notes as ten men took seats around the stone fire pit in the center of the room. The tower room overlooked the panorama of the city, with the lake to the west and the rest of Clarys in a circle around them. Caol expected some sort of furtive meeting, a gathering of men wanting to keep secrets safe, but with thick glass windows hung between marble pillars, their location was hardly secretive. Other gdhededhá, servants, and visitors to Hes Dhágdhuán and Chellé Udhan could be seen passing to and fro on the stone paths below, some occasionally glancing up at the men gathered here, but they continued along without giving the meeting a thought. The gathering was high enough above the ground that what could be seen from below was not clear to anyone, and normal enough not to arouse suspicion.

Or perhaps they did question the meeting but kept their thoughts private or shared them in secret with companions and family. Hwensen assured Caol that everyone in the complex had been told the k'gdhededhá was ailing; any who knew differently were sworn to secrecy, and the Elyri aide gave Caol strict instructions not to speak, not to hint of what he knew to anyone…though it was a warning he did not fully heed. All anyone knew was that he was a novice brought to assist Hwensen while the k'gdhededhá was ill. With four other novices, one of whom was Teren, there to take notes as well, Caol's attendance did not appear suspicious. And when the other

Teren fellow chose to gossip, Caol did likewise in the hopes of gaining any small hint of how those living here viewed the situation.

Caol studied each person who entered the room, making mental notes that could not be put to paper but would be provided to Kavan later. Perhaps their focus was on the four names he had been given, but the other six gdhededhá were equally worth watching. If these were men of influence within the Faith, then any sway they might have on the investigation into Dórímyr's death, any connection to him no matter how tenuous, deserved investigation.

gdhededhá Ylár, the first to arrive, was the only Elyri Caol had ever seen, or heard of, without hair upon his head. Purple scarring over much of his scalp suggested burning, perhaps the cause for the absence of hair, and gave the man a menacing, haunting appearance. Judging by his hunched shoulders and the gentle tone of voice with which he spoke to the man he pushed into the room in a rolling chair, however, he was less intimidating than his appearance foretold.

The man in the chair, gdhededhá Tumm, stretched back to hear him, his wrinkled skin stretched taut to the bones beneath. His blue eyes were bright and alert, however, causing Caol to wonder how old the man was and how serious of a contender he was for the position of k'gdhededhá. Five hundred years he had heard? Perhaps six? The oldest known Elyri Caol had heard tell of was said to be shy of seven hundred years old when he died. Caol was willing to bet money that this fellow was nearly that age. In any case, he did not seem capable of poisoning someone, not if he was confined to the chair in which he sat. His voice was harsh, crackling, rough, and deep, and as the day wore on and he spoke more and more frequently, Caol quickly determined that Tumm was a man of firm beliefs who was not afraid to speak them or to share his position on sensitive topics. Perhaps he was not physically capable of murder, but Caol judged that if Tumm had planned to do away with Dórímyr for any reason, or anyone else, he would have no qualms with seeing a plan through to have it done.

Lláhy, the youngest of the Clarys candidates, barely spoke as they debated first the nature of Dórímyr's sudden illness, the seriousness of it, and what preparations the Faith Council should make in case their leader was to die. Lláhy's pale red hair, shorn in the middle and tonsured short, made his head appear quite round, an effect that was offset by his too large hazel eyes. He seemed less of a leader, more of an observer, a follower, but when asked his opinion directly, he voiced it succinctly, with carefully chosen words that left no room for misinterpretation. When an argument arose, it was Lláhy that the others turned to for a final opinion or word on some sticking theological or moral point. He was the youngest, but well studied and intelligent. Intelligent enough, Caol wondered, to orchestrate a poisoning without leaving a trail? Or too intelligent to need to resort to any such act to be elected to the highest position in the Faith?

Most of the others in the room were lesser gdhededhá who served the Faithful and led some of the orders who held their headquarters here. For the first few hours, the fourth gdhededhá Kavan had named did not appear, leading Caol to suspect mischief or at least forgetfulness. When Kluín did burst through the door, his disheveled blond hair having escaped the ribbon that held it back, he was panting, out of breath. He smoothed his green and gold robes and sat in the one empty chair in the room with muttered apologies and Caol's first impression evaporated. The man's clothes were mud-splattered, his hair damp from the rain that had begun falling early that morning, and his hands, also rain-soaked and muddy, bore a redness that suggested he had been outdoors somewhere working with his hands, likely digging. None of the others seemed surprised at his tardiness; most smiled or nodded, welcoming him with kind greetings and gestures. Kluín, like Lláhy, seemed well-liked by the others, or at least accepted, even though he bore the robes and insignia of the Order of Saint Kóráhm.

None of them, to Caol, seemed like assassins, but he knew from experience that visual perceptions of behavior, appearance, and personality could be misleading. And a man not likely to kill with his hands might be willing to direct someone else to do it. By the time he left the compound, the sun having set long ago, his feet and back aching from standing in one place for the majority of the day, he hoped Kavan had come up with something more definitive.

But the bard had little success either, having searched the compound's massive kitchen as best as his cat form allowed, hoping for a trace of poison, for anything amongst the kitchen and serving staff that suggested animosity towards the deceased man. As it turned out, enmity was prevalent; Dórímyr had not been well-liked by any of the staff. He was too quick to express dislike of his meals, too unwilling to forgive, too unwilling to extend a kind word, too hasty with condemnation and insults when someone did or said something against his sensibilities or moods. The nickname "Old Marble", something Kavan had learned long ago from Tíbhyan, took on life in the tales of the man's unmoving rigidness in personality and belief. Kavan had not been the only one, he discovered, to be threatened with heresy, though most had been threatened on such flimsy grounds as not showing the proper acquiescence on a Feast Day or not being prompt enough with a meal or in cleaning his clothes or his suite. His bitter, close-mindedness was enough to leave him with many enemies, or at least with a string of people who would not be disappointed about his passing. There were no indications, however, that any of these bitter, resentful men and women wished him dead.

It was easy to gain access to the private quarters of the four potential candidates while the men attended their meeting. There were few servants going in and out, and with doors rarely locked within a compound where none had cause to fear for their lives, Kavan was able to enter with a touch of his mind to those he passed who might recognize him. Forced contact with unsuspecting Elyri minds was discouraged by the rules of common courtesy, and normally it was something Kavan despised. Today, however, while he could not argue that a man's life depended on his actions, for that man was already dead, he could argue that his life depended on this action, on his learning the truth. Keeping others from recognizing him or helping them forget they had seen him seemed the wisest thing to do. If by some strange twist, an Elyri murderer resided in the halls of the Faith, and was in any way connected to k'gdhededhá Claide, then there could be many more lives at stake. That, to Kavan, was justification enough.

There was little in any of the four suites to suggest the men were capable of poisoning their superior, or to hint that they had done so, but there were small clues of their relationships left that others might miss, details that could not be found without touching and reading object after object. It was a form of invasion into personal privacy, welcoming the host of images forced into his head by each object he lifted or brushed his fingers over. But there was no other way. Most other Elyri would shun the repetitive absorption of information, but the expenditure of energy was a relief for Kavan and each tidbit might, he hoped, bring him closer to an answer.

A ring, a gift to Lláhy, a token of favoritism from Dórímyr was thrown haphazardly with disgust amidst the clutter on the nightstand. A falling out then, though there was no hint, in touching the band, what the matter of contention between the men had been. A crumpled parchment carrying traces of anger, on which Ylár had begun to write, with Dórímyr's name in the place of address. A series of memos and letters between Tumm and Dórímyr, suggesting they had known each other long before Dórímyr's appointment to office and suggesting that the surviving Tumm knew something, a secret, that Dórímyr had not wanted to be revealed. It also seemed that there was some detail of equal importance that Dórímyr had held over Tumm, something that prevented the chair-bound man from revealing that secret. Was either mystery enough, Kavan wondered as he worked his way around Kluin's rooms, to warrant murder?

Sounds in the corridor, the approaching nearness of the room's owner, alerted Kavan to the completion of the day's meeting, to the late hour and the hunger in his belly. Though curious to meet this particular man, this was not the place nor circumstance for such a meeting, not even if Kluín might be inclined to sympathize with Kavan's position and offer assistance. Kavan was not prepared for that risk, not until he ruled the young gdhededhá out as a suspect. Each of the four, it seemed, had cause to dislike Dórímyr, cause to wish him out of their lives, and though Kavan found no compelling evidence to suggest any of them had been involved in murder, he was not ready to say they were not.

Tonight it was time to compare what he knew with whatever Caol had learned. If that did not present answers, he would be forced to speak with each of the four in person. That would be a much more precarious undertaking that he was not looking forward to.

❧Chapter 9❧

"Y ou must come to visit," Prince Kjell said with a merry smile, resisting the temptation to put his arm around Princess Asta's shoulders. It had been intriguing to learn that Enesfel's acting inquisitor was a woman barely older than a child. She might be a Dugan, the daughter of the best Inquisitor Enesfel had ever had, who had provided her the highest level of training to be found, but she was too young to be involved with the likes of him. Such a relationship would be complicated, but oh the possibilities he could imagine for both Enesfel and Neth.

Sensing the scathing glare of the young Elyri healer, however, Kjell accepted that the Princess was not only young, she was also spoken for. Perhaps not officially, but there was no doubt she and Gaelán Cáner were destined for one another. Her devotion to the healer and his protectiveness of her did not prevent her from flirting with the Neth prince and had not kept her from flirting with Fen Geli before his departure from Rhidam earlier. He sensed secrets between the Inquisitor and her new Cordashian ally, but Kjell chose not to pry. He was in Enesfel to learn, to win favor with the Lachlans, both Queen and, as it turned out, Inquisitor, in the hopes of finding ways to work together against the man he reluctantly called brother who ruled on the throne of Neth.

He anticipated that Merkar was either beside himself with fury in thinking Kjell was not returning, thinking him a traitor, or was relieved that his closest rival for the throne would not come back to fight him for it. Perhaps he even believed Kjell to be dead. His return home would have to be cautious and carefully played, but Kjell had little fear of his brother or General Glucke. He had been talking his way around such men since the day he began to put words together. He could do it again.

"What a scandal that would be," the princess laughed, looking over her shoulder to smile and wink at Gaelán, hoping the look would be enough to soothe his jealousy. No matter her actions when pursuing duty, her heart did not waver in its devotion and she hoped he would come to believe that. "Someday perhaps…"

"I will pave the way," Kjell said with a bow and another smile. A page surrendered the reins of the prince's horse. "Your Majesty," this time his bow and smile were for the Queen who had come to bid him farewell. The empty wagons returning north with him had already pulled out of the castle courtyard to begin weaving through the muddy Rhidam streets. "Should you desire anything I can give, tell my cousin…" He smiled at Owain. "He will know how to reach me."

"I assure you I shall," Diona agreed, accepting the kiss placed on her hand before he swung up on his horse. "Your visit has been enlightening…and encouraging."

"Likewise. I'm pleased my visit was well met."

"Good speed and safe travels."

He bowed his head. "And best wishes for the resolution of your difficulties." Kjell waved as he turned the horse and galloped away with the cluster of retainers who waited for him. There was stronger suspicion within him now regarding his brother's involvement in Enesfel's difficulties, not based on anything that had been said or shown to him, but rather on a gut feeling he had long ago learned not to ignore. His objective was to return home and dig, to find out if that feeling was accurate, to get to the root of the interference, if there was one, and thus prove his honest intents to the Lachlan Queen in actions as well as words. Having her as an ally would be a good thing. He wanted that alliance to be good for her too.

❧*❧

A kid's sting,
like bitter honey,
to a world torn,
by apathy's rage,
it collapses upon him,
and consumes the burning grey sky.

"There are similarities in language and style, you must admit," Prince Espen said, the words Diona read aloud after her return from bidding Prince Kjell farewell still echoing in his ears. The departure of first Geli and then Kjell had left a void of sorts, a calm undisturbed by violence, that almost made the palace seem dull...until the arrival of this peculiar verse interjected a touch of mystery into their day. Espen had been grateful for the opportunity to enjoy his new marriage in the sanctuary of the back garden, but that enjoyment had now been, once again, interrupted.

"And the reference to grey sky...and a kid..." Stretching, Owain leaned back in the chair with a frown, frustrated that he could not offer his niece the answers she hoped for.

Diona frowned as well, smoothing the scroll with her hand and reading it again. She too was disappointed with the interruption, but a second message, similar to the first, was noteworthy, and, she was certain, important. "But what does it mean?"

"Does it mean anything? Who says it must?" A practical man, Justice Corbin was skeptical about this second note too vague to be a practical clue. "A poet looking for an audience, perhaps."

Asta shook her head in disagreement. "It is a clue, pointing to someone or something, that we don't know how to interpret yet."

"Of what use is it then?" huffed the Justice, arms folded across his chest. "If someone knows something they should come to tell…"

"And risk their lives like the last fellow? Obscurity might be their means of self-preservation." After Hagan's failure to protect a witness, Diona did not expect the public to have faith in the Crown's willingness, or ability, to protect them. People might not know as much about that failing as she did, but surely, there was gossip.

Owain leaned forward, took the scroll from the table, and read the lines again. His fingers traced the words, his brow furrowed, and his mouth moved to their cadence. He could think of three people who might be able to give meaning to these words…and those three were unavailable.

"Uncle?"

He looked up from the parchment into the Queen's eyes, comfortable with the familial label between them instead of a formal title. "In the absence of the writer…there are few who might resolve this…and none are here. Caol's wide range of experience might find some meaning in this, but Kavan is likely our best hope."

"Lord Cliáth?" Prince Espen did not know the bard well, though he knew the duke had tutored the Lachlan children and knew there must be more reasons than music behind King Arlan's choice of the White Bard as chief adviser and confidant. He also knew the man spoke several languages and as Elyri could read impressions on objects that no Teren could see.

"The most well-read man I know," Owain replied. "If there is anyone who might glean information, either in reading or in the meaning of the words, I would trust him to do so. He helped decipher clues that allowed us to find Princes Bertram and Wilred when they were boys. If there are clues here…"

The memory of her brother's kidnapping and death brought a pang to Diona's chest. She had not asked for details, how he had died, how they had found him, what the men, especially Kavan, had gone through to bring the boys home. All she had seen or cared about in the days and weeks following their return had been the grief of others, and the return of Espen and the troops from Neth's battlefields. But Owain had been there during that rescue, knew how instrumental Kavan had been, and she suspected that, without Kavan, the boys might not have been found and brought home.

"Then I suggest we get his assistance...if any one of us sees him...and I will send a request through Ártur. If these messages are telling us anything meaningful..."

The morning room door was pushed ajar and the young page Peter squeezed into the room without knocking, a scroll tube in his hand. He bowed, avoiding eye contact with anyone as he waited for permission to speak.

"What is it?" Diona asked, hoping it was not another cryptic poem. The boy was wet, his hair tousled by the wind and he shivered from cold. "Come by the fire and tell me what you have."

"A message...for the princess..." he said through chattering teeth, obeying the offer to get warm and dry at the hearth. "The messenger said it is from Mr. Elotti."

Excited, Asta took the case, popped open the hinged top of the tube that protected the contents from the rain, and removed the pages within. Seven of the drawings Ártur had made were included, four with carefully drawn lines crossing through the ink-etched faces. She hastily read the enclosed letter as the others passed the drawings around. It had been weeks since she had heard from the bounty hunter; the fact that he traveled and investigated in the worsening winter weather kept her and the Queen from despairing that the job was being ignored. As expected, they would hear from Elotti when there was news to report.

"These…donors…" Asta began, using the term Wace had written, "are missing or dead…"

The Queen frowned as the Justice grumbled, "Dead?"

"Died or disappeared during the worst of the Coryllien violence. He gives details…two merchants, a woodsman, a farmer. All from different villages and cities. No connections between them…"

"Except that they donated into that gift…" It was possibly a coincidence, but the Queen did not believe it was.

Scowling, the Justice asked, "What gift?"

The Queen shook her head. Prince Espen knew the tale, but none of the other men in the room did, and thus far she and Asta had kept the news of k'gdhededhá Dórímyr's death from spreading. No one, not even Claide or Tusánt, had brought official news through the Faith, nor, as far as she knew, had they received any, and Diona felt confident they would speak of such a tragedy when the time came.

"It is nothing…clues Lady Inquisitor was asked to investigate, nothing more. When we know what those clues mean, you will be given every detail, Justice Corbin. Please…" She rose, gestured to Asta to follow her, and continued, "Excuse us."

The men looked at one another, shrugging their confusion, acceptance, or discontent. Diona was queen, sharing information was her prerogative, but none were pleased with being left directionless.

❧*❧

Sóbhán and Gaelán were escorted with Rouvyn by several Lachlan soldiers, passing through the streets in tense silence. Late Elcalum rains had brought an assortment of ailments to the men living and working in the drafty homes and shops they struggled to repair before the rain turned to snow. The Queen had requested that Physician Talis and Healer Cáner go to Hes á Redh Náós as a goodwill gesture to tend to the ailing townsfolk. It was a duty Gaelán took pride in and was happy to fulfill. Sóbhán was neither healer nor physician yet had come because it was the day for the choir's rehearsal, because he knew he could help distribute tonics and remedies, and because staying alone in the castle when he had come to spend the day with Gaelán was not his choice of pleasures.

But slogging through the mud, protected by soldiers who served as a reminder of the dangers to their race, their people, was not pleasurable either. A year ago Sóbhán had lived on these streets, in the rafters of the náós, alone, hungry, cold and afraid. Always afraid. The fear was mostly gone now, replaced by new friends and the family of men and women who had taken him in and made him one of them. Kavan had not needed to do it. The White Bard could have sent him back to the village where he had been born, where he would have become a ward of the Faith, or some other local family who had known his parents, his uncle. No law or regulation dictated that Kavan had any responsibility for him, and Sóbhán had never asked for his protection. What Kavan gave, he gave freely, offering the chance for an education he would not have found elsewhere...in Rhidam and Bhryell, with healers, soldiers, harpmakers, and the private tutelage of one of Elyriá's prominent bhydáni. Those opportunities, and the bard's selfless acceptance, fostered in Sóbhán the love of family...not a parent, as he still adored the memories of parents he would not forget...but as an uncle and respected mentor.

His distracted thoughts of belonging plagued him as their work began in the Gathering Hall, where enough repairs had been completed to keep the worst of the drafts and weather out. It was too early for the choir to rehearse, too early for any except the gdhededhá and those still finding shelter within these walls to be awake, but there was already a line of needy townsfolk awaiting the healers' help. Sunken eyes, blotchy faces, sniffling and coughing, people stooped and shuffling with age and a variety of ailments. Most were not ailments an Elyri could cure; only herbals and poultices and bed rest could treat many of the symptoms. But sometimes, someone came with cuts, burns, broken bones or the like, allowing Gaelán to happily put his ever-increasing skills to use, and Sóbhán had the joy of watching it happen. Tiny injuries, he could have tended to, but his random hint of healing skill was something he rarely used on anyone but himself and he had not told Gaelán, or Kavan, or anyone else in the castle about it.

He was no healer. Sóbhán was not yet sure what he was.

There was one in the queue, however, who appeared neither sick nor injured; he was a tall, broad-shouldered man, reddish-gold stubble across his square chin, his coppery hair tied back from his face. His bearing was regal and confident despite the same plain, dirty, threadbare clothing of the others in the line. He wore no cloak, only a blanket around his shoulders and his tattered shoes, though once well-made, were worn through with age, but he appeared neither uncomfortable nor miserable. Despite his determination not to stare, Sóbhán watched him shuffle closer, his skin prickling with excited uneasiness as every one of his senses grew more certain that, despite the Teren-characteristic facial hair, this man was Elyri. Or at least one of his parents or grandparents had been Elyri, else the tell-tale energy traces the man exuded could not have existed.

"Níkóá." The stranger said no more as he reached the front of his line. Rouvyn was explaining a curative to a woman with a cranky, red-faced child, and did not notice the man in front of Gaelán.

Having paid little attention to the people in line, his focused set on each individual as he treated them, Gaelán was startled by the man before him. This man loomed tall in his memory, the executioner who visited his nightmares too frequently since the killing of the Corylliens. His appearance was unmistakable, though he had not spoken that day for Gaelán to recognize his voice and they had been too far apart for Gaelán to have a clear view of his face. Still, Gaelán knew it was him, and his clammy hands began to tremble as the color drained from his cheeks.

Níkóá reached for his hand, but upon seeing the young man's fear, he frowned, a sad expression for he did not understand that reaction. His hand dropped, but his other came from within the pocket of his muddy trousers. Again, Gaelán jerked away, suggesting to the stranger that the healer was afraid of being hurt though there seemed no reason for his fear.

Being Elyri, however, surrounded by anti-Elyri violence, might have been reason enough.

"I wish to leave this with you…and ask that you deliver it to Duke Cliáth…if you can." There was no other Elyri, save Ártur MacLyr, regularly in Rhidam. Since the elder healer was not here, these two young men would have to suffice as messengers.

Sóbhán accepted the offering when Gaelán would not and studied the small stone box they were given. It was not marble, rather some more common form of stone, granite or limestone perhaps, but he still understood that such a box was worth enough that the man before them could sell it and buy new clothing sufficient for the coming winter. Though curious about its contents, there was no way to see inside without breaking the wax seal or the metal band clamped around it. That secretive precaution made him scowl.

The copper-haired man laughed. "Do not fear…there is no poison, no threat to him or anyone else. I want to deliver this to him with the hopes he will appreciate its contents."

"Who do I say…?"

"I am no one of import…"

"What if he asks…?"

Níkóá laughed, a friendly warm sound that filled Sóbhán with ease. "If his curiosity demands satisfaction…he will know where to find me, I suspect. I am not hard to find."

The words should have eased his mind, but Gaelán's fear made it difficult for Sóbhán to trust the stranger any further. He said, "I will see that he gets it…when I can." He did not expect that to be soon.

With Kavan indefinitely away from Bhryell, there was no way of knowing when the box might be delivered.

"Thank you." Níkóá bowed, the noble gesture contradicting his unkempt appearance, and drew away from the line to allow others in need of aid to step forward. He remained in the shadows, unseen, for nearly an hour more, watching or taking advantage of the building's warmth. Sóbhán could not tell. Eventually, when he looked into that alcove one more time, the man was gone and Sóbhán frowned. Later he would discuss this with Gaelán. After that, he would decide what should be done with the box now in his possession.

Kavan expected to confront at least one of the four Clarys gdhededhá about their relations with Dórímyr in the morning but a middle of the night door-to-door raid by apostolic soldiers prompted a hasty escape from Clarys through the window of Caol's rented room. Caol guarded the scrolled parchment given to Kavan by the High Mother, a card of protection they decided to play as a last resort only if the need arose. The bird that flew through the window could not take it with him.

As the white kestrel circled the city, watching the ecclesiastical footmen banging on doors to eventually clash with the Kyne's secular forces over the boundaries of authority they had crossed, Kavan realized this could turn into a much larger battle between politics and Faith, something avoided since the ancient establishment of the Elyri state. Having no desire to be the focal point of politico-religious bloodshed, bloodshed unheard of in Elyri history, believing that the search for him would herald the public announcement of Dórímyr's death, Kavan chose to wait out the night beyond the city walls in a grove on the northern shore of Lake Eladhán that he had often visited as a boy. The cold and snow of early winter mattered little. Keeping his family and friends safe while continuing his quest for answers did.

Three days later, when Caol was able to join him at the agreed-upon spot, it was with news that, in that night-long search, before the intervention of the High Mother's forces, the ecclesiastical soldiers had searched without revealing what, or who, they were seeking. Such a hunt was a violation of the authority they were granted by charter agreement between the Faith and the High Mother. It was for that reason the Kyne had become involved. Because few but the Tribunal knew the truth about the bard's arrest, she had taken up Kavan's cause, arguing that they had no grounds on which to arrest or hold him if he was not being publically accused of a crime against the Faith or against her.

When the Kyne took responsibility for Kavan's release, and with the Tribunal unwilling to make an accusation of murder of a man publically still claimed to be alive, they were given no choice but to relinquish their charges and suspend their search, for the time being at least. As long as the k'gdhededhá was proclaimed to live, or if his death was at some point attributed to the unanticipated illness the Tribunal openly announced to everyone as the cause of his dereliction of duty, Kavan could not be accused or condemned for his death. Kavan had the right, by the Kyne's decree, to seek acquittal, and she commanded that the investigation of the prelate's death was entirely into Kavan's hands.

Such a decree surprised Kavan and, as expected, sat ill with the majority of the Tribunal. It was word from Hwensen that alerted Caol to the continuing, albeit secretive, hunt for the White Bard. If, Caol reasoned, Kavan stayed out of Clarys for a few weeks, focused his efforts elsewhere, the tension in the royal city should ease enough for him to return and complete what he had begun. By that time, it was expected that the prelate's death would be public knowledge, and, unless they asserted murder, Kavan would remain free of arrest and prosecution.

How Kavan and Caol could investigate a murder, if one was never admitted, would be a tricky matter.

With a few names supplied by Hwensen and by gdhededhá Bhílári during one of Kavan's late-night visits to Hes Índári Náós in Bhryell, Kavan turned his attention from Clarys and followed the trail of other likely candidates for leadership of the Faith. Caol, meanwhile, opted to remain in Clarys, maintaining his rented room, striving to lay the groundwork for an information network that no Teren had ever established. If news came of Dórímyr's death, or if word came from Enesfel, he wanted to be where he was expected to be to receive it. Ártur, thus Diona and his daughter, were aware of his approximate location. It was best he remained where he was until he was due to return to Rhidam at the summons of Anri Heward.

Fortune brought Kavan, the night he stepped into Káhrmycá's airy, spacious náós, into a room warmed by the ancient fire pit at its heart, something no other náós in Elyriá had any longer. Surprised that the fire burned, though his knowledge of Faith lore should have prepared him for it, he was not alone as expected at such a late hour. The familiar presence, not any of those he most often encountered in such holy places, belonged to the man who lay prone, face down before the altar, his body too rigid in position to be dead, the sounds of mumbling and occasional deep sighs and groans escaping his unseen lips. Kavan hesitated, not wishing to interrupt a man in prayer, particularly a man he was fond of.

But the blonde, un-tonsured head turned to face him before he could retreat, and Khwílen Kesábhá scrambled to his feet. "My lord...I did not expect to see you here..."

"Nor I you," Kavan admitted, grasping the offered hand firmly. He knew of the gdhededhá's activities throughout Elyriá and wondered, reading tumult in the man's touch, if that work was why some force, be it Kóráhm or some higher power, had brought their paths to cross in this place. "I mean no interruption."

"k'Ádhá forgive me…but I think such a disruption is excusable. I have spent too many nights in this place, seeking guidance without answers; now you are here…and as you gave me answers before…a purpose…perhaps you are here to do so again."

Kavan drew him down upon the steps of the fire pit, a comfortable place for his soul and heart, and after exposure to the winter chill, a place of comfort for his body as well. "I will offer what I can, Khwílen. What troubles you?"

"You know why I am here…in Elyriá…?"

The bard nodded. "A task no longer necessary I…"

Eyes wide with unexpected hope, he squeezed Kavan's hands. "No longer? Has peace been made between Rhidam and Clarys? Has Claide been removed from his post?"

"Unfortunately no…at least, he was not when I last received news from Rhidam."

"Then you are no longer in Rhidam?" As dangerous as that city had become for Elyri, departure from it was no surprise.

"Circumstances drew me to Bhryell…Rhidam is no longer safe for my family and I dare say may never be safe if the course of history is not corrected." He shook his head, hesitating before adding, "k'gdhededhá Dórímyr has been poisoned."

"Poi…" Khwílen's angelic countenance turned ashen in the fire's shadows.

"Nearly a week past." Kavan continued, anticipating what questions would be asked. "For now, he is proclaimed ill…to avoid the scandal of murder. The Tribunal is debating the wisdom of announcing his death by sickness or admitting to murder in order to persecute their primary suspect."

"They have a suspect? Who…?"

Sighing, Kavan released the other man's hands before he spoke because he did not want to read either astonishment or the revulsion he expected towards a man accused of such a heinous crime. "Me." He swallowed before continuing. "I was with him when he died, circumstances brought me to warn him of a threat. He went to Rhidam unexpectedly days before without announcing his intentions, and brought back tainted gifts...but I arrived too late..."

"He went to Rhidam with Claide in charge and no one suspects Claide?" Khwílen spat.

"None in the Faith...that I know of...save Hwensen and Tusánt. Few others know of his death...and with the focus on hiding the truth, there is no proper investigation underway. Only my own...at Kyne's insistence and my own desire. I have theories, but too many suspects. I am meeting potential candidates for his post to establish possible motives..."

Khwílen's grey face twisted into an expression of horror. "You suspect one of us? One of the gdhededhá?"

"It is an unfortunate possibility, given what I know...and as long as it is possible, I must investigate until I can rule it out or am left with the guilty."

The blonde Elyri leaned back, his fingers nervously twisting at his robes, raking and flexing in their frustration. Kavan did not interrupt his thoughts but instead used the silence to regain his composure. He did not like explaining this, repeating his suspected guilt, but Khwílen could be the ally he needed. The man had spent months traveling Elyriá, village to village, seeking justice for k'gdhededhá Jermyn's unnecessary death. Now there was another death, another...

Khwílen gulped. "They will suspect me." Perhaps not of the murder itself, as he could easily prove to have been elsewhere at the time of the man's death, but Khwílen could be accused of inciting discontent that might have contributed to the man's murder.

"I do not believe they would dare…but they could, should they reach the point of desperation," Kavan reluctantly agreed. He hoped not, and hoped that his handpicked leader of St. Kóráhm's would return to the chellé where he would be safe if the worst happened.

But Khwílen was not that sort of man; it was evident in his choice of Orders in which to study, in his acceptance of a post outside Elyriá, in his decision to confront every parish in Elyri with their prelate's apathy. Kavan was not surprised when Khwílen shook his head, his expression set with determination.

"You have come to speak to gdhededhá Bhín and Syán? How will you…?"

"I do not know." He could not openly ask if they had killed, or would kill, the leader of their Faith, nor could he directly ask about their desire to be k'gdhededhá. He hoped that an interview, a meeting, a talk, a shaking of hands, would be enough to test their mettle and give him an inkling as to their potential guilt or innocence. It would not, however, be enough to prove the truth either way. "I pray k'Ádhá and Kóráhm will guide me…"

"Perhaps I can save you effort." Khwílen offered his hands. "I have met and spoken to many gdhededhá during my time here…what I know may be enough to direct your search." He could not think of a single man who might take a life, or willingly orchestrate the taking of one, but at the time, he had not been seeking that sort of detail. "I can tell you, the brothers do not seem likely candidates for murder…"

It was the same conclusion Kavan reached when he took Khwílen's hands and read the details within his mind. As frequently happened in most rare cases of Elyri twins, Bhín and Syán functioned as a team in everything they did. The elder, Bhín, had been born deaf, and the young Syán had lost his eyesight in infancy. Always together, they had entered the Faith, serving as each other's eyes and ears, inseparable even in sleep. They were two of the most devoted men of Faith Khwílen had ever met, living in poverty, teaching and preaching and tending the needs of others during their every waking moment. To the people of the region, they were beloved, kind, gentle men whom many believed deserved to spearhead the Faith, the best men available with the humility to undertake such a job with wisdom and respect. To their superiors, they were men who never caused controversy, never argued, and never complained. They had the support of the people and the Faith alike…but not, Kavan sensed, the drive to pursue the path of leadership. One would not go without the other, and yet two had never been ordained to hold a single post. All the brothers wanted was to serve the Faith together for the rest of their days.

And serving precluded murdering the leader of the establishment around which their lives revolved.

There were others, dozens of them, from parishes large and small, wealthy and modest, popular and unpopular, most of whom had no desire to rise above the station in which they found themselves. Many gdhededhá, upon ordination, frequently returned to the towns and villages where they had been born or grown up, to serve the people they had known all of their lives. Others chose to be assigned elsewhere, having no desire to learn the secrets of family and friends. In recent decades there had been fewer applicants for the priesthood, thus the teaching orders had diminished in size, but the Faith was in no danger of suffering extinction. Indeed, Kavan mused as he sifted through Khwílen's memories, if the Faith could survive this crisis and reconcile with the Teren church, and with itself, there might be a renewed surge of those eager to work towards peace.

Three-quarters of Elyriá had been visited, three-quarters of the population aware on some level of Dórímyr's questionable judgments and actions. Sixteen names fell out of that sifting, those Hwensen and Bhílári had given Kavan and several others. Two of those men were ambitious enough to take potentially ruthless action, but Kavan sensed nothing in the others that warranted overt suspicion. Some were dedicated friends or followers of the late leader, some too meek and non-confrontational to take the risk of murder. The rest, men of faith and conviction, strongly believed that something needed to be done to make right the death of Jermyn Tythilius. But did any of them, or the ambitious two, have it in them to break one of Elyriá's most sacred laws?

Kavan was going to have to meet each one to learn the truth.

"Thank you," he murmured as he pulled away, gaze lowered to give Khwílen the chance to regain his composure as many often needed to do after such a reading. Not many, Elyri or Teren, willingly allowed such intimate and invasive contact. When someone gave him that trust, Kavan deeply appreciated it. "I know what I must do next...where I must go."

"As do I." Khwílen wiped his hands on his robe, a determined smile on his face. "I will continue to do what I have been doing...as though I do not know what has happened. To do otherwise would be to suggest foreknowledge of his death and arouse suspicion. I will continue my campaign, meet with as many gdhededhá as possible before you and I meet again, and I shall tell you anything I learn. Until this matter is resolved...or I am no longer needed here, k'Ádhá granted my request for direction and I shall take it."

Head bowed, Kavan agreed. "And you have given me mine. záphyr be with you, Khwílen...keep you safe."

"And you, my lord."

❧Chapter 10❧

The world was rain grey and Caol was cold and sick of the damp. Such weather was expected at this time of year, even Rhidam was likely to be caught in the grip of early winter, and soon the rain would turn to snow. The early precipitation dampened Caol's first St. Kóráhm's Festival, but the weather was not bad enough to draw it to a premature end. Here, close to Lake Eladhán and the sea, snow was unlikely, or so the people Caol spoke to in the inns, in the streets, or in the shops along Clarys' streets claimed, and though the rain was heavier than usual for the date, such amounts were not unheard of. Those who here as vendors moved their stalls indoors, into bathhouses and public reading rooms and beneath large open gazebos where people met to converse or conduct business, or into any other unused shelter they could find or create around the city center. Colorful waxed canvases were strung to protect these marquees, porches, and awning-covered storefronts from the weather, and those interested in art, theatre, music, and the array of autumn harvest foods, continued to make their way between exhibits as if the downpour was an everyday occurrence.

Clarys did not have the dark underbelly Caol was accustomed to in Enesfel, dirty streets where the destitute and outcast congregated for the security of numbers. With no criminal class, getting the desired information was a monumental task. But as anywhere else, men were men, Elyri or Teren. Caol's relationship to the Lachlan Crown bought influence with some, and gambling could gain coins, coins that could buy information from others. Sometimes people talked because they enjoyed the titillating rush of rumor. Gossip about the ailing k'gdhededhá and about who might be selected to replace him if he died was prevalent, as fear and speculation filled the void of official proclamation. Everyone had their theories, the gdhededhá they hoped would lead their vision of the Faith, and knowing that most gossip tended to have some kernel of truth at its core, gossip was the place Caol began.

No one had cause to think ill of Caol, to be coy or distant, as long as the ecclesiastical soldiers were not about. Posing, for most, as a merchant seeking potential business for his family in Durham, he was amiable, well-versed in the gossip from elsewhere in the Sovereignties, and was willing to give any information or gossip he could offer about Elyri in Enesfel, about the state of Rhidam, about the Teren church, or even about the ruling families of the distant lands he had traveled or knew tell of through discussions with others at court. Such chatter gained him tidbits to investigate, details to pass to Kavan, but he did not know when he would see the bard next. It felt as if it had been too long without word from him, though experience had taught Caol that Kavan worked best alone and that he would return in time to return Caol to Rhidam. Caol had to continue as he was, whether or not Kavan returned, and seek another possible route to Rhidam should Kavan fail to come.

Here in this place, he could not take justice into his own hands, did not know the proper authorities and channels to go through to get information to those in power who should have it, but Caol could take his findings to his daughter and Queen Diona. What, he mused as he wiped condensation and rain from the open window of his room before closing it to return to the streets, the Crown might do with that information, he could not guess.

❧*❧

"You cannot tell me who I may talk to," Asta exclaimed with a petulant stomp of her foot. Not since her mother's death had anyone tried to dictate whom she could speak with. Her father encouraged her to talk to everyone, for the experience of it and the learning of others' customs and languages. Yes, there were customs, some level of propriety that dictated the way a woman of noble birth was to conduct herself, but her father's influence had dictated that she was a Dugan first and foremost, and a princess second, and her chosen direction in life, to assume the mantle of Royal Inquisitor, demanded freedoms that she would not otherwise be permitted. She was not about to allow anyone, except perhaps her cousin, the Queen, to dictate her behavior.

Gaelán pouted and bunched his fists. "I'm not trying to…"

"You are! I speak with a man and you react like a spoiled child. You have to trust my busi…"

"I do trust you!" He was thankful they were in the stables and that there was no one around to overhear them, but still, he kept his voice as low as the heat of emotion allowed. There were servants in their quarters, readying for the night as the sun sank into darkness in the west, and soldiers making their evening rounds. But the majority of the day's work was done, and in the raging storm that dimmed the distant lights of the castle, few could be seen wandering the grounds. Clapping thunder spooked the horses, and the clatter of nervous hooves, the nickering and echoing rumbles across the sky kept his disagreement with Asta from spreading beyond the stable walls.

"No…you do not. I am the Inquisitor and…"

"You are not…"

❧169❧

"I am!" Perhaps not officially, since her father still held the title on official documents, but with Caol absent indefinitely, Asta had been granted every right and responsibility the title of Inquisitor held. "Or I will be one day. Talking to people is my duty, and if you cannot accept that Gaelán Cáner…"

Her frustrated tone reminded Gaelán of his mother, the scolding way she used to bring him and his brother in line when they refused to listen to her, or their father, in the way they should. It was a tone that made him flush with indignation, made him feel like the child Asta was accusing him of being, and he turned away to hide his embarrassment and frustration. "If I cannot then…what?" he asked without looking at her.

She sighed, made it to the stable door, and looked back at him. "Then there can be no future for us."

Asta tried to argue, as she stalked away, that she understood his jealousy, but she could not understand something that, in her heart, was unwarranted. Not long ago, perhaps, there had been a cause for wonder, as she had flirted in their growing up years with him, his brother, Hagan, and many other young men who came and went through the keep. But she had turned down Hagan's marriage proposal and when the feud had begun between the Cáner boys when Tayte had turned against his younger brother, it was Gaelán Asta sided with. He was the one she chose to spend her free time with, the one she trusted with her secrets, the one she turned to when she needed someone to listen. He was also the one she had chosen to give her chastity to. Was that not proof enough, she thought, as she wiped tears and rain from her cheeks, of loyalty and devotion? Surely he did not think she was the sort of woman to bed every man she talked to. The notion that he might think that of her was the most painful thing she could imagine. Her choice to surrender to him might have been a mistake. Perhaps he regretted it. She did not know and was afraid to ask.

Gaelán did not hear her leave, but when she said no more, when the night grew still of thunder and anxious horses, he knew he was alone. Regret was the furthest thing from his thoughts, except when he wondered if perhaps she regretted their impulsive act. In his head, he knew she was right. He was behaving childishly. He had known her too long to believe she would ever share what she had shared with him with anyone else. Asta, for all the liberties her father had taken in her upbringing, had been raised to be more honorable than that. As had Gaelán. His head knew better, trusted her, and deep in his soul, he trusted her too. Somewhere in the middle, however, where his heart lived, those flashes of jealousy continued to rule his head and he did not know how to win the battle against them. He did not want to drive her out of his life before he had his father's answer, before he could ask her the question burning to be asked.

"Something troubles you, Gaelán?"

Not having heard anyone's approach, the young healer started and turned to find Kavan in the dim light where Asta had been moments before. "k'aendhá," he exclaimed; not caring if it was childlike or not, he threw his arms around the bard and hugged him.

Kavan welcomed the embrace of the boy he had grown closer to in the months Gaelán had lived in Rhidam. Gaelán was as tall as he was, something Kavan had not paid attention to before, and though he lacked Bhríd's breadth of shoulder, he was filling out into a strong young man. And his center of power was stronger, more focused, something Kavan believed was due more to Tíbhyan's added training than anything Kavan or Ártur had taught him. He was not, however, trained enough to keep his thoughts under control, and the fears and feelings towards Asta that occupied much of his waking time were easy for Kavan to read.

The bard chose not to speak of them, however, preferring to let Gaelán bring up his troubles if he wished, now that Kavan had offered to hear him. He had not come to Rhidam to bring news or ease pains. He had come to see Ártur and Gaelán, since he was aware that the elder healer was still in Rhidam this night, tending the ailing gdhededhá Tusánt. It was not a serious ailment, the contact with his cousin across the miles had confirmed that, but the Elyri gdhededhá trusted no other physician as much as he trusted the man who had served in Rhidam far longer than anyone else.

"I did not think to see you again," Gaelán murmured against Kavan's shoulder. There was a touch of jealousy in those words, as there had been towards Asta minutes ago, but Gaelán did not try to hide it from Kavan as he had tried to hide it from her.

Kavan drew back but held on to Gaelán's shoulders tenderly. "Your brother has damaged your trust, Gaelán..." Perhaps his mother had as well, since Madalyn made little effort to disguise her favoritism towards her eldest son, favoritism she appeared not to see. Gaelán's father following her to Levonne, leaving Gaelán alone during such troubling times, had not helped. "But you must overcome that. Duty draws me elsewhere, but that does not mean I love you any less...nor does your father...or Asta."

The younger man looked away and freed himself from Kavan's hands. "I know...but sometimes..."

Kavan looked at his empty palms, the sudden impression gained from his cousin a strange and unexpected one. "Sometimes it is difficult to trust when much around you has changed. But circumstances and duties should not change a person's heart. Your parents will always love you. And tonight, I am here for you."

"Me?"

He nodded. "Bhryell is dangerous for me...and would be for the others there if I was to go back...and tonight I wish not to be alone."

"Not to be...?" Gaelán's features twisted with suspicion for a moment before he grinned with a touch of embarrassment and regret that he had not remembered sooner. "It is your birth day."

"It is St. Kóráhm's day," Kavan corrected, though Kóráhm was not the reason Kavan wanted company. True, the saint's company had been absent from his life for several weeks and Kavan had not had the opportunity to retrieve his harp, to play in prayer in order to summon his patron and mentor to him. But tonight it was something else, some other longing in his core to see Gaelán, to touch the young man and be with him, and it was that longing Kavan chose to follow instead of risking Wortham or his children by returning to Bhryell. They might be expecting him this night, but he would not go there. It might have been Gaelán's emotional need that drew him, but here was where Kavan felt he needed to be.

"It is, yes," Gaelán agreed, "but he is not why you are here."

Instead of contradicting him or second-guessing his words, Kavan changed the subject, assuring him of something Gaelán needed to remember. "The princess is not to be distrusted wrongly, Gaelán. You know the Dugans are an honorable family. She would not disgrace herself, or you, by showing unfaithfulness or infidelity as your heart accuses…"

Gaelán did not ask how Kavan knew about Asta, or what he knew, and he did not look into the man's face for fear of seeing a deeper understanding of recent developments between him and Asta than Gaelán was prepared to admit to. He might have been there listening before she left. It was the easiest reason to believe. "I know…" he mumbled, chastised.

"Prove it to her. Do not tell her, but show her. Give her your trust and she will give you what you seek. She will not betray you, Gaelán. I can assure you of that."

As they stepped into the dwindling rain to stroll through the gardens, to talk and share one another's company, Gaelán's mood lifted. If Kavan said something was true, then it was. Kavan would not lie to him. He had insight…and the Sight. It was up to Gaelán to trust him too.

ॐ*ॐ

Nerves rattled, Bhríd thundered up the stairs of his home, intending to demand information that he suspected his wife had but had not yet shared with him. The woman, heavily pregnant with what Ártur said would be twins, had been weak and unwell as the pregnancy continued, and Bhríd strove every day to take her health into consideration. But the continuing blind favoritism of their troubled eldest son was wearing thin and frightened him more than he admitted. He had not seen Tayte in weeks, but he always knew when the young man had been home. He knew it in the fearful silence of the newly hired staff, knew it in the tension he could feel in the air, knew it in the way Madalyn kept her distance. Tayte's last visit had been three days ago, while Bhríd had spent the day amongst the vineyard workers preparing the last of the vines for winter. Snow was uncommon in Levonne, but the cold and the storms that blew in from the sea could still damage the sensitive plants.

"Where has he gone?"

Though the hour was late, Madalyn waited quietly on her sewing bench at the window, hands in her lap, staring wistfully, her thoughts seemingly far away or else deep within. But Bhríd knew she had heard him coming up the stairs and saw, in the set of her shoulders and jaw, that she was prepared for confrontation.

When she did not reply, he thundered across the room and threw the rolled parchment he carried onto her lap. "Have you seen this? Have you read it?"

At first, she did not move, did not look at the scroll he had thrown at her, but gradually she recognized that his mood was rooted in fear rather than fury. She smoothed it open and read its contents. She read it a second time, her face showing more confusion with each word, until she looked wide-eyed at her husband.

"No...I...when did you...where did you...?

"I found it in his room! According to the servants, it arrived three days ago for me...when he was last here..."

Her pale cheeks lost more color, turning deathly grey. The implications of Tayte intercepting such a letter from his brother, not sharing it with her or his father, and then disappearing, were chilling. "It does not mean..." she began, stammering, unable to believe the implications her husband was fearfully making.

"I pray you are right," Bhríd snorted, yanking the scroll away. "I am going to Rhidam...now...to find our boys. If you love them both...pray that Tayte is no fool."

The thought of what could be waiting burned within as he stepped into the rarely used house Gate and left Levonne.

❧*❧

They strolled the grounds the better part of the evening, until the midnight bells tolled and Kavan stole away to spend a short while with Ártur before returning to Elyriá. Gaelán knew he would regret the late hour come daybreak, but he felt more confident in his relationship with Asta and was happy that Kavan had chosen to spend time with him at the start of this important day. Their circle of the gardens and grounds brought them to a rear entrance of the castle, where servants entered each morning and exited each evening. Soaked to the skin and cold, Gaelán nevertheless remained outdoors, his mind and heart too awhirl to consider sleep. There were benches here, where the servants sometimes took their rest, and Gaelán waited there, watching the last of the clouds dissipate and follow the now-vanished rain to the north of the city.

He had been there over two hours, past the tolling of the second-hour bell, when footsteps roused his attention from his daydreams. Asta, perhaps, or Ártur returned from the náós and his visit with Kavan, or a servant making a late night or early start. Shifting on the bench, turning to see who was there, he stared in shock into the face of his older brother, features twisted with rage and hatred that Gaelán still found hard to comprehend.

"You will not marry before me," Tayte spat, eyes flashing, the short sword in his hand poised to swing. "You will never marry her!"

"What...?" started Gaelán, scrambling to his feet, intending to back away from his brother's blade.

"You will not defile her with your poison the way he has done to our mother!"

Gaelán was too far away for the slashing sword to reach him. But the stone courtyard was wet, puddles from the downpour gathered in the depressions and crevices, and when Tayte's next lunge came, Gaelán lost his footing as he scrambled out of the way, yelping as he fell. His skull impacted with the stone beneath him and he lost consciousness.

Mid-flight, having chosen to fly before returning to Elyriá, a sharp pain in his skull, in his shoulder, brought blackness to Kavan's vision, paralyzed him, and sent the white kestrel spiraling out of the sky, crashing through trees and bushes, until he landed, his own form resumed, in a twisted, unconscious heap in the brambles.

"Tayte!"

The young man, bloody sword yanked free of his brother's body, spun, wild-eyed, to see his father and healer cousin emerging from the castle through the door he had used. Still enraged, Tayte bellowed and charged at his father, slashing and swinging as Ártur raced past to Gaelán's side to press his hands to the boy's injury. His lungs were filling with blood, an injury that had to be tended first and quickly, if Gaelán was to have any chance of living, but the rear of his head was misshapen, bloody, and Ártur feared the worst, though he worked as if he could save his protégé's life, intending to do precisely that.

When the sword sliced through his arm, survival instincts kicked in, and the fact that this was his son was pushed out of Bhríd's head. The younger man was intent on killing him, as he had been intent on killing Gaelán, and Bhríd decided at that moment to never allow this boy, full of hate, to kill another. Heedless of the blade, not caring about the damage it might do, when it swung Bhríd charged, hitting Tayte's sword arm with enough force to break bone. He knocked the blade from Tayte's hand and brought his son to the ground, pinning him beneath his weight. Tayte continued to struggle, but he had neither the mass nor the experience to break free from the Lachlan's Champion and his broken arm hindered his efforts as well.

"You will die for what you have done!" Bhríd snarled, his fury momentarily overpowering the grief of what his words meant.

"Then kill me! You know you want to!"

"Silence!" He struck Tayte's scarred face hard enough to draw blood from his nose and lip and hard enough to silence him, though not hard enough to crack the bone beneath. He did not want this discussion, not when he felt the nearly overwhelming urge to do what Tayte was goading him to do. He yanked the young man to his feet as five palace guards ran into the garden, drawn by the commotion. "Retrieve his sword…take him to the dungeon…wrap his arm…and stay with him…" Shoved into their waiting arms, it gave Tayte the chance to struggle, hoping for freedom or to at least draw blood from his captors. But they were five strong, and when one of them punched him low in the back, without Bhríd's protest, Tayte spluttered, coughed, and stopped fighting.

"I want no harm to come to him, is that understood?"

Yet one had already harmed him with that punch, and Tayte sneered, presuming this to be yet another indicator of weakness in his father. He did not look at his brother as the soldiers dragged him away. Nor did he see the glint in Bhríd's eyes, the weight of fury that would have told him the request for no harm was no matter of weakness but rather a matter of struggling with the longing to cause that harm himself. There would be punishment, one way or another, even if Tayte believed otherwise.

With the night quiet once more, the heavy boots of the soldiers on wet stone and Tayte's growls and spat curses having faded behind the closed door, Bhríd dared to squat beside Ártur to see his other son's injuries for the first time.

"Is he...?" There was blood, too much of it in his opinion. Blood across Gaelán's shoulder and upper torso, blood on the ground beneath where the sword had cut through, blood on Ártur's hands that gingerly cradled the young healer's head. Bhríd could not see the extent of the damage there, but there was more blood on the stones where Gaelán's head had been, enough blood to hint at the severity of the wound. Ártur did not immediately reply, and though Bhríd was anxious for an answer, he knew he could not interrupt, could not rush the healer, if he wanted his son to live.

When Ártur eventually looked at him with glazed eyes, he murmured, "We'll take him to his room." He barely had the strength to rise, but Bhríd helped him to his feet as he lifted his boy, and together they staggered through the servants' entrance. One of the returning sentries, coming back to report that Tayte was safely in custody, took Ártur's weight from Bhríd's shoulder and accompanied them to Gaelán's room. They made little noise, but something, the commotion in the garden perhaps, brought the Queen to them. Perhaps, Bhríd mused as he stripped Gaelán's bloody, wet clothing away and laid him on his bed, someone had roused her with the news of Tayte's arrest within the keep's confines. Why should they not? Tayte's being in Rhidam, being in the courtyard against the Queen's ruling, was treason. What he had done to his brother, and his father who sported gashes across his face, neck, and arms, were further damning evidence against him.

"Gaelán?" began the Queen, noting the blood all three men bore. Though Ártur tried to rise from the chair where he had collapsed, his legs would not support him.

"I do not know, Your Majesty," the healer mumbled, wanting to spare his cousin the necessity of speaking the painful explanation for the evidence before them. "The blood loss has been stopped…and what is in his lungs should not kill him, though it will take him time to recover from it. But his head wound…" He had seen too many head injuries in battle. Sometimes men survived them without incident. Sometimes men died. Sometimes, as with Bhríd's long-dead brother Phaedr, a man lost some physical capacity…sight, hearing, movement of his limbs, his ability to speak…but remained alive. "We will only know more…in time…"

"Who has done this?"

"My…" The second word stuck in Bhríd's throat and would not break free. "Tayte." He spat out the name with icy disdain.

The Queen felt no need to say or ask more. The spark that had led to this attack did not matter. She knew of Tayte's threats against his brother; it was enough that he had followed through with them, had come back against his banishment orders, had snuck into the grounds to do this heinous thing. "We will speak later," she murmured, her hand light on the dark-haired Elyri's uninjured shoulder before backing out of the room. It was best to leave the men to their wounded kin. Her duty was to decide the fate of a young man she had grown up with, had liked, had once called friend. A young man who had tried, perhaps successfully, to kill his brother for no reason other than that he bore Elyri gifts, Elyri blood, and had proclaimed himself Elyri. The same blood Tayte carried, but a proclamation he could not make.

White Purgator

❧Chapter 11❧

C oincidence or fate brought Níkóá out of his home as the rain stopped falling. He heard nothing unusual, saw no trace of any disturbance that should have interrupted his slumber. Pleased to see the stars, he stretched, his hands behind his back until his spine cracked, and sighed with relief. In that position, he saw the white hawk struggling to stay aloft, snap backward as if struck by a stone or arrow, and plummet towards the thicket nearby. It was the unique coloring of the bird, and the fact that he knew of no one who would be near enough to his home to harm the creature in that fashion, that made him sprint across the clearing to find the creature. Watching as it fell, he was the single witness to the transformation that occurred moments before the body crashed through the trees. A man. A man falling from the sky.

A white-skinned man.

He found the unconscious form amidst the brambles, exposed skin scratched by thorns but otherwise, he seemed unharmed. Disengaging the stranger from the twisted branches, fabric snagging and tearing as he worked, Níkóá brought him into his single room shelter, stripped off his wet clothing, and laid him on a spread of furs before the fire. Wherever his fingers brushed skin, the tiny cuts and scratches disappeared without any conscious effort on Níkóá's part.

The clothes were hung to dry before he settled cross-legged on the floor beside his unexpected guest.

He had heard the stories; few in Enesfel had not heard tell of the White Bard. He had heard tell of miracles and of the great musical talent that had seduced his father. Hope had led him to seek the bard out, but he had not expected a meeting such as this. No, the Elyri's path over the cabin had been circumstantial. He had been in Rhidam most likely, on business. Having made his first contact with the Lachlans, anything that involved them was of interest, and if it was something of enough import to bring the Elyri harper back when he had heard the bard had left Enesfel, then it must be significant.

He watched, further scrapes and pricks healed beneath his curious fingers, and still the man did not wake. Having seen no head injury, Níkóá had no idea what might keep the man from waking. The sky was beginning to brighten, dawn creeping into the air, by the time he decided he should have breakfast prepared in case his guest awoke. He knew where the last of the autumn berries grew, where the bees stored their honey, and he had bread that would suffice for a meager morning meal. With one more glance at the sleeping man, Níkóá frowned with worry but went out into the cold morning. This would prove to be an interesting day.

"Your Highness, I must see him at once."

Once again, k'gdhededhá Claide burst in on the Queen's breakfast, making demands as if she was there to obey his whims and wishes. Though angered and irritable, she was too weary from a long night's worry to launch into the tirade she felt the man deserved.

"Who?" She knew, of course, because there was but one other prisoner held by the Crown, one Claide had shown no previous interest in, and there was no one else in the keep she thought him likely to demand to see. No statement had been made of last night's events outside of the castle walls, no mention of this particular prisoner or the charges he might be accused of. No servants had been commanded to take him breakfast, none, to her knowledge, had been told about Gaelán Cáner's tenuous condition. The five soldiers who had come to Bhríd's aid last night, and those keeping watch in the dungeon below were the sole witnesses, and they were sworn to silence, but that did not mean that one of them could not have spoken to a man of Faith despite his oath to the Queen.

"Master Cáner, of course," the bald man said in a rushed tone, not realizing his knowledge might not be public. "I must speak with him. No man should be convicted without the chance of atonement."

"k'dedhá." The Queen cut his diatribe short. "No one has been tried or condemned, and no one…including you…will be allowed to see him before I do."

"You must allow…"

"I must," she paused for emphasis, "do no such thing."

"His work is too important to allow this feud with his brother to be his downfall. We need him…"

"Work? We?" The words were spoken quietly, but with no mock innocence or ignorance in Diona's voice. The weight of them, however, was enough to cut the prelate short, his mouth open mid-thought, his words buried beneath the suspicion he had brought upon himself. "What work, k'dedhá? Who needs him?"

The older man's face stilled with a blank expression that might have hinted at boredom if not for a trace of what Diona thought was fear or panic. "His family does, of course…and the work he must do to prove worthy of your favor and grace…"

The Queen wrinkled her nose as her husband entered the morning room behind Claide. He had been there long enough to hear her questions and Claide's reply, though she did not think he had heard more of the discussion. "k'dedhá," she said with a dismissive wave, "I do not believe you are that naïve to the nature of men. You will not see him; no one shall, until I have spoken with him. Then, if he desires it, you shall be permitted to see him."

Claide hesitated as if internally debating pressing his argument, but then stalked from the room without excusing himself or offering a good day greeting and without acknowledging or apologizing to the prince he pushed past. Espen swallowed back the bark on his lips and looked at his wife who gestured at the empty chair across from her and the meal spread for them to share.

"The noose tightens," she murmured before pushing the man from her thoughts. Hunger was far from her mind, but sharing these quiet moments with Espen before confronting the friend in her custody was a needed balm. Espen's hand over hers helped take away some of the pain this day had yet to heap upon her.

Alone in an unfamiliar rustic room when he opened his eyes and rolled towards the warmth of a fire, Kavan judged it to be a hunter's cabin, or a peasant's dwelling, as sparse and simple as the furnishings were. He rose slowly, aware of the throbbing in his skull that spoke of a powerful psychic jolt or the expending of too much energy too quickly. As his last clear memory was of flight, an easy feat he had done hundreds of times before, he knew he had done nothing unusual that would account for the ache in his temples, behind his eyes, at the crown and back of his head. Whatever had happened had been incapacitating enough that he could not recall coming here, undressing, or the night passing into day. His clothes, hanging over the back of a rickety pair of wooden chairs, were dry; he rose with painful slowness to dress, expecting that his host, whoever it was, would return shortly. Kavan owed them gratitude for their kindness, whether they had saved his life or not.

As he drew his torn tunic down over his head, however, causing a strain in the muscles of his back and left shoulder, other memories of the night came to him and with it, an image, in that pain, a face that made him choke and hasten his dressing. Gaelán. Gaelán had been harmed. Gaelán needed him. He intended to return here later, after Gaelán was safe, to give his appreciation to whoever owned this cabin. Now, however, he forced the change and flew back towards Rhidam as swiftly as his aching wings would carry him.

❧*❧

"You don't understand, Lord Healer…I don't care if he's not awake…I have to see him! Now!"

Ártur took pity on the young woman, her round face tear-stained and stricken in its expression, and stepped back to allow her into the room despite Bhríd's admonition that no one be allowed to enter. The jolt he received when the princess grasped his hands in pleading was the deciding factor, a factor he doubted even Bhríd would protest. He watched Asta fall onto the bed beside Gaelán's unmoving form, her arm across his chest as she cried. He frowned. Did he dare speak to her of what he knew?

Instead, he murmured, "I will leave you alone and return soon." He doubted, as he stepped from the room, that she heard him.

All that Asta could do was cry into Gaelán's red hair. Their fight last night seemed petty now, foolish, particularly since she had heard from the Queen that he might die and, as he lay still, his chest barely rising, his head wrapped with bandages meant to absorb the blood in his hair, that appeared to be true. She did not know what had happened because the Queen did not yet have the details, but those details were unimportant. Gaelán had been alone when she should have been with him, had been attacked when he would not be able to offer defense, and she risked losing the person she cherished most.

"This is my fault," she sobbed. "I'm sorry, Gaelán…this would not have happened if I'd been there…"

"You did not cause this, my princess; you could not have prevented it."

The girl lifted her wet face to gaze at the bard she had not heard enter the room. Her eyes brightened with a spot of hope at the sight of him, but she mumbled, "I would have heard his attacker coming. I could have fought them off. No oaths prevent me from…"

"He has yet to take any oaths…could have fought if he had been armed…but I can say truthfully that he does not blame you for this."

Kavan inched closer to the bed, staring at the young man, itching to touch him but afraid to. He did not yet know how this had happened, was reluctant to learn the truth, but a single touch to Gaelán's hand would tell him, show him, everything. Kavan felt ill-prepared to face that revelation.

"Oh, I think he would," she sniffed. "We had a terrible fight and I stormed away. I never gave him a chance to…I didn't tell him I…"

"I believe he can hear you…that he knows we are with him, that he knows how you feel. I spoke with him last night…before…" He frowned. He had been gone less than two hours before the attack had come. If anyone was to blame for not protecting Gaelán, it might be Kavan, and he felt cold and ashamed of that failing. "I know he has been…difficult…recently…but love makes us irrational at times."

"You think he…loves me?"

"I know he does." Gaelán had not used those words, but he did not have to for Kavan to hear them. Reaching Asta's side, where she perched on the edge of the bed, he clasped her shoulder tenderly…and flinched with the jolt that drove through him. "Do you know he sent word to his father…for permission to approach the Queen…to pursue your hand…?" he whispered.

Asta shook her head, wide-eyed and struggling to breathe. "He wants to…marry me? I did not know…he did not say…" But, she chided herself, she should have guessed. She was a master of small details, of reading signs, but had missed any he expressed. Perhaps this explained his stronger jealousy of late. Perhaps he was afraid he would not have the opportunity to ask her if her affections strayed.

Kavan sank onto the bedside stool to look eye to eye at the young woman. A girl no longer, no matter her age. Keeping his voice low, in case anyone should pass in the corridor beyond the closed door, he asked, "Do you know you are with child?"

The way she stared at him, slack-jawed and pale, her eyes wider than before, was reply enough. "I am with…but he will…Diona said he will likely…"

Wanting to address her unspoken questions and fears, praying that some miracle would pass through him, Kavan reached for Gaelán's limp hand and tightened his grip around it. He saw, he felt, the attack as it had happened, Tayte's hatred, the sword through Gaelán's breast, a strike that in itself might have killed him if not for Ártur and Bhríd's timely arrival…and the blow to the head as he slipped on the rain-slicked stone. Kavan followed the faint trail of power to the young man's center, to its source, and then sighed as he reluctantly pulled the tendrils of power away, though his hand remained around Gaelán's.

There had been no miracle in that touch. Not this time.

"He will not die." His heart, his body, were strong. But the damage done within his head, despite Ártur's care, was extensive and devastating. Kavan could not predict when, or if, the young healer would awaken and he knew that, if he did not awaken soon, eventually that strong body would wither and cease to be. That was information, however, he chose not to share.

"If he dies…or cannot…I will be disgraced." Not that she cared about such things, not in her heart, but the Queen might, and her duties as Inquisitor might be stripped from her. And what, she wondered with a sudden stab of fear, would her father think?

"Bhríd knows his intent, I believe…if he agrees, and if the Queen consent to it, there may yet be a way to…and if you would like your father to be here…"

She frowned, lost in thought, and Kavan did not push for an answer. There had been no miracle to reverse Gaelán's injuries. He should return to Elyriá, as he did not relish being discovered here, but Asta's predicament changed everything. Whether Gaelán lived or died, this was not a decision the young woman could make lightly. If she needed, or wanted, someone to intercede on her behalf to the Queen, Kavan would gladly take that duty for her, or bring Caol here to do it if there was deemed time enough.

"Kavan!" Ártur, having returned with a freshly scrubbed face and a breakfast he was not likely to eat, set the tray on the nightstand and embraced his cousin, noticing in the same instant that nothing about Gaelán's condition had changed and that he had interrupted something private between the bard and the princess, who quickly scooted away from Kavan now that the healer had returned.

"Last night you said…"

"Yes, but that was before…"

Ártur stared at his patient. "He is why you came back? To help?"

"I wish I could," Kavan sighed, meeting Bhríd's gaze over the healer's shoulder, his tone full of the pain he felt for Gaelán's father. It was difficult enough to face losing a child. To lose one child at the hands of another was the sort of devastating pain Kavan hoped he would be spared. Feeling it in Bhríd's aura was enough. Asta, heavy-hearted with the unexpected news as well as fear and grief, collapsed against Bhríd and held him as she would have embraced her father if he were present. She had known this man all of her life.

Surprised, the black-haired Elyri hugged her back, glancing from her to Kavan in question.

"There is…a matter we should discuss…" Kavan hesitated as Asta looked back at him. Her head did not nod but he saw the permission he needed in her eyes. There would be no hiding this indefinitely, and she knew it made more sense to confront it, to trust Kavan's assessment of the situation and follow his lead.

"He is not going to die," Bhríd grunted, expecting some discussion over where Gaelán was to be buried or how he should deal with his eldest son.

"No...not for some time," Kavan agreed. "But as you know, it is impossible to judge when he will awaken...when his mind and body will be his own...and there is something that cannot wait for that day to come." He could feel Ártur's scowl, knowing how the healer hated it when he, a non-healer, was able to dispense medical information that even Ártur was uncertain of. Kavan took a breath, looked at Bhríd, and asked, "Gaelán reached out to you...regarding marriage to Princess Asta?"

"Aye...he did...though I hardly see why this is pressing." Bhríd looked at Asta, wondering if she had known of Gaelán's intention and regretting that his abrupt words might sting. "I am sorry, Asta."

She shook her head and sniffed back a sob. There was no reason for him to apologize. Normally he would have been right; there was no reason that marriage should be important when one party was incapacitated and potentially near death.

"The princess is carrying Gaelán's child."

Both men stared at Kavan, Bhríd more shocked and disbelieving than Ártur, who had suspected the same thing after their earlier contact. Asta held one shaking hand to the healer and whispered, "Read me." She prayed he would, for though she did not doubt Kavan's pronouncement, hearing it from the healer would cement the truth...and if Kavan was wrong it would mean no more than a few minutes of embarrassment. Ártur touched his fingertips to hers; no more was needed to confirm what his cousin claimed.

"It is…you are…" He looked at Bhríd as Asta awkwardly freed herself from the man's embrace, believing he must think ill of her. "No more than a few days…or weeks…I would say."

"To prevent…difficulties," Kavan continued as Bhríd struggled to find words, "I am prepared to persuade the Queen to permit this marriage…and will speak to her father…" No one immediately questioned how Kavan might know where to find a man presumed to be abducted…or dead.

"But he is incapable of…"

"You know his intent, Bhríd. We know it was his desire. You, as his father, could speak on his behalf. If Asta is willing…a private ceremony…those of us here…the Queen…Caol if he is able…Espen and Madalyn if she chooses to…"

Bhríd shook his head with a deep frown. "No. I do not think she should…she will…" Her health was not good enough to allow travel, even through the Gate. As it was, he feared what news of this act between brothers would do to his wife's fragile condition, feared what she would do if she saw Gaelán like this, feared the demands she might make to protect Tayte. Torn between his anger and his love for his family, Bhríd did not believe he could afford to be persuaded by the woman's pleading.

As it was not a choice Kavan felt he could advise on, a choice that should remain between husband and wife, he decided not to intervene. "gdhededhá Tusánt would do this if we ask. No declaration has been made regarding the attack or his health. There will be little cause for any to suspect a child conceived before marriage…before his injury…it would be best for those concerned."

From the practical side, having been both chancellor and chamberlain, Bhríd understood that such an arrangement would protect the child, the princess, and the Crown. Though Gaelán had no assets or title to bring to a marriage, Bhríd could arrange for the younger brother's share of inheritance to be transferred to him, a wedding gift bestowed before Tayte ever faced punishment and word of this nightmare became public. And if, as he feared despite his bravado, he was to lose both sons at once, and the state of his unborn twins hanging on the thread of his wife's poor physical and mental health, then a grandchild, should it survive, would provide an heir to the Dubuais-Cáner estates that Madalyn had been concerned enough with to risk marriage to an Elyri at the start.

On the emotional side of their predicament, how could Bhríd deny this young woman he was fond of, the woman his son loved...deny his beloved son and the grandchild he had never dreamed of having...any protection he could afford? The protection of a legitimate marriage, and his love and support, were the most vital gifts he could give.

"I will talk to the Queen," Bhríd promised solemnly. "In light of what has happened...I can persuade her."

"We can persuade her," added Asta, slipping her hand into his. In a way, he was a second father, and she trusted him.

Kavan nodded, relieved. "Do it now...and bring gdhededhá Tusánt. I will seek Caol and return as quickly as I am able...before the day ends and word spreads..."

He did not know, as he kissed Gaelán's forehead and each left Ártur alone at the young man's bedside, that word had already reached k'gdhededhá Claide, that the man might have spoken what he knew to others. The Queen and Prince Espen alone knew that, and when Bhríd and Asta went before her to present their dilemma and the solution Kavan offered, to argue the rationale for the marriage, Diona's worry for the state of Enesfel was enough that she nearly exploded with rage at her cousin's irresponsibility.

Once again, Kavan had been in Rhidam and had not come to her.

It was that anger, however, that Bhríd's experience with King Arlan enabled him to turn to Asta and Gaelán's favor. The Queen could not afford to send her cousin away, both because of the potential of dishonor to the Dugan and Lachlan names, and because she needed the best Inquisitor Enesfel had until the Coryllien threat was behind her. Gaelán carried enough Elyri blood to be a healer, but his family, on both of his parents' sides, was well respected in most corners of the kingdom. Though it broke his heart to admit it, the scandal of this attack, brother against brother, had the potential to further sway the gradually turning tide of anti-Elyri violence back towards peace…but only if it was handled with finesse.

Barring some catastrophe, Asta was unlikely to sit on Enesfel's throne. Should Diona pass without an heir, her throne was already pledged to Prince Muir, the most capable Lachlan she knew, whether he carried Lachlan blood or not. Marriage to a Court Healer would keep Asta here, where the Queen wanted her to stay. Diona liked Gaelán and believed without seeing the letter he had sent to his father regarding his intent to marry, that the younger couple, whom the Queen had grown up with, would have ended up together, married, regardless of their present circumstances.

For those reasons, because it was what Asta wanted, what Gaelán wanted, and to honor her ex-chamberlain who was facing too many sorrows with both sons and his ailing, pregnant wife, the Queen agreed to a quietly arranged marriage. She alone helped Asta to dress while Ártur brought Gaelán to the upper oratory and Bhríd left to bring the still ailing, though much improved, dedhá Tusánt to the keep. The matter, this bittersweet wedding to legitimize an unborn Cáner-Dugan child and give Asta the marriage she wanted…and might not otherwise have…had to be dealt with first. Afterward, there would be time enough to see to the fate of the one responsible for this overwhelming heartache.

⮞*⮜

Returning to Clarys during the Feast of Saint Kóráhm was a risk, but for Asta's sake, there was no choice. Beneath the cloak meant to shield him from rain and gloves meant to disguise his hands, he did not believe he would be recognized as he paused outside of the door of the tiny prayer chapel on the far side of Clarys, one of the few Gates in the city he could safely access without fear of discovery. The crowd was thin here; most of the city's population gravitated towards the center of town and the magnificent structure that housed the core of their Faith. It allowed Kavan the chance to dig within the power to detect Caol's presence across the whole of Clarys. It did not surprise him to realize the man still slept in the rented room; the hour was early and the majority of those out at this time were either on their way to a Gathering or else were merchants preparing for the festivities of the day.

The memories of other festivals, when Kavan had been here to participate in the Showcase, added to the disheartened ache already inside. He needed music, he needed prayer, he needed his family, needed Kóráhm's presence to still his soul, but he could not seek any of those things. Others were waiting, perhaps already gathered in the oratory if the Queen gave no fight to the request made, and he had to know if Caol would come back to Rhidam for his daughter, or if he would choose to remain in Clarys, undercover. Kavan had no intention of judging his decision. That was not his place.

A small white raven crossed the width of Clarys faster and safer than Kavan could on foot, raising no questions or glances even when it landed on the windowsill of the room where Caol slept. It took several minutes of rapping on the glass before the sleepy figure, his red hair again growing in, stumbled out of bed to the window. They stared at one another until Caol, with the fogginess of sleep gradually lifting, realized that a white bird with emerald eyes meant one thing. He opened the window and the wet bird hopped inside.

"Sorry...I should have realized...but you could have used the door like anyone else..." Caol yawned as he plopped onto the nearest chair and scrubbed his face with his hands.

"I could not risk being seen."

"A white raven banging on the window certainly wasn't going to attract attention." The redhead smirked and wiped his eyes with his thumbs. "Didn't expect to see you..."

"I have come to bring you to Rhidam...if you will come."

"To Rhi..." Caol sat up, his interest peaked. "Has Claide..."

"No, this is for your daughter. Asta needs you."

Caol could have asked a myriad of questions that would have delayed the inevitable decision. But he knew Asta could manage on her own except in the direst of circumstances. He also knew that Kavan would not make such a request if the need were not great. He began to dress, not caring about his clothes' lack of tidiness. "Meet me at St. Bhyrínt's as soon as you are able. I have one other errand to complete and then we shall go."

"Saint...where is...?" The answer came with the press of Kavan's hand on his bare chest and a flash of imagery, the layout of Clarys with the route to the chapel clearly indicated, and then Kavan was gone, out the window the way he had come.

By the time Caol was dressed, his dagger tucked into his boot, and he found his way through the morning's thickening crowd to the dimly lit chapel, Kavan had accomplished what he had set out to do. The bard was near the altar with a young Elyri boy at his side who looked pale and horror-struck. "Come." The bard gave Caol no time for questions before pulling him into the Purification Chamber and manipulating the Gate to deposit them in Rhidam's upper oratory where a small congregation of people was gathered. Syl was there; Kavan had taken the time to notify her of her brother's dilemma and she now waited beside him, arms around his waist, her head pressed against his chest as both struggled not to weep. Gaelán lay on the altar, dressed in the finest clothing Prince Espen had been able to supply on such short notice, and it was to his friend's side that Sóbhán rushed. The prince nodded, eyes turned to Caol, but none seemed surprised to see him there, at least not as surprised as Caol was to see each of them and they were to see him. gdhededhá Tusánt waited quietly on the other side of the altar, head bowed in prayer, and did not look up when Caol, Kavan, and Sóbhán arrived.

Something was wrong with Gaelán, Caol deduced quickly, and knowing his daughter's fondness for the young healer, he wagered she was deeply upset. Was this why Kavan believed she needed him? He turned to the bard, about to ask, when the door of the oratory opened and Asta entered, dressed in a formal blue gown Caol had once seen upon Diona, with the Queen directly behind her. Though she appeared unharmed, her face showed traces of distress and anxiety, emotions briefly replaced with relief at the sight of him. He ran to embrace her, his fear that she too had been badly injured quickly subsiding.

"Asta..." he muttered with a shaky breath.

"Please do not be angry...please tell me you are not angry; please don't say no..." she squeaked with her face buried in his chest. It was a little girl sound, a little girl voice, and he regretted the paths that had forced her to grow up too quickly.

"Angry for what? What is it, Asta? What do you need of me?"

"I must marry Gaelán now...today...I must!" she gushed. "He might d...and we have to protect our child..."

"Child?" Caol stumbled back, pulling her with him as his arms stayed around her until he bumped into the nearest bench and collapsed onto it. He looked over his shoulder at the young man on the altar and then up at Kavan as if the bard could explain everything...or should have to prepare him for his daughter's words.

The Queen spoke next, feeling that her authority might make some difference to the tension in the room. "Timing is imperative, Uncle...I cannot go forward with the trial until I know that both Gaelán and Asta are protected."

"He was going to ask me...ask you...do this properly," Asta added morosely, "but then Tayte..."

Tayte had attempted to kill his brother? May yet succeed if the young healer succumbed to injuries Caol could not see. No wonder Bhríd seemed smaller, withdrawn and broken.

"A marriage decreed today is soon enough that, when the child comes due, there will be few questions about the timing of conception," Kavan said gently. There was a chance of talk regardless, as a hasty, secretive marriage for a Lachlan princess could be seen as suspect. But given Asta's distance from the throne, and this marriage being to a man of Elyri blood, claiming the marriage had taken place in Elyriá, according to Elyri practice, could provide the cover she would need to suspend those questions. It was a detail Kavan would discuss with them later, to be certain they each reported the same story to any who asked. The necessity of the falsehoods made him uneasy, but he could see no other way to protect everyone concerned...and do what was best for Enesfel.

Still reeling from the unexpected news, Caol stared at his daughter and she stared back at him, fear of rejection slowly filling her eyes. She had not intended to disappoint him, had struggled throughout her young life to be someone he could be proud of, and that he might no longer have faith in her was a difficult mistake to face. Eventually, however, he brought her hands to his lips and held them there, his hands trembling as much as hers.

"Then a marriage we shall have," he said, his tone strong and decided, "if it is what you want." If this was something they could do legally, despite Gaelán's condition, they would do it. He would protect his daughter, his second grandchild, the Crown, and even Gaelán in this way if he could.

There were no formal vows to be said, as Gaelán could not repeat them and seemed unable to hear them spoken. Bhríd spoke for him, promising the fealty he knew his noble son would have pledged to his bride if he was able. Asta made promises against the young man's ear, in the hopes that he was listening somewhere inside of the darkness that trapped him, and then the documents Prince Espen had helped Bhríd draft were signed, by the gdhededhá, by Asta and Caol, by Bhríd on behalf of his son, and finally by the Queen. There would be more documents later, once the matter of property was decided, but for now, the critical task of protecting lives through this legality was accomplished. Asta was a Dugan no more, and Caol, after several shared moments alone with his daughter, and then in embracing those he had not seen in too long, returned to duty in Clarys as a soon-to-be grandfather for the second time. It was not the future he had envisioned for his daughter, and it was not the start to this day he had expected, but it was what fate had dealt him. Had dealt each of them. k'Ádhá help them, he prayed for the young troubled couple. k'Ádhá help us all.

◈Chapter 12◈

Bhríd did not know what he expected to find when he entered the castle dungeon to confront his eldest son. A broken, fearful boy? A defiant, raging man? When he came around the corner of the row of cells where Tayte was housed, to see the hunched shoulders followed by the tilted head and a look of hatred on Tayte's face, what Bhríd saw was a young man he did not know. The single other individual in the castle dungeon was Idal Gottfrid, whose family had yet to pay the fine for his release.

Bhríd remembered the child Tayte used to be. Easygoing, jovial, loyal, and brave. A boy who protected his little brother more often than not, who tried to take the blame for mischief even when his parents knew the truth, the boy he had taught to ride, to wield a sword, to know the growing of grapes and the making of wine in the way the Dubuais had done for generations. A boy who enjoyed his company, followed him everywhere, eager to learn, eager to love. More open, in truth, to his father's attention and affection than Gaelán had been.

When, Bhríd wondered, had that changed? Why? Was it the changes in Gaelán, the emergence of Elyri power in the younger Cáner, and the tightening of bonds between Gaelán and his father that had opened the rift? Was it jealousy for something his brother shared with their father that Tayte could not? Or was it something else? And why, Bhríd wondered, had his efforts to reach Tayte, to reconcile their bond, failed? He had held out hope at the rise and close of each day, that he would be given another chance, that he would find the key he needed to unlock Tayte's love.

That chance, he knew with growing certainty, would not come.

"Where is my mother? Bring her at once," Tayte demanded, lurching to stand. His lunge at his father failed when the chains that bound his wrists and ankles to an iron ring on the floor jerked him off his feet.

Bhríd scowled at the demand and crossed his arms, thankful there were iron bars between them. Studying Tayte's face, struggling to see himself in his son, he snorted, "Your mother cannot protect you. Do you honestly want her to see you here…like this? To see what you have done to your brother? Do you know what that would do to her?"

"She would lose the bastards she's carrying," Tayte spat, distaste in his voice but something else in his eyes, an emotion Bhríd latched onto as soon as he saw it.

"Which would kill her, in heart, in spirit, and likely in body. Is that what you want for her? Do you despise her that much?"

"I don't desp…" The exclamation cut short and Tayte did his best to emulate his father's stance, trying to cross his arms before him with the chains restricting his movement.

"Then what? What is this burning need you have for her to witness your downfall?"

"I don't hate her. I hate what she…what you and she…"

"You hate yourself?" For what he was not, Bhríd wondered, or for what he was…by blood or by the acts he had committed?

"I hate you!"

The older man did his best not to flinch, not to show the despair those words inflicted. His son wanted a reaction, wanted to hurt him, but Bhríd was determined not to give him the satisfaction of seeing it. "Yes…I do not doubt that. But you do love your mother, as she loves you. I will not bring her here to watch you die."

"I will not die. Diona would never…"

"No? You think her such a weak Queen? What choice has she? You were forbidden to come here, banished from Rhidam. You broke banishment and tried to kill…"

"Killed!"

"Tried," Bhríd repeated. "He is not dead…and has married despite your efforts to prevent it." He was not going to tell Tayte his brother's true condition. Let him think his actions were for naught. Perhaps he would come to regret them.

Tayte's face turned ashen but the look quickly passed. "You are lying. You've never been good at lying."

"I have never lied to you." It was no surprise that Tayte chose to believe the words were a lie. How much harder it must be to face inevitable execution believing his efforts had failed. "I may have failed you and your brother in other ways, but I have never lied to either of you."

"You failed us by fathering us!"

The regret and pain of that accusation cracked Bhríd's otherwise calm features. "Perhaps that is true," he conceded quietly, "but the man you have become is not entirely of my making, Tayte. You were given every advantage of your birth and title. The estate was to be yours. Your future could have been anything you wished it to be…"

"Lies! Your blood has poisoned me!"

"Hatred has poisoned you. Blood does not rule a man's actions, his heart, his soul, his head. You are exceptionally bright…and yet k'Ádhá knows why you have chosen the path you have. We tried, your mother and I…your brother…the princess and the Queen…to guide you, direct you…yet you have chosen the path of hatred."

He stepped away from the cell to where the shadows fell over his face, obscuring the tears in his eyes. "Perhaps I have been too lenient in sparing you from consequences in the past…perhaps your mother shielded you too well. But we cannot shield you this time, Tayte. I cannot undo what you have done…though saints and záphyr know I have tried…"

"No, you haven't! You want me to die for killing your precious Elyri son…"

"I have never wanted you to…"

"That choice is not his to make." Neither man had paid heed to the approaching footsteps until the Queen stopped beside Bhríd to stare at someone she had thought she had known so well. "I alone hold the choice, Tayte. You held it once…when you chose to aid in killing a man…and again when you chose to ignore my commands and return to Rhidam…to attack your brother within these walls where you were forbidden to be. The law is clear. Disobedience of the Crown's command is treason. That offense alone demands execution. Attempted murder does as well."

Her voice was remarkably cool and callous, as unfeeling as Bhríd had ever heard it, but the demands of the Crown denied her any other choice. She could not give in to sentiment, to emotion, nor to the affection she once had for the man before her. Bhríd did not envy her position, as it was as difficult as his in its way. Making the decision, giving the order, was a burden he was thankful he did not have to make. When faced with his son's future, he did not believe he could do it.

"I did what I had to do," Tayte snarled, lunging again though this time with less force, intending that this act would startle or frighten her. The Queen did not flinch.

"Had to do? As ordered by whom? The Corylliens? k'dedhá Claide?"

The unexpected question drew Bhríd's gaze off his son; he did not see Tayte's reaction. He felt it, however, the flash of fear in Tayte's aura, the shakiness of his resolve, the hesitation that suggested he might yet be saved if he gave the Queen something in exchange for his life. The sensation was strong enough for Bhríd to whip his head around to stare at Tayte and demand, "Tell her! If it is so...speak it!" There was a chance, however slim, that Diona might be swayed to leniency if Tayte had damning information about either the remaining Coryliens or the k'gdhededhá she believed lay at the heart of the violence. It would not erase his crimes, particularly the attempt on his brother's life, but a confession might condemn him to a life of imprisonment...which was surely better than execution.

Tayte, however, recovered from the shock of the question, squared his shoulders, and replied, "I have nothing to tell."

"Come now, Tayte," Diona cajoled, the first hint of desperate emotion in her voice, the first indication that she would rather find a way out of a likely execution than to have to proceed with it. "k'gdhededhá Claide has already been here...asking to see you...he mentioned the Coryliens..."

The corners of Tayte's mouth twitched and his shoulders slumped and Bhríd believed he saw fear, a moment when his son almost gave in. But the slender shoulders drew back a second time and any fear that might have tried to emerge was buried. "There is nothing to tell."

The Queen might have sighed, but there was no sound as she stepped back between the attendants who accompanied her. "You leave me no choice, Master Cáner. When my decision is made final, you will know of it. In the meantime...shall I send k'gdhededhá Claide to see you, hear your confession? He was adamant about his return...should you wish it..."

A flicker flashed in Tayte's pale green eyes, an emotion, a decision, which Bhríd tried to identify but failed to understand. Chin lifted, defiance settling on his face, Tayte replied, "I don't want to see him. Tell him his services are no longer…are not necessary."

Diona bowed her head in acceptance of the request and started away. That refusal told her as much as anything else he had said. "Lord Cáner…if you please," she requested, believing there was no other way he would leave his wayward son. No matter how deeply Bhríd loved him, remaining in the sphere of Tayte's venom would be no good for either of them. Though she trusted the man who had faithfully served her father, brother and herself, she suspected he would, in time, feel an overwhelming compulsion to free his son from the fate he faced, However hurt and angry he was, how could he not try to save the one rather than risk losing both?

Bhríd took a long look at Tayte, who turned away and refused to look at him. Knowing this could be the last time he saw his son, since he doubted he would have the fortitude to watch the young man's likely execution, he sighed, fought for something to say, and in the end chose to not even utter the word farewell. "I love you, Tayte," he murmured before following the Queen.

Tayte made no reply, none Bhríd could see, hear, or feel. With his eyes closed against the choking pain, Bhríd made it out of the dungeon without sound or incident, having no notion what he would do next.

"My lord…Kavan…"

No one had told him of the bard's return. Understanding the danger he and the children and Kavan's extended family could be in if he was discovered in Bhryell, Wortham had not expected to see the bard for many weeks. He was not even aware yet of Sóbhán's absence. It was a shock to find Kavan seated on the floor in the corner of Dhóri's room with the child held against his chest, knees drawn up into a posture that Wortham recognized as a protective one, a shield against fear. With the shutters closed, the room was as dark as the fingers of daylight prying around the edges allowed, but Wortham did not need light to know Kavan was weeping. It was the tears that brought the captain to the man's side, his bear-like arms wrapping around both bard and child as he fell to his knees.

"What is it? Speak to me."

Kavan could not utter the words aloud, that his kinsman faced the death of two sons, one through murder, the other through execution for that murder. He could not express the pain of Gaelán's condition, the empathy he felt for Bhríd now that he too was responsible for rearing children as more than their tutor or mentor, guiding them in life, preparing them for an uncertain future in a tumultuous world. He had no words to explain how afraid he felt, afraid for Dhóri and Sóbhán, afraid of his own shortcomings, of failure, of how the boys might one day come to see him no matter what choices he made in raising them. Kavan was heartsick and terrified and with those emotions came one of the rare instances when he could not hold back his tears.

There was no need for words, however, not with Wortham, the one Teren he had known to willingly initiate contact with an Elyri mind. The captain did that now, holding Kavan's face between his big hands, using his thumbs to brush away tears as he pressed their foreheads together. Kavan knew the request without Wortham voicing it, and willingly, though with reluctance in sharing the pain, opened his thoughts and fears, the day's events and those which were yet to come, to the man he trusted more than any other.

Equally devastated by the news, the possibility of Gaelán's death, the guarded wedding and the unborn child, and an execution that could not be staved off, Wortham wept too, his tears erupting with snuffling and wheezing and gasping for air through emotions that constricted his lungs. There was temptation there, in Kavan's core, to free Tayte, to save at least one of Bhríd's sons from death since there had been no miracle pass through him that might save Gaelán, but both knew it was a futile, fruitless thought. This heinous act must carry consequences. Should Gaelán live to discover his brother escaped justice, the repercussions would be too painful to think about. And there was, to Kavan's mind, nowhere for Tayte to go. He had to remain hopeful, believe that Gaelán would live, that Tayte would see reason, even if it was too late, and that, when this was over, there would be love and forgiveness between father and son, and one good and honorable son left alive.

Wortham's arms slid down to embrace Kavan but his forehead remained pressed against the bard's, the two men rocking side to side, grieving with the child between them. Falling asleep that way, in the throes of grief, was not the way Kavan had wanted to spend his birth day. Accepting the comforting touch and embrace of his dearest friend, with his child in his arms, were the things that made the day, and the fear and despair that came with it, bearable.

≈*≈

They told her she should not do it, but Asta had not been raised to passively accept fate…or to casually accept the restrictions placed on her by her gender or society. No one had forbidden her to go, though they had strongly recommended she not confront the source of her distress. To her credit, she had resisted the lure to bring a knife or any item that might be used as a weapon. The temptation to use it would be too great, and she already knew the fate of those who took justice out of the hands of the Queen. As furious as Asta was, she did not wish for the death of one who had once been a good friend.

"Why?" she demanded when he came into view, before she reached the cell, rousing him from his appeared sleep. She did not care if he had been sleeping. She wanted answers.

"Asta…" There was less bravado than she had imagined there would be, but nor did she see any of the regret or sorrow she had hoped for, things that might have stirred pity for him.

"Why did you do it?" she demanded, fists balled at her sides.

He sat and faced her, seeing her more like the equal they had always been instead of as an enemy the way his father was. "Are you…he said you were…"

"I thought we were friends, Tayte. You and me and Hagan and Gaelán…"

"But why did you have to marry him? Why sully the Lachlan line with…?"

He believed what he said. Asta did not know if she should feel anger, disgust, or pity. "I am a Dugan. Or I was a Dugan. Not a Lachlan. Now I'm a Cáner…as are you…"

His nose wrinkled. "You could have done better."

"By marrying you? Is that why you've done this thing?" Unlike Gaelán, Tayte had never expressed anything towards her that she could have called romantic interest. Perhaps she had been too enraptured with Gaelán to see it.

"He is Elyri! I have done what needed to be…"

"So are you! You may not be a healer…you may not be able to do the things Elyri do…but it is in your blood. You share the same father…"

"That man is not my father!"

Asta gripped the bars of his cell and glared at him. "So you slander your mother by accusing her of infidelity?"

"Marriage to an Elyri is not a true marriage. k'dedhá Claide says…"

Nostrils flaring at the mention of Claide, her disbelief that he would listen to anything that man said as strong as her annoyance, she shot, "Claide says a lot of things that aren't true…and if you thought about them, you would know it. When did you become a follower, Tayte? When did you stop thinking for…?"

"The day my brother became one of them!"

Asta shook her head. Tayte was arguing in circles, arguing hatred for something he was, as if pruning that branch of the family would somehow erase his heritage, would atone for it in the eyes of the Faith…or someone else. There was no reasoning with a man who argued that way. That was one of many lessons she had learned from her father.

"My marriage is real…before k'Ádhá, before the Faith…before my father and the Crown and the law. And our child…ren…Elyri gifted or not…will be loved and cherished and will grow up knowing that hatred between brothers…or sisters…is the worst sin imaginable."

"Being Elyri…"

"Is as much a matter of birth and blood as being a boy or girl," she said with a sigh. "I am sorry you cannot see that, Tayte…that you cannot see your father's love…that you blame him for things he cannot control. But Gaelán is not dead…and one day he will fully recover and spend his life mourning his older brother. Remember that while you can, Tayte. He adored you…worshipped you. Remember you have killed nothing more than his respect…and yourself…and I…we…will pray that you find peace."

And, she thought, wiping her eyes, turning away without allowing him to rebut her words, I will pray that the one who has twisted your heart against your kin, against yourself, rots in the darkest pit of torment for eternity.

❧*❦

It took a lengthy discussion with the Queen, and pleading on Bhríd's part of which he was not ashamed, to avoid the public execution of his son. He understood why the Queen wanted it public.

Public execution of someone of Tayte's status…the son of a lord, a favored advisor, a man trusted by three Lachlan monarchs, the Lachlan Champion…would send a clear message to the whole of Enesfel. Noble, merchant, or peasant, none defied the Queen and Crown, and none attempted to kill another on the grounds of race. And if, as she suspected, Claide was in any way connected to Tayte's actions, it would, she believed, send him a message as well, a message that said if she caught him entangled with Corylliens, found him to be guilty of the death of k'gdhededhá Jermyn or anyone else, he would not escape justice either.

But it was a lesson the people of Rhidam, indeed throughout Enesfel, seemed to be learning without Tayte's public execution. A weariness of violence and the lack of Elyri in the land, the great Rhidam fire, and the deaths of two Lachlan kings in such a short span had worn them down. The core of anti-Elyri violence in Rhidam was imploding as Coryllien after Coryllien was captured and executed, and the compassion with which gdhededhá Tusánt served the Faithful in the face of oppression was gradually winning all but the staunchest anti-Elyri proponents. Whether it was the dwindling presence of Elyri to ease irritation or the declining number of Corylliens to murder, torture, and destroy in the effort to spread terror and hatred, the effect was a slowly growing peace, one that, in Bhríd's eyes did not need Tayte's execution to enhance.

With the number of public executions Rhidam had recently witnessed, was one more truly required to teach Enesfel that there were severe consequences for treason?

He admitted freely that his fight against a public execution was personal. Watching his son die would be difficult enough without it being a public spectacle. He neither wanted to have Tayte spew his hatred and anti-Elyri beliefs for others to hear, nor risk the young man crumbling into fright and crying in front of the world. Bhríd wanted to be seen as the good father he believed he had been, and neither end for Tayte guaranteed that familial image.

His main concern, however, and the one which held the most sway with the Queen, was the effect a public execution would have on his weak, fragile wife. It was no secret the great love mother held for her son. The shocking news, the attempt on Gaelán's life and his condition, the private wedding and eventual grandchild, Tayte's capture and execution, public or otherwise, would destroy her and possibly harm the children she carried. With Kavan's warning ever in mind, that his wife would be taken from him sooner than he desired, Bhríd had no wish to hasten that day's arrival, or to allow his wife to share the crippling pain he carried. If he could keep the truth from her, allow her to live the remainder of her days in peace and the belief that both sons were alive, even if that belief was based on deception, Bhríd was determined to remain silent.

It was consideration for the Duchess and out of respect for the decades of service Bhríd had given her family that influenced the Queen to accept Bhríd's petition for privacy. Four of the soldiers who had arrived on the scene of the attempted murder were serving as Tayte's guards and Ártur had been the one permitted to deliver meals to his kinsman. Other than them, Espen, and Asta, Syl and any other family Kavan might have notified in Elyriá, only Rouvyn Talis and gdhededhá Tusánt knew the details. Diona trusted each of them to keep the matter silent. The man she did not trust was the soldier who had informed Claide of the murder attempt and arrest, a soldier the Queen had the good sense to send north to serve on the border between Neth and Enesfel.

And there was Claide.

Diona did not, however, believe Claide was ready to play his hand through public confrontation, and he would not be able to prove Tayte's fate if she controlled the number of people who knew.

It was with further respect that she agreed to allow the execution to be as clean and painless as possible. Afterward, the young man's body would be taken to Bhryell and buried beside the marker that commemorated Bhríd's brother. Should word of Tayte's return to Rhidam spread, it would be said that he had been banished to Hatu, where the Harcourts could monitor his actions. If Gaelán succumbed to damage that could not be healed, word would be given that he passed due to a protracted illness, not attempted murder. Thus would end the House of Dubuais-Cáner, until the birth of twins, should they survive, to provide heirs to the estate. Bhríd no more relished the lies than did Ártur or Kavan, but to protect the Crown, and his wife, he would do what was necessary.

Those decisions were what brought him into the dungeon, his way lit by smoky torches and lamps as the setting of the winter sun stole daylight from the sky, and from the few small windows along one side of the dungeon, windows that revealed the ground level outside passed by occasional booted feet and the clopping of horses' hooves. He was accompanied past Idal's cell by two of the attending soldiers, men the Queen insisted on being with him in case anything should go wrong. They were men with orders, prepared to carry them out if he could not, unless Bhríd stopped them.

Not even the Queen believed Bhríd Cáner would do such a thing.

As they had done each time they had accompanied the healer down for the day's previous two meals, the soldiers unbound Tayte's hands to allow him to eat. His broken arm was bandaged still because he refused to allow Ártur to heal it, he held his good arm up to take the tray. Bhríd hesitated long enough to make his son suspicious, but it was the contents of the tray, small portions of pheasant, lamb, potatoes, sweetcakes, water, and wine, that told Tayte more than he wanted to know.

"My last meal," he spat, though with a tremor in his voice that belied the fear he felt now that he was nearer the execution he stubbornly chose to believe would be avoided.

"Aye," Bhríd murmured. "I argued for your favorites…the pheasant and lamb were all the Queen would spare."

Tayte grunted, accepted the tray without getting up, and side-eyed his father when the man did not move. "You don't have to wait for the tray. They'll take it when I'm done. I'm not going to kill myself with a tray."

"No…you will not."

Tray balanced precariously on his lap, detecting the hitch in the man's voice, and a note of sorrow, Tayte looked at him, his mouth full of food, his hand reaching for the glass of wine but hesitating as he touched it. He began to tremble.

"k'ykurích," Bhríd said to the unspoken question.

"What is that?" came the questioning growl.

Bhríd knelt on the stone floor, out of Tayte's reach but at eye level with him. "It is," he choked, "the sole form of execution allowed in Elyriá…so rare that I have not heard of a single use of it in the last seven hundred years…"

The young man's eyes narrowed. "I do not want an Elyri execution…" He was tempted to throw the tray, but if his meal was poisoned, he suspected there would be little use in that. He had already partaken, and such an act would probably get him struck down by the attending guards. As hungry as he was, as delicious as the meal smelled, it seemed a pity to waste it if he was due to die at the end of it.

"I do not want your execution; I would stay it if I could, take your place, but the Queen will not…it was either this or beheading."

Bhríd could almost imagine, almost feel, his son's heart twisting within his chest. Despite the bravado and the very public statement of his attempt on his brother's life, he was no martyr, had no desire to be made into a spectacle for public derision.

"Will it be quick? Painless?"

"Yes...relatively so." As long as the dosage was correct. He had heard horrible tales of agonizing deaths taking hours when too little was administered, and brutal seizures when too much was given. But Bhríd trusted Ártur. Though under oath to not knowingly, willingly, take a life, the proper use and dosage of this one substance was something taught to all healers, by decree; so that in the rare event of a scheduled execution in Elyriá, any Elyri healer would be able to prevent either agonizing end through proper dosage and would proclaim the death valid afterward. No healer ever administered it; they prepared it and provided it to the judicial authorities who would carry out the execution. No healer ever desired to be called on for this duty, especially when it was to be used on beloved kin. Ártur had resisted as long as it took Bhríd to explain its use to the Queen. If execution was unavoidable, sparing both father and son humiliation was the most compassionate thing Ártur could do...regardless of how deeply he hated it.

Tayte's dark head of hair bobbed and he returned to eating, though with less enthusiasm than he had begun. Neither spoke as the meal, then the water, gradually disappeared. When he reached for the wine, its bouquet telling him it was from his family's vineyards, he heard his father's breath catch. Lips against the untipped glass, meeting the other man's gaze over the rim of crystal, Tayte swallowed hard, cleared his throat, tried to steady his hand, and then drained the cup in one long drought, an acceptance of his fate that Bhríd hated to see. Tayte could have resisted, could have dumped it out or set the glass back upon the tray, pushing Bhríd to either force him to drink it or pushing the guards to be the ones to take his life. Tayte chose the inevitable, chose the Elyri way...regardless of his hatred for the blood he carried. Empty, it tumbled from his hand and shattered amidst the straw and dust that lined the cold floor. "You will stay with me? Until it's…over…bhydhá?"

The tears Bhríd had held back since Tayte's arrest spilled free. In those words, in the use of the Elyri word father, in the frightened tone of voice that followed the acceptance of death, he witnessed the return of the little boy he had feared lost forever. To hear his return, however, when there was no hope of going back, no hope of redemption, brought a crushing weight onto his chest and shoulders.

It was too late to reverse what had been done. Perhaps because he believed his father would smash the cup, seek some form of rescue, Tayte had, in his last act, taken the choice from him. There would be no further defamation of the Dubuais-Cáner name or the family. No chance to disobey the Queen's commands or destroy the future of his unborn siblings…Elyri blood in their veins or no. Tayte had surrendered to the personal, private war he had been waging, giving back to his family, to his father, the one thing he could give to undo the harm he had caused.

Bhríd nodded and motioned for the guards to unbind Tayte's ankles. There would be no escape, even if Tayte were to overpower them in an attempt, he would likely make it no further than the dungeon steps before his nervous system began to fail. When Tayte's legs were free, Bhríd scooted on his knees to close the distance between them and reached for his child as the first tremors of physical collapse began. Tayte's limbs twitched and convulsed and he clutched tight to the arms that held him, welcoming them despite his earlier claims of hatred.

"You're right…no pain…" The body's struggle for breath began soon after, the signals within that controlled such functions flashed and sputtered, connecting and disconnecting in rapid succession. Tayte tried to reach his father's face, but he lacked control over his arm. Bhríd caught the flailing limb and pressed the hand beneath his to his face. "Tell mother…tell…Gaelán…not your fault…"

Bhríd heard the breathing of the guards beneath the shallow breaths of his son. He heard the hiss of the wind through the shuttered dungeon windows. He heard his own heartbeat as it struggled to pull Tayte's with it, fought to keep him strong, fought to keep him alive. He heard the rattle, heard the sigh of expiration as the hand against his face lost the last of its warmth. Then there was nothing to hear but the silence of a broken heart.

❧Chapter 13❧

Despite the danger, Kavan insisted on being there for his family, lingering in the branches of the nearest tree as a small white raven, watching as Tayte was laid to earth near the burial marker of the uncle he had not had the opportunity to meet. All that any in Elyriá knew, save for Syl and Bhen, was that Tayte had been poisoned. There was no mention made of his attempt to kill his brother, no hint from any of those who knew that the k'ykurích had been administered to claim one of their own. Though not a Cliáth, Tám MacLyr, and perhaps many of the townsfolk, would have demanded the burial be elsewhere if they had known the truth and Bhríd would not be satisfied with a burial anywhere else. The young man could not be buried in a marked grave in Rhidam or Levonne, as there was too high a risk of word reaching his mother, and an unmarked grave for Bhríd's son was unacceptable. It had been bad enough to bury Phaedr on the battlefield away from his family. He would not allow a similar end for his son.

Long after the family departed for their homes and the comfort of loved ones, Kavan remained at the grave, the white raven perched on the marker sending up a song of mourning to k'Ádhá, to the záphyr, to Dhágdhuán, to any saint who would listen, a song seeking blessing for his broken kinsman, the man who would not find comfort at home and little of it in Rhidam. Bhríd would return to the keep, to his remaining son and new daughter-in-law, but his stay would be brief. Being too long away from his wife would raise questions, and for the sake of her health and that of the unborn children, he could not afford to answer them. Kavan did not envy his position and wished there was something he could do, some miracle that would restore Gaelán's health and life so that one son was saved.

Sóbhán, brave boy that he was, insisted on continuing the bi-weekly trips to Rhidam, both for the training he could receive there and to visit his friend and help with his care. Syl acquiesced to allow Ártur to remain full-time in Rhidam until Gaelán's fate was decided, a concession to her brother's wishes, so long as Ártur promised not to leave the keep, not even to go to the náós and he would, when he could, spend his nights with her in Bhryell. Enough family had been lost; she did not want her husband to be next. Too many people needed him. For the time being, Gaelán had constant supervision, family, friends, or carefully chosen servants who would remain with him. With the use of the Gates, even Bhríd would be able to spend time each day with him with no one in Levonne ever knowing. Kavan wished he could be there as well, but duty called.

A day and night of pleading song brought no solution, no hint of hope that he could change the path winding into the unseen before them. Kavan reluctantly left that place and his family to resume his mission. A resolution in Clarys would not be put off indefinitely.

Another week, perhaps two or three, and he would have visited every candidate in the outer reaches of Elyriá who might desire or have a chance at obtaining the topmost leadership position in the Faith, a position second only to the Kyne in relevance and as influential in its own way. None so far, as far as he was able to determine, had either the means or the drive to poison the k'gdhededhá in the hopes of gaining his title. No matter how strong the desire for the position, their Faith, either strict or relaxed, forbid such crimes as murder, and that adherence to Elyri mores and Faith tenants kept the thought from ever crossing most peoples' minds. Even those Khwílen had visited who accepted the truth of Dórímyr's failings for the Faith, for his people, showed a strong preference for allowing the wheels of ecclesiastical justice to take care of the matter instead of taking the decision into their own hands.

No one, other than a few in his immediate family and gdhededhá Bhílári, knew that Kavan had been in Bhryell. The hands of ecclesiastical justice would not reach him here, and none he loved would be harmed. Trusting their silence, and trusting Caol to continue his digging in Clarys, Kavan would follow his Faith, his heart, until Dórímyr's death knew justice…regardless of what that man had thought of him.

ᕔ*ᕚ

When he was not summoned back to the castle to hear the final act of penance from Tayte, Claide had been livid that the young man might be denied a Rite of the Faithful to be made clean before k'Ádhá before death claimed him. He was even less pleased with Tusánt's summoning shortly thereafter, for the young man would surely never accept words of purification from an unclean Elyri. Not now. Not after many months of righteous faithfulness.

He growled and paced the width of the naós, ignoring the altar and the homeless still taking refuge in the spacious, dark building. As long as they thought him to be in restless prayer, they would not trouble him. His agitation sprung from one nagging thought, one that should have, he believed, been put to rest by the news that Gaelán Cáner was not dead. Even though it meant failure on Tayte's part, it also meant that the Queen might be swayed to leniency, might be persuaded by Tayte's father to allow him to live, to send him away where the matter could be laid to rest without fuss. That could be,

Claide admitted, a better outcome than he had anticipated, for if the Queen allowed Tayte to live despite the treason of returning to Rhidam and the castle after banishment, it would show a royal preference for Elyri, show the people that Elyri could break the law without fear of punishment, whereas punishment for Teren perpetrators of similar crimes was swift and brutal.

It would mean turning Tayte's blood against him, but Claide was not against using the situation in his favor, regardless of the position it put Tayte in or what it did to the young man's view of himself.

But with no news from the keep, he could not press his advantage and had to pray that the people learned of it some other way, discovered the truth of the ways Elyri manipulated the Crown to their benefit, see how dangerous that race truly was. The seed of Claide's unease lay in the possibility that, in facing death, Tayte's courage could fail him, that he might reveal what he knew to Tusánt and the Queen. While he did not know much, it could be enough to endanger Claide and his work.

Nothing had been made public. The Crown had not pursued any leads they might have and punishment had not been administered. Perhaps they were waiting for the revival or death of the young healer. Perhaps Tayte's life similarly hung in the balance, awaiting that outcome as well. Perhaps, Claide thought with flexing fists, the devious Queen was saving her information, whatever she thought she knew, for the moment Claide attacked with accusations against the Crown. Again, she had him at an impasse and that, more than the danger he faced or the fate of the Cáner boys, made him angry.

Enesfel needed a new monarch. Diona Lachlan was not meant to rule from that throne and Claide was determined to have her out of it.

But who, if he took that step, could rule in her place?

❧*❧

There were few of them left. The Lachlans' Coryllien hunt was effectively weeding them out of Enesfel's population like the pests they were, but the few who remained were not idle. Leaderless, with Layton dead and Alty missing, the survivors continued to meet, to act on their own, though with little thought and planning to their activities or the consequences. With few Elyri to harass, there was no need for murder, kidnapping, or threats to existing citizens. But being bored and angry over the Elyri still known to be in Enesfel, they resorted to acts of vandalism, using blood, wine, feces, or anything they could find to leave messages of hate scattered around the city. With reconstruction still in progress, the effort required to remove the slander was an irritation, time spent that could be better directed elsewhere. But the Queen refused to leave such displays visible, and bounties were set on the heads of those defacing the city with salacious words or symbols. The announcement of a bounty brought a brief halt to the defacement and the arrest of a few individuals, but after a short period of silence, it began again.

Though aware of the continuing destruction, gdhededhá Tusánt did not expect to find it occurring in the náós when he, unable to sleep, came in to pray. With fewer threats of violence, though still aware of the menace his superior might pose, Tusánt felt no need to wake Edward or Saul to accompany him to his prayers. At this hour, those still housed here, fewer and fewer in numbers as homes and shops were repaired and rebuilt for families to return to, slept soundly, but even they, he felt, would protect him from harm. It seemed illogical to think that anyone would be foolish enough to enter in the middle of the night to desecrate the altar with waste and the small wood and straw effigy he found there.

The two men placing it, having come in quietly and gone about their work without disturbing the sleeping guests, stared at Tusánt with the same surprise and alarm with which he stared at them.

He could shout for help, could speak loudly enough to awaken those scattered about the náós. He chose to do neither. He chose not to exhibit fear or alarm, chose not to retreat and instead held his ground, watching as the pair struggled with what they should do next. Caught mid-act, there was no logic in trying to finish what they started or denying it. One began to run but tripped on the altar steps, falling to his face with a clatter and loud swearing. The second, more clear-headed, produced a knife from a waist sheath and threw it. It was ill-balanced for throwing; the wobbling projectile flew wide but managed to slice across Tusánt's upper arm. He yelped as the blade clattered against the wall behind him and those sounds, combined with that of the first man tripping, woke others, many of whom scrambled up with shouts and cries and surrounded the two outlaws who struggled to be free. Outnumbered, the effort was futile.

"dedhá?"

Though not life-threatening, the wound on his shoulder was painful and blood stained the fabric of his sleeve. Tusánt barely noticed as a woman approached and began to wrap her headscarf around his upper arm to cover the wound and stop the bleeding. Trembling as the initial adrenalin and shock seeped out, he stared at the vandals, allowing her efforts until someone spoke directly to him. He barely heard the cacophony of chatter amongst the others before that moment. His focus was on the captives.

"What shall we do with them, dedhá?" a burly fellow with missing teeth asked.

Tusánt opened his mouth but two warring impulses kept the words from forming. He knew what the Crown expected, what these people around him expected. He could hear it in their thoughts without actively trying to read them. But it was not the action Tusánt felt compelled to take. He could not be sure, without touching the two, that they were Corylliens, and there had been, in his opinion, too much killing in recent months. Things in Rhidam, in Enesfel, needed to change, and that change could begin with him.

Covering his injury with his other hand to lessen the throbbing, Tusánt fought to steady his voice and said, "Let them go."

The surprise had to wear off before the order was obeyed and the two captured men ogled the Elyri with shock and fear. He expected disdain as he continued, "You trespass in k'Ádhá's house...defiling the altar of Faith...that is a sin against the Faith, not against me."

"But he..."

Tusánt glanced at his bloody arm where the speaker pointed and allowed his gaze to travel over every person he could see. "A frightened man lashes out. Which one of us has not done something similar when afraid?" He gave those words a moment to sink in before continuing. "However misguided these acts are...it is not my place to pass judgment..."

"But they are Corylliens!" someone shouted.

"If you know that to be true...and have not reported them to the Justice or the Crown, then you are as guilty of their crimes as they are." Tusánt felt the discomfort in the gathering though he made no effort to judge its source or reason. If the accusation was true, then it was that person's burden to bear. "Judge me as you will," he murmured as he approached the two men still held, though no longer tightly, by the crowd. "Elyri or Teren...we are the same in k'Ádhá's eyes...judged by our deeds and the lightness or darkness of our souls. You have killed no one here...nor do I believe you attempted to. I cannot judge you by motives I do not know...I do not know your hearts. Therefore, I forgive you...and release you...with the single instruction that you lay your hearts open before Dhágdhuán and make peace with him."

Before someone chooses to take that option away from you, Tusánt thought with a sigh as the men were released and slowly backed down the aisle and out the door. With the fear of Coryllien violence still in the air, he half suspected the two men would be caught and killed, before the night was over. He prayed not, prayed that he had given them a lesson in humility and forgiveness and that they would have time to take it to heart.

Perhaps they would learn that Elyri were not the monsters they feared.

꘠*꘠

Bhríd's return to Levonne was burdened by the knowledge he could never share with his wife. If she lived past the birth of the children she carried, then perhaps there would be time to tell her the truth…and bear the wrath he knew would come upon the tail of that revelation. Her worry for her sons had driven her to bed, and after his initial visit to her bedside, when he gave her the impression that he had not seen Tayte and that their youngest son was well, she refused to see him, refused to allow him into the room they had once shared. Perhaps she knew he was lying. Perhaps she believed he had taken action to prevent Tayte from coming home. Or perhaps she no longer had the strength of will, of mind, of body, to want to confront or solve the situation. Heartsick with the reality he carried, he decided it was just as well she did not want to talk.

He threw himself into the winter work of winemaking, of running the estate, of living with the hopes of new children. And each night, long after he was certain Madalyn and the rest of the household slept, he took the Gate to the Lachlan keep, to spend two hours at his unconscious son's side praying he would wake, would smile, would laugh. The turn of the new year was approaching and Bhríd could not stomach the thought of his sons not spending another festival season with him, of spending the season alone, without even his wife at his side to celebrate.

꘠*꘠

The onset of winter snow and freezing temperatures did not hinder Kavan's travels, as the Gates took him from one village, town, or city to another, but the weight on his heart dragged at him, pulled him to Rhidam each night for hours spent quietly at Gaelán's bedside. Though legally wed, Asta had not taken to spending her nights in the unconscious man's bed, to allow both Kavan and Bhríd time alone with him. Kavan prayed for him, begged k'Ádhá for mercy and healing, but none came, and as the final two months of the year passed, they were left with the growing realization that Gaelán, while breathing without help and swallowing when fed, might never wake. Kavan had heard of such cases, particularly amongst Elyri who suffered head injuries. There was a facility in Clarys where those who suffered thus could be taken and cared for in the event the family was incapable of providing care. Kavan had visited there once, when he was young, asked to play for the unresponsive residents in the hopes that, wherever they were trapped within their heads, they would be able to hear the music. He had not learned until much later that two of the over forty patients had awakened during the night after his performance, and though he was reluctant to claim any part of their recovery, others claimed it for him. Ártur, knowing of that occasion, begged Kavan to give Gaelán that same gift, bring him a song, wake him with the power of music.

Thus far, Kavan had resisted. It was not a miracle he feared, but rather the failure to be granted one. Giving others false hope, and then failing them, was a burden he had not yet learned to accept.

Failure was, to his dismay, his constant companion. He had spent the anniversaries of Arlan's birth and death alone, unable to grieve with a harp in his hands, but still able to give the man's memory voice in prayer, pleading with the dead to forgive him for failing Hagan, for failing Diona, for failing Enesfel. The year was drawing to a close, and not only did his cleansing of the chapel seem to have given no obvious results, he had yet to find a single clue as to who had murdered Dórímyr.

Not one of those he met, spoke with, or observed revealed any inclination or proclivity towards murder, or a desire for such. It should have been reassuring, learning that his faith in Elyri nonviolence, the strength of the Faith, and common decency and morality, was upheld by most in a position to sway the minds of believers. Though some bordered on fanatical in their faith, Kavan had found none he could not accept as k'gdhededhá, should they pursue the as yet unannounced vacancy. Failing to solve that crime, feeling his time slipping short, he had at least proven, as he stepped into the k'rylag in Hes Índári Náós, Bhryell, who the criminals were not. A brief visit with Wortham and the boys in the safety of Bhryell's náós on the final night of what had proven to be a largely dark, unbearable year, brought him back to Clarys, back to the beginning with the hopes that Caol had learned something, anything, they might be able to use to end the running. Once Kavan had been a wanderer, a traveler. Now he wanted to be home with his family. He wanted to make music again.

It was a risk and he knew it, but something he had heard in the Udhár sermon, or perhaps heard or felt in the bald prelate's tone of voice, his choice of words, the nervousness in his rigidly contained movement, had told him this was an opportunity not to be missed. It had never been his plan, had never been considered, as he had little legitimate claim that could suggest success. He was not interested in succeeding, as he was happy with his life the way it was…aside from the constant danger Enesfel presented in these days. And there was a chance, however small, that the k'gdhededhá would recognize him. Yet if he was lucky and Claide did not, if he could win the man's trust, there was no telling how far he might be able to go.

He might be able to help bring an end to the violence. Would not that be worth something to the royal family?

The Faithful who had homes to go to filed into the cold night streets adorned with colored lanterns, the air filled with music and the smell of hot buttered brandy cakes and spiced apple rum for the Udhár festival. This last longest night of the old year, which gave way to the season of rebirth, gave hope that it would bring peace and prosperity to the beleaguered city and kingdom. Yet he remained, hiding in the shadows as the gdhededhá bid the Faithful farewell and imparted Udhár blessings on them. Many who would return here for the night had gone out into the festivities, some of the gdhededhá as well, until only the youngest of them, Valgis, remained alone to clear away the traces of the night's Gathering. k'gdhededhá Claide was about to disappear through the side door that led to the wing where the gdhededhá lived when the stranger emerged from his hiding place and called, "k'gdhededhá...a word please..."

Claide turned with barely masked annoyance to stare at the bearded redhead who was hurrying down the center aisle. Valgis, concerned about a potential attacker, left what he was doing to hurry to Claide's side, but the hawkish man waved him off. He did not recognize the stranger but felt no threat from him.

"k'dedhá..." he bowed when he reached his target, a show of respect he did not feel, and added, "Please, I require Purification. I have not been able to...I do not wish to face a new year without a clean slate."

Claide's brow crept up. It was not an odd request; many in the Faith had come throughout the last three days for Purification as the change of season drew nigh. But Claide took pride in a higher than average level of astuteness and realized that what this man wanted was privacy to talk. Not anonymity, or he would not be here face to face, but the sort of privacy that the panels and curtains of the Purification chamber could provide from outsiders, as well as, he mused, the level of confidence and secrecy it could afford. Hoping for good news, he gestured towards the chamber and said, "Of course, sir...this way."

No time was wasted; as soon as the curtain-enclosed them in the chamber, he began to speak. "If there was another Lachlan...would you be interested in meeting him?"

"Another...?" How could that be? Had King Arlan fathered a bastard child, or Owain Lachlan perhaps? Perhaps this fellow referred to Prince Owain, who had once been king and might still harbor dreams of resuming the throne, despite the apparent loyalty he showed to the Queen and even to Lord Cliáth. No, Claide thought with a frown. Not Prince Owain. Not a man with ties to the Elyri. If there was to be anyone to assume the throne in the place of the quarrelsome Queen, it had to be someone with no Elyri sympathies, someone he could manipulate or at least trust to have a similar agenda and vision for Enesfel's future.

"Not a legitimate Lachlan heir...but a Lachlan nonetheless...an heir of the late King Farrell..."

Behind the curtain, he could feel the smile spreading across Claide's face, the hope that flamed to life in the man's breast. The late king had been well known for his liaisons, both with aristocrats and women of less than noble social status, and with more than a few men as well. Rumors had flown wildly at the time that Farrell had fathered several illegitimate children, but none were ever publically recognized as his and none had ever come forth to lay claims against him. It was assumed that part of his lavish spending had gone towards the upkeep of at least a few of those mistresses and children, but the majority received nothing more than the child they gave birth to and a chance to live.

Claide had not served in Rhidam in those years; the Faith had not been active and he had been a boy at the time. Those rumors had not reached his ears until much later, until he had first come to serve with Jermyn Tythilius in Rhidam's newly refurbished náós. As it had been information irrelevant at the time, he had pushed it from his thoughts, so far from them that, until this stranger mentioned it, Claide had not considered such an individual to be the solution to his problem with the monarchy. A son would be of age to assume the throne, old enough to have children and perhaps grandchildren, but if he was of sound body and mind, what did his age matter? If the heir was a grandson, laying claim might be more difficult to prove, but youth would also mean strength and determination…and, he hoped, no qualms about doing what would need to be done to secure the throne. Or herself. Perhaps the heir was a woman. Claide cared little, as long as he could mold and guide them.

"There is such an heir?" he asked, forcing his voice to be casual, not thinking for a moment that the other man might detect his racing emotional state.

"I know him."

A prince then. Claide might not care if the heir was a man or woman, but a prince would find it easier to win public support and would be less likely swayed by a marriage partner. Not, he frowned, that anyone had ever been able to sway Queen Diona's mind or path from what she determined best. "It will not be an easy thing to accomplish…to overthrow the rightful heir. He would be willing?"

"Best things in life are not obtained easily. Willing…I do not know…but he would not be…adverse…to ruling." He was grateful for the skills and gifts he had polished over the years. It allowed him to keep a steady voice though he felt anything but steady within.

"I would like to meet him."

"No," the redhead said hastily. "That is not safe, not yet. Risking his life should someone recognize his lineage or get wind of our discussion. No. I will humbly serve as liaison until he feels assured of his safety."

It was a rational request and precaution, but Claide pouted in frustration. What if this man was a spy? He had risked his veiled sermon because no Lachlans or courtly advisors had been present at the Gathering tonight, and he had not expected anyone to understand what his hopes and dreams were for Enesfel's future. Nor had he expected anyone to present a solution. It seemed too convenient, and it worried him. "How do I know he is who you claim?"

"Shall I bring you proof? What would suffice…other than his head? Is there an Elyri you would care to have read…?"

"No." The adamant word was spat with distaste. There was no denying the accuracy of that Elyri skill, but an honorable Elyri would also likely present such information, and possibly Claide's intentions, to the Crown. That was a risk he could not afford. It left him the risk of trusting this stranger, or refusing the offer altogether.

Chuckling, the redhead leaned close to the grating between them. "I can bring proof but you will have to give me time to obtain it…"

"He is not in Rhidam then?"

"Of course not. Can't risk royal recognition. If you need to speak to me…to reach me…leave word at the Duck and Quail."

"Is that where you are staying?"

"That is where you can leave word," he repeated smugly. He was not going to leave an opening for spies, or potential assassins, by revealing the location of his bed. "Blessed Udhár to you, k'dedhá."

Claide heard the curtain draw back, opening and then closing, as the other man left, but he did not immediately react, though he was tempted to part the curtain to look at the stranger one more time. He remembered red hair…and the beard…but there were no other features of note. Would he be able to pick him out of a crowd later?

What he did know was that there were people he had to contact, plans to be made. The náós bell above chimed the end of the day, the end of the year, and Claide smiled. The sun had not yet risen and his new year was already off to a fortuitous beginning.

❧Chapter 14❧

He was not surprised to find that Layton had died during his absence. That had been a foregone conclusion when he had last seen the injured man. Nor was he surprised that most of the remaining Corylliens had taken his advice to heart, leaving town or lying low to not be found in Rhidam. Knowing their families in many cases, however, it was not difficult to find where most had gone. Friends in the country, other towns, and villages, or in a few cases travel out of the kingdom had been the solutions for many in response to his instructions to lay low. It was those he did not find, or could not locate, that perturbed him.

When he heard about the two defectors caught in the act of defiling Hes á Redh, men the Elyri gdhededhá allowed to go free when he could have had them arrested, the news had infuriated him and he wasted no time in finding the pair and taking care of the matter on his own. Vandalizing a náós while there were people within had been a foolhardy risk; they deserved, in his opinion, to be punished for their stupidity. But it was not their stupidity that needed addressing. It was their reversal of position, their growing belief that Elyri, or at least gdhededhá Tusánt, were not the monstrous enemies they once believed them to be. It mattered little that their loss reduced his supporters to a handful; better this loss than a spread of the taint of Elyri support they had begun to espouse. The bleeding of that particular poison needed to be done.

He regretted the arrest of the young Cáner boy, the one he had believed, as had others, held so much promise and who he had meant to groom for a position of leadership. The young man was no longer held prisoner; he guessed that Tayte had been exiled far away. If he had been king, he would not have missed the opportunity of the value of public execution for such a traitor, but he, like others in his circle, had little faith in the Queen's ability to do the right thing. That she might have exiled the son of a favored Elyri advisor rather than execute him seemed to have proven his point. Thus far, though he had tried, he could find no trace of where the young man might have been exiled to. He suspected either Hatu, where King Noreis would have less difficulty executing him if need be, or somewhere in the heart of Elyriá where he might be detained and indoctrinated into a love of his Elyri blood that Layton, Claide, the Gottfrids, and others had struggled to burn out of him. If he could be found, he could be saved and brought back to finish their work.

But Heward was only one man, and those he located in Rhidam or its outskirts were not capable of the tasks of finding Tayte Cáner, bringing him back, or even leading the remaining few to prominence. There was but one man who might be able to do all of that...the resourceful and intelligent Alty.

He had not met the man face to face, but he had heard Layton's reports. Alty was less a man of action than a planner. Like Heward, he was a man who preferred to keep his hands clean, but he was also a man who saw dangers where others failed to see them and had proven his ability to find ways out of even the most difficult situations. The man had long-range priorities and avoided foolish risk. Heward had made sure that Alty got out of town until the heat on the Corylliens subsided. They should have met while Heward had the days to spare in Rhidam, before he returned to the other duty he was being paid to accomplish. But Alty was not in Rhidam, and as the man had no known family or friends, there were no clues as to where he might have gone into hiding. It was logical that the news of the unsanctioned spate of vandalism which had brought about another Coryllien manhunt had reached Alty and he had chosen to extend his vacation in hiding. A wise decision, even though it left Heward with unanswered questions about what information network Alty had at his disposal if no one knew him…and whether he should be concerned about the secrecy of it or not.

❧*❧

Asta toyed with the folded message left at the gate for Sóbhán and Gaelán, a message she had, at first, resisted reading out of respect for the two men it was addressed to. But with the approach of dawn and the first snowfall of the year, despair crept in as she lay curled at Gaelán's side, unable to sleep. More than a month had passed with no change in Gaelán's condition. He still breathed, food passed through him, but to appearances he slept, a sleep from which no amount of movement or sound could awaken him. She talked to him often throughout the day, any time duty did not require her to be elsewhere, secrets of state she could discuss with no one else shared in a low voice to keep others in the corridor from overhearing, or gossip, or the highlights of her lessons for the day. She shared everything in those long hours.

It was in that spirit of sharing, and the despair that he might never know the child they had created, that she gave in and read the delivered message aloud to him.

The reading told her little, fueled more questions than answers as it referred to things Gaelán had not spoken about to her. Perhaps he had meant to, that last night when they argued. She chose to believe it was true, however, and when Ártur brought Sóbhán shortly after daybreak for his promised visit, she shoved the message into the other young man's hand when the healer was focused on Gaelán.

"No change?" Ártur asked, not expecting any but asking out of habit. None of his healing skills seemed able to reach beyond the wall within Gaelán to draw him back to consciousness, a dismaying fact that left the healer sadder with each passing day.

"I thought he groaned...when I came to him, as Lord Cliáth...but..." Asta shrugged her shoulders with a sigh. She might have been hearing what she wanted to hear, or attributed some other sound in the room...wind pushing through cracks around the shutters perhaps...to him, as no other sound followed and he had not moved.

"Kavan was here?" It was not news. Every morning's exam revealed the bard's presence in the room, sprigs of pine and fragrant woodland flora left to give life to the otherwise still chamber, the rumpled edge of the bed where he sat each time, the tended fire, the sometimes cracked open window each a clue that Kavan was keeping vigil over Gaelán's life and soul. But there had been no sign that Kavan had touched the young man again, despite Ártur's hopes to the contrary. He guessed that Kavan feared failure...or perhaps feared success...but either would have been better than not knowing if there was something the man often called Bhryell Saint could do. Ártur knew Kavan would not leave Gaelán alone, knew that someone had to see him when they exchanged duties, but it was never Ártur, and the healer felt sure his cousin was avoiding him.

He did not see Asta's nod but he did not expect an answer to his question. "Still strong." He picked up his healer's bag and slung it over his shoulder. "I will come at noon and we shall see to your studies, Sóbhán. Rouvyn will be here soon. Mind him until I return."

"Yes, sir," the boy said. There was no need for those instructions. This was the routine, on the days when Sóbhán came to Rhidam. Any studying done was done in this room, often with Gaelán's hand in Sóbhán's, as though the younger boy intended the knowledge to pass through him and into Gaelán. Because he felt privileged to be receiving an education of the sort few had the opportunity for, Sóbhán was determined not to waste the advantage he was given. He would not, however, leave his friend's side if he did not have to.

For the moment, lessons could wait, as the healer made his early rounds of the palace staff, visiting nobility, and the Queen's private household. Asta normally retreated for her early duties as Inquisitor, but this morning she waited until the healer was gone and she was alone with Sóbhán. Her duties included that mysterious note, and she expected answers from the other individual it was addressed to.

"What does that mean?" she asked without preamble, pointing at the folded parchment in his hand.

"How would I know?" he retorted, the question, or rather her demanding tone not what troubled him. Rather, it was the sensation he got from the parchment, a reminder of something he had yet to do. "I haven't…"

"Then read it. What did that person give you? Who is he? What did he want delivered to Lord Cliáth?"

"I don't know." Seeing her exasperation and suspicion, he hastily continued without reading. "I don't. The day we served in Hes á Redh with Rouvyn, a bearded man gave us a stone box…asked us to see that Lord Cliáth got it. We did not open it to know…"

"You should have! It could have been poisoned!"

"And be poisoned ourselves?" He understood that was not her intent, that her concern was a threat to Kavan, but his question pointed out the fault in her thinking. "We did not give it to him yet."

"Good. Give it to me."

"I cannot." He swallowed and shook his head to the protest she was about to make. "It is in Bhryell, safely hidden until I could give it to him…but I haven't seen him to…"

Asta huffed and rolled her eyes in annoyance. "Well, he wants it back, whatever it is…you can bring it in two days…and I can set up a trap to…"

"He is not a criminal. He is not going to…"

"You don't know that. And…" she narrowed her gaze at him then looked down at Gaelán, "we cannot be too cautious. If you did not suspect him, you would have given…"

"I have not seen Kavan to…"

"But you know he comes here. You could have left it here at any time…if you weren't suspicious too."

Sóbhán frowned. Was he suspicious? He was not sure. He wanted to give it to Kavan in person, that was his sole certainty. "I did not want anyone else to take it," he finished lamely. "I…if I bring it…we give it to aendhá…and let him decide what to do." Some part of him did not want to deliver that box, as Asta accused, though he did not consider himself suspicious. He just did not want to. But it was better that than return a potentially deadly package into the hands of a stranger who might harm someone else with it. If it was dangerous, Kavan would surely know and avoid being harmed.

Folding her arms across her chest, Asta stared, her expression of exasperation mirroring his frown. "Very well. We allow Lord Cliáth to decide. It might be an important clue."

"And it might be nothing," Sóbhán reminded her. It might be a gift that was none of their business. Whatever it was, it would not rouse Gaelán, and Sóbhán believed he would have agreed with their decision to allow Kavan to decide the box's future.

᠙*᠙

It was a long shot. If Níkóá had known this opportunity would come, he would not have tried to get that message, that single item, into Lord Cliáth's hands. He doubted the message had been delivered, for he felt certain the bard would have come to him if he received it, thus the boys must still possess the box. Perhaps they had not seen Kavan to deliver it, someone had taken it from them…or they had kept it for themselves. The possibilities were numerous, presenting problems he did not want to think about. If he could not get it back, what else could he offer as the proof Claide needed?

There had to be another way. He would give the young men time to return it, or for the White Bard to find him, but it would not be much time. Claide would not wait indefinitely. Nor, the redhead thought as he spurred his horse to the east of Rhidam, away from the castle, sure that his message had been received, would he.

❧*☙

There should be screaming. There should be cries. But Bhríd heard nothing, even when he stopped his furious pacing and pressed his ear to the thick oak door of the bedroom. Hasty footsteps made him jump back before the door flew open. His cousin, bloody towel in hand, looked at him with distress.

"I must take the children now, Bhríd…or we risk them as well."

The strength rushed out of his bones and Bhríd sank against the doorpost and slid to the floor, staring beyond the healer at the still woman on the bed. "She is…?"

"Not yet…but she has no more strength…and there is too much bleeding. Rouvyn and I can try to save her…but the children may be lost…and our efforts will likely fail." Ártur hated bearing that sort of ill news, but this was no time to be delicate. "We must act at once…"

Bhríd took three long breaths, fought to his feet, and stumbled into the room, past midwives and the two physicians, to sink down on the bedside and grasp Madalyn's hand to his chest. He had known this moment would come; Kavan had warned him of it months ago…but the children were early, their chance at life slim at best…and he had hoped to have her with him longer. When she did not respond to his touch, neither blink nor speak, her flushed skin already beginning to grey despite the rapid rise and fall of her chest as she fought for breath, he could feel life leaving her, feel her slipping too far away from him to return.

"k'Ádhá forgive me…" he croaked with a nod at his kinsman. He had to let her go. There was no other choice if the children were to live.

"She will feel no pain, I promise," Ártur murmured solemnly as he pressed his hands on both sides of her distended abdomen. He could see to that, leaving the task of cutting, of saving the children, to Rouvyn and the midwives who hovered nearby with towels, hot water, and sharp knives.

But it was not the possibility of pain Bhríd was apologizing for, nor even the choosing the children's lives over her already fading one. He was apologizing for the lies he had told about their sons, lies meant to spare her heartache in her last days and keep her love, what remained of it, in their final weeks together. Should he tell her, he wondered, keeping his thoughts busy, his eyes on her face as the others feverishly worked behind him.

No. He made his decision as the first cry of an infant filled the room. At that moment, as the hand in his lost warmth, he became hyper-aware of the smell of wet earth from beyond the partially opened window, aware of the crackle of the hearth fire, the splash of the towel in the washbasin and the rubbing sound of it on tender skin. He held his breath, trying to block out each of his senses, to lock his thoughts and heart away. Gaelán should be here, assisting. Tayte should be here, taking his new sibling from his brother's arms and holding it affectionately. And Madalyn should be here, eyes wide and bright, her radiant smile beaming proudly with love at what they had created together. But none would ever open their eyes for him, he feared, at least two of them would not, and as a second cry joined the first, punctuating his reverie, he turned from the bed, suddenly sick in body as well as in spirit, to vomit on the floor…and faint.

The room was dark when his senses came back, the open shutters revealing that it was evening, or night, that hours had passed since his last memory of being sick at the feet of whichever midwife had been closest to him at his wife's bedside. He groaned and rolled sideways to rise, no longer feeling ill but still cold, empty, and alone. He needed no healer to tell him Madalyn was gone. The emptiness within told him that when he eventually acknowledged it was there.

"Drink this." He looked at Ártur, blinking in confusion, not having realized anyone else was in the room. His room, the one he had been using since the distance between him and his wife had begun to grow. He did not resist, did not refuse, but dutifully drank what he assumed would be some sort of elixir to clear his head and ease the ache inside.

It was water.

"Are they…?"

"Your little girls are beautiful, Bhríd," he replied gently. "Small…for being early twins…but healthy and strong. There is a wet-nurse with them; they are both eating heartily. As long as they continue to eat and are kept warm, they stand every chance of living…"

"Is she…" he began with panic.

"I interviewed her, read her myself, as you asked. Editt will not harm your children, I swear it."

"I want them here…with me…"

"Bhríd…"

"This room is warmest…or it will be when the fire is stoked. They and the nurse will stay with me. A pallet will be brought for her. I want them where I can see them…where I know they are safe,"

Ártur decided not to argue. It was not customary to keep a wet nurse close at hand in a father's private room, but after his recent losses, steeped in anti-Elyri hatred and the failings of mortality, Bhríd could hardly be blamed for feeling over-protective of his newborn children or for not trusting the woman hired to mother them in Madalyn's stead.

"I will see to it immediately."

"And tell the Queen the legalities will be addressed…when it is time." For there would be much to settle. With Madalyn's passing, the largest vineyard estate in Enesfel came into Bhríd's hands. It would have, should have, gone to Tayte, but his eldest son's choices had guaranteed that could never happen. Bhríd had no desire to remain here without Madalyn, would have preferred to place the running of the estate into Gaelán's hands and leave, but that son was not fit for the duty, and would not have wanted it if he were, and the newborns, of course, were too young.

That meant that, as per his agreement with Madalyn at the time of their marriage, should there be no suitable heir at the time of her death, Bhríd would become sole lord of Levonne and the vineyard her family had owned for generations. He would dutifully manage it, run it, lord over it as the second unmarried Elyri duke in Enesfel until his daughters were old enough to assume the responsibility. Some would not like the change in ownership, in leadership, and Bhríd was aware of the violence Madalyn's death and the change might cause, but he would not turn the lands over to strangers. He would fortify his home, protect his daughters, and do everything he could to honor Madayln's legacy. It was the best he could do.

"And tell Gaelán…I am sorry I cannot…"

Ártur understood. Until the girls' lives were secured, until the risk of their premature births was passed, Bhríd would not spare time away to visit his comatose son. Bhríd prayed Gaelán would understand, wherever he was within himself. Ártur did not think Gaelán would know the difference.

❧*❧

The Bhryell náós was the first place he thought to go, a place to pray, to pour his music, his heart, out to any powerful force that might be listening tonight. The number of deaths of loved ones in such a short time weighed heavily in his soul, and he was trying to push past this new pain, trying to ignore it for the good of Enesfel, the Faith, Elyriá, all men and women of the realms. He had not been close to Madalyn, though he had liked and respected her as his cousin's wife, but her passing, something he felt without being told it had happened, broke his resolve tonight and pulled him here.

Particularly since he had the gnawing feeling that this would not be the last death he was soon to face. Logic told him it would be Gaelán's passing, his loss of the battle he was fighting every day seeming to be inevitable, but Kavan prayed death would not come for the boy who had barely had the chance to live. Bhríd had suffered enough. No more, he thought, his eyes pleading with the figure suspended on the wall above the altar. Spare the lands such losses, and I will suffer anything you ask of me.

The harp between his hands, silent though he had brought it from home specifically to play, was the reassurance that things could be right in the world. He plucked absently at the strings, seeking a melody that would soothe him, that would summon záphyr or Kóráhm, but the music would not come.

"Kavan!" gdhededhá Bhílári burst into the sanctuary, face red with alarm upon hearing those barely audible notes. His presence surprised Kavan, for it most often seemed that when he sought solace in this place, the man he had known since childhood was not here. In his distraction and despair, he had not thought to discover if the man was here this night. "Stop, I pray you. You must go quickly…before you are heard…"

"Heard by…?"

"They're here…asking questions…looking for you…"

They.

Kavan realized who they would be as soon as Bhílári began speaking. Terrified, not for his own safety but for his family's, should any discover he was here, Kavan took no time to speak or thank the gdhededhá but instead scrambled into the chamber where the k'rylag was located. Harp clutched to his chest, he made the connection to Clarys, the one place they would not expect him to go while he was being hunted, as one of the unwanted visitors to Bhryell's náós entered in search of sounds he thought he had heard.

"Who is here?"

"No one," Bhílári replied, turning abruptly mid hum to face his guest. His shaky voice might have been due to being startled and not by the panic he had felt for Kavan's safety.

"I heard music."

"Look around you. Since when is praying aloud and humming a crime in the eyes of the k'phóredhet or the Faith?"

The other man, small and plain with nothing intimidating about him except the authority he was given on behalf of those who knew of Dórímyr's death, scowled and did as Bhílári suggested, walking the whole of the sanctuary, peering into every crevice and nook a man might fit in. Thankfully he, like the majority of Elyri, was unschooled in the use and locating of Gates, or refused to use them if they could; he either did not notice the presence of the k'rylag in the dhín bhólibh or else did not believe Kavan would have used it had he been here. Arrogance and folly were on Kavan's side, for which Bhílári gave a silent prayer of deep gratitude.

"If Kavan Cliáth shows himself, you must detain him…report his presence to the authorities…"

"Which authorities, sir, and on what grounds?" Bhílári asked innocently. "Of what crimes is he being accused?"

"Heresy and crimes against the Faith."

"Heresy? Surely not." So that was the spin the officials were putting on the manhunt, although Bhílári had not heard tell of such a kingdom-wide search for a single heretic in all of his years. They could not accuse Kavan of murder without revealing the patriarch's death, and thus they were forced to fabricate charges. He was aware there were philosophical differences between Kavan's beliefs and those of k'gdhededhá Dórímyr, but he did not know what those differences were, had not sought details, and he could not imagine they were of a nature to warrant this manner of witch-hunt. What experience had taught Bhílári was that he had never met a more devoted and believing follower in the Faith than Kavan Cliáth. Heresy was as far-fetched as believing Kavan could, or would, murder the prelate.

Kavan entered the night streets of Clarys to the tolling of the náós bells, a sound he paused to listen to, a sound that sent a chilling shiver down his spine and into his belly. Not the midnight tolling, as that was normally a combination of melodic bells chiming in sequence. This was the deep tolling of a single low toned bell, a cry into the night, the announcement at last of the death of k'gdhededhá Dórímyr. People came out of their homes, out of inns and taverns, gathered as families or on street corners or in open doorways with strangers to stare in the direction of the bell, of the spires of the seat of their Faith. He knew it was customary, a practice that went back at least to the years of the Great Plague when many had died, to acknowledge the death of a Faith leader thus, but passing through streets of people gathering with candles in hand, heads bowed in prayer or else staring at the sky or the spires of the náós, was an eerie, nerve-wracking thing. Even his hooded grey cloak might not protect him should patrols spot him, question his lack of stationary reverence, or if someone recognized him and choose to raise an alarm.

But no one paid him no heed, allowing him to reach the inn where Caol huddled in the doorway, shivering, bleary-eyed in the cold with no cloak or coat to protect him from the gently falling snow. No one else might recognize him, but the official Inquisitor of Enesfel did, and when Kavan beckoned him back into the building, he gratefully followed.

"What is happening?" he asked in a low voice, though there was no one around to overhear.

"They announce Dórímyr's death."

Caol swore under his breath and wiped snow out of his hair. "How long do you think we have?"

The bard perched on a stool at the bar, watching the door, still clutching his harp to his chest. If those outside noticed the two men not paying homage as expected, while they might excuse Caol, they would certainly not excuse Kavan's lack of respect. "I do not know. That will depend on whether they continue to espouse the claim that he was ill, or whether they declare his death to be murder. Either way, I must speak to the candidates here in Clarys at once..." Not tonight, perhaps, perhaps not even tomorrow night since the halls would be abustle with mourners and diplomats, but it would have to be soon, before the other candidates converged on Clarys and were sequestered for the election.

"Then you found nothing." That was both good news and bad, and might explain the bard's sullen mood.

"Nor did you, I presume."

Caol shook his head. "Nothing damning. There are rumors. Illegitimate children, affairs, bribery, but nothing I have been able to substantiate. If gdhededhá Hwensen knows anything about these rumors, he has not been forthcoming." He shrugged. "He does not trust me. Can't say I blame him…a foreign Teren amid all these Elyri…a Lachlan agent. It's a wonder no one has tried to read me to figure out why I am here…who I am."

"As a whole, we are more trusting than that…particularly inside those walls and our own borders." Relatively few Teren lived in Elyriá and Teren novices underwent a rigorous screening before being accepted into the Holy Halls. Hwensen had vouched for him, at Kavan's request, thus the others did not question his right to be there nor suspect him of ulterior motives. Why Hwensen might distrust him, however, Kavan would have to investigate.

"That's probably how someone got to him." Caol raked his hand through his hair that was growing out into its normal red. When Kavan glanced at him, gauging the truth in those words, he shrugged again. "I have a few more trails I can follow, but honestly, I don't believe I'll be of any more use here…and I have to return to Rhidam. If he hasn't gone back already and been looking for me, Heward will soon enough…and I'm not done with that duty yet."

"I do not need to remind you to be cautious with him?"

"Cautious is all I can be. I imagine he'll first ask to recruit new blood…it's going to be difficult to accomplish anything without more supporters. I think I've got a grip on how that is going to go…but I'd prefer to be done with him…with all of this…before I'm asked to do something more illegal than vandalism or theft."

"Indeed." Kavan wondered if he dared reveal his premonition of death to Caol. What the man was doing was dangerous; the possibility that this was his death flirting with the edges of Kavan's Sight was a high one. But death was a risk Caol was fully aware of, and well prepared for. The man would take every precaution and Kavan chose to believe he would remain safe. With another grandchild soon to be in his family, Caol had much to live for, and Kavan expected him to have the chance to enjoy it.

❧Chapter 15❧

The Queen stared at her healer, expression wide-eyed and faintly terrified with disbelief. "You cannot be serious…"

"Pardon, Your Majesty…"

Their privacy in the morning room interrupted, Diona motioned for Owain to enter. The man she called uncle had settled easily into the role of Chamberlain, and she knew by his formal address that what he had come to tell her was state business, not some personal or family matter. He had not been to see his wife, his daughter-in-law, or his sons in many weeks; she expected soon he would make that request but did not think this would be that time. He had missed the holy days with them, remaining in Rhidam out of duty; with an uneasy peace drawn over the kingdom by the chill of winter and the continuing efforts to rebuild Rhidam, there was little reason for Owain not to visit them or his lands in the north.

She suspected he stayed in Rhidam in the hopes of seeing Kavan.

But Kavan had not come, or at least he did not visit the rest of the Royal household, only Gaelán. No one but Asta or Rouvyn crossed paths with him regularly. Owain, a man dear to Kavan's heart, was suffering his absence as were many others, and the Queen wondered often if he would be happier if he was released from duty to go to Bhryell, to reside with the bard, with Captain Delamo, with those he cherished, it sometimes seemed, more than his blood kin.

Now, however, his was not an expression of mourning or loneliness, but rather the pale flush of sickness she saw, something that made her frown. "You may wish to see this…or you may not…"

Not the plague, she thought with a stab of pain in her chest. He was not coming to announce that, was he? There had been reports of plague in the south, limited to a single village in Enesfel and another in Hatu, and she worried every day that it would find its way to Rhidam. After the worst of the Coryllien violence and the fire, a plague was the last horror Enesfel needed.

"What is it? Tell me."

Owain nodded, swallowing hard. "Two more Corylliens…or so they seem to be…at the náós…"

Wondering who the Corylliens had attacked this time, the Queen was on her feet, striding from the room with both men close behind. The matter she had been discussing with the healer would have to wait. She feared for gdhededhá Tusánt, one of the few targets left for anti-Elyri hatred. The second target was at her heels, and too late she considered that she should have demanded he stay inside the keep. But if Tusánt needed healing, Ártur was his best choice, thus she said nothing but swung up on Owain's horse behind him as best her gown would allow, while the healer joined General Agis on his.

It was not Tusánt, thankfully, found hanging from thick tree limbs outside of Hes á Redh, but rather two men, long dead, the flesh of their limbs stripped to the bone at hip and shoulder, their life bled out onto the holy ground beneath. A sign hung about each man's broken neck, reading, 'Traitor'. Tusánt at the entrance steps wrung his hands while gdhededhá Rankin had the novices at work digging graves. A scan of the gathered crowd as she slid from the horse told the Queen that Claide was not here, but Valgis could be seen through the open doors attempting to soothe agitated parishioners, though he spoke and gestured like a man frightened and disgusted.

"Corylliens? Are you sure?" Diona asked, joining Tusánt on the steps.

"Yes…I assume so," he said with a nod and more clenching of his hands. "Several weeks back I caught them desecrating the altar. I let them go, let them live, in the hopes that kindness would win them. I have spoken with both since, in Purification and in person. Both showed a marked change in opinion and disposition…of belief…a shift away from hatred and towards acceptance…and now this…" He gestured to the two who swung in the cold wind.

"Someone did not want them to change," Agis grunted as the first body was cut down. The healer was already beside the dead man, kneeling to touch, to read him, seeking details of whatever the fellow might have seen in his final moments. Saucer-eyed, the last thing the dead man had seen had been his partner's suffering, although there was a lingering trace of memories of family, of friends, of a small farmstead to the northwest of Rhidam. Feeling the tightening cord around his neck, evidence of strangulation that had incapacitated but not killed him, Ártur began to choke and cough and quickly removed his hands to grasp his own throat. He shuddered and glanced up at the General while absently placing a hand on the second man being laid out on his other side.

"They do not need to speak to tell a tale," Ártur croaked. There were no extraneous memories within this man's mind, only the last several minutes before he lost consciousness. Trying to flee, stumbling, crashing to the floor over a fallen chair, choking. Before that, however, a cord around his companion's neck, the hands that tightened it, the features of the man behind the hands, the man whose dark eyes burned with contempt and disregard for the one he strangled. A man with little regard for anyone, Ártur thought with another shudder before pulling his hands into his lap and closing his eyes as he gulped for breath.

"Parchment…paper…pen and ink…"

"Lord Healer?" asked the Queen, pressing for details despite her Healer's distress.

"I can draw him; I can give him a face again. But we already know who he is."

"Who?" Justice Corbin was wiping out the blood on the ground with the toe of his boot. "The killer?"

"Anri Heward."

☙*⅍

He seemed, to Kavan, the least likely suspect, a man of controversy who sprung from the Order of St. Kóráhm and climbed the ranks of the order as far as he could before stepping outside of it to serve in the ranks of Hes Dhágdhuán's multitude of clergy. Most gdhededhá who joined orders remained within them. Once in a while, one would renounce the vows and take up a secular life, while an equally rare few set their vows aside for the higher calling of leading a náós or serving as co-leader in a náós that housed multiple gdhededhá. In Clarys, the chance was more common than elsewhere, as the seat of the Faith supported twenty to thirty gdhededhá at any given time to fulfill the needs of the city's vast population.

This was the path Kluín had taken. Though not having been among their ranks during Kavan's previous visits to Clarys, the gdhededhá had built a reputation for his tireless efforts in aiding the sick, the orphaned, the needy, and for being a patron of the arts, modeling his life after the Heretic-Saint's. Such a popular servant of the people had not escaped Dórímyr's notice and the prelate had drawn him into Hes Dhágdhuán's ranks despite their differing views on Kóráhm. It had been a wise choice, as the náós had seen a swell in attendance and donations after Kluín's appointment, cementing the

man's popularity with his fellow gdhededhá as well. In Kavan's
opinion, Kluín owed Dórímyr his position, and thus seemed unlikely
to have wished the prelate's death. But Kavan had to begin with one
of the five, and Kluín seemed easiest…and safest.

The curly blonde hair hung loose as the gdhededhá knelt in
prayer, alone in this small private chapel of which there were many
scattered through the Hes Dhágdhuán complex. It was not yet dawn
but few within these halls had returned to sleep after the tolling bell
had awakened them with the grim news. Kavan remained by the
door, having closed it quietly behind him, and waited as Kluín
continued his prayers for the deceased. Having avoided detection
thus far, Kavan wanted no trouble. There was no k'rylag here for a
swift escape should he need it. He would have to rely on Kluín's
kindness and pray he had not misjudged the other man.

When the blonde head lifted, Kluín turned on his knees to see
who had come to share this chapel with him. He smiled when he saw
who it was. "Lord Cliáth…a pleasant surprise…"

"Is it?" There was no surprise in being recognized, identified.
His features were such that any who had heard of him would know
him, and he had been in Clarys often enough since his first Festival
at the age of sixteen that Kluín, a contemporary in age to Ártur the
bard suspected, was likely to have seen him at least once.

"Indeed. I heard much about you from gdhededhá Jermyn before
he left us…and have followed the tales of you that have come to
Clarys in the years since. Not," he smiled with a gesture to draw
Kavan closer as he rose to welcome him, "that I believe every rumor
I hear. gdhededhá Kesábhá speaks highly of you, and when two men
I admire speak well of someone, there is good cause for it."

Kavan nodded his head, bowing slightly as he accepted Kluín's
offered hand, a hand the man brought to his lips to kiss the ring the
bard wore, the token of St. Kóráhm's that any adherent would
recognize if they had seen the paintings and depictions of the

Heretic-Saint. Though uncertain if the act of reverence was towards him or Kóráhm, Kavan pushed aside his disquiet.

"What brings you to Clarys? You have heard the news I presume?" It did not seem to trouble or perplex him that Kavan could know of the death of the prelate that had been announced only hours earlier.

"In a manner of speaking…yes. I am here on behalf of Kyne Morné…seeking a murderer."

"Someone has been murdered?" Kluín asked, stricken and appalled. "One of her family? What do you hope to find here in Hes Dhágdhuán? How might I be of assistance?"

"Not one of her family, thankfully. I am seeking anyone who might have had a motive, means, and access to Dórímyr, to his routine, his rooms, to poison him…"

"Poison?" Kluín's legs began to buckle and Kavan caught him.

Easing him to the floor, Kavan nodded. "I was there…I saw him die…I found several poisons in his room, working in unison to kill him. Two of them, the strongest ones, have sources I understand…" At least, he knew where to look for their origins and knew what he expected to find. "The others came from someone near to him, someone close enough to provide extended exposure, over a month at least, likely longer."

"You believe someone…in Hes Dhágdhuán has…" Kluín swallowed hard and wiped his mouth on the back of his hand. "You do not suspect me?"

"I suspect no one…yet. I know Dórímyr was not a well-liked man…that some disliked his politics, his policies, his character…and with whom he has likely battled over the decades, for I am among those. But that hardly seems motive enough to poison him. The most likely motive I can deduce is to gain his position."

Kluín nodded. "Yes…I can see that would be a motive for some…but I assure you, I have not…"

"I believe you, gdhededhá…"

"Kluín, please."

Kavan bobbed his head in acceptance of the lowering of formality. In catching the man moments before, the physical contact was enough to assure him that Kluín was not the suspect he sought. "I have spoken to potential candidates from the whole of Elyriá, save for those in Clarys, and I have found no cause, no guilt…"

"Then the bells…last night…?" The blonde scowled.

"Were long overdue," Kavan sighed.

"The Tribunal has been lying…?" It was difficult to believe. An organization of Faith that he had grown up to respect and revere should not be responsible for misleading its followers. Not here; not in Elyriá. Not with something as important as this.

"Avoiding panic," Kavan offered. It was lying, but he had been witness to politics in Rhidam long enough to understand why such a falsehood might be necessary for the greater good of the land. He did not like it, hated dishonesty, but he did understand it, and he could, in extreme circumstances, excuse and forgive it.

"This is why they hunt you? They accuse you of heresy to protect themselves?"

Uncomfortable, Kavan took a step back. Given the other man's warm greeting, he had not considered that Kluín might know he was being hunted or accused of heresy. "They accuse me because they believe I killed him…despite proof to the contrary…and they could not hunt me as a killer without revealing that he has been dead for some time. The Kyne has granted me the opportunity to find the guilty, as I am the one who knows Rhidam…who knows those in Hes á Redh who want him…"

"And because she believes in your innocence." Kluín's shoulders hunched as his face creased in thought. "I have heard…well, there has been no secret of his opinion of you…at least not amongst the gdhededhásur here, or in the Tribunal. He was never specific about the reason…but whatever the disagreement between you has been, I find it hard to believe you would poison a man over doctrinal friction. There's more of that in Hes Dhágdhuán than anyone outside these walls knows. Murder does not fit what I know of you." He shook his head as Kavan began to protest those rumors and tales. "Prompting Khwílen to undertake an effort to undermine Dórímyr's credibility, his support, is more your style. Not poison and murder. Is there anything I can do?"

Again Kavan's head shook. "With you no longer a suspect in my mind, that leaves three others amongst those in Clarys who might stand to gain by his death…but gaining access to any of them will not be easy in the time I have remaining before seclusion begins and a vote is taken. Hwensen has been invaluable…"

"But his access is limited and his position, his life too, might be at risk…"

Kavan frowned. He had not considered that the aide might be in danger by continuing contact with him. Surely the murderer would not compound his or her guilt by killing another. Hwensen had worked at Dórímyr's side for nearly a century. If anyone knew the man's secrets, it would be his aide, and the killer would know it.

"I will watch over him as best I can," Kluín promised, "and will tell you anything I learn that might be of use…of anyone here." He knew who the other candidates for this post would likely be, though he was surprised that Kavan believed him to be one of them.

"I can tell you this." He glanced at the closed door to be sure no one was there, or beyond it, and then lowered his voice to a whisper. "Ylár has a mistress." Seeing that the news did not surprise Kavan, Kluín continued. "Not within these walls…I have seen him many times leaving Hes Dhágdhuán late at night…sometimes he misses morning services. Tumm knows this, of course…we all do. It is hard not to miss him when both are absent from their offices. Those absences are frequently explained by Tumm's health…he has stomach issues that often incapacitate him, but I believe Dórímyr knew the truth. I overheard the ends of fights between them, Dórímyr and Tumm, about Ylár. Not enough to learn details, just enough…the sudden dying of loud voices when someone approached."

A mistress was not, in itself, a motive for murder, but it could be enough of a reason to prevent a man from being appointed to the highest duty within the Faith. Many gdhededhá over the centuries had mistresses, but such secrets and indiscretions were not talked about, kept hidden, as long as they did not interfere in the daily running of the Faith. But if there was some reason this affair could harm Ylár's chances at the prelacy, either an inappropriate mistress or a lack of discretion that posed an embarrassment to Dórímyr or the Faith, perhaps Ylár had motive…to keep his affair from being exposed. And perhaps Tumm cared enough for his friend and caretaker that he too had a motive.

It was worth investigating, although involving himself in a man's personal life made Kavan uneasy. "I will look into that…if you will do likewise…for him, for Tumm, and for Lláhy?"

Eagerly nodding, Kluín offered his hand and Kavan helped him to his feet. "I will. Of course I will. I do not want a murderer to lead our Faithful. I will help as I can. How shall I reach you?"

"Through Hwensen. He is the best source." Kavan squeezed the hand in his and added, "k'Ádhá be with you, Kluín. The Faith needs more men like you. I pray for divine will to be done through you."

"And through you, Lord Cliáth. If the Faith needs any men to lead it…it is men like you."

⁊*⁊

Diona paced the Great Hall, her emotions jumbled, chaotic, though her thoughts themselves were not. She had endured the day's events, the death of the two Corylliens and the subsequent rush to get

Heward's newest sketch into the hands of the Lord Justice, Lord General, Rhidam's sheriff, her Chancellor and her Chamberlain, Princess Asta and her Association contacts, and Tusánt. A copy had was south to Hatu, in case the man took refuge there, and one north to Prince Kjell, in the hopes that someone, anyone, in Neth would recognize Heward. His capture might not stop Claide, but it would be a significant step towards peace. She would send one to Káliel, and hoped to get a copy into Kavan's hands, and thus into Caol's. She had hope and faith that soon that man would be brought to justice. Ultimately, Diona blamed him for Hagan's death, as she blamed Claide, and she wanted both to suffer the most undignified death imaginable for the suffering they had inflicted on Enesfel.

Now the sketches were sent and the night was still, with snow falling beyond the castle walls, blanketing the keep in a winter chill, and with that calm came the stillness of thought that brought to focus what Ártur had said early that morning. There was no cause for him to lie about such a thing, and it was inevitable, she knew, but it surprised her nonetheless. Surprised her and frightened her. She was not ready for this. Not now. Not when there was still much to do, many duties that needed her time and attention.

"I thought I would find you here."

Espen entered the room, his robe and gown tied about his waist, his hair rumpled in a way that told her he had awoken to find her absent from their bed and had come looking for her without bothering to make himself presentable. It did not matter to her that they each had a room; she preferred to sleep in the same room, the same bed with him now that she had discovered that luxury, and he, despite an upbringing that encouraged segregation of the sexes, preferred to share hers. It was an arrangement that suited them both, but it meant that, when she wanted privacy at night, she was forced to go elsewhere in the keep to find it. Sometimes she chose the day room, sometimes the library, but often she ended up here, where there was room to pace without the impediment of chairs and tables.

She faced him, and though her words should have come forth more graciously, they blurted unhindered and raw. "I am with child."

The prince's footsteps faltered as he, taken aback by the abrupt announcement, felt the air sucked from his lungs. He did not yet know of her fears, of the worries of following in her mother's wake, dying in labor from complications of childbirth. "When..." he stammered. "How...?"

The last question broke her tension and caused her to laugh. "You know perfectly well how. As for...I learned of it this morning...at breakfast..."

That, on top of the Coryllien business, explained her distraction and avoidance. Was she angry, he wondered? She did not appear to be, but she did appear unsettled and afraid. He closed the distance between them and embraced her. "Did Ártur say more?"

"No." She shook her head but her face remained buried against his chest. Sometimes, being held this way reminded her of how her father had hugged her to belay her childhood fears. But this did not feel childish. Voice small, she continued, "He says I am healthy. It is too early to know much, except that the child too is healthy."

He understood then, in her tone, in the words she did not say, the reasons that had kept her from the marriage bed, the things she feared. How could she not be afraid after witnessing her mother's death and hearing of the loss of siblings during or shortly after childbirth? Madalyn's recent death had undoubtedly brought those fears back to the surface.

"And you shall both remain thus," Espen assured her, smoothing her hair and kissing the top of her head. "Ártur will see to it, as will I...and I will be here with you throughout every moment, Diona. You need not fear. We will heed Ártur's advice and I shall do what I must, what I can, to keep you both safe."

I pray it is enough, she thought and held him tighter. After hearing the news about Madalyn, Diona's nightmares had returned, and she did not think they would leave until the child was safely born. She was not going to feel secure in her condition until Kavan could remove her doubts. More than anyone else, if he said she would be well, that her child would be well, she would believe him. Kavan would never lie to her…even if she felt like she deserved it.

〜*〜

There was a mistake. There had to be. Khwílen reread the summons and wondered what in the name of k'Ádhá had possessed anyone to put his name on this list…and who that someone was. His name was not well known outside of the Order of St. Kóráhm, not in Enesfel or Elyriá. It had to be someone within the order, but who? Who, he asked the air as he bundled his belongings and prepared for the journey to Clarys early the next morning, would think him an ideal candidate to lead the Faith in k'gdhededhá Dórímyr's stead?

He did not want the job, would not accept the nomination, but he would, at least, go to Hes Dhágdhuán to decline the offer in person. His home was no longer in Clarys where the Order's motherhouse stood. His home was in Alberni, in the family of Faith Kavan had placed in his hands, a place he had been away from for too long already. With the prelate's death made public, with no reason to continue his crusade against Dórímyr any longer, home was where he would return…as soon as he faced this nomination.

〜*〜

Caol was restless, eager for something to do that provided more challenge than talking to people for information that no one seemed to have or wanted to share, thus Kavan set him to the task of watching Hes Dhágdhuán for Ylár's departure, with the instructions to follow him, learn where he went at night, and if possible, who he was to see. There was no guarantee that the man would leave the complex, since Dórímyr's death had brought attention to those living there, but they could not miss the opportunity to learn the truth if it presented itself.

Perhaps it was not an affair that pulled the man out on those nights, perhaps he had family nearby, or perhaps he was tending to someone in need. Kavan did not plant any seeds of direction in Caol's mind, told him no more than that the gdhededhá's activities had aroused suspicions and thus warranted investigation. Caol accepted the mission gladly, a little midnight skulking through empty streets, darting through shadows and scaling trees and walls, each an activity he had not had the opportunity to practice in too long.

It freed Kavan to go to Rhidam to keep his nightly appointment at Gaelán's bedside. Kavan suspected that circumstances would soon interfere with his efforts, as he drew closer to finding whoever was responsible for Dórímyr's death, but he was not yet ready to leave the young man alone. He wanted Gaelán to know he had been there as much as possible, should he awaken to inquire.

Tonight, instead of finding Asta at Gaelán's side, as usual, Kavan also found Sóbhán, which both surprised and worried him. "You should not be here…" The tense words made the boy's expression fall but brought the princess to her feet in his defense.

"He is here because I asked him to be," she said. "He is safe…I swear it. But we needed to…"

"I needed to see you," Sóbhán said in a small, sad voice. "The captain is kind…as are Ártur and Bhen and…but they are not you…"

His tone, the hurt Kavan felt in those words, in his voice, made the bard reach for the young man and pull him into his embrace. "I miss you as well, Sóbhán…and I am sorry that circumstances keep us apart. It is not my wish, believe me."

"I know it's not your fault; I hear the talk..." he sniffed. Asta busied herself with Gaelán's blanket rather than watch the reunion.

"Perhaps it is not, but..."

"Everything will be right soon...won't it?"

Kavan sighed and kissed the top of his head, a rare gesture reserved almost exclusively for children. "I hope so."

"Good." Sóbhán stepped back with a teary smile. "We...there is something I was supposed to give you before..."

"Before?" There was a visual exchange between Sóbhán and Asta, and a glance at Gaelán that Kavan interpreted to mean that it was a secret the young healer had also been involved in, a secret from before his long sleep. Asta opened the drawer of the bedside table and gave the small stone box hidden there to Sóbhán, who fumbled with it nervously as if he did not know what to do with it.

"The day he...before..."

"The day he and Tayte..." Asta started, trying to help but finding the words sticking in her throat, choking her as they did Sóbhán.

Kavan touched them both lovingly, flesh to flesh contact that took away distress in so many people for reasons Kavan had never understood. It worked now, as both calmed, their trembling stilled, and they tried to relay their gratitude for his support with smiles.

Sóbhán continued, "A man gave this to us in Hes á Redh. Gaelán recognized him but would not tell me who he was. He seemed afraid of him. I did not find him frightening...just...odd..."

"Odd?" The box had not yet been handed to Kavan, but he was looking at it as it turned in Sóbhán's hands and passed back and forth from one to the other.

"Like...I should know him. He was poorly dressed...a pauper in appearance...but his speech, his bearing...I do not think he was either poor or uneducated, despite his appearance. He gave this to us...asked us to be sure you received it...but I was afraid it was a trap and I hid it...and I did not see you before. I forgot about it until he delivered a message, asking to have it back…like he knew I had not given it to you…that I still have it."

Asta's lips pursed. "If it is dangerous, I do not think we should give it back…and if opening it might harm you…"

"Let me have it, Sóbhán," Kavan said.

"But…"

Kavan's hand was open, waiting, and Sóbhán was already handing it over despite his protest. Asta attempted to snatch it, still concerned that it was dangerous, but Kavan's fingers closed around it and drew it back quickly, his eyes blinking rapidly at the sensations present on the stone. His mouth opened but no sound came out.

"See!" Asta proclaimed, taking the bard's expression to be one of pain. "We shouldn't have…"

The bard shook his head as he pushed the collection of bombarding images aside. "No, it is not…I know him…"

"Know him?" Sóbhán and Asta exchanged looks. "Who is he?"

"Not know him…precisely," Kavan corrected. "But we have met before, after a fashion." Or rather, what he felt in that box was identical to the presence he had felt in that woodsman's cottage the morning after Gaelán's attack. This red-haired man with a strong aura, a powerful life force, had found him, cared for him, and was reaching out in the only way he knew. How else would anyone seek the White Bard except through the Lachlans, Ártur, or someone else from within the castle?

The face he saw, however, shadowed as it was, seemed familiar too, a sliver of a long-ago dream, but what he felt was something else, and the dichotomy of the two bits of knowledge forced Kavan to break the seal on the box and open it cautiously.

"aendhá!" Sóbhán squeaked.

"Lord Cliáth…" warned the princess.

A glimpse within the velvet-lined box was all Kavan permitted himself before he snapped it closed, a whisper of surprise and alarm warning him to keep this tidbit of knowledge secret until he had the opportunity to prove what could not be, should not be, possible.

"What is it?"

"I...where did he ask you to take it? How were you to deliver it to him? When?"

"The Duck and Quail. He said to deliver it to the tavern keeper. I think he was expecting it before, but I did not have it in Rhidam."

"And we don't want to give it to him if it's going to hurt someone," Asta interjected.

"Hurt someone? No...I do not believe it will do that." At least he was not going to permit such a thing. He shoved the box into the pocket of his vest where neither Asta nor Sóbhán were likely to get it from him. "I will see that he gets it. If you hear from him, if you learn anything about him..."

"His name," Sóbhán said. "His name is Níkóá. He told me when he gave it to me."

Kavan allowed the word to roll around his head as he nodded. "Thank you. Please tell him...if he calls...that I will find him soon." Not tonight, however, and perhaps he would not go to the Duck and Quail alone. That, he decided, might best be undertaken by Caol. Caol had said it was time to return to Rhidam. It appeared the time was right indeed. But soon, Kavan would meet this man face to face and gain the answers to the mystery this box represented. A mystery that seemed impossibly unreal.

"General Glucke!"

Prince Kjell sounded more startled at running into the old general than he felt. His stroll through the castle halls, seeking a private refuge in a place that seemed, since his return from Enesfel, too busy with strangers, advisors, and soldiers coming and going, had brought him past the door onto the garden terrace where Gluck's loud voice could be heard for quite a distance. If the man's conversation with someone Kjell did not recognize in passing was meant to be private, he should not have been so vocal about his distress. The other man was already leaving when Kjell appeared to inadvertently stumble into the terrace as if unaware it was occupied. Given his simple reputation for social clumsiness, such a faux pas would not be surprising.

But for once, though Gluck's expression shifted to his usual one of condescending flattery and tolerance, Kjell caught a hint of something else in the man's eyes, something that made the hairs on the back of his neck prick up in warning.

"My apologies, General. I was hoping to enjoy this little scrap of morning sun before the snow clouds rob us again."

Glucke looked at the clear blue morning sky, the pink traces of dawn finally faded though in their wake traces of clouds could be seen on the eastern horizon. The crisp heaviness in the air did indeed threaten snow, and this was, he knew, a place Kjell had favored since he was old enough to scamper out of his caregivers' sight. "Enjoy it, my prince."

He started towards the door, brushing past the prince's arm without a word of apology for the contact. That new attitude was hard not to notice. Kjell barely managed to keep the frown of disapproval off his face. Not that the man ever showed the prince great respect, usually just enough to keep Kjell mollified by a show of obedience. But this, the prince determined, was different. Perhaps the other man had brought bad news or perhaps Gluck was preoccupied. Perhaps he and the King had not believed Kjell's tales from Rhidam, or had heard something different, something damning.

Perhaps it was something to do with the name Kjell had overheard, had not been meant to overhear, and was suspected of overhearing.

Mr. Heward.

It was news he had to get into the Lachlan Queen's hands...but cautiously. He wished he had seen the other man's face well enough to describe him.

If only, he thought much later when his messenger's horse returned to the castle alone, its saddle askew, he could get a message through. He knew what that empty horse of his false messenger meant. Merkar might not doubt his innocence and ineptitude, but it was beginning to appear that General Glucke did. That was a misfortune Kjell was going to have to correct before he found himself at the end of an assassin's blade.

ᢒᗉChapter 16ᗉᗉ

The Duck and Quail was a tiny tavern on the north end of Rhidam, a building separated from the main structures of the city by a collection of tanneries, blacksmiths, and stockyards which had kept the business free of the ravaging fire of months before. The tavern had seen an increase of business since other taverns throughout Rhidam had been damaged or destroyed, but at this early hour of the day there were few customers, allowing Caol to sit at a corner table where he could see the comings and goings, and, he hoped, easily identify the man Kavan had sent him to find. On the off chance that he failed to recognize the redhead the bard had shown him, he had shown the stone box to the tavern owner and told them he was here to deliver it to a man named Níkóá. Some might have been frightened off by that direct approach, but Kavan seemed to believe it would not scare away this particular man.

The other face he watched for was a man he did not expect to find in this place. Having arrived in Rhidam a short time ago, he had not taken the time to contact any remaining Corylliens, had made no attempt to announce his arrival, but had instead come straight to the tavern, preferring this duty to that of coming face to face with Heward, a fellow he would recognize thanks to the many drawings

Ártur had made, including the most recent one that had come through Kavan from Asta. While giving Kavan what few details he could of his night's activities, Caol had memorized every crevice, every pockmark, every angle and roundness of detail on that drawing, features a man could not easily hide regardless of disguise. He had no recollections of having ever seen that man before his interactions had begun with the Corylliens, nor in his years of contact with the Rhidam or Durham branches of the Association, except on the drawings the healer made. The Association network was vast, however, and Heward could be involved in one faction from anywhere between the northern sea in Cordash to the southern border of Hatu without crossing a Dugan's path before.

If he was Association, Caol intended to find out, as soon as he located the man Kavan wanted him to find. What part this stranger had in the affairs at hand, Caol could but guess, but if he was important to Asta, and to Kavan, he was important to Caol as well.

෫*෫

"Kyne."

Kavan bowed to the elderly woman, the longest living, and reigning, Kyne Elyriá had ever known. Mórne's once blonde hair was pale silver, elegantly braided and arranged on her head in a fashion that gave her taller than average height several more inches, adding to the imposing figure she made as she drew near to her six-hundredth birthday. None expected her to remain at her hereditary post to see that day arrive, but Kavan suspected she was stubbornly holding on to power in the hopes that there would be peace between Elyri and Teren and the bleeding, fractured Faith that bound them.

She glided with unexpected grace, although slowly, and drew Kavan to his feet with her steady hands on his shoulders, and after an unanticipated embrace, she settled on the nearest chair and motioned for him to take another. They were distant kin, several generations removed, but Kavan did not feel that kinship. She was nobility, in the Elyri sense, and he was a harper, no more. Nobility in Enesfel, it was true, a title that carried weight even here, and a title he hoped to one day bestow on his sons, but a title that meant little to him. Only music, knowledge, and Faith mattered, and it had been too long since he had been able to indulge in any of those things.

Her gaze traveled from his face to his hands and lingered there, the evidence of their healing bringing a thankful smile to her face. "Have you made progress in your search?" she asked instead of inquiring about what miracle had restored his hands. "I do not know how much longer I can hold the Tribunal's dogs at bay."

He watched her arrange the folds of her startlingly blue gown across her lap and sighed. "If ruling out the innocent is progress, then yes…but I have not yet found the guilty."

"Then k'gdhededhá Claide is not…?"

"Oh, I am sure he is…but there were other sources of the poisons found in Dórímyr's rooms, and Claide cannot be blamed for all of them. Two sources appear to have been administered over some time, suggesting a source closer to him, someone within Hes Dhágdhuán."

The woman bobbed her head but showed no thought or emotion on her face and Kavan did not dare attempt to probe her thoughts. He did not know the extent of her gifts, whether she would sense such efforts or be able to counter them, but his respect for her age, position, and kinship, prevented him from trying.

Kavan continued. "Hwensen is examining the staff and servants, those who had access to Dórímyr regularly. Thus far he has found nothing concrete, which leaves either those I have not investigated, or suggests someone who is not a member of the clergy."

"There is another possibility." Her voice trailed off, her gaze shifting to a point far away, or far within, where Kavan could not go.

Whatever that possibility was, he did not see it, and continued with the business he had come about. "There are three who might benefit from his death…now that his position is vacant…the three most likely to be elected to his position…"

"Only three?"

"I have spoken to, and ruled out, every other known potential candidate in Elyriá. We know from experience that the k'gdhededhá is most frequently selected from those serving within Hes Dhágdhuán. I believe the Króel twins have a chance equal to those here…a better chance, most likely, than gdhededhá Kluín whom I have spoken to and cleared of this crime. And they, because of their impairments and beliefs, have no interest in the position."

"But they would take it if elected?"

Kavan pondered the question. "Yes…I suspect they would, out of duty to what the Faith asks of them. But they would not seek that path themselves, which rules out murder to obtain it."

"You are certain gaining leadership is the motive?"

The bard nodded. "To gain it…or protect someone else's chances of gaining it. I have no proof, but it is the motive that makes sense to me. I have yet to speak to the remaining three, as access to them is difficult, but I have learned something of one of them that I am hoping you can assist me with."

"If I can assist you, I shall."

After a deep, nervous breath, Kavan straightened in his chair and began, "gdhededhá Ylár has been witnessed coming and going from this place many nights over the years. It is believed by some that he has a mistress…"

"He would not be the first gdhededhá to…" the woman began evasively.

"Indeed…and it would not necessarily be enough to deny him the election, since others will not want to expose him and run the risk of exposing their secrets and shortcomings. But if he felt he was at risk…or if someone else believed…"

"gdhededhá Tumm?"

"Yes," Kavan nodded with an exhaled breath. "Perhaps some effort has been made to keep that detail from being known."

"Not by either of them, I assure you."

"If I could, perhaps, speak with your staff…the servants…"

"There is no need, Kavan." The woman pushed to her feet and poured two glasses of serbháló, something one of her staff members would have done had one been present. But as they had frequently done during Kavan's visits over the years, they had left the Matriarch alone with the White Bard at her insistence, and she had no qualms about serving him. She was one of the few who treated him not as a saint or an anomaly but rather as an equal, something he appreciated though he did not see himself as her equal.

"If I were to know then I could…"

"I know…and that is enough." She caught his quizzical expression as she pressed the glass into his hand and gave him what he thought to be an unusually awkward smile. She motioned him to the window and gestured into the courtyard below, where a woman and six children varying in ages from newborn to late teens were scattered about, some at lessons, some at play. "You have met my great-granddaughter Lláná?"

Kavan watched the woman and the children, deducing them to be hers by the similarity of features and hair color, but he quickly realized something else, something in the face of the eldest son, and when the realization struck, his mouth opened, he blinked several times, and then he bowed his head.

"Yes," he murmured, ashamed for pressing for an answer. How could he have known the gdhededhá was entangled with a member of the High Mother's family? He had met Lláná years before, knew at the time that she had three children though he had not met her husband. Who would have guessed at this situation? Believing the High Mother's bloodline to be fiercely protected, Kavan was surprised that such a thing could be permitted or accepted.

It dawned on him that it normally was not, which was precisely why the Kyne was reluctant to speak of it, why it had never been made public, both to protect Lláná and Ylár.

Watching the emotion play across Kavan's face, Mórne sighed. "They are husband and wife in every way except the ceremony…which the Faith denies them because of his rank. He will not abandon his duties, forsake those vows save this one…an archaic vow meant for people incapable of controlling their impulses without it…and not even with it. We are meant to procreate. It is absurd to deny our basic nature in the name of religion…as long as no one is harmed…" She smiled wistfully. "Do you find this heretical?"

Kavan shook his head. "No. I have reached such conclusions myself…and wonder often why the Faith demands things of leaders who do not, in turn, obey the mandates. But Ylár…?"

"Has been honorable and faithful to her for over one hundred years…and she to him. She is a strong-willed child…like many in my family…" She smiled, this time directly at him, knowing that he too was strong-willed in his way. "My desire for my kin is that they have happy, prosperous lives. She has what she wants…and he supports her well. There is nothing more I could ask of him, and she asks for nothing more than he can give."

After draining his glass, Kavan turned from the window. "How many know?"

"You are asking if any of my children…or grandchildren…or even great-grandchildren…if they might kill to protect this secret? Only she and I know the truth; I have seen to that. Not even their children know, though when it is time, she may tell them. Ylár is a good man; he has told no one save his father…"

"Where might I find his father?"

With an enigmatic expression, she set her empty glass on the sill. "You already know him."

"I do?"

There was a knock on the door, interrupting before she could reply. A young man Kavan deemed to be another grandson or great-grandson appeared in the opening, bowed and said, "The k'lómesté is convened and awaiting your arrival, Kyne."

"I will be there shortly." She took Kavan's hands and kissed them both, murmuring, "I pray you are wrong...that Ylár is not guilty of this thing...nor his father...but I can tell you this much..." Her voice lowered to a whisper; they were alone but she was taking no chances on being heard should anyone be near. "Journey south, to the village of Bhórdh...Dórímyr...Tumm...it may be that the clue you seek is there."

"What is in...?"

Mórne shook her head. If she knew what he might discover there, she was not going to say, but Kavan saw in her eyes that even she was not certain what was there or how it might connect to Dórímyr's death. Bhórdh was a tiny mining village, one of the smallest and oldest in Elyriá, but there was something in that word that Kavan felt he should remember, something he had learned long ago in his childhood studies with Tíbhyan that had been buried beneath other, more pressing bits of knowledge. He scowled in frustration but bowed and watched the woman depart. He had come here for answers but was leaving with questions and the sequester drew ever nearer. He needed more time.

⊱*⊰

The redhead at the bar eyed the bald man in the corner, knowing he was being scrutinized in turn without having to stare. This was no Lachlan, nor was it the White Bard, but he supposed it had been wishful thinking to expect the bard to be the one to return his treasure directly, and he had not expected either the apprentice healer or his young dark-haired friend to be the ones to deliver it when he made the request. An intermediary, the man he had taken to Clarys if his memory was correct. Good enough. He took the bottle of wine the bartender gave him, and two cups, to the stranger's table and sat without asking or waiting for an invitation. He knew he was expected. Why ask?

Caol watched as the man settled across from him, poured a cup of wine, and slid it across the table before speaking. "Níkóá." He knew the man's face now. Whoever this man was, whatever he was, he had been the one to take him to Clarys in Ártur's stead. What were the odds, he mused, of this being the same man, of them meeting twice?

The redhead tucked loose curls behind his ear as he stretched out his legs and met the man's gaze. He knew he was recognized, but decided it was not worth mentioning. "You have something of mine." He wondered how this man knew the White Bard.

"I have something you gave…a gift, I believe?"

He produced a small stone box and Níkóá frowned, noting that the seal had been broken. "I did not think I would need it…"

"But you do." Caol had no idea what the box contained, or what it had contained before he thought with a wry twist of his lips as he pushed it across the table. "You are lucky he still had it…"

Níkóá's frown grew, and when he cracked open the lid, his frown became an angry scowl. "What is this? I need the contents…"

"If you want that," Caol said with a shrug, "you will meet him at the cabin in two days."

"Two days?" Níkóá did not ask which cabin. Because he had taken Kavan inside the structure he called home, it was not difficult to imagine that the bard could find his way back to it. Having promised the k'gdhededhá he would be in touch soon with proof, he hated further delays, but there was nothing to be done about it. He had many resources and skills at hand, but he did not know how to track the bard across the Sovereignties to find him sooner. "I will be there. If he is not…"

Chuckling, Caol finished the offered wine and got up. "I would not threaten him if I were you. It will be the last mistake you make."

"It wasn't a threat." Níkóá stopped, shrugged apologetically, and muttered, "Two days." It was a message he would have to leave with the tavern owner, should Claide arrive he would have to specify three days. "Tell him I will wait two days." He had no choice. After that, if Kavan did not come, he was going to need to rethink his strategy with Claide.

ᘒ*ᘒ

Though calm to the eyes of the Faithful who watched his bright career with interest and fervor, Lláhy had, when Kavan found him speaking amidst a group of young gdhededhá within the thóres courtyard where they gathered for their midday meal, an air of conceit and cockiness, an assurance that his views and opinions were infallible, that he knew the words and intentions of the Intercessor more surely than any man alive. It was the same sort of surety that Kavan had experienced firsthand with k'gdhededhá Dórímyr, the sort of self-righteousness that set the bard on edge with annoyance and despair. The ring he had seen discarded on the man's nightstand was worn on his hand now as he spoke to his companions of Dórímyr's greatness as a man, as a leader, as a follower of the Faith.

The Kyne's bidding him go to Bhórdh would have to wait. Come nightfall, he was due to meet Caol in Hes á Redh, and he felt he owed Bhríd a visit, to meet the children and to offer comfort to his grieving cousin. He did not know what words he could offer that might help, as he had sorely failed King Arlan when the man had grieved the death of his wife, but Kavan felt obligated to try.

Not knowing what the upcoming days would hold as gdhededhá from across Elyriá arrived in Clarys, it was vital that he completed his investigations of the remaining three men on his list. But with the Tribunal still determined to capture this particular heretic, though on what grounds was becoming increasingly unclear, Kavan dared not be seen in the thóres or in Hes Dhágdhuán. It seemed the accusations against him were not common knowledge, as Hwensen assured him he had heard no talk of it amongst the gdhededhá, but avoiding talk did not mean lack of knowledge of the charges. It might mean that no one else deemed the matter important enough to talk about, even though there had been no official arrests or charges of heresy made in several generations. That alone, Kavan thought, should make him a topic of interest. Regardless, he was unwilling to take the risks that public appearances in Hes Dhágdhuán could be.

Without resorting to probing the man's thoughts, the white dove, the cat, the mouse, each shadowed Lláhy throughout what remained of the day in the hopes that something could be learned of the man, his ideals, his motivations, his goals and temperament which would either exonerate him or point towards possible guilt. Though Lláhy's expressed grief over the prelate's death seemed forced and contrived, expressed through the wearing of that ring and his continual praise of the man to any who would listen, it was not enough to suggest he was involved in murder. To Kavan, it was political posturing, nothing more, the actions of a man interested in gaining enough support to advance in power.

Lláhy was the sole man the bard could find who was actively campaigning for the position of k'gdhededhá. Perhaps that was the only proof Kavan needed.

᚛*᚜

Duty complete, too much ale and the glass of wine slept off in the security of an Association safe house, Caol took to the streets of

Rhidam with relief and relish. He may not have been in Clarys long, but it had been long enough to develop an unexpected case of homesickness. He was happy to be back at what he hoped was the start of the final hunt for Heward and an end to the Corylliens. A final hunt meant higher stakes, a higher risk of death, but it needed to be done and he knew of no other man or woman who could do it…just as Kavan was the best man to delve behind the veneer of the Faith and weed out the infection that had claimed one man's life and had possibly spawned the deaths of many more. Caol did not believe he had been of much help to the bard, but he had succeeded in making a few Elyri contacts, merchants and traders and a few minstrels, men and women who traded as much in information as they did in goods and music, the first such contacts in Elyriá that any Teren Inquisitor had ever made to his knowledge. They were names he had already sent to Asta in the hopes she too would be able to make use of them. Those contacts made his stay in Clarys worthwhile, but he was happy to be back in Rhidam.

Responding to what Kavan had told him of the deaths of two suspected Corylliens, Caol approached Tusánt in the Purification chamber and learned as much as the man was willing to share with someone he believed to be a contact of Lord Cliáth's. Further questioning of one of the sheriff's underlings and those Association members and townsfolk he could locate who had known the two men brought Caol to the same conclusion.

Heward had been in Rhidam. Heward had killed two of his followers with his own hands. Perhaps as traitors to the cause, as it seemed, but that detail was less important to Caol than was the most glaring one. Rather than win them back, Heward was not above killing any man who crossed him. If he had any sense that Caol was not who he claimed to be, that he was a traitor far worse than either of those two men, he would not hesitate to kill Caol either.

Caol was going to have to kill him first.

To reassert his cover, though he hated to terrorize innocent people, Caol found, and vandalized, the dead men's homes with anti-Elyri slander painted across their doors in pig's blood. As Alty, he left a cryptic message hinting at a meeting in the Merry Ewe for anyone of anti-Elyri bent, then he spent the greater part of his evening there, waiting to see what would happen.

He did not expect anyone to show. He could see and feel the shift in public opinion in the streets and in the chatter of both taverns he had loitered in that day. The great fire which some tried to attribute to Elyri causes had shown that the Elyri, those already in Rhidam and those who brought aide or came do heal, were not the enemy. The murder of the Elyri within the castle courtyard had backfired on the perpetrators, turning the population against hatred and toward a path of tolerance that Tusánt fought to preach every time he stood at the náós podium. While there would always be men of bias, the residents of Rhidam, at least, were tired of fighting a struggle that had resulted in the deaths of more Teren than Elyri and had destroyed much of their city. The tide could easily have gone the other way, towards full-fledged anti-Elyri warfare; those behind the fire had taken a gamble and lost. Not even the murder of King Hagan had fanned the flames of that hatred. If it still existed, Caol was going to have to find each morsel to woo Heward, whom he was unable to find, into the open, to find him so that he could end the hunt.

The other reason he did not expect anyone to come was Claide. If the k'dedhá saw the message and suspected entrapment in that offered meeting, if he thought it an adverse risk backed by the Crown, he would ignore it and encourage others to do the same. It was a risk for Caol as well, signing it with the authority of a man he had not yet met, as it might negatively draw the man's attention, but drawing him out was a risk Caol was willing to face.

If Claide responded, it would be the cleanest proof, in Caol's eyes, that Claide and the Corylliens were bound to one another, that

Heward and the k'gdhededhá knew one another at least enough to make contact and utilize the other's resources. It would be proof of Claide's anti-Elyri stance, proof the Crown could use for an arrest, perhaps. Not the sort of risk easily taken if one wanted to protect their life from an angry Queen.

The hours ticked by, with Caol nursing his drink, playing dice with a couple of old men, chatting with patrons as if he, like they, was killing time before heading home for the night, enjoying a place of warmth rather than remaining outdoor in the cold. Having been a popular tavern with the less affluent for as long as Caol had lived in Rhidam, it was a frequent haven for those down on their luck and a frequent stop for members of the Association to meet. And, in recent times, it served as a frequent exchange location for information within the Coryllien ranks, anyone who recognized Caol in this place would have thought little of his presence. The Association would know not to interfere in his business, and if there were Corylliens here, they would know how to signal Alty without risk.

But no signals came, no faces he recognized, none who made an effort to approach or who looked suspicious. While not surprised, he was disappointed, and at the last call for drinks, he decided his best recourse was to call it a night and return the following evening, and every evening thereafter, until he made contact with any remaining Corylliens or potential members. Wondering if he should consider hiring a few Association contacts to pose as Corylliens with him, with the intent of showing Heward he was recruiting should the man be in Rhidam and watching from a distance, he turned up the collar of his cloak, pulled his knit cap down over his ears, and headed into the street, pondering where he should room for the night. Not the safe house, nor the room he had rented before. He wanted Heward to know he was back, but he did not want the man to find him while he was vulnerable in sleep. In the end, he decided that bedding amongst those homeless still lodged in Hes á Redh would be a safe choice and started towards the náós. As long as he avoided further contact with the gdhededhá, there was little cause for worry.

Little cause except for the quartet of shadows who fell into step far behind him as he passed through the deserted streets. He did not turn to look or acknowledge their presence, but he sensed them there, large, bulky, seemingly inebriated brutish men who slowed when he slowed, turned when he turned even if it was through an alley shortcut, quickened pace when he did or stopped when he halted to piss and adjust his twisted cloak.

The sound of melting snow dripping from the roof in this narrow alley, no longer spattering on solid ground but rather on the softness of leather, told him how far away they were when he stopped to stomp mud off his boots in an empty doorway. Their proximity set off alarms in Caol's head. He ducked into the burned hulk of a gutted building where he waited long enough to be satisfied that the men had ceased following him; they passed by, their guffaws and slurred chatter fading as they drifted away from his location. He crept through the ruins, found a rear exit, and after another long pause, listening and counting the distance to the sounds he could hear, he began forward again. The pounding in his chest had subsided, along with the fear that someone, Claide or Heward, had sent men to apprehend or kill him.

His relief lasted as long as it took to reach the crossroads that would take him to the náós across the intersection, north into the garment district or south to the castle. With no starlight to guide him and no streetlamps to light his way, his knowledge of Rhidam's streets was enough to make him confident of his steps. That confidence betrayed him as he did not see or hear those who leaped at him from the left and the right, swinging fists, kicking boots, a wooden pole and a length of metal knocking him to the ground before he had the opportunity to draw his sword or avoid the attack. He was small and fast, agile, and well-trained, but he was no match for four larger opponents who had caught him unaware. He rolled, crawled sideways and back, avoiding some of the blows but not all, and with no one to aid him, he was smart enough to know that should they knock him unconscious, it would be his death. His attackers were unlikely to leave the job unfinished. This was no warning. This was a cease and desist order that left Caol with a single choice.

"Sanctuary!" he bellowed at the top of his voice, a word with enough force and volume that it should bring anyone from within the náós to his rescue. He was right, in that he caught a bright burst of light from a lantern through the open náós door, but the flash was the last thing he saw, the crack of wood over his head the last thing he felt, and the sounds of shouting and footsteps running through the mud the last sounds he heard before the world turned dark and still.

❧Chapter 17❧

"Why am I here?" The bright winter sun reflected off the freshly fallen snow as Khwílen strolled side by side with Hwensen through one of Hes Dhágdhuán's many courtyards. His arrival last night had been too late to meet with the man he believed had summoned him, or with anyone who might have answered his questions, but he wasted no time this morning in finding the man who had once been Dórímyr's top aide, the man who many suspected would be the top aide to the next prelate as well since he had the most intimate knowledge of the Faith's inner political workings. The two shared an early meal before the first Gathering of the day, a Gathering that proved there were other gdhededhá present from outside of Clarys. He knew each face, had met each man during his aborted circuit around Elyriá, and though he knew why each of them was here, they no doubt were perplexed by his attendance. He had neither the seniority nor experience that most of them had, he was an adherent of St. Kóráhm's teaching which put him on the fringes of the Faith, and his post in Alberni put him outside of Elyriá's jurisdiction, put him in what some deemed to be dangerous enemy territory.

"Your candidacy is registered," Hwensen said with a shrug.

"Yes…but why did you nominate me?"

"Me?" The aide's steps did not falter. The nervous energy of recent weeks had prompted him to walk here multiple times each day. Today he was thankful to have someone with him. "I have made no nominations. If I had, my choice of nominees would be mocked…at the very least.

"Lord Cliáth." That deduction was easy to make. There had been other non-gdhededhá candidates in the past, men who were well-learned in the Faith, scholarly, pious men with charisma and the gift of oratory. Only one had ever been elected to the Holy Seat, and as the first such outsider to be elected, set future precedent for similar candidates. There had yet to be another outsider elected, however, and Khwílen knew the bard was unlikely to accept a nomination if it was made. If by some miracle he did, he would never likely be elected. He was beloved by the people, but his personal views on matters of the Faith, while not well known, would cause friction amongst the gdhededhá, particularly since he already had the invisible threat of heresy hanging over his head from the shadows of the dead. "If not you…who?"

Hwensen shrugged. "If I had to guess…Kluín. You and he are friends and contemporaries, are you not?"

That was a possibility Khwílen had not considered. "He must know I am satisfied with my position in…"

"Perhaps he wants you here for moral support and thought this the best way to guarantee it." Kluín had been nominated, as many had anticipated he would be, the sole member of St. Kóráhm's Order to receive nomination, aside from Khwílen. He had a moderate chance of election, and Khwílen knew that, were he in Kluín's place, he would desire the support of a friend as well. "Or perhaps your campaign against Dórímyr has been noticed by those amongst the gdhededhá who feel it is time for a change in leadership style. You have been in these halls before, serving as I have…your familiarity with the duties makes you a fitting candidate."

Khwílen frowned but nodded. He might not have garnered a lot of ecclesiastical supporters for his cause, but he did have them. Any of those people might have nominated him. He had left the position as Dórímyr's aide after less than ten years of service, due to doctrinal differences, but he had served in Clarys in other ways for many years before and after that, long enough to be a recognizable face and name. "Have they found Dórímyr's…?"

Hwensen's hand rose to stop him as they approached a collection of women gathered in prayer at the foot of a statue of Saint Bhílycá that adorned the open terrace. The men bowed to respectively to them and continued on their way and Hwensen spoke only when he was confident they were beyond the easy hearing range of the women. "It is said he died of fever on Udhár, only the Tribunal, I, and a handful of ecclesiastical guards know differently. And Kavan and the Kyne of course."

"But they still assert, amongst themselves, that Lord Cliáth…?"

"It seems they must. They have recalled many sent to actively seek his arrest, needing them here during the upcoming weeks, but the charge of heresy stands and probably will remain viable until he can satisfy them with proof murder. Perchance it will remain even then. Politics is a sticky business…"

"Indeed…all the more reason I do not want to be part of it." Khwílen closed his eyes while sending up prayers to Kóráhm, k'Ádhá, Dhágdhuán, and any who might hear him, for Kavan's safety. Opening them again as he continued walking, he added, "I will accept the nomination in order to attend the sequester…remain long enough to help Lord Cliáth uncover the truth…but I do not want the position. I will not accept it if I am selected. In Faith, I cannot."

"Think on that, Khwílen," Hwensen said earnestly, clasping the man's hand. "If k'Ádhá sees fit to present you the office…think on your choice, on what good you could offer the Faithful, before you dismiss election entirely." Perhaps he would still refuse, but after many decades beneath Dórímyr's tight-fisted guidance, a man like Khwílen Kesábhá might be what the Faith needed most.

But he, like Khwílen, doubted the man would progress beyond initial nomination. The wheels of bureaucracy were slow to change even when the need for change would be best for everyone. Still, he could pray that Khwílen, or Kluín, or another like them would have the chance to change the course of Elyriá, and perhaps the fate of the Faith throughout the Five Sovereignties.

๖๏*๏๖

Prince Kjell watched the ball of parchment shrivel, darken and disintegrate into charred ash as the hearth fire did its work, removing evidence of what existed in his mind alone. Such evidence had to be kept out of General Glucke's hands. Possibly Merkar's as well, but the prince had found no reason to believe that any plot the general was hatching had anything to do with the Nethite King, and was being carried out without the monarch's knowledge. Merkar lacked political finesse and foresight, being a heavy-handed man, and he had little to back his time on the throne beyond the taking of it and his belief in his right and superiority to rule. Glucke, despite his advanced years and diminishing physical capacity, was the sort of man to take advantage of those things to procure advancement. There was nowhere else for him to advance to except the throne, and advancement was undoubtedly what Glucke intended.

Until recently, the general had seemed willing to settle for manipulating the prince behind the scenes and ruling through him once Merkar was off the throne. Kjell did not know what had changed, but something had. Perhaps Glucke was tired of waiting for Merkar to die of overindulgence. Perhaps he was frustrated that he had yet to find an opportunity to kill the king or to wheedle Kjell into doing it. Or perhaps, after what appeared to be Kjell's successful foray into Enesfel which had given Merkar enough tidbits of information to satisfy his needs for spying without endangering anyone in Rhidam or Kjell himself, the general was beginning to suspect that the prince would not be as easily manipulated on the throne as he hoped.

What the prince was sure of was that the man who had been the scourge of Enesfel was connected to Neth's topmost military leader. The face on the sketch his uncle had sent to him, a delivery that had, for once, gotten past both the king and the general unopened, was without a doubt the face of the man Kjell had seen with Glucke on the terrace. While that did not guarantee the general's involvement in Enesfel's troubles, or even suggest Merkar's involvement, it was strong enough evidence to suggest that it was time to be rid of General Glucke. The man had served his purpose, but Prince Kjell had other military backers and no longer needed the sort of trouble Glucke could bring. Glucke had to go.

☙*☙

Bhórdh was one of the oldest settlements in Elyriá, a quaint community of single-level gray stone structures established at the southern edge of the Relzá River that wound north through valleys, plains, and forests until it emptied into Lake Eladhán at Clarys' threshold. The river here was a collection of trickling snowmelt rivulets from the heights of the Llaethlágárá Mountains, bringing sediment and silver from the ancient rock above. As deposits accumulated in the crevices of the riverbed, the earliest Elyri to pass over the mountains found a ready source of easily attained wealth on which to build the kingdom that Elyriá would become.

But Bhórdh, for reasons few understood, had not benefitted from that wealth, despite being the source of it. It had grown little beyond its collection of initial families, had barely spread beyond the original homes and structures built there, and had rarely drawn attention to itself for anything other than the silver mines that founded it, and later the gold mines discovered further up the sometimes sheer walls of the Llaethlágárá.

Why then, Kavan wondered as flight brought him to the perimeter of the tiny settlement, did the village's name stick in his memory with teasing persistence?

The cold night was clear and cloudless, allowing the kestrel eyes to study the streets from the safety of the sky as he searched for anything out of place that would suggest why he had been sent here. Beyond the eternal rumble of the waterwheel at the head of the river where much of the mining occurred, and the rush of the bubbling water through the middle of the village, the community was quiet, its inhabitants asleep beneath blankets and furs. No lights showed except for the faint glow of hearth fires around shuttered windows and a single lantern on a post outside of the village náós, a structure about twice the size of the upper oratory Kavan favored in the Lachlan castle. North and east of the village were small farms with snow-laden fields, and a collection of wooly cattle and shaggy goats, the source of most of Bhórdh's food. Unlike many larger settlements, Bhórdh was largely self-sufficient, and what they could not produce came in trade for the ore they wrung from the earth. How the village had not prospered was a mystery Kavan did not have time to pursue. He had a single day here, a single day to learn what the Kyne thought he should know, before he had to be in Rhidam. But without a hint of an established school or library, he wondered where, or how, he was meant to learn anything.

He could ask the villagers, but he did not know what his questions should be.

If there were any secrets to uncover in this place, they would not be given up easily.

The náós perhaps. That structure, or the lómesté lodge beside it, seemed the places most likely to house whatever documents, official or educational, the village possessed. Confident of not being seen, the white kestrel came down before the Gathering Hall where he resumed his normal form, paused to listen for anyone who might be near, then genuflected respectfully and pressed his hand to the oak door to push it open. There was no jolt of power, no presence of anything sacred, and though the door fed him images of those who most recently passed through it, he did not believe they had entered to worship. That perplexed him, but not as much as the inlaid silver symbol set into the frame to his left. The symbol, a stylized eye, or a flame perhaps, was something he had seen before, but at a glance, he could not recall where or what it meant. Not a common symbol, something arcane that he suspected few beyond the borders of Bhórdh would recognize, but it was, he discovered when he traced it with his fingertip, a symbol of power.

A symbol of the same power detected as flight brought him nearer to the village. There were places throughout the Sovereignties, glens and caves of natural power and ruins whose origin and power were believed to reside with the k'kairá. Finding such a place in Elyriá, the first to his knowledge, would be a joyous discovery. Though the symbol looked like no k'kairá symbol he had seen before, that did not mean it was not. What Kavan quickly decided was that it was neither Elyri nor High Elyri in origin, and it was not, as far as he could determine, a symbol of the Faith.

He shivered and lowered his hand before turning from the door. He was not going to find what he sought here. It was the source of this power he needed to find, for at the center of it he believed he would discover the truth. What truth, what connection k'gdhededhá Dórímyr might have to this place, he could not imagine, but he would find it. He faced south, found the thread of power that wove away from Bhórdh, and began the slow trek through the snow into the forest at the edge of the village, anticipating what he might find when the wellspring of power was reached.

❧*❧

Caol faded in and out of awareness under the care of Tusánt, Edward, and Saul, after a single visit from the court healer to ascertain his condition and tend any life-threatening injuries received in that beating. None of those who broke up the fight or carried the beaten man into the náós recognized him, not even Edward or Saul. But Tusánt had, this time, and was the one to insist Caol be brought to his private room and kept there with one of them with him constantly until he was well enough to leave. Tusánt did not speak his patient's name, pretending he did not know the man, and no one asked the reason for such caution. Someone had tried to kill the poor fellow. It made sense to protect him until he could protect himself.

To Tusánt's knowledge, most in Rhidam had not seen the Inquisitor in many months, not since his journey to Durham to see his new granddaughter and had afterward gone missing. Many talked about him as if he was dead. Tusánt guessed, by Healer MacLyr's surprise at seeing him, that this was the first time Caol had returned to Rhidam other than for his daughter's unexpected, secretive marriage. He had no notion what such secrecy meant, what it was attempting to accomplish, but it was not his place to ask questions. Tusánt considered sharing the news of the man's condition with the Queen, but the healer advised against it and thus Caol's return and care remained hidden as the new day dawned. Keeping that secret from Claide was going to be difficult as tales of the night's attack circulated and, as he washed the last of the man's blood from his shorn head, Tusánt had no idea what he would do or say if Claide asked. He had to hope that did not happen until Caol was well enough to be away.

❧*❧

Through the denseness of the forest, conifers packed tightly leaving no easy path between them, the greying sky was barely visible, but Kavan could feel the encroaching dawn in the air. The snow was light here, the branches preventing most of it from reaching the forest floor, a positive thing as snow would have made passage more difficult. Flying to his destination, to wherever this path of power led, would have been quicker, but he would have missed the slow build of energy as he drew nearer to it and might have been overpowered by its strength if he had simply dropped into the middle of it. By the time he entered the grove, with a scattering of large mountain stones in a circle at the center, the sensation of power raking across his senses was almost overwhelming.

Once before he had felt power like this, in a similar clearing littered with stone relics, dancing figures, and a harper he was sure was k'kairá. Perhaps they had all been. There was no music now, no dancers, no k'kairá, but there was unmistakable power, raw, hungry, and vaguely dangerous, growing stronger as he neared the circle stones. Not the malevolence encountered with Coryllien's spirit, but something dark enough to make his skin crawl.

He encircled the forms of mottled gray sandstone, following a packed earth and rock path partly overgrown with grass beneath the recent snowfall. People still came here. Perhaps not for the purpose originally intended, but at least out of curiosity. The grouping was similar to what he had found in Hatu...a toppled stone ring that contained the Gate that had taken him to Arlan the night the king had died. He sought a mark on each stone, a sigil, any indication of their purpose, but there was none visible, and there was no Gate. There were more stones in place here, a near-solid wall of them, with an entrance arch at the east and west of the circle. Some of the stones lay on their sides at an angle that a man could have stood or sat on, but he did not think it was their original position.

The earth mounded at their bases, covered with the stubble of winter grass and pine needles, showed signs of having been pushed up, disturbed when the stones fell on some distant day. The scoring that had shaped them was worn with weather and the touch of centuries of hands, supporting his suspicion that this was a shrine, a place of worship, sacrifice, and celebration nearly as ancient as the land itself, from a time before Elyri had come here. The power, however, while of an equally ancient source, was recently fed, not within his lifetime perhaps, but within the past generation, three to five hundred years at most. It felt odd that he should know that, and that the time frame felt significant, but no stranger than other things he 'knew' without consciously seeking to learn them.

He passed warily beneath the eastern arch, gazing up at the wide flat stone above him, unmarred by anything other than centuries of elemental exposure. Directly in front of him was a single flat stone as wide as his arm span and two to three feet across, standing to the height of his hips. The snow had not stuck here, perhaps having been melted off by whatever heat the stone absorbed during the day. Shadowy faded brown stains on the sun-bleached stone spread down the sides of it as if having dripped there, hinting at sacrifices made, but none, he was relieved to sense as his hand passed over the weather-smoothed surface without touching it, appeared to be Elyri or Teren. He wondered if anyone in Bhórdh could tell him the history of this place, the tale of it, or if anyone even knew. As old as it was, it might not have been used by anyone living, and what stories they might know might be no more than legend and folklore handed down to children to frighten them away from a place no one understood.

Four pillar stones stood equidistant around the inner space, the intermediate markers between the cardinal directions that designated an inner circle within the outer. And in the center, raised within three circles of steps, a pillar taller than the rest, an obelisk that Kavan envisioned had marked the passage of time as the sun's path across the sky cast the stones' shadow around the space that protected it.

To the south, where the outer stone wall met the mounded earth behind it, as if shoring up a collapsing hillside, a smaller arch yawned into blackness beneath the earth, a tunnel or a burial mound or some gateway to a secret treasure that would require ducking into, crawling, to get inside.

Kavan sensed nothing there. No power, no presence, not even the movement of air that might hint at an open passage on the other end of wherever that chasm led. He was curious as to its origins, to the secrets it might protect or that might have been removed from its earthly bowels, but not so curious as to turn away from the mission that had brought him here.

He had come for the power, power that emanated from the mossy obelisk protruding from the raised-stepped center which had withstood untold centuries alone in this nearly forgotten place.

He drew closer, reverence and the perusal of everything around him demanding a slow approach. It towered above him beyond the tips of his fingers when he stretched his arm upwards to gauge its height. Arcane etchings marred every visible surface, but many were filled with dust or had been worn down by the elements, making them difficult to see, particularly in the still dim early morning light. But on each cardinal face, placed at eye-height to a man standing on the ground, throat-height to a man standing on the first raised step, or heart-height to a man standing on the final raised step, was a symbol identical to the one on the doorpost of the Bhórdh náós. A symbol filled with a metal that, without touching it, Kavan believed was the same as the crescent pendant he wore, the pendant that bound him to the Lachlan House. A metal unidentified and unfamiliar to any of the metalsmiths Kavan had questioned over the years.

He reached to touch it, feeling a prickle of static race up his arm towards the smoky grey crystal Muir had given him, producing an audible pop-pop when he made contact. The sensation was not painful and did not feel dangerous, merely a transfer of some sort of earthly energy from the symbol, to Kavan, and back again.

What the contact did do, however, was reveal a memory flash of this same image in Claide's room, in a book open on the table near his breakfast tray. This flame-eye symbol was the connection between Dórímyr and Bhórdh, but how did Tumm fit in? What was the binding thread between the three the High Mother had insinuated when sending Kavan here? What did it mean?

The bard turned slowly, studying the entire circle from this raised, central vantage, seeing it with an unexpected degree of familiarity. Dórímyr had been here. This place had existed in the prelate's memory, one of those final images forced into Kavan's head, a memory image eroded with time in the old man's mind but vivid enough to suggest it had been an oft-visited remembrance.

Kavan wanted to understand, needed to know if this was what Kyne meant him to find. What did she know about the connection between the two men and this place? Imagining nothing that might foster the need for murder, only a knowledge of the arcane or a historical event intertwined with the earliest roots of the Faith, Kavan pressed one palm flat over the encrusted icon, his mind open to what the stone or symbol's power might reveal. Unprepared for the assault of power that erupted beneath his hand, he flinched and began to shake as images, sounds, smells and emotions blasted through him with the force of an uncorked, pressurized bottle of spirits.

Saint Zythán. Heretic Zythán.

Breath sucked from his lungs, Kavan's knees buckled, his body twisting awkwardly as it tried to collapse though his hand on the stone refused to pull free. He slouched as if hanging by one arm chained to a wall, feeling his shoulder wrench in its socket, before unseen arms bolstered him up, steadied him, the touch and sense of

Kóráhm's presence giving Kavan the strength to push to his feet as his head filled with images of a sort he would rather not see.

Bhórdh. Zythán. How had he not remembered the association of those two words? In his student years, in an attempt to understand what a heretic was and why Kóráhm was considered to be one by some within the Faith, Kavan had read the mythos of Zythán, tales that had given him uncomfortable, nearly tangible dreams for weeks after reading them. But as no one claimed knowledge about the mythological figure, not even Tíbhyan, or they refused to discuss it if they did have anything to tell, Kavan had pushed the details into the recesses of his mind, not expecting to ever encounter that name again in any context that would require remembrance of what he had read.

A prophet and saint without identity or gender, Zythán's story had been absorbed into the early Elyri church, coming into the Faith as the first saint, the earliest force to be adopted by the fledgling Faith as it took roots among the people in this new land. For surely, someone with the power over life and death, weather and winds and seas, had hands entwined with k'Ádhá's.

But it was these gifts that soon drove a wedge between the Faithful and the small but loyal adherents of the Cult of Saint Zythán. As the array of powers attributed to him, or her as Zythán was sometimes called, grew ever more fanciful and dangerous, some began to equate Zythán with k'Ádhá. Some even worshipped Zythán as a deity, a faceless, capricious deity with little regard for anyone, even his followers. Wild, bloody orgies were a substantiated trademark amongst those worshipers, and more than a few were given the 'gift' of the power to kill without touch. A skill that, when Kavan learned of it, was, he suspected, the same ability he carried, the inborn defense he possessed when threatened that first manifest when he accidentally harmed Prince Owain at six years old. That had been the source of Kavan's nightmares, thinking that somehow he was part of that outcast group, that shunned name, whether he wished to be or not. He had feared, and sometimes still did in the depths of his nightmares, that the difference he bore that turned others against him had some eerie, unnatural connection to that mythological name.

A killing spree, the only one in recorded Elyri history, began in Bhórdh, as Zythánites began to kill any Faithful, gdhededhá and commoners alike, who opposed their orgiastic lifestyle and who systematically persecuted, arrested and imprisoned those who professed belief in Zythán. The cultists believed they had every right, being a persecuted party, to fight back, had every right to be accepted by those in Clarys who decided policies of Faith, despite the self-centered, hedonistic beliefs that ran contrary to everything the Faith embraced. The factions battled for nearly one hundred years, the Faith finding it difficult to arrest those who could kill without touch or warning, but in the end, it appeared that the Zythánite cult was subverted. Any followers who remained went deep into hiding, disappearing from common life as nothing more than legend in some Faith circles…and out of memory in most others.

Once or twice in every generation, tales of a Zythánites coven were reported, someone telling of a witnessed orgy, Zythánite sigils left on doors, walls, or scorched into the side of cattle, or a series of unexplained deaths attributed to the heretical spirit. When the great plague first erupted in Elyriá, it was blamed on Zythán's followers until the reality of the spreading pestilence became fully realized. Having been away from Elyriá for too long, Kavan was not aware of any reported appearances of the cult in his lifetime. This, what he learned from the violent power of memory in this stone, was the first contact he had ever had with the cult. Though the events burned into his mind's eye, the last such episode to occur within this grove, had been long before Kavan's birth, even before the great plague, the fingers of repercussion were still clawing across Elyriá.

Two men brought up in the Faith. One man, older and believed wiser by the other, coming from a long line of Zythánite followers, living his whole life in the small village where Zythánism had first sprung up and dug its deepest roots into the family. One man, weak in power but strong in the conviction that his family's long-held beliefs were harmless and compatible with the teachings of the core of the Faith. A younger man, impressionable, not yet firm in his views of the world, traveling to Bhórdh with his merchant father, drawn by the charisma and novelty of the elder. Staying on the pretext of securing better trading rights, learning at the feet of one older still…one called Ámállá, a woman with the wiles to lure many to her, mainly men but some women as well. A woman who led her followers from the secrecy of this difficult-to-reach grove of prehistoric pines and power, where every depravity of their 'saint' was followed, down to the practice of a skill that would kill.

An objective…to kill the k'gdhededhá, the leader of the Faith she professed, and her followers believed, to be the greatest evil the Sovereignties had ever witnessed. Two men trained and sent to do this, hidden in the guise of gdhededhá as they worked their way through the Faith to positions of prominence. Two men who, when the time came, found they could not do what was asked of them; two men who returned to Bhórdh, men still young enough to have a future, two men who, together, butchered Ámállá and every Zythánite they found gathered in the grove that night.

Cries of horror and agony, new grass washed crimson with the flow of Elyri blood, a village nearly wiped from existence by a single night of frenzy beneath the fullness of the moon. Cries carried into the world on the wings of frightened birds, scattered insects, panicked animals, the only beings, except for those two men, to take the secret knowledge away from this place.

Two men who returned to Clarys carrying their secret deed with them, no one else knowing the dual life they had led, the blood they had shed to protect themselves and to prevent further attempts on the leader of their Faith. While killing Ámállá might have been excusable, might have been sanctioned if the matter had gone before the ecclesiastical council, the murder of dozens of other men, women, and children was unforgivable and both knew without a doubt that, should their secret come to light, they would have no future within the Faith leadership.

Why those who remained alive in Bhórdh had never spoken of the horror was impossible to say. They must have known the cause of the absence of so many of their number. The screeches and yowlings in the night must have burned echos into every pore, living or otherwise, of the village. Not even the ever-running rush of the river could have washed that horror completely away.

Why then had it never been spoken of beyond this place? Why then, did the annals of Elyri history bear no whisper of it?

A secret worth killing to protect. Who had killed who, how much blood was on each man's hands, Kavan could not guess. This had not been murder of the mind, murder by power, but murder with knives and hands…although what Kavan sensed in the power embedded in the stone was that the majority of deaths were not caused by the two men, but rather by the woman they had trusted. A woman who would rather destroy her followers and erase all memory of herself than risk capture and indoctrination by the Faith leaders and population at large. But the two men fleeing here to return to a more civilized world had not known that, had never learned the truth as they had gone on to lives of prosperity and influence.

One man, forever silent as if that night had been a horror in his sleep. One man who, in a backlash against the shadow of heresy, made it his personal crusade when elected to the position of ultimate authority, elected to replace the man he had once been sent to kill, to stamp out all heresy in its many forms.

Who would suspect such a man of heresy himself?

The man who, before his death, branded Kavan a heretic on the order of Kóráhm…who he had hated as fiercely as he had come to hate Ámállá, Zythán, and the mysteries of their cult…despite clinging to a few of those beliefs until the day of his death in Kavan's arms.

Horrific images of the massacre passed, the power expended in those deaths resulting in a painful pounding in his skull. Kavan freed his hand and staggered backward until his unsteady legs gave out and left him jumbled on the snowy earth. Dórímyr's hatred and persecution made sense now, even if it was, in his opinion, inexcusable and hypocritical. Zythán, whether Elyri, k'kairá, deity, or the fabrication of man, was believed to hold powers beyond comprehension…just as Kavan did. His teachings had not been mainstream…as Kavan's beliefs were not. In Kavan were mirrored many of the things Dórímyr had chased in his youth…and had later come to hate. Kavan became the virus Dórímyr had to stamp out, in the same way he had hoped to eliminate the lingering seeds of the virus Ámállá had planted in him. That made Kavan the enemy, eradicating Kavan the only way to justify the murder of so many that long-ago night.

Did Kyne know of this history Dórímyr and Tumm shared, or was she at least aware of their early affiliation with the Zythánites? Kavan assumed she must know, although how she could have learned of it, he could not imagine. Nor did he want to know, for the first conclusion he made was that she might somehow have been part of this as well, and that thought sickened him. No, someone else must have told her, perhaps one of the men themselves or, he mused as another logical connection was made, the information had come from Ylár. Tumm's son…a boy fathered in Bhórdh and taken to Clarys to be raised on the death of his mother after that frenzied killing was over. A child raised in the orphan home that was part of Hes Dhágdhuán's many sub-structures, taught the ways of Faith by the man who sired him, whether or not he had known it. Kavan believed Ylár knew now, though it was a secret only they, Dórímyr, and the Kyne had come to share. If Tumm, like Dórímyr, clung to any of the teachings inherent in Zythán's cult, it stood to reason that Ylár might have grown up knowing them too…at least the ones that permitted relations outside of marriage and outside of the priesthood, that did not prevent gdhededhá from having spouses and children and actively encouraged it.

Thus Dórímyr had held multiple threats over Tumm, the ability to expose him as Ylár's father, as a remnant of the feared and despised Cult of Zythán, and a murderer. That might have given the more ancient man cause to seek Dórímyr's death…to protect himself and his son. It might have given Ylár the same cause to protect himself, his father, and his family. Or, if Tumm believed that those long-ago events required Dórímyr's death to achieve atonement, that could have been cause as well. Tumm, with his shared knowledge, had been a threat to Dórímyr too, something the k'gdhededhá may have tried to use against him. Despite their friendship, they had been a threat to each other, and in the end, perhaps one of them had to die if the other was to find peace.

Learning the truth would require a confrontation Kavan was not keen to have, but it would not happen today. Already, the exchange of power and information had lasted well into the new day, and he was cold, hungry, and weary. Tonight, perhaps…or after his scheduled meeting in Enesfel. It would likely take him that long to assimilate everything that had been dumped into his head, and even longer to decipher what any of it meant.

❧Chapter 18❧

W hen Prince Kjell decided to spend the day riding, possibly hunting if anything worthwhile crossed his path, he intended to go alone. Bumping into General Glucke was unexpected, and when the man offered to go with him, bringing three other soldiers for protection, the prince's first impulse was to insistently refuse. He needed time to think, to decide how best to deal with the threats he perceived, threats to himself and Enesfel, and he would not be able to give the matters proper consideration with Glucke looming over his shoulder. But the general was unrelenting and soon the five men were gathered near the castle gate.

"Lord General, by my faith…there is no need for you to abandon your duties," the prince said with his well-practiced airy laugh, a sound that had, in the past, contributed to the King and general failing to take him seriously.

Glucke adjusted the fingers of his gloves as his horse fidgeted beneath him. "But there is, my prince. Have you not heard the threats against yourself and the King?"

"Threats?" Kjell eyed the other three men with him. Two he knew, one quite well, a captain in Neth's militia, the second an underling with no rank but a man trusted by Glucke and the king and destined to rise through the ranks if he lived long enough. The third man was a known associate of the general's, although he too had no rank to speak of. Rumored to be the general's illegitimate son, he was someone the prince did not trust, particularly when he was in Glucke's company.

"Against the Crown."

"There's always a threat," the prince laughed, one more attempt to dissuade the general from accompanying him. Threats were part of being a de Corrmick, being a Nethite.

The general frowned at not being taken seriously. "One conspirator was caught this morning." He thumbed over his shoulder to the headless remains of two men in the gibbet across the drawbridge. "He said there were others…but he died during questioning…and was followed by his careless torturer. The King is not safe…nor are you. He bid me see to your security and I shall."

It was Kjell's turn to scowl, a grimacing look as he stared at the executed men, a look intended to express his disgust at the dead rather than to mirror the forced jumble of thoughts in his head. A man under torture might say anything to make the pain stop, and one of the two showed unmistakable marks of torture on his barely clothed body. The prince suspected the second man, if he had indeed been a soldier, the torturer, had been killed to protect Glucke's official story rather than for the accidental death of the victim.

Movement out of the corner of his eye, as well as Glucke's sudden shift in gaze made Kjell turn in his saddle to see the King in the doorway. The prince nodded, smiled, and waved as if to thank him for generously providing protection for the day, but he felt no such gratitude. A threat against the King should have resulted in Merkar keeping Gluck nearby to protect himself. Either Merkar believed Glucke to be part of the threat to the throne, and thus was sending him out of the castle out of paranoia, or the plot was not against the King, but rather against Kjell. If that were true, Glucke might even be behind the plotting, or was put to it by the King.

Kjell could not imagine Merkar was concerned about his brother's safety. Kjell's death would mean one less contender to worry about.

Any assessment of risk, any dark thought or fear had to be hidden. Kjell heeled his horse's flanks and the animal took off at a gallop, leaving the others to catch up. The direction of the day's ride was altered considerably now that he had suspicion on his side, and the prince needed time to decide what to do. The one thing he was not going to do, regardless of Glucke's intention, was die.

❧*❧

"Thank you," Caol murmured to Tusánt, as he dressed in the pale blue robe one of the two novices delivered. "Are you sure he's..."

"Claide's not here, I swear it. I saw him and Valgis to the gate and watched them go into the city. This is your best opportunity to be away...if you feel well enough..."

Caol stretched, rolled his shoulders, and flexed his arms and legs. He was stiff and sore, his body covered in purple and yellow bruises left by the beating, though the injuries that had caused the bruising were healed already. Ártur's care, and the hours of straight, uninterrupted sleep, had been enough to leave him capable of rising when he might otherwise be dead. "I have to be. I don't think he knows who I am...if he knows I'm here...but he may suspect me of duplicity." Well-deserved as it was, Caol was not going to wait for the truth to be learned. "I'm not safe this close to him."

"Him? Claide?" Tusánt helped draw the cloak over the other man's shoulders and tied it loosely at his throat.

"Aye." He was not going to explain, not risk blowing his cover or endangering Tusánt, even though he believed he could trust the

Elyri who had tended him. "No one must know I was here. Not Claide…not the Queen…no one." Ártur knew, obviously, and Caol suspected his daughter knew, but the girl had been wise enough to stay away. "I've got work to do."

Tusánt nodded, his expression grave. "I have sworn Edward and Saul to secrecy, and you know I shall not speak of this. Healer MacLyr made us swear to your protection. I presume he will also speak to no one. You are safe here, should you need a haven."

"Good to know; hopefully it won't be necessary much longer."

The gdhededhá was smart enough not to ask what the Inquisitor meant. Politics were none of his concern, and he preferred to stay out of them as much as his position in the Faith would allow. His concern was for the people he served, what was best for them, and that meant bringing an end to the cycle of violence that had circled the realm for too long. He could not do it, not alone. He could only offer prayers, lessons to parishioners, and use his public and private actions as examples for the congregation to follow; anything else he happily left to the Queen and her staff.

"I pray you are right. The suffering has gone on for too long." As he opened the door and peered into the corridor, making sure no one was about, Caol repositioned the hood of the robe and then the two made it out of the room to the nearest door to the outside world. They passed through the kitchen to get to it, and Tusánt snatched up a loaf of bread and a slab of ham to press into the Inquisitor's palms before he departed. "Take these…and good luck."

Caol nodded and slunk away, tucking the offering under his cloak so he would not be accused of theft. He had to come up with a strategy to recruit Corylliens, or at least people who could look like Corylliens. His last effort had nearly cost his life. There were few men he deemed trustworthy and skilled enough to pose in such roles. Finding those few would take him the rest of the day. There was time to eat, however, once he located a safe place to do so; afterward, it was time to begin. He had to be ready when Heward tracked him down. Ready to perform, ready to pose...ready to kill.

❧*❧

Rather than venture into the forest, Prince Kjell limited his ride to the plains south of the city. Little chance of deer there, but there were rabbits to be found, and quail and pheasant. Without a hunting dog at his side, such hunting would largely be futile, however. He would rather forgo a prosperous hunt than run the risk of Glucke using the forest's cover against him. One of the three soldiers rode before them, one behind, and one, most often, rode to his left while Glucke remained on his right, sometimes chatting but mostly silent, watching for prey with a distraction that raised further flags of alarm for Kjell. There was no friendship between them, and when Kjell did speak it was of paltry matters that had little significance to anyone except those in the castle without power, intelligence, or need to focus on matters of importance. Silly triflings that gave credence to Kjell's perceived lack of intelligence, disinterest in the throne, and non-threatening irresponsibility. As usual, Glucke tolerated the fanciful turns of conversation, the antics the prince pulled to make those with him smile or laugh, but he did not initiate most exchanges. He was intent on his mission, or perhaps he was bored with Kjell's undignified behavior. It did not matter to the prince, as long as he kept Glucke off-balance enough to not suspect anything.

Mid-day they stopped by a creek for the prince to eat the meal he had brought. The general and his men, seeming to have believed their ride would not be a long one, had brought nothing, not even water, and while each shared his wine, only the young captain accepted a portion of the plentiful meal Kjell had brought. Kjell noted the look of disdain and distrust the general gave the captain and wondered what it meant. A connection to be nurtured, perhaps, was what the prince saw, and he decided it was a relationship he would explore once they returned to court and were away from Glucke's hawk-like observance.

❧*☙

After circling the small cabin nestled in the copse of oaks in a snow-laden vale, several passes made seeking signs of danger, an ambush or trap set for him, the white kestrel set down far enough away that none within the cabin would see the alteration from bird to man. Cautiously he approached, listening, toying with the velvet pouch he carried in his pocket containing an item he doubted few others living would recognize or remember…except perhaps Ártur. Kavan had not shown this to his cousin, would show it to no one, until he verified what it meant.

While he was several yards away from the cabin, the door opened and the red-haired man stepped across the threshold. His hair hung loosely about his shoulders, thick and wavy, a sign of a man in good health. He wore brown breeches perfectly tailored to fit his form, and a leather and fur outer coat unbuttoned; his linen shirt was open, revealing a chest fit and lean, a man in his prime and use to physical exertion. Brilliant blue eyes shone from a sun-kissed complexion and when he smiled, though his jaw-line showed no trace of hair, none was needed for Kavan to recognize the physical characteristics he expected to see.

"Lord Cliáth." There was no one else the snowy complexion could belong to, but the words still came out as more of a question than he intended. He offered his hand when the bard reached him, pleased to find him of equal height. He was more pleased when Kavan, after a glance at his hand, accepted the greeting with the barest of hesitation. From what he had heard about the White Bard, he had not expected an offer of physical contact to be accepted.

❧304☙

"Níkóá." Kavan resisted reading him through that touch but he did not need to confirm what he already believed to be true.

"They told you my name."

"Sóbhán did, yes. He thought it would help me find you."

Níkóá gestured into the cabin. "You did not need it to find me though, did you?" he asked with a chuckle as he closed the door behind them. The small crude wooden table before the hearth was set with mutton, turnips, flatbread, and serbháló…something not easy to come by in Enesfel. This was no pauper's meal despite its simplicity.

"I have been here." Kavan looked around him, studying the room more closely than he had before. He felt no drafts, the candle flames did not flicker, and the single room home was considerably warmer than the winter day outside. Though modest in décor, a bed, a table with two chairs, a cabinet and chest at the foot of the bed, none of those items were shabby or of poor quality. They were not new, but they were in good condition, well taken care of and lovingly used.

"True. Please. Sit. Join me. I do not often have visitors or guests. To be honest," he smiled wistfully, leaving the chair nearest the fire for Kavan, a place of honor for a guest to find warmth, "there has been no one here since my sister passed."

"I am sorry to hear it. Older? Or younger?"

"Older by nearly seven years…my mother's only child by her husband…"

The way his voice trailed off told Kavan as much about Níkóá's life and upbringing as the words he did not say. Whether she had been raped or had an affair, Níkóá was the product of relations outside of marriage and Kavan suspected that his sister looked much nearer her actual age than this man did.

"Did you know her? Your mother?" Kavan asked, hoping his question was not insensitive.

Níkóá nodded. "As well as an eight-year-old boy can. I did not know him…either of them…but there were stories…I felt like I did.

My sister cared for me until she married; I was thirteen. He beat her for many years until he died in his drink. He believed we...I...had money...but I never told the truth...where it was. She was not strong enough to hide it from him as I was. I suppose if I had...perhaps she..." He shrugged. "Afterward she remained with me...until her mind left her and she had no will to live. It wasn't hard for the fever to take her; she wanted to be strong to care for me...but I had to be strong for both of us in the end."

"I have no clear memories of my parents...a fire, and the Great Plague, claimed them and there were no siblings. Only my aunt, my uncle, my cousins..." Kavan toyed with his cup before drinking. "I would have liked to have had a brother or a sister, older or younger."

"No one else knows quite how alone that can make a person," Níkóá agreed. He wondered how often Kavan spoke of his past, how privileged he was to hear even a small portion of those private stories, but he did not inquire. Let the bard speak of what he wished. Níkóá was content to hear anything he would share. Kavan was in his home. That was more of an honor than any dialogue they might share. "You did not bring your harp."

"No." There had seemed no need for it, although it did not surprise him that this man might have hoped for a song or two in exchange for a shared meal.

"I've not heard you play...one day, perhaps, I will. I have heard it is...mesmerizing." He smiled, a mischievous, boyish expression that brought a twisting pain within Kavan's breast. Any doubt he carried was shrinking. Oh, how he missed that smile.

To cover the unexpected pain, he set down his fork and folded his hands on his lap, feeling the small pouch in the pocket beneath them. "You asked me here for a reason."

Expression serious, though disappointed his friendly efforts seemed to have gone unnoticed, Níkóá said, "You know why. You have something of mine. I need it back."

"I have a gift given to my ward to be delivered to me…"

Níkóá flushed. "Yes…yes, I know…but that was before…now I need it. It is of no use to you…"

The object was presented in his open palm, the gold ring with the large crimson stone, carved in the shape of an eagle's head, set in a nest of small amber chips. "On the contrary," Kavan corrected, "Farrell Lachlan's ring could be quite useful…should anyone have the foresight, the courage…the folly…to use it…"

Níkóá's tanned face lost color, his hand hovering inches away from the ring as he stared, feeling suddenly afraid to take it, as if the bard might think he had some ill intent. He had expected Kavan to recognize it, but it still surprised him to be casually uncovered.

"You must be…forty-five? Give or take a number of years? If he left this with your mother…either a gift to her or meant for you…she could not have sold it…or shown it to another…without fear of royal repercussion, particularly after his death. Bowen would have killed you both. Did he know what she was? Your stepfather? Your sister?"

The red hair shook as his head bobbed side to side. "Half-sister…she and her father…were Teren. I do not think either ever knew…" he mumbled, staring at his sleeve as he twisted it in his fingers. "If she had not died of a lung-sickness when I was very young, I am sure both would have learned the truth in time. It spared her the dangerous times we live in…for I do not believe she would have left Enesfel without me." His glance stole to the ring. "And I have too many reasons to stay."

"Indeed?"

Níkóá pushed away from the table and crossed the small room to look out the window. He did not, to Kavan's eye, appear to be staring at anything in particular, but rather putting distance between them, and perhaps between himself and his thoughts. Arlan Lachlan had often done the same thing. "I've killed those I've found, Corylliens that is. When my beard grows in, I can pass as Teren…infiltrate their ranks when I choose…one village after another."

Kavan swallowed his surprise. Most Elyri, with standard Elyri upbringing, would not consider the life of a vigilante. A soldier or a mercenary, perhaps, as Bhríd had become in the service of Prince Arlan, but never a vigilante. But Níkóá, like Gabrielle, had been born of an Elyri woman and a Teren man, raised outside of Elyriá, both by people who knew little of Elyri ways. Teren were, it seemed by their nature, more ferocious and prone to violence when it came to resolving problems, and growing up in that atmosphere, without his mother to guide him, it was of little surprise that Níkóá had taken a darker path.

"Do not fret, sir," Níkóá said without turning. "There was no bloodshed by these hands…save for the beheadings…"

"Then it was you…" Ártur had told him of the stranger, the redhead who had conducted the Queen's executions, the Elyri who avenged the deaths of those killed within the castle courtyard. None had known he was Elyri save the Queen and Espen, Justice Corbin, the men who had been executed, and later by the healer when the detail came out in a conversation with the Justice. Caol suspected the executioner had been the one to take him to Elyriá when the healer could not. Whether others knew the executioner had been Elyri, Kavan did not know.

Another thought leaped to mind, one that brought Kavan to his feet. With a startled blink, he murmured, "You are hwonághk…"

He had to be. Perhaps, like Gabrielle, he had experienced some rudimentary training before their mothers had left their lives, but after that, outside of Elyriá, Elyri training would have been impossible to find. Gabrielle had used the Gates, and she had some vestiges of other rarely used innate skills. Most of her gifts had faded or the skills were too difficult to practice any longer as her access to power dwindled. What Kavan sensed here, however, in Níkóá's detection of his surprise, in the hinted bloodless killing, the tingle of power in the cabin that he had felt upon approaching, the strength of it that he experienced when entering and in that welcoming handshake, was considerably more power than Gabrielle possessed.

Níkóá's shoulders twitched. "Technically...yes." He turned to face Kavan with an expression, an emotion behind it, which struck close to Kavan's heart. It suggested that, whatever his training, he recognized the sometimes derogatory word Kavan had used.

"I mean no insult." Kavan closed the distance between them and clasped the man's broad shoulder, resisting the urge to use the touch for a more in-depth glimpse into the power Níkóá possessed. "But you are untrained."

Níkóá covered the white hand with his and managed a familiar crooked smile. "I trained myself, as much as I could, and I spent several years after Janette passed in Elyriá, seeking what knowledge I could find. I was an adult by then, of course...and not many bhydáni are willing to train an adult..."

Kavan nodded as his hand fell. "An untrained, unfocused child is safer...usually. There is little risk of a bhydáni being harmed should the child make an error."

It had been one of the reasons many bhydáni had debated Kavan's initial education, as his early show of substantial power had been frightening even then. Over the years, as Kavan learned more about the nature of power, how Elyri learned to detect it, manifest it, harness it, control and use it, he had grown to admire Tíbhyan much more for the risk he assumed in undertaking Kavan's sole tutelage. To teach an adult, even one who was half Teren, meant possibly tapping into stronger, if unfocused, power, and risking a mistake that could kill student and teacher alike. If Níkóá carried enough power to train himself in its use, had learned the skill of bloodless killing without a teacher, how dangerous would he be to a bhydáni?

"Fortunately, a few were willing to accept the risk…for a price…and with the number of our people who are not fully trained as children…and my own skills…it was not difficult to seek a bit of knowledge here…some there…as I traveled. Not as much as I wanted…but enough to suffice."

"For what purpose?" Kavan felt a swell of pride that this man identified as Elyri despite his parentage and upbringing, and he wondered if there might come a day when he could offer training as well. There was too much upheaval in his life, both in Elyriá and Enesfel, for Kavan to consider it now, but it was something he would gladly offer in time. Having tutored the Lachlan children, and now mentoring Sóbhán when he could, Kavan realized more and more that sharing what he knew was one of the few passions he possessed after seeking knowledge and making music.

"Do I need a purpose?" Níkóá chuckled and returned to the table and his meal. "I have been given a unique opportunity…Elyri power…Lachlan blood. I did not intend to make use of that blood when I undertook some further degree of mastery…but now…now I can use it, use them both, to my advantage…and I intend to…"

A violent tremor passed through Kavan's body, clawing down into his soul, knotting his stomach, causing him to clutch the table as he lowered onto the chair. The ring he had been holding clattered to the wooden planked floor, but Níkóá did not notice as he sprung up to catch the bard as the man missed the chair and sank to his knees. Kavan gasped for breath, struggled for consciousness and air, his complexion turning slightly bluish as his fingers tore into the other man's arms in search of a lifeline as his sight began to darken.

"Lord Cliáth!"

❧*❧

Sóbhán threw open the door into the corridor, not wanting to turn his back on the young man behind him, but having the sense to seek help when he did not know what was happening. "Ártur!" he shouted, forgoing titles or formalities. "Lord Talis!" When neither man immediately appeared at his call, he cried out their names again before dashing back to the bedside to try to restrain the convulsing body that, until this moment, had shown no indication of life or movement beyond breathing.

What he felt in that contact, what Ártur felt when he burst into the room and took Gaelán's head between his hands, was the presence of one neither expected to feel there.

The healer groaned in fear, and as he fought to keep Gaelán's unprotected mind from damage, he murmured, "Kavan...sínréc..." hoping that his cousin would hear him and that whatever was happening to Kavan, both bard and novice healer could survive.

❧*❧

The six ships, tall, mismatched, barely sea-worthy and sailing in a haphazard formation, bore down on Pháne not out of the fog but out of the glare of the low-setting sun on the glassy sea. There was no reason to think them a threat at first, as their intent might have been to trade on Káliel, but as they drew nearer and ignored the warning trumpet blats given to steer them away from Pháne, it became obvious to those stationed in that tiny outpost that the ships meant business of an unfriendly nature. It gave Prince Muir's soldiers time to prepare, to launch the ships kept moored for protection and time to gather every weapon at their disposal.

The two were not warships, however, as the pacifist, isolationist islands had never had a use for vessels of war, but they were equipped with every manner of weaponry Káliel was able to supply. Outnumbered, they fought valiantly, possessing one thing the others did not...desperation. The Prince watched as attackers and Káliel men alike fell over the rails into the sea. He watched as two enemy ships turned into billowing, belching clouds of black smoke and a third, large, heavy and unwieldy, having gotten too close to the dangerous sharp outcroppings submerged beneath the bay, was gutted. It quickly succumbed to the saltwater it swallowed and tipped sideways as it began to sink.

The enemy captains, refusing to let their ships be confiscated to use against them, set the damaged vessels alight when it became evident that their efforts were doomed to failure.

The outpost, Prince Muir and the men under his command, had to fend for themselves as the Káliel ships struggled to fend off the remaining three vessels.

❧✳❧

"A…k'rylag…" Kavan rasped when air began to refill his lungs. "I need a k'rylag…"

Níkóá knew panic when he saw it, understood fear, and with one of Kavan's arms about his shoulders, he helped the man to his feet and pulled him through the cabin door. Having feared he had inadvertently poisoned the man he was hoping would be a friend, he was glad to see the blue-grey smudge of death leaving the bard's skin, but he was still afraid of what he did not understand.

"There is one about a mile east of here…a náós…"

A mile. Too far to walk or even run. If he did not hurry, he would be too late. Death was clawing and gnashing at the edges of his perceptions and he had to thwart its mission. "Too far…I will return…just…" He shrugged free of Níkóá's grasp to stand on his own. "Do nothing…do not use that ring…until I return. Swear it…"

He had no reason to believe Kavan would return, no reason to trust that the bard knew of what he spoke in that command, but he had heard rumors, and rumors were enough. He nodded his head with a croaked, "Yes…" moments before the bard's shape was replaced with that of a white kestrel that took to the sky on unsteady wings and headed east as Níkóá had indicated.

"k'Ádhá be with you…" Níkóá whispered, not knowing what else he could offer to the man fleeing with such distress. It was not a danger here from which he fled. It was towards danger elsewhere, and Níkóá wished he had some means of helping beyond prayers.

❧*❧

Prince Kjell's horse faltered sideways with a whinny of surprise as the second horse slammed into its side. The knife blade, inches from Kjell's throat, missed its target because the horse stumbled and went down. The Prince might have gone down with it if not for an arm suddenly wrapped around his neck that kept him from being pinned beneath the animal's flailing weight.

The grip was tight and growing tighter, no gesture to save him but exactly the opposite. It took no look to know that the man who held him, who drew his sword with a free hand intending a fatal strike, was Glucke. Though he half-expected an attack when he set out on his hunt that morning, the Prince was ill-prepared at this moment, and though calmly certain he would die, he was equally certain he would not die without a fight as his older brothers had, murdered by political intrigue for the betterment of King Merkar.

The first attacker could not reach him as the fallen horse struggled to its feet and the captain with whom Kjell had shared his meal kept the attacker from further attempts with a sword through his back and belly. The third soldier, leading the column, turned back to engage the captain, as the captain appeared to be fighting on the prince's behalf. Kjell could not be certain it was not some larger plan by which Glucke meant to strengthen his alibi, an elaborate ruse of how two traitors turned on the de Corrmick prince and were killed in the fight for their crime.

Kjell kicked as he fought free of the crushing arm. Glucke was a seasoned warrior and strong, but he was a man past his prime fighting against a younger, stronger opponent and he was perched on an animal that, despite being trained for combat, would not willingly tolerate the sharp elbow Kjell jabbed into its tender belly. When the horse bucked, rearing in response to the unanticipated pain, Gluck lost the grip of his knees on the horse's sides and tumbled off its back. The fall resulted in his grip releasing around Kjell's neck as the general sought to break his fall and roll away from the horse's crushing hooves.

The prince fell face first onto the snowy ground but avoided the riderless horses trying to escape the strong emotions of the men. With his sword embedded in a dead man, the captain was fighting barehanded with the other soldier, whose sword had been kicked out of reach in the skirmish. In no position to draw his weapon as he scrambled away from Glucke's angry surge to his feet, Kjell found the discarded sword when his hand slashed over the blade. The cut was not painful enough or deep enough to cause the loss of the use of his hand, but it hurt enough to elicit a scream. The sound morphed into one of outrage when he closed his fist around the blade and brought it up as Glucke lunged. The general's sword drove into Kjell's left shoulder, pinning him to the earth, the intended deathblow missing its target when Kjell rolled. Glucke's lunge was, instead, met with the bite of the prince's weapon sinking between ribs, through his lungs and lodging against his spine.

For a moment Gluck hovered above the prince, suspended in time in a position of frozen amazement, fury, and fear before he toppled to the side, narrowly missing landing on the prince. The last expression Kjell noted on the man's face was one of disdain and, he believed, a healthy dose of humiliation, for how could a naïve simpleton be the one to end his hopes, his career...his life? The Prince grimaced as he yanked the embedded sword free of his shoulder and fought to his feet, expecting to fight one more man, whether it was the captain or the soldier the captain had been fighting. He knew he was not yet safe.

❧*❧

One of the remaining ships inched north, in the direction of Pháne's cave. Or where it had been. Kavan had destroyed it, and the entrance to it, meaning that the attackers, should they gain access to the island, would never find what they sought…if that cave was indeed their objective. As the last two ships drew closer, as close as the jagged outcroppings would allow, an exchange of fire-tipped arrows began, fire being the one thing that could win either side an advantage. Several rowboats dropped over the ships' sides, filling with men whom Muir's forces picked off with precision. The archery practice he put them through every day was paying off.

Men screaming, men scrambling to douse pockets of flame as they erupted wherever arrows made it through. There was no need for Muir to bark orders; the men knew what to do if they were to survive. The third ship was temporarily put out of their thoughts. These were the opponents they needed to stop. Whatever their mission, the Prince was determined to see it unfulfilled.

❧*❧

"What is…why…?"

Ártur had no explanation to offer that the Teren physician might understand as Rouvyn obeyed directions, binding arms and legs to the bedposts in the hopes of keeping Gaelán from being harmed by his thrashing. Asta had come and had, on seeing what was happening, knotted the kerchief she carried and thrust it into her cataleptic husband's mouth to keep him from biting his tongue, watching him thereafter in case he showed signs of choking or drowning in his own fluids. She had heard it was the right thing to do and the physicians were too busy to tell her differently. The Elyri healer found nothing wrong that had not been previously wrong, no sign of injury or trauma or failing bodily function. No bleeding within his brain that might result in convulsions.

All he found was the frantic, fluctuating power of Kavan's presence as he sought something, knowingly or not, through the young healer's mind. Ártur tried to touch it, tap into it, make his cousin aware of what he was doing, stop him…or help him. He could do nothing more than balance on the edge of the bard's great power, blinded by Kavan's distress, and try to keep his healer's strength between Kavan and Gaelán to lessen any effect this might have on the helpless young man.

His destination had no k'rylag of its own, only an exit point he had once used to escape a deadly collapse with his life barely intact. The k'rylag Níkóá had directed him to, in a long-unused crumbling Gathering Hall, surrounded by a largely abandoned cluster of peasant hovels, would not take Kavan to that exit point, but it could take him close, into a closet from which he burst forth. Soldiers, servants, and a woman's familiar voice followed as he sprinted through the hall to the outer door. He took no time to greet anyone or explain, and made no effort to hide the rapidly forced shapechange to kestrel that came as soon as he was clear of the villa. The Sight had shown him flash after flash, image after image, causing his heart to thunder with exertion and horror. He was not certain what he would find at the end of his flight but he knew he was running out of time.

❧*❧

"Lay down your sword, Captain."

The young captain, near in age to Prince Kjell, had killed the second soldier Glucke had brought, leaving the captain to face the prince alone with three bodies at their feet. A glance at the three as he dropped the blade he held and the captain said, "I mean no harm, My Prince." His face was bloody from a cut down the left side and his hands and chest were splattered with blood. He was breathless from exertion, but he was still standing.

"So you say." Kjell had no reason to believe him…except that he had saved Kjell's life. But in Neth, saving a life often meant no more than the desire for a royal favor for the furthering of one's own goals. It rarely, in Kjell's experience, had anything to do with kindness or morality or even duty. "The knife too."

The captain obeyed without question or hesitation. "Why would the general…?"

"I'm de Corrmick. Why wouldn't he?" But the question had taken root in Kjell's belly too. The obvious answer was that it was done for Glucke's protection or advancement, either because he decided that the prince was a liability, a threat, or a stepping stone to favor with the King, or because Merkar had perceived his brother to be a menace. None of those questions mattered since the man Kjell had groomed was dead…dead by his own hands. He looked at his bloody palm dispassionately and wondered if he should feel disgusted by what he had done. Unlike many de Corrmick princes who had experienced warfare first hand, this was Kjell's first kill…and he was slightly troubled that he felt nothing. No shame, no disgust. Were all de Corrmick's bred to kill without concern?

The question that troubled him most, however, was whether or not his brother, the King, was involved in, or aware of, Glucke's intentions, and what, if anything, this had to do with Enesfel and a man named Anri Heward.

The captain neither spoke nor moved as the prince studied his situation with a calm stillness of body and soul. Had Kjell been the

King or any preceding de Corrmick ancestor, the captain would be dead and the bodies left to rot as he thundered home to bluster and seek vengeance on any he believed, rightly or wrongly, had been involved in the plot. The prince's levelheadedness, the calm with which he surveyed the dead, the steadiness of his hand as he kept his sword trained on the captain, suggested that Kjell was not the flighty, insipid weakling many at court, and in the de Corrmick employ, believed. It was a refreshing, welcome change of pace and a sign that gave the captain hope.

Unless that façade was the calm before a terrible storm.

"I can help…"

Kjell snapped alert, took a step closer bringing the point of his sword to the man's throat. "I'm sure you can. If you think I need a cover…"

"No…no…nothing like that, My Lord," the captain squeaked. A more rational man, perhaps, but Kjell was still a product of a de Corrmick upbringing, which meant that a degree of paranoia was the best means of staying alive. "There are others…like me…we would support you…back you…if you…"

Wanted to take the throne. He did not need to finish the statement for Kjell to know the words. Someone was always interested in taking sides against a de Corrmick king. It was the nature of Nethite politics.

Voices in the distance, however, interrupted his thoughts and brought him to more immediate, practical matters. "We get them onto the horses…back to the castle…" And deal with the repercussions then, for he did not doubt that repercussions would come. Perhaps he mused, as the captain helped him secure bodies to their horses, the captain might be of use after all.

᷂*᷂

Ártur blinked. Stared. Pushed his thoughts deeper. Kavan was still there; nothing about that link to the young man had changed.

But Gaelán had gone still between Ártur's hands, as if something had happened…and the healer could detect no reason for it.

❧*❧

Despite their efforts, one rowboat containing seven men reached the rocky outcropping that served as the single accessible footpath from the sea to the outpost. Seven men, joined by three more who washed to shore alive, ten who sliced and swung and fought their way up the stone path until they were less than fifteen yards from the outpost's postern. Having lost too many good men, Prince Muir charged through the open gate with a half dozen more behind him. The odds were in his favor, and growing with the loss of another enemy ship and the litter of bodies floating in the sea. On the prow of the remaining enemy vessel, a man watched alone, his expression one of callous observation; though the prince felt familiarity, as they locked eyes with one another over the great distance between them, it was impossible to be certain. That was the man Muir wanted, the leader, and he killed another combatant in his efforts to reach the rowboat that could take him to that ship.

He did not hear the screech from the sky above, the warning cry of a bird of prey that folded its wings and plummeted like a stone towards the earth. Nor did Muir hear the distant twang of a released bowstring. No sound registered, no conscious thought or recognition of a billow of white hair that appeared directly before him in the same instant that a flash of pain spread through his breast. Both bodies, the bigger blonde and the slighter silver-haired man, stumbled and crashed to the wet, rocky earth.

"Muir!" A blinding sting scored along his ribs, an agony Kavan believed to be caused by the puncture of the arrow he had fought to

keep from reaching its target. But when he pushed up with one arm
to see if the prince had survived the fall to the sea-soaked stones, all
he could see was failure. The arrow had found its way between his
arm and torso to bite deep into the young man's upper chest.

Power and the sudden scent of Kóráhm in his nostrils alerted
Kavan to movement behind him. He roared, twisted his body with
one hand outstretched, and each living attacker was thrown away
from them with enough force that, when they hit rock it was with the
sickening crack of bone, and those who were tossed into the water
were held there, sinking, unable to tear free of the unseen hand that
bound them even when Kavan turned his focus back to the prince.

"Didn't...expect...to see you...today..." Prince Muir's lips
twisted into a wry, but happy smile, as he focused his blurry vision
on the bard's face. Men rushed by, grabbing rowboats, emptying
them of bodies and pulling them ashore where those still in the last
assault vessel could not get to them.

"I didn't expect to be here." Though no healer, Kavan worked
threads of power down around the arrowhead and shaft inside of
Muir's body. He could not remove it, not without killing the young
man, but he could try to dull the pain the prince was feeling as his
lungs filled with blood.

He clutched Kavan's free hand in his. "Did we...?"

"You have won, Muir. They will not return to Pháne." Perhaps
someone else would try, but none of these men would trouble the
islands again.

"Good." He coughed, struggled for breath, but his grip on
Kavan's hand held fast. If he was fading, slipping beyond where
Kavan could follow, he showed no sign of it and expressed no fear.
Perhaps it was the nearby presence of Kóráhm that soothed him, or
Kavan's proximity and touch that filled him with calm and grace.
"Did I...do good...?"

"You did." Trembling with growing grief and the outpouring of energy, Kavan sought a hold on the prince's soul that would keep him close as long as possible. There was something else there, that trail of orange energy that had entered Muir's body months ago, an attack that Kavan had not prevented but seemed to have dissipated as soon as it had begun, and it struggled against Kavan's efforts, intending to push Kavan out and hold the arrow within. It made Muir's life force slippery. It ran through fingers of power like flour through a sifter; the harder Kavan tried, the faster it retreated. There was no miracle. Time and life were nearly gone...and Kavan could not reverse it.

"Go with my love, Muir..." Mindful of the arrow, he brought the young man up against his chest in a loving embrace, no longer pouring power into Muir but rather the love and acceptance and pride the blonde prince had sought his entire life. It was not his father's love, or his wife's, and it was not the love of the man who had raised him or the love of his sole surviving sibling. But it was love all the same, and Kavan awkwardly felt that, through the peace in Muir's soul, his might be the love that mattered most in those final moments before Muir's hand fell limp and his soul slipped away. The lethal energy within him escaped with his final breath and the orange of it faded to black and dissipated above them.

Kavan closed his eyes, pressed his face into the golden curls that had freed themselves from the tie at the back of Muir's head, and wept as he had never wept before.

❧Chapter 19❧

The news of an attempt on Prince Kjell's life by General Gluck and two of his soldiers, whether prompted or supported by King Merkar or not, gave birth to a purge of the military that was, in Kjell's mind, long overdue. As within the castle halls, corruption in the Nethite military scored deep. The King, either because he was relying on Kjell's outrage to backfire or provide clear evidence of corruption, gave the Prince and Captain Stone reign to carry out the questioning, to bring every man or woman they believed to have been responsible for this attack on the de Corrmick House to the King for justice. With the captain's aid, and his own knowledge of the men who worked with Glucke or within the walls of the castle closest to the royal family, Kjell brought forth nineteen men he knew to be untrustworthy, men who were a threat...mostly to him but also to his brother. The culling would leave a core of soldiers more loyal to him, should he face his brother's wrath someday, a necessity for survival in the de Corrmick house that Kjell regretted but knew how to use.

King Merkar, not content with dismissal, commanded the death of each person. Not satisfied with the amount of bloodshed, he sought out and slaughtered another three dozen people before the night was over. The carnage ended when another man, a wizened, gnarled, crafty captain by the name of Fraen, took the king aside, offered him wine, and soothed him with words the prince was not permitted to hear. The look the king gave his brother afterward was one that made Kjell's skin crawl and one that, when coupled with a servant's tale a few hours later of another, more secretive purge of close to forty soldiers, officers, and servants whose favor Kjell had been covertly grooming over the years sent the prince on the run. If Merkar suspected him, saw him as a threat, staying alive meant disappearing, taking Captain Stone with him as far as the dawn kissed edges of the city. Captain Stone, convinced he could live through any purge, that he could better serve the prince within the ranks, returned to the de Corrmick castle to try to undo the damage Fraen had done in the mind of the King, leaving Prince Kjell to seek safe haven somewhere his brother would not think to look.

Pale rose and amber crept over the sea and the crest of Pháne's mountain ridge, reaching the battered outpost before the men deemed themselves safe from those who had ravaged their tiny island. Built mainly of stone rather than its original wood, the structure had suffered little damage, and save for the sailors who had lost their lives, no more than a handful of outpost soldiers had perished. The wounded and those sailors brought to shore were tended while the captured enemy vessel was scoured from top to bottom in search of identifying clues. The man who had perched on her stern had dived overboard and swam to the retreating ship, which circled the island cave-side and returned as the fight neared its end. That ship, its captain and the man Kavan had watched escape from them, decided against further action, decided to retreat, leaving unanswered questions in their wake and the death of many innocent, or less than innocent, men. The expedition leader had not been near enough for anyone to see clearly, none could identify him, but Kavan knew in his gut who that man was, knew the identity of the one who had ripped Prince Muir from him.

If Caol did not bring Anri Heward to justice, Kavan would.

He and two soldiers trained as Káliel Guards took a rowboat across the channel to the main island, but Kavan sent them back to aid their comrades as he adjusted the prince's limp body in his arms. Many had wanted to travel with him, take one of their ships, give Muir a proper full escort home, but Muir's second in command, a young freckle-faced fellow with a stern expression, talked them down. Duty kept them where they were. Abandoning their post after a battle would send the wrong message to any follow-up attackers who might come in search of their comrades. Kavan would have to make this trip alone, the sole escort for their leader. The escort he understood Muir would have wanted.

Kavan glanced at the island bathed in the glow of morning colors, with the halo of the sun beyond it, and sighed. He could complete the journey to the villa by nightfall if he pressed on; there was no need for horses as there had been the last time he had made this trek. Long ago when he made this journey, his energy had been spent on trying to keep Prince Bertram alive. He knew the path without the use of his eyes. This time, there was no need to expend energy to sustain a life already gone. For a while, as his steps found their way through the tangled foliage that overgrew the path in places, Kavan could do nothing but berate himself for not arriving in time, for not being faster, not saving the boy he had tutored, mentored, raised like his son, one of the few he entrusted with the secrets of his soul. Though he had known Muir would never be king as his father and adopted father before him had both been, he had carried such hope for great things in the life of that kind, gentle, strong-hearted young man.

And it had come to this. For nothing. Kavan, despite his powers and gifts, had been unable to save him.

His anger turned in time to Kóráhm, Dhágdhuán, and k'Ádhá, anyone who might have intervened, any of whom might have given him the ability, the chance, to keep Muir alive. He had not been granted a miracle; they had taken another young life and he could not easily forgive the cruelty of such callous disregard.

By the time his forced march brought him within viewing distance of the villa, the sun was nearing the western horizon, bringing encroaching darkness to those who lived within. With that darkness, however, Kavan had shed his anger and in its place felt sorrow, loneliness, and an empty ache that would take years to heal...if it ever did. Fate, some higher purpose shielded from his knowledge, had taken Muir too soon, and being bitter, angry, or resentful was a useless waste of emotion. Whatever the reason k'Ádhá had called the prince to peace, it was not Kavan's place to question or judge.

Men at the gate recognized both Kavan and Muir, and, after closing and latching the iron-barred gate behind them, escorted the bard to the villa without a word. There was no need for speaking. The reason for this visit was obvious. One opened the door and Kavan entered as the two women he needed, but dreaded, to see came from the corridor to his right, the direction of the Prime Magistrate's office. Everyone stopped. Both stared from Kavan to Muir and back to Kavan. Kavan maintained eye contact with one, then the other, despite the difficulty, until Clianthe, at her mother's side, collapsed to the floor in a faint.

"The study." There was no need to take the prince to a bed, and the study was the nearest room. Gabrielle knelt beside her daughter, but when Clianthe did not stir or awaken, the woman had her taken to her room, while she, instead, followed Kavan.

The bard did not wait for the study door to close before saying, "Pháne was attacked...six ships...one of your ships was lost...the other suffered heavy damage but was afloat when I left. Four of the enemy vessels were sunk, one captured, one escaped. Many lives were lost, but the outpost stands...and more live than were lost amongst your men."

Understanding the flat tone in which he reported, knowing that the moment of duty had to be dispensed, Gabrielle nodded, cursing the Council beneath her breath for their refusal to act as necessary and their shortsightedness in action when they did take a step. If they had allowed the number of ships and total resources of weapons and commodities she had asked for at Muir's behest, this death, and the others as well, might have been avoided.

"Did he...is he...?"

"I was with him in his last moments," Kavan whispered, guilt settling heavier upon his shoulders. "He is at peace...I am...sorry..."

"This is not your doing, Kavan. No one blames you." She squeezed his arm gently. "At least he had you...which is as it should be." The prince loved her daughter, Gabrielle had no doubt, and would have wanted his wife at his side as he passed, would have wanted to say farewell to her. But Clianthe, especially in her condition, did not belong in a combat region and he would not have wanted her in the heart of battle. As dear as Kavan was to Muir, having the bard beside him had probably been the most precious gift he could have in his last moments. "He would want to be buried in Rhidam, as a Lachlan, with his family."

"You and Clianthe and Piran are his..."

"I know, but this was already discussed. I know this is what he desired."

"And Clianthe?"

"I will speak to her and join you shortly." This news was going to hit her husband hard; she would be in Rhidam to share his grief.

It was breaking that news in Rhidam, to Owain and Diona, which Kavan could barely stomach facing. As he waited without putting Muir's body down on the study desk cleared for it, he listened to the screamed words, the wails, the crash of shattering glass or ceramics breaking upstairs, and closed his eyes. Clianthe had every right to be angry…with Muir, with fate, with her mother, with Kavan…for this tragic turn of events. When Gabrielle returned to him, a single bag hastily packed and Piran at her side, it was without her daughter. The little boy was visibly devastated as he approached to touch Muir's dangling hand, trying to hold it in his grasp and pouting through tears that he could not hold back. This was the first time death had personally touched the child, and Kavan knew how difficult this moment was.

"She will not come." Gabrielle's voice trembled but she did not hesitate to lead them into the closet that housed one of the few island Gates. "I left instructions for her to be watched…I do not think it is safe for her to be alone…but I have to do this…for Owain…"

Kavan nodded grimly. With both being seasoned travelers by k'rylag, they knew to touch him, and each other, forming a circle of power that allowed the connection to Rhidam to be made. In the keep, Kavan laid the prince on the altar, relinquishing him to the divine because there was no other choice. "Ártur may not be here…but send him when you find him. I will…stay…with him…"

He would not be able to hide in the oratory indefinitely, and he would not leave Rhidam until he saw to Muir's final rest, but he was not eager to step into castle life and face those he believed he had failed. Remaining at Muir's side, with Piran hoisted on his hip, was the place Kavan needed to be.

➤*➥

The tavern was customarily quiet at this early hour, as few began their day with a drink. But on a brisk winter day, with the wind howling and blowing last night's fallen snow into drifts, such places offered warmth, thus Níkóá was not the sole patron here and did not look out of place as he waited at a corner table for the man he was to meet. Having established a rapport with the tavern's owner, Níkóá knew he had nothing to fear from that man, but he waited with his back in a corner to watch the room as he trusted no one else. When the one he waited for entered, the novice priest with him, Níkóá frowned but did not otherwise react. He had not invited two, but they were no threat to him as long as he stayed watchful.

His guest was not going to be pleased with him either.

But the younger man trudged up the stairs to the boarding rooms above after a short conversation with the bartender, while the hawkish man ordered a drink and brought it to Níkóá's table where he sat without invitation or preamble.

"You were supposed to contact me…"

"You're here, aren't you…I'm here as well?"

Claide grunted and drank deeply of the potent spirits his large mug held. Níkóá could smell it but could not identify it. It surprised him to see the other man drinking. "Did you bring it?"

Fingering what he carried in his pocket beneath the table, Níkóá turned his cup of mulled cider in his other hand and took a small sip as if testing its temperature. "Not yet."

"You said you would…"

"You want me to steal proof? You think that will gain his cooperation and trust?" He snorted and took a longer drink of the cooler liquid. He was not sure why he had suddenly changed his mind about offering that bit of proof to the gdhededhá…except that Kavan had demanded Níkóá not use the ring until his return. The bard's distress when he fled the previous day still troubled Níkóá; he had not slept during the night in his worry over the man's health or what might have driven him away. There were stories, rumors, that the White Bard could foresee the events of the future, that he possessed something called the Sight, that he was touched by divinity as no other was or had ever been. If it had been one of those things that pulled him abruptly away, had possibly filled him with fear of Níkóá, it made the redhead even more anxious. Something bad had happened, or was happening...or would happen...and the feeling that he was suddenly part of a much larger picture, a much larger world, through the acquaintance with the White Bard, was enough to make Níkóá second-guess himself.

"He will come. Soon."

"When?"

Níkóá's brow and the corners of his mouth twitched with annoyance. "When the time is right. There are many factors to consider beyond his safety. When he is ready, you will know it." Seeing an impending protest, he continued, "If he feels pushed, he may decide to work alone...please have patience. I can bring him around to favor you, but you know the atmosphere in Rhidam...you know care must be taken..."

Claide frowned, thinking of the man who had tried to make contact with him a few nights previous, the one dissuaded from trying again. He wondered, as he tried to decipher the thoughts behind this other man's deep blue eyes, if that fellow had been working with this one, if perhaps it had been the man himself on whom Claide was waiting. If he had ruined his chance by that hasty inspired action. He did not want to mention it, to offer an apology, in case his hand in that assault was not already known. Why accept the blame for something when his involvement might not be presumed?

"I will need something...some sort of assurance that he exists...that your honesty..."

With a heavy sigh, Níkóá finished his drink. "As will I," he countered. "But know this...the next time we meet there will be news. It should be soon. In good faith, if his life and identity are safe with you..." Movement drew his attention to where Valgis was coming down from the boarding rooms towards the bar for a drink. "...you will come alone next time...and not put me at risk by identifying me to others when we meet."

He caught the barman's eye and left coins on the table as he rose...contact made to let the man know he had paid...and who to blame if theft of the coins was involved. "I will be in touch," he grunted, annoyed by the other man's unrealistic expectation. Kavan might be right. This might be the path he needed to reconsider. But that reconsideration would not come today.

❧*❧

With his back turned to the door, Kavan recognized the heavy running footsteps before the door burst open with a shout of, "Say it is not...!" The demand went unfinished, as it ended with a bellow of grief as the steps continued charging forward and the man shoved Kavan aside.

"I tried to..." the bard began, setting Piran down, watching the older blonde bend over the other, seeking signs of life. But there were none, and Kavan's attempt at offered comfort was aborted when the broader man lashed out, roaring, his swinging fist striking Kavan in the jaw with enough force to crack bone and drive the bard to his knees. The sound, seeing Kavan sink beneath the unintended assault, brought another cry from Owain, this one a reflection of horror and dismay for what he had done. He dropped down beside the bard and crushed him to his chest, weeping into his white hair, his slender shoulder, hands grasping at fabric, at muscle, looking for something, anything he could do to rectify what he had done.

"I am sorry," Kavan whispered, returning the embrace, the wall he had built to contain his pain now crumbling as he tried to ease Owain's. Piran's presence, where the boy stood nearby watching with horror-stricken, sad eyes, was momentarily forgotten. "I did everything I could..." He did not feel it had been enough, believed he should have done more, but realistically, there had been nothing else he could have done. If he had stopped long enough to bring

Ártur with him, the prince would have been dead before Kavan reached him. The snippets of Sight he was given had warned of this end but as with any other time he attempted to thwart fate, he arrived unable to change anything.

One day, perhaps, he would accept that fate, the hand of k'Ádhá, or whatever one chose to call it, could not be averted, had to be accepted as inevitable, but Kavan's desire to protect those he loved meant that day would not likely come soon…or easily.

For a long while neither spoke, the powerful initial grief seeking an end, an out, an understanding from another who shared it fully. Eventually, when the oratory door opened, this time bringing Gabrielle, Ártur, and the Queen into the room, it was Owain who pulled free of the hug and pushed weakly to his feet. Piran rushed into his mother's embrace and buried his face against her belly. Kavan kept his head down, waiting for more shock, more grief, more anger and blame, to wash over him. The healer's eye assessed the situation, determined with remorse at a glance that he could do nothing for Prince Muir, and then helped Kavan to his feet. Seeing the already spreading bruise across Kavan's cheek, Ártur touched the area with his fingertips, sending probing power beneath the surface to knit cracked bone, stretched muscle, and torn blood vessels.

"How did this happen?" Diona demanded, brushing the hair from her brother's face, the only sibling she had, the only other Lachlan of her generation, if Lachlan in name alone. Making the demand for answers was easier than confronting her grief. Her free hand absently came to her belly.

"Pháne was attacked…six ships…"

"Whose?"

Kavan shrugged and shook his head. "No kingdom's ships. No fleet. Four were destroyed…one captured…another fled. I did not know the voices…the accents…of the few I heard…but I trust my instinct that the man in command was Heward." This meant, to

Kavan, that if Heward had been in Rhidam recently, at least within the past four months, he had to have met those ships somewhere within easy traveling distance. Unless Heward was Elyri, carried Elyri blood, he could not have met ships in Cordash and sailed around the coasts to the islands, not in the storms this time of year brought. Such a feat would have been barely possible for fleet ships and seasoned seamen. An Enesfel port seemed more likely, and easier for the Queen to investigate, which, he judged by her expression, she intended to do.

"Heward did this?"

"I..." Kavan sighed. "I am not certain...but I believe so." In his grief and shock, he had not thought to touch the murdering arrow, removed by one of Muir's men so that he would not have to travel to his rest with the weapon intact, nor had Kavan looked to see where it had come from. The trajectory he had Seen, however, that he imagined in his mind's eye, and the fact that someone on that captured ship had to have taken the shot...and that the man on the prow, whom he believed to be Heward, made him the one person Kavan could recall being there who might have made such a shot. No one else had been near enough...or so equipped. "I am sorry I did not pursue him...but I..."

Gabrielle's hand on his shoulder, as she stood with her other arm around her husband, silenced him. "You stayed with Muir. No one faults you for that."

Diona opened her mouth, intending to disagree, to express her first impulsive feeling of blame, but the sorrow on Kavan's face stopped her. If not for Kavan, Muir would have died alone. "Lady Dilyn is right, staying with him was more important..."

Kavan had been with her father at his death, with her mother, and with her brother Bertram. Others had prevented him from being with Hagan and she had seen how much that had hurt him. She wondered often how Hagan had felt without Kavan there, whether he had passed into the arms of family or had suffered some other fate without Kavan there to guide his way. Being at Muir's side had been for the best, and she wondered, as she looked at him, if he would be with her when her time came. "Where is Clianthe?"

"She would not come," Gabrielle sighed. "She does not want to accept this."

"Nor do I," the Queen agreed, trying to imagine how the other young woman must feel, how she would feel if she lost Espen as she was due to bring his child into the world.

Gabrielle continued, "He wished to be buried here…with the Lachlans…if you will permit…"

There was no hesitation from Diona. "Of course, we will. He is a Lachlan, my brother." He might not have been Arlan's son, but he was Owain's, and though Owain was not a Lachlan by birth either, he had long ago been accepted by the Lachlans as one of their own…as had Prince Muir. To the outside world, where there was no inkling that Owain had been neither King Innis' child nor King Bowen's, he was as much a Lachlan as any other, causing others to believe Muir was one as well. Public perception mattered, though not as much as Muir's wishes or the Queen's. She wanted him close enough to talk to, even if he would never offer her advice again.

"He will be afforded every honor," Diona promised. "Lord Healer, will you preserve him until arrangements are made?"

Ártur bowed stiffly, thankful that his trembling was noticeable only to his cousin. Yet another Teren child he had welcomed into the world, another Lachlan, was lost, and his heavy heart made him choke on his grief. "Of course. Will he be moved or…?"

"No." The Queen looked at Kavan, grateful to see him, grateful that he was here, that he had been with Muir as her brother had given his last breath to the air. With the moment of outrage dampened, she was able to settle into her gratitude. "He shall rest here, on this altar...until he can be laid to rest...if that is acceptable, Lord Cliáth?" This was his place, a holy place. His wishes mattered.

Head still bowed, Kavan murmured, "There is no offense in it." He did not think k'Ádhá would find fault with their choice, and Kavan could re-consecrate it afterward if he felt compelled to. At least one other Lachlan had rested here after death, as had Muir's grandfather. "He will be safe here...and it is private, should any feel the need to be alone with him..."

"I will set Logros and Waljan to watch," the Queen promised. "Both are set to retire to Káliel...I will beg this final duty of them and send them back with you, Lady Dilyn, if you accept?"

The Prime Magistrate nodded. Long ago, she had sent five men, men hired by her father to serve and protect her, to Enesfel to serve Prince Arlan in his bid for the throne. The five had taken their duty to heart, remaining in Enesfel after the throne was won, and one of the five had taken it upon himself to serve Kavan throughout his life. Of the other four, Logros and Waljan were the eldest, and after long, distinguished careers in the Lachlan employ, it was time, they felt, to take their families to the home of their hearts. Avner was already retired from active duty but remained in Rhidam to recruit others and mentor them in the style of the Káliel Guard. Denyan assisted him, though he was still considered an active-duty member of the Lachlan Guard, but with Wortham gone from Rhidam and the others leaving service, the Queen suspected Denyan too would soon retire. Diona considered requesting further guardsmen from the Prime Magistrate, but those Avner and Denyan had trained were enough. Enesfel had men of her own, and right now Káliel needed as many fighting men as it could muster.

"Prime Magistrate," the Queen said in the tone of an unexpected, spur of the moment decision, "if you will meet with me later...I have a proposition to make. Lord Cliáth...will you stay for the burial?"

Though many matters were pressing on him, Kavan nodded. A few days more or less were not likely to make a difference to the state of Enesfel or Elyriá. He would be here, where he was needed, and then resume his quests for secrets, for information that would bring peace to their lands, if not to their hearts and souls and Faith.

"I shall take this news to Bhríd…and to Wortham…and return."

"Good. Then I ask you to meet with me later as well. I require your expertise on a matter of state. No one else has been able to discern the meanings of documents I received. We hope you might be able to offer insight.

Curious, since this was something not spoken of to Ártur, who had not mentioned puzzling documents, Kavan nodded. Though reluctant to leave the prince, the young man's care was in good hands, and Owain would want to be alone with his sons and wife. Kavan would give them that since there was nothing more to give. He would have chance enough to mourn during the night.

꙳*꙳

"Good morning, gdhededhá."

Khwílen turned from the gradually brightening sky, surprised to be interrupted here but not surprised that Kluín was the one to do so. Thus far he had little opportunity to speak to anyone in private save Hwensen who had, at Kavan's insistence, given him the details of Dórímyr's death. Khwílen doubted it was everything there was to know, suspected that Kavan would withhold details he was either uncertain of or felt might threaten any who knew them. The bard would not knowingly put someone at risk.

"It looks to be a stormy one," Khwílen nodded with a sigh.

"Within and without," the other man agreed. Khwílen cocked his brow and Kluín shrugged. "There are but five or six candidates yet to arrive…and the others are restless for the election to proceed. Their unrest is fostering bitterness…which does not bode well for a pleasant process. Men of Faith should have more patience, but the possibility of power corrupts even here."

"Few are immune," Khwílen muttered in agreement. "Except perhaps Lord Cliáth."

"If only he would accept nomination."

"Indeed, but we know it will never be. I do not believe the Faith is ready for such as him...and his heart is not in leadership."

Shouts from the corridor behind made them turn as gdhededhá Tumm rolled his chair across the arched portal at the most furious pace his thin arms would allow. Ylár followed, his face crimson and creased with fury lines across his forehead and at the corners of his mouth and eyes, demanding Tumm wait, that he not roll away in disrespect. But the elder did not listen, taking their cross words beyond the hearing distance of the men on the balcony.

Hwensen frowned. Noting Khwílen's curiosity, he smoothed the front of his robe to take a moment with his thoughts. "In all my years...I have not seen them...heard them..."

"Perhaps, as you say, the waiting..." Both were aspirants for nomination and even dear friends could chafe under such weight.

"Perhaps."

"We could speak with them separately?" There was little chance of learning anything, and Khwílen doubted their tiff had any connection to k'gdhededhá Dórímyr's death, but it might be worth the effort made to try.

"You go to Ylár...I will speak with Tumm." Having been Dórímyr's aide, Hwensen knew the late man's friend well enough that a show of concern after hearing that fight would not be unusual. Tumm might even trust him. Ylár, younger and more outgoing, was more open to those he served beside. It made sense to divide their efforts this way.

"Return here later today...we shall speak again."

Khwílen nodded with anticipation. At last, something he could do that did not involve summits or topics of Faith and election. Something he hoped might benefit Kavan when the bard returned to Clarys.

❧Chapter 20❧

There were few reliable options for Prince Kjell as he sought somewhere to hide from his brother. Those he knew in the city, soldiers and nobles, the houses of peasants, servants, and merchants he had been generous to in the past, would not be safe if he took refuge there. Merkar would eventually think to look in such places, to threaten torture and execution to any who offered shelter, and the prince would not be able to fault any of them for breaking under the threat. Merkar might even follow through on those threats without Kjell being in any one of those places, but at least the innocent would remain innocent and any blame for their torture or death would fall on the King. The de Corrmicks had ruled for centuries on a platform of violence, cruelty, capriciousness, and unrelenting iron-fisted decrees. The kingdom was cowed into submission long ago. Someone would have to lead the people by example, as well as word, before they could ever be expected to show loyalty to a de Corrmick. Kjell had fought to foster such loyalty for years, but when up against the might of the King, that loyalty was likely to weather badly. No, Kjell would not submit any of those important to him to near-certain death to protect himself.

Nor could he flee south to his cousin's home. The King had likely sent an envoy there in search of him, on the off chance that

Kjell would make such a bold and brazen visit, and this was not the time to draw Owain and Enesfel into a confrontation with Neth and her King. This was a matter the prince was determined to resolve on his own. Once Merkar calmed, once the newest influence at the King's ear was neutralized as Captain Stone promised to do, Kjell believed he would be able to soothe his brother's fears and convince him of his innocence. He had no plot against the throne, no desire…yet…for it. He would convince Merkar of that. It would either be supremely simple to do, or else impossible, and Kjell was, as always, confident of his ability to play the innocent fool.

It was the decision to win back Merkar's trust that led Prince Kjell to hide in plain sight. He knew the de Corrmick castle better than anyone, he believed, having made sport of memorizing the rooms, the halls, the tunnels and passages created by one paranoid monarch after another. Kjell could pass through them, stay in rooms rarely or never used by family or staff, and when the time came, he could honestly claim to have been in the palace the whole time people were searching for him. None but a fool would be expected to hide close to the source of danger…a fool or a very wise man…and if Kjell made no attempt on the King during those days, or weeks, then surely he would be seen as no threat to his brother. He would prove Fraen, and anyone else who suspected him of duplicity, wrong.

❧*❦

"Lord Cáner…welcome back…" He was welcome, but the words were difficult to say as she studied the grief-stricken features of her former chamberlain. He, a wife and one son lost, facing the suspended life of the other and the death of someone he had known so well, should not have come; Diona would have understood if he had not. She had insisted that Kavan give Bhríd the option to decline attendance. She believed he would not come. The woman behind him, holding the man's infant daughters, one in each arm, looked nervous about being in the castle, for what was likely her first time. Whatever Ártur and Kavan had said to him, or perhaps his own reasoning, it had been enough to draw him back to Rhidam. Perhaps he believed being here was a duty to both her and the fallen prince. Loving the Royal Champion as she did, the Queen was grateful to see him, even under these painful, trying circumstances.

"My Queen." Bhríd bowed, held her hand in his trembling one, and kissed her ring. She had never known him to tremble, to show any manner of weakness, and it grieved her to note it now. "May k'Ádhá comfort you in your loss."

"And you in yours, my lord," she replied with heartfelt earnestness. "I thank you for coming. Are these…?"

Thankful to stray away from the topic of what was lost, to focus instead on what had been gained, on the newness of life, focuses he dared not let out of his sight for more than a few moments, he motioned the wet nurse forward with a sincere, if melancholy, tender expression. "Alyná and Sylyhá Dubuais-Cáner…our daughters." Though small, the babes appeared healthy, rosy-cheeked and alert, wrapped in soft blankets and, the Queen mused, seemingly hungry as each gnawed on tiny fists.

"Welcome, children…" Diona laid her hand across each forehead, noting that neither had much hair and what they had bore little color. The girls were too pink, too wrinkled and round still for her to say which parent they were most like, or whether their features would be similar to each other in appearance or not. She remembered thinking that Hagan looked more like Lord McHador and his mother than his father and it set her to wondering what her child might look like. The thought, the secret of it, made her blush as she removed her hand and stepped back. "They, like you, shall always be welcome in Rhidam, Lord Cáner."

"My thanks, Your Majesty. May we settle in?" His desire to see his son, not dead but still beyond his reach, pulled at his heart. He had not been here in many days and now that he was, he realized how important it was for his daughters to know their brother from this moment onward, for however long that was possible. Family was what mattered, particularly in times of great darkness.

"Your room is untouched..." Gaelán would wait. A fleeting thought of Prince Espen flittered across her mind and after an impromptu hug to one of the many people who had helped guide her in her youth, she hastened out of the Hall to find her husband. Her brother might be gone, but she did have her husband waiting for her, someone she needed now more than she ever had before.

❧*❧

"I will not go! He will be here soon! He promised!" Clianthe pulled from her mother's hold on her elbow, the twist causing her to stumble into Ártur's arms. As the burial preparations formed throughout the day, Owain felt strongly that Muir's wife and unborn child should be present, a united family to preserve Muir's memory. Ártur came with Owain and Gabrielle to Káliel, as Kavan undertook other arrangements with gdhededhá Tusánt and went to Bhryell with the news that kept the healer away from his family.

Gabrielle found her daughter singing, laughing, smiling as she bustled about the villa in preparation for the return of her husband from duty. It was as if she had never received the devastating news, and Gabrielle's efforts to speak to her fell on deaf ears.

The healer shook his head when Gabrielle began to speak. Hugging Clianthe tenderly, he murmured, "Of course he will...but you will be gone a few hours, no more. We will leave word with the staff so he knows where you are, and he will wait for you. The Queen is expecting us..."

"The Queen! I like the Queen. She is his sister, you know. She invited us to a feast? Of course, I shall attend. Lord Healer, you will bring him later, won't you? He will join and dine with us? She would surely invite him too…"

"Of course, he is invited."

Clianthe smiled and took her mother's hand. "Mother, help me choose a gown…we must hurry. The Queen is waiting…"

Gabrielle glanced at Ártur as she followed her daughter up the marble stairs, worry and terror in her eyes. Ártur held his breath, choosing to say nothing until the women were out of sight. He ran his hand through his hair with a groaning sigh.

"She knows he's gone," started Owain. "She was here when…"

The healer nodded. "Knowing it, believing and accepting it, are different things. She is…I have seen this before…a spouse unable to bear the loss…with a child on the way, she cannot accept that she must raise it alone…or else marry again…"

"Not alone," Owain grunted, a sound of frustration rather than anger. "Gabrielle and I will…"

"Of course, you will be…but you know that is not the same. Perhaps attending the burial will aide in her acceptance…but you should be prepared for no change…or for her to take leave of her senses all together for a time. I suggest you watch her closely, whatever the case, lest she endangers herself or the…"

"Endanger…?"

A scream from upstairs ripped through his words, a scream that sent both men running to the girl's room where she was found in a corner, arms wrapped around her drawn knees, banging her head side to side against the stone walls as she continued to shout.

"Clianthe!"

Ártur pushed past Owain and Gabrielle and dropped to his knees before the young woman, catching her head between her hands, forcing the movement to still as he made her look into his eyes. Watching the healer, trusting what he was doing without understanding it, Owain pulled his wife against his side and croaked, "What happened?"

"I do not know..." Gabrielle admitted, her voice stretched and small. "She drew dresses from the closet, threw them on the bed, and began to scream..."

Clianthe's head lolled to one side, her eyes closed in slumber. "A reminder, I imagine," Ártur said, "something that jarred her memory enough to bring back this morning...even if for a moment." He stepped back to allow Owain to lift her from the corner.

"I will stay with her..."

Ártur sighed, "I fear that may not be enough, my lady. If such reminders continue to produce distress...the sooner she accepts his death, the better off she will be. She should come...she should be there...for him...and for herself too..."

"But if she..." started Gabrielle.

"You said it may get worse if she..." Owain began.

"May," Ártur agreed, "but it may also help her. There is no way to tell, to guess...but if this chance is missed, we will never know. If she does not come...one day she may regret it. Being away from here for a few days may be beneficial." He held Clianthe's hand, seeking signs of injury or physical distress, but there were none he was able to detect. "I cannot guarantee the outcome...you alone must decide if the risks are worth taking for her sake."

Owain and Gabrielle gazed at one another as he continued to hold Clianthe and her mother toyed with her hair. Neither spoke, but when their silent dialogue was over, the Prime Magistrate, whispered, "We will take the risk...for her."

"And stay with her," the healer warned. "No matter how sane she seems...how calm or rational...do not yet believe her words." Not, he thought, until Kavan could see her. If anyone might be able to help her, Ártur believed his cousin could.

৯*৯

Although Diona had asked to see him, by the time Kavan returned to the castle the hour was late, the corridors dark. He doubted anyone slept…or slept well. Much of his day had been spent in Rhidam's great náós, making arrangements with Tusánt and discussing the state of the city and the Faith in Enesfel. The Elyri gdhededhá knew Clarys' top candidates in passing; he had been young, new to Clarys, when the late k'gdhededhá Jermyn had chosen him to serve in Enesfel at his side, an idealistic mind that the martyred man believed would serve Enesfel well. Tusánt could not offer Kavan details about the men he was investigating, but he was ideally tuned into the situation in Enesfel.

Despite his increase in popularity amongst the Faithful and the gradual shift towards tolerance at the heart of the people in Rhidam, there were many amongst the Teren gdhededhá who, disappointed with Dórímyr's continued apathy and the mother náós' overall indifference towards the troubles that plagued Enesfel, continued to support a break from Clarys and the founding of a new center of Faith in Rhidam. On the surface, Kavan accepted the choice, but he feared the results of such a schism. Two centers of Faith leadership would undoubtedly lead to divergent doctrine, and as he had yet to reconcile his own divergent personal beliefs with those the Faith officially taught, the idea of separation made him uncomfortable.

Once darkness fell, Kavan spent over an hour following the man's twisted trail through Rhidam before eventually locating Caol to relay the news of Prince Muir's death. After the Prince's contribution to the rescue of his cousin Wilred, Caol and he had shared a bond that few others could touch. They were not particularly close, as Muir's destiny had drawn him away from Rhidam, first to his father's home in Fiara and subsequently to Káliel. Their respect and trust of one another, their understanding of each other, were things few missed on the occasions when the prince came to Rhidam for festivals, feasts, and family occasions. Kavan knew Caol would want to hear of the young man's passing from someone in the keep, not as gossip in the streets, even if he was unable to attend the service, the burial, or mourn with the family.

Kavan alone knew of Caol's increasing closeness to the Corylliens' core, and the fact that Heward was, in all likelihood, the prince's murderer was more reason for Caol to stay on course. He could calculate when Heward might return to Rhidam from the approximate speed of ships to port, and he would be ready for him. When that was done, he would return to his family and mourn properly for those lost while duty kept him away.

Afterward, Kavan took the risk of returning to his own family, needing to share the grim news with both Wortham and Syl and needing to see the boys. Weeping openly, Wortham fought to return to Rhidam with him for the burial service despite Kavan's fear for his children. Dhóri's wet nurse would not travel to Rhidam, an option Kavan could not consider asking of her, though Wortham did ask without hesitation. Kavan refused to pressure her, yet did not want the boys and women left alone in Bhryell without Wortham to protect them. Normally, in a land free of most forms of crime, particularly violent ones, there was no cause for fear, but with the threat of arrest for heresy hanging over his head, Kavan did not trust his family to be safe from the one institution which should be safest of all.

After Wortham took the news to Syl, while Kavan visited the boys and marveled at how quickly Dhóri was changing, he went to one of the few men he knew Kavan trusted and returned with Syl and Bhen in tow. Bhen did not know Prince Muir but he understood the young man's importance to his cousin. As he had done for Ártur and Syl, Bhen offered a solution Kavan could accept. When the burial hour came, the boys and women would go to the MacLyr house under Bhen's care while Syl brought Wortham to Rhidam. Kavan could trust his family to be safe in his kinsmen's care for the few hours the ceremony and burial would take. Despite the differences between him and his uncle, Kavan believed that Tám and his wife would do their part to protect innocent children. Tám, like most Elyri, did not believe in a child sharing the sins of his father. Dhóri was not Kavan. Kavan had not even told Tám, or anyone else, that the child was biologically his son.

With a plan in place and Kavan's grief temporarily assuaged by the nearness of his boys, he returned to Prince Muir's side, harp in hand, to offer prayers and music he had not been able to offer King Hagan and had yet to give to Gaelán. Though no one was in the oratory, he sensed Owain and Gabrielle's recent presence in the air and the spread of hellebore and snowdrops on Muir's breast. Kavan wished he could take away Owain's grief, but not even music, he knew, would do that. Though Kavan had not experienced the loss of his children, Muir felt to be his son, as he had served as much more than the prince's tutor in the years when King Arlan had been unable to see past Muir's parentage, unable to see the boy as an individual rather than a duplicate or extension of his father. Muir's death weighed on Kavan, despite knowing there was nothing he could have done to alter the events of the day before.

"Not everything is your fault, átaelás mai; you cannot save the world."

Caught in grief and remembrance, paying little attention to his surroundings in a place he felt safe, Kavan had not felt the arrival of the man beside him. He recognized the feel of him, the voice, at the same moment and barely resisted the compulsion to turn against the saint's shoulder to weep. "Not the world, but I would give everything to save the ones I love from such pain and death and grief."

Kóráhm covered Kavan's hand with his, curling as if to pull the hand from Muir's body. Kavan, still hoping for the slimmest chance of a miracle, refused to be drawn away and Kóráhm relented. "Pain and death are part of what it means to live. We cannot know joy and appreciation without them." Kavan snorted and the corners of Kóráhm's mouth twitched. "Yes, even you. By now I would think you have a significant share of joy due you. Know that he is at peace, beyond harm, and he mourns to see you in such pain. As do I."

"It will pass." Arlan's death had been the pain most comparable to what he felt now, heightened, perhaps, by his self-destructive self-loathing at the time it had occurred. There were moments still when the loss crept in, sank into his core, and filled him with crushing melancholy, but that death had been relatively recent, barely a year. If that grief could lessen, as it was beginning to with time, then this pain would as well, although Kavan swore he would honor both men's memories for as long as he lived, even if it meant clinging to some sliver of pain indefinitely.

Kóráhm sighed. Some things, like Kavan's propensity to relish pain, carrying it unnecessarily, were difficult to change. The bard had grown much over the past year, but this personality trait would likely take him years to outgrow...if he ever did.

Though Kavan's shoulders tensed at the sound, and a tickle of shame for a failing he had such difficulty mastering slithered through his center, he did not speak. Prince Muir, like King Arlan, had given much to Kavan, supported and aided him in some of his darkest hours merely by being present. They deserved remembrance for that.

"Shall I play for you?"

The saint shook his head though Kavan did not see it. "I must not remain long...but I have been too long away from you and thought you would appreciate my company, however brief it might be."

"Thank you...for considering me." Though he did not understand the rules that regulated Kóráhm's comings and goings, he did appreciate every moment the saint spent with him.

"And I've come to offer you this…not all that you read is as it seems on the surface."

Kavan turned to look at Kóráhm, to question his meaning, but the saint was gone as silently as he had come. Kavan did not doubt that Kóráhm's advice was meaningful, but why, he wondered as his hand dropped from Muir's chest and he knelt before the altar to give over to the too-long silent harp strings, was the advice so cryptic?

❧*✖

Though the gathering at the Lachlan crypt was small for a royal burial, consisting of family, friends, and a large collection of staff, servants, and soldiers, there were more faces present than Kavan expected to see. Most in the keep, except for the servants, knew Prince Muir was not Arlan's son, and also knew who his father was. The older he had grown, the more like Owain he looked. As most had never seen the adult Owain beside his father, a secret kept tightly controlled by the Lachlans, public opinion was that Muir was as much a Lachlan as the Queen, a grandson of King Innis, which afforded him the rights of any Lachlan to be buried with those he considered family.

He had proven an adept leader and soldier like his grandfather, as evidenced by the tales of his exploits on Pháne that Gabrielle recounted for those gathered.

Those reasons, as much as Muir's kind-heartedness and fair-mindedness, brought respectful mourners together in a way that touched Owain's heart. With his arm around Clianthe's shoulders and hers around Piran's, he stared at his son's body, while Clianthe rocked back and forth on her heels, her eyes closed, humming softly the same snatch of tune over and over. Kavan recognized it as the song he had written for her wedding to Muir, even if no one else did. Having heard about her behavior the night before from Ártur, Kavan decided he would try to reach her, although by what he sensed in her aura, he believed her to be as far beyond his reach as Gaelán was.

He wished he could block Muir's death from her mind, but that seemed a cruel act that would leave her the torment of desertion, or a sense of shame for a pregnancy she might be unable to account for. He would leave her memories as they were.

Wortham, having come to Rhidam with Syl' Ártur, and Sóbhán, was with his countrymen, on either side of the stone slab which, when pushed into the empty chasm, would be Muir's final resting place. With two of his comrades returning to Káliel, it was likely he would not see them again after their many years of service together, and Kavan suspected Wortham would seek to spend time with them before leaving Rhidam, one last round of drinks and a recounting of their adventures over their long careers. Though reluctant to leave his infant son without his friend's care, Kavan felt he owed the man, who had given him so much, those few hours of camaraderie. And he did trust Bhen. As Kavan had yet to meet with Diona on the matter she deemed an important use of his time, perhaps that would provide time enough for the friends to gather. Though there would be no lessons today, Sóbhán, who had insisted on attending the ceremony and stood with his hand in Kavan's, a steadying influence for both of them, intended to make the most of an unexpected visit to Gaelán and Asta to learn about the man they were about to entomb.

General Agis, as he had done at the burials of both Arlan and Hagan, gave the prince the Cíbhóló anointing of honor as well as prayers and blessings to pave his journey into the afterlife with accolades and tributes befitting royalty. It mattered not that Muir had not been a king; he had been an honorable man and the Cíbhóló respected honor above nearly everything else. He did not recite the man's genealogy as he had with those other burials; an astute man, he knew Prince Muir's parentage, and with Owain an accepted member of the family, there was no need to dredge up unpleasant family history. This day was not about scandal or accusation, but about valuing a man none had ever expected to die in conflict.

It was to no one's surprise that k'gdhededhá Claide was not present, although every other gdhededhá who served in Rhidam gathered to pay respect to the Queen and her brother lost. Claide had been seen less at the keep since King Hagan's death, even less since Tayte's arrest, and less outside of the náós. Save for the Gatherings at which he presided, he was seen even less within the holy walls as well. Frequently he was said to be traveling, the newly elected patriarch seeming intent on visiting every náós in Enesfel, at least those furthest from Rhidam where Asta's resources could not quickly or easily verify his claims. Another such trip was the excuse for his absence this day, although he had been in Rhidam when the news of Muir's death had arrived the day before, giving him ample opportunity to change plans.

That he chose traveling over the burial service of royalty was viewed by most, including those citizens and Faithful who were not aware of the animosity the Queen carried towards the k'gdhededhá, as an insult to the Crown. Kavan did not understand the man's choice, as his absence would earn Tusánt, who spoke with fondness of his memories of Muir, further support from the population of Rhidam. If there was logic to Claide's actions, Kavan failed to see it.

All he could see, as Tusánt finished speaking and stepped back into the gathered crowd, was the Káliel guardsmen pushing the slab into its tomb. All he heard was the sound of stone upon stone as the vault closed, all he could smell was the compound which would seal the grave forever. There was no music, as he could not share any of the tunes he had composed and played for the prince during the night. Those were for Muir's ears, his soul, alone and he did not have the heart to open his soul to anyone else tonight. Songs were the only gifts, since he had been unable to spare or restore Muir's life, which Kavan was able to give. As the gathered mourners dispersed to grieve in small groups or privately away from the polished bronze marker of death, Kavan wished again that he could give more.

<h2 align="center">⚭Chapter 21⚬</h2>

"Kavan, come in."

The Queen, dabbing her eyes with a kerchief where she sat before the hearth fire in the dayroom with Prince Espen and Owain, looked weary as she gestured the bard into the room, but she succeeded in offering a welcoming smile. To Kavan, it felt as if he had never left this place, as if nothing had changed, but he knew it had. It seemed, with Muir's death, that everything had changed, ties cut between them that could not be recovered.

Syl, after spending time with her brother and husband and giving supporting words to the Queen, had returned to Bhryell. Peace might be slowly returning to Enesfel, but as she did not yet feel safe here, she refused to place her children at risk in Rhidam. Bhríd too had departed, returning with his daughters and their nursemaid to Levonne, with barely a word spoken. Kavan encountered Gabrielle in the corridor near the library as she followed her daughter's absent wanderings and tried to talk to the younger woman of happy matters to draw her out of her collapsing mind. Though he offered to help as he could, both Gabrielle and Kavan knew there was little he could do unless some miracle was sent through his hands. That was something Kavan could not control and Gabrielle's responsibilities to her daughter were too pressing, and so they parted after the briefest of exchanges. Ártur would see that Sóbhán and Wortham were returned to Bhryell later that evening, should neither be prepared to depart when Kavan's business was complete, and Kavan, eager to finish what he had begun in Clarys to put this dark chapter of history behind him, wanted to tend that business quickly.

"If I am intruding…"

"It is a welcome intrusion. It has been too long since you spent time here, though I am grieved it is not under better circumstances…" It hardly seemed fair that death and tragedy were the things to bring Kavan back to Rhidam.

Kavan bowed but kept his eyes averted. "As are we all," he murmured, barely able to say the words. "I did not believe I would see this day…"

"You will outlive us all," Espen said with a forced chuckle.

"Perhaps." The bard's eyes closed. On days like this, he could not bear to consider Elyri mortality.

"Peter." The Queen beckoned to the page by the door. "Take this…bring the small wooden trunk from the wine cabinet in the state room…do not give this key to anyone else and return both it and the trunk to me at once."

"Yes, Your Majesty." The boy took the key she held and scurried from the room, leaving her alone with the two men who had been royal advisors and one who was her husband and the dearest advisor among them.

"Kavan…sit…please…"

He took the empty chair nearest her with a nod of gratitude. "You wished to see me?"

"Yes…when Peter returns."

"No gifts…" He had not been there to receive acknowledgment of his birth day; he hoped that was not the reason for the summons.

His words and expression made her chuckle, despite the dark mood of the day. "I know you have no desire for gifts, Kavan…I would never ignore your wishes…" She paused, remembering a time when she had done precisely that and what it had cost Kavan and everyone he knew. "Not unless I discover something rare and unusual I think you should have. No…this is something else."

Relieved, Kavan shifted in his chair to a more comfortable position, noting Owain's absent gaze towards the window. He wondered why the man was there instead of with his wife. "We have anonymously received two scrolls," Diona continued. "Poems or clues or threats, we are unsure which. Perhaps they are each of those things. Each of my advisors has read them except for Ártur…but no one can tell me what they are…what they mean. I do not accept they are merely poems; I hope you can prove me right…or prove me wrong…tell me what, if anything, they mean."

"I will try," he agreed, though the distraction from Clarys was unwanted. Kóráhm's advice of the night before flitted across his mind. If these poems, as the Queen called them, were a sort of encrypted message, something more than their surface words alluded to, perhaps he could decipher them. Kóráhm had intimated as much.

"It was mentioned that you had considerable success translating other documents…"

"Translating?" Kavan looked back and forth from Espen to the Queen.

Espen, embarrassed, tried to smile. "Perhaps not translating but rather…" He struggled to find the word he wanted, and when it came, it was presented in Hatuish, a language that Kavan had some experience with though not a lot. He was, however, able to understand and nodded his head.

"Interpreting…yes…some," he agreed. As many hours as he spent studying a variety of texts, in a wide array of languages, he believed himself adequate, at least, in discerning meaning in written words. Peter came back, flushed features and breathless gulps for air suggesting he had been running in his haste to obey the Queen's command, and handed her the wooden box and key. From the pouch at her hip, Diona produced a second, smaller key that unlocked the box. She returned it to her pouch before opening the lid and removing one of the scrolls. She unrolled it, read the first line silently, then put it back to give Kavan the other scroll first.

"This came first."

Kavan took it to the window where there was more light to read by and smoothed it on the round table there, reading the impressions in the parchment, studying its weave, its age, the color of the ink, and the style of the hand that had written the words as he absorbed the short four line verse.

Wrath burns
When the kid stands
Beneath the grey sky
Of a faithless heart.

He scowled as he reread the words a second time. The author, or at least the man who had put the words into writing, was a simple man, educated to read and write, but he was not an author or poet.

"The second?"

The Queen put it into his open hand though he did not look up from the first. This parchment too was spread beside the other, Kavan taking in the same details from it as he had from the first.

The kid's sting
is bitter honey
to a world torn
by apathy's rage;
it collapses upon him,
consumes the burning grey sky.

"The penman is the same," he commented, "the parchment and ink of the same source…though the quills are different." The press of the point into the parchment on the second was finer suggesting the use of a new quill. He sniffed at each parchment and the ink upon them. "They carry the aroma of tallow…medicinal herbs…a faint trace of metal." Between those clues and the image of the man he could see bent over a narrow writing desk, Kavan believed he could find the one who had written the words. "But he is not the author," he continued, cutting the Queen off before she could ask questions. "There was someone else, someone dictating what was put down…"

"Can you find them both?"

Prince Espen, like most Teren, had no idea how reading an object or person worked, what the limitations were, how much an Elyri might be able to learn from an attempt…or how little. Even Kavan could not properly explain the how of it. He could show another Elyri how to do it, but explaining the mechanics of something that was, on many levels, intuitive for most Elyri, to a Teren who did not share the Power, was almost impossible.

The bard shook his head. "No…I can sense him there…but I cannot hear his voice…or see any more of him than his legs." There was something familiar in the air, however, but he had not yet deduced what it was. If he found the scribe, he might be able to locate the author, but doing both would take more time then he felt he could spare. "My Queen…may I copy these?"

"Peter."

The page produced parchment, ink, and a quill from a desk drawer and set them for the bard to use. Kavan quickly copied both short poems onto one page in the order they had been received. "Is there nothing else?" the Queen asked impatiently.

Kavan looked up with mild vexation. "I will need time to study them…and it will be easier to do where I have considerably more resources." He shook his head to the Queen's impending protest. "This library is extensive…but what I need is not here." Mainly he needed uninterrupted solitude in a place where his thoughts would not draw constantly to Prince Muir. Somewhere the Queen would not hover. "These verses are poetry…but the imagery is not typical…and I do not believe that the author's native language is Teren…"

"Elyri then?" Few Elyri resided in Rhidam, or Enesfel, any longer. For any to have survived hidden from view, to deliver such messages to the Queen, made the messages seem more important than before. "Not Ártur…or Bhríd…or dedhá Tusánt…?" She did not consider Gaelán or Sóbhán to be the author, for neither seemed capable of writing something this peculiar.

"No." Kavan knew Ártur and Bhríd well enough to believe that, if they had knowledge to share, or a warning, they would do so without poetic verse and hidden meaning. While Tusánt was capable of such wordage, as a man who had to teach from the altar several times a week, sometimes multiple times a day, explaining concepts in words and imagery the people would understand, deliberately twisting words or hiding meaning in them was not his doing.

If anything, Claide was more adept at hiding meaning in his orations. The man was familiar with the Elyri language, had probably read Elyri poetry in its many forms, but as much as the man hated all things Elyri, why might he write, and then deliver, something to the Crown couched in what felt to be Elyri phrasing and cadence? If not a warning, then perhaps these were threats. Kavan shivered and returned the quill and ink to Peter before rerolling the scrolls.

"I will study this further. I will take them to St. Kóráhm's and return my findings as quickly as I can." He did not express his fears of a threat, for it was but a feeling, a supposition, and he wanted more proof before causing panic. He bowed to take his leave. "If any more of these arrive…please ask Ártur to contact me at once. I will try to return by evening…if I can." He needed to return to Clarys, but this matter deserved his undivided attention and today his heart was not in matters of Faith and future. This, however, was the sort of task that would distract him from grief.

Distraction was the best he could hope for.

Prince Owain sighed as Ártur stepped into the Purification chamber to take his wife, son, and daughter-in-law back to Káliel. He was torn between duty to the Crown and the desire to go with them, to help Gabrielle manage a young boy and a grown woman who seemed to have lost the best of herself, as well as her governing duties to her people. Gabrielle made no requests of him, nor did he expect she would, but Piran's sad, teary face had wrenched his gut and heart as Owain bid them farewell. As dear as Queen Diona was to him, she was less family than his sole surviving child, and watching the boy leave when he had missed out on Muir's childhood was a difficult burden to carry. His heart pulled one way, his head another, and with Kavan again away with barely an exchange of words…something that was more Owain's fault than Kavan's, it was a decision the prince knew he was going to have to make alone.

It was not going to be an easy choice.

❧*❦

St. Kóráhm's was a maze of corridors and hidden alcoves, with small oratories and prayer chambers where those who lived within its walls, or who came for study or refuge, could seek privacy for reading and reflection. For those desiring fellowship, there were the Gathering Hall, the courtyard, the grotto, the dining hall, the gardens, and the cemetery. The library and scriptorium were separate, where residents carried out the valuable work of copying and cataloging with quiet reverence the many books and documents that arrived from every corner of the realms. The library contained several small side alcoves for study and discussion, and it was into one of those that Kavan had retreated with his copied parchment, several blank sheets on which to make notes, candles to see by, and ink and quill with which to write. He did not know if he would need the library's ever-growing resources, but he wanted the books and scrolls nearby should he need them as he puzzled through the two small collections of words. One of the three individuals whose duty it was to keep the catalog records could bring him anything he needed, which would save him the time of scouring the shelves on his own.

Convinced that the verses were Elyri in nature, if not authored by an Elyri than by someone who knew and understood the language, Kavan wrote out the translations in Elyri to compare them side by side. After two hours of studying both, comparing word usage with possible translation errors, he felt no closer to deciphering any meaning or potential threat from the metaphors the author used. If the author's original language was Elyri, there was no hint of special meaning to be found.

On a whim, Kavan translated the words from Trade into the base languages of Enesfel, Cordash, Neth, Hatu, Káliel, and the Cíbhóló. He translated as accurately as he could into the language of Zelenka's people as well, although he had not had the chance to put significant time into the study of her tongue and resorted to books in the chellé's library for assistance. It was a long shot, for if there were no clues found in the commonly used Teren languages, he did not expect to find one in a language as obscure as hers, or that of the western nomads.

Frustrated with his lack of success, he stalked to the window to stare at the darkening eastern sky. The Queen was expecting him, and he should return to Clarys, but the puzzle had hold of him, and as he was rarely one to give in to defeat, he was determined to solve this mystery before leaving St. Kóráhm's.

He pushed the window open enough to let in a tendril of cold air. Eyes closed, he breathed deep, smelling damp earth, sea salt, and a hint of rain although there were no clouds from Alberni to the crest of the Llaethlágárá. The wind, however, was blowing from the south, off the Bay of Phállá; perhaps the storm was out to sea blowing in to engulf them overnight. It might bring rain, a welcome change after days of snow and bitter cold. He sank into his senses, listening to the whistles and gushes of wind, tasting the salt, smelling the freshness, feeling the cold across his skin, watching the dark sky littered with glittering shimmers of light when he chose to open his eyes. Those sensory perceptions banished thought, giving his tumultuous mind a break from his daylong endeavor to untangle the obscure language used in the pair of poems.

Obscure language.

His eyes popped open and his breath caught. To most in the Five Sovereignties, Teren and Elyri alike, there were four languages deemed obscure, for most did not count the languages of any group of people south of Hatu. Of those three, Cíbhóló was common enough along the western borders of Cordash and Enesfel, where trade with the nomads flourished. Though trade conditions had waned during these troubled times, there were still some who conversed with the nomads in their native tongue, for few nomads bothered to learn to speak Trade. Kavan had translated the verses into the nomadic tongue already, however, and had gained no insight into their meaning.

The second, the native language of Káliel, was barely spoken even amongst the islanders who had long ago begun to settle into Trade as their language of preference. The mother language seemed to bear no commonality between any other language in the Sovereignties, although some words sounded to have an Elyri root. Only the oldest families carried the old language with them, and those who wished to enter the political realm learned it as well, since all of the islands' laws were written in it, and the oaths of office were exchanged in it. Their reluctance to move beyond their entrenched ancient ways, and their determination to hold on to their heritage, prevented the translation of those things into any other language.

Kavan tested the mysterious verses into Kálysh, but again found nothing in that translation that was of use.

The third, and most obscure of any language known to him, was one most were not even sure existed. But examples of an elaborate written system of symbols led most scholars to assume it to be an alphabet, though none had any idea what the symbols meant, what sounds each might represent. Those symbols, of which Kavan wore a constant example around his neck, were assigned to the elusive phae k'kairá. Despite his experiences with those he believed to be descendant from that race, Kavan did not know their language, could not say he had ever heard it spoken, and thus had no way of attempting such a translation. It was unlikely that anyone else could have written, or intended to write, these lines in the long-dead language of the k'kairá; it was not an option worth pursuing.

The fourth language, however, was one that he, and approximately one-fifth of Elyri, had learned, some to read and write, others to speak as well. Most who learned it were gdhededhá or historians and scholars, members of the ancient noble Bhíncári House, or else musicians, storytellers, and other artists seeking to keep an ancient language alive. With the help of gdhededhá Bhílári and bhydáni Tíbhyan, as well as Kavan's own stubborn persistence, he had become one of Elyriá's foremost experts in the High Elyri language, beginning the study of it earlier than most children began their first reading and writing lessons in Standard Elyri. It had come naturally to him, as if he had been born to speak it and he felt at home with the ancient words.

He turned from the window to stare at the papers strewn across the table in this chosen alcove. In the distance, he heard the dinner bell chime but ignored it as if the sound came from an intangible place of memory. With his thoughts already translating words he had now memorized, Kavan scowled. No threat then, at least not from Claide, for he knew the k'gdhededhá did not know the Old

Language. The words, if High Elyri indeed, had to have come from an Elyri author, someone of learning, but he knew of none in Rhidam, save his cousin and Tusánt, who knew any of that form. Had he been wrong? Was one of those men he thought he knew well trying to relay something to the Queen that they were, for some reason, afraid to share in person?

Another blank sheet was taken out and he hastily wrote out the High Elyri translation to see with his eyes the words that crowded into his head. When the first poem was complete, he stared at it, dissecting root words, prefixes, and minor misspellings that could happen sometimes in translation from ancient texts or unfamiliar, obscure tongues.

> *cógdhut thórgae*
> *bhol chínzé íth ededhór*
> *hne íth zaene ghymae*
> *phain et hes naiaehállys.*

What if, he mused, the original word was thurgag, consumes, instead of burns? That minor potential alteration set off a landslide of similar differences in his head and he quickly wrote out the second poem as well, to follow through on his hunch.

> *íth aegaenag íth ededhór aelás*
> *ibh nec aeturgaeag*
> *sun et k'dhedoc*
> *phain methag aelás k'stomaeph*
> *íth phyghóth keh gaeth*
> *thurgag íth thórgae zaene ghymae.*

Many minutely possible changes, a letter here, a prefix or suffix there, a tense or word shift that, when written out as a whole, spoke a much different picture to the reader than that which was delivered to the Queen. Verses that, to Kavan's eye and ear, seemed not like threats but rather evidence, or at least the hints of evidence from someone who had seen and heard things they were not meant to know. Evidence witnessed by someone Kavan would never have suspected…until now.

He needed answers tonight before he faced the Queen with what he had found. He gathered his notes, determined not to leave a single one on the off chance he was somehow wrong, and left the alcove after blowing out the candles. The hour had grown late, but he did not care. If his assessments, his interpretations, were right, he might hold the key the Queen needed to restoring peace to Enesfel.

❧Chapter 22❦

"**Y**our Majesty…"

Diona knew, by the use of her title, that whatever her uncle had come to discuss, it was not personal but duty-related, according to his station. Normally that would not trouble her, but today, after burying her brother, the man's son, business was not something she expected Owain to be concerned with. Knowing that the remainder of his family had returned to Káliel, leaving him alone, she was worried and thus, despite the late hour, agreed to see him. Not that she had yet to sleep; Kavan had said he would return tonight and she held on to hope that he would arrive soon, if for no other reason than to tell her he had yet to learn anything helpful.

"How are you, Uncle?"

"I have been better," he admitted heavily as he sank onto the steps near the throne on which she sat. It seemed common for the Lachlans to come to the Great Hall when troubled, as Owain remembered King Innis pacing here, knew that Arlan had done it, and Owain had walked these stones in agitation. Diona did not seem one to pace but finding her here for the second time did not surprise him. "Lord Cliáth…?"

"He will return tonight; he promised he would when his investigation of those poems is complete."

"I'm sure he will." Perhaps, he thought, if he waited in the oratory, he would see the bard, talk to him at length in a place of privacy and sort out the chaos in his head.

"If I see him before you do, I shall tell him to seek you out."

Owain bowed his head. "I would appreciate that." He rubbed the back of his neck, not sure how to say what needed to be said.

"I thought you would be with your family."

"I have duties to attend…as does Gabrielle…and we thought it best for Clianthe to return to more familiar surroundings."

Diona nodded. She had seen the woman wandering the castle corridors, looking for something, or someone, she was not going to find. A few times Clianthe stopped to stare at Owain with elation, and Diona expected her to call him Muir, but then her expression would fall flat and she would wander again. As far as she was into her pregnancy, her family was right to be concerned.

"When Lord MacLyr returned, he said the first thing she did upon leaving the Gate was fall into hysterical weeping and wailing. He was forced to make her sleep, see her put to bed…but I fear she may not recover from this shock. It is why…" He paused and cleared his throat. "I wish to resign my duties to be with them, on Káliel, until she is recovered…or for as long as Gabrielle needs me."

Expecting the Queen to protest, he continued, "She cannot manage Piran, her duties, and Clianthe in this condition. Extra staff can be hired to see to Clianthe's care, but it would not be the same, and the toll it will take on Gabrielle, as she manages the consequences of the battle on Pháne with the Council and the future of the islands, are too great. My estate is in good hands and I am sure you can find another to serve as chamberlain."

Diona took a deep breath to stay an impulsive outburst, and after another breath, and the release of it, she said, "Temporarily, you understand, Lord Lachlan," in a clipped tone, the tone and the use of title the sole conveyance of her displeasure. She was not angry about these circumstances, but she was disappointed and worried about the sudden need to replace a key advisor from a dwindling pool of those she trusted. She would not hesitate to offer the position to Kavan, if she believed he would accept it, or to offer it once more to Bhríd, but neither man was likely to take the job. Perhaps she could convince Espen to assume some of those duties temporarily, redistribute others to her chancellor and her justice, and even to her acting inquisitor, but that was not a satisfactory long-term solution. There was no guarantee Clianthe would ever recover from the devastating loss of her husband. It was something Diona would have to discuss with Kavan, she decided, when he returned.

"Temporary, yes." Owain hoped it would be temporary, for Clianthe's sake, and Gabrielle's, as well as his own. He was happy here in Rhidam, where he had the opportunity to see Kavan periodically, here where he had once ruled as king. He had no desire to abandon Rhidam while the kingdom still needed his support. "I will remain through the week, and then go to Káliel...if that is acceptable. Perhaps by then you will have found a substitute."

"Perhaps." Grief quickly replaced her displeasure and she leaned against his broader form, hugging him tightly. "I am sorry, Uncle. I...this isn't fair. He shouldn't be...I hope you...that Clianthe...can find solace. Muir would not want you to mourn him indefinitely..."

"Nor you." His son had died bravely, a leader in battle, with Kavan at his side. The only thing better Muir could have asked for would have been to live long enough to welcome his child into the world...a child Owain was determined to do right by no matter what it took. "I believe he is here with us. We will see him again...he will not abandon us."

The Queen nodded but stayed in her uncle's embrace, allowing this rare moment of weakness. She wished her faith was as strong as Kavan's. She wanted to believe her uncle's words were true.

Tonight, however, she believed in very little…except that Kavan would return with answers as he had promised.

≈*≈

"What do you know?"

Despite the hour, Kavan had not knocked on the cabin door to announce himself to the man sleeping within, and Níkóá, jarred awake by the voice and proximity of someone in his home, bolted upright with a knife in his hand, drawn from beneath his pillow. Kavan, however, was too far away to reach, and from the man's posture, the redhead was not certain if an actual voice had roused him or if that voice had been inside his head.

"About what?" His words croaked as he struggled to wake and stay calm. He did not believe Kavan was a threat, but how could he be certain? He barely knew him, and what he did know was rumor.

In High Elyri, Kavan spoke the translated poems, the versions he believed to be accurate.

cógdhut thurgag
bhol chínzé íth dedhá
hne íth zaene ghymag
phain et hys naiaehállys.

Níkóá's face lost color but he shifted on his bed until his legs hung over, bare feet on the floor, his blankets covering what Kavan presumed to be his naked waist.

Kavan continued with the second translation, now unnecessary.

Íth aegaent íth dedhá aelás
ibh nyek aeturbhae
sun et k'dedhá bhithár
phain bhemethán k'stómaer
íth phyróth kóh
thórgae íth thurgag zaene gymag.

Níkóá closed his eyes. "I didn't…" He had hoped someone in the keep could decipher those words, but now that Kavan had, he felt awkward for having gone to such lengths to obscure what he knew.

"You wrote these." He half-expected the man to deny it but was satisfied instead when Níkóá nodded.

"Yes."

Though he did not say it, Kavan was impressed with the attention to detail that had gone into the crafting of those phrases. It took mastery of both Elyri and High Elyri, or else a great amount of time with books and someone who knew the old tongue, to piece together words that were just similar enough in spelling, in meaning, in pronunciation to create a multitude of layered meanings. "You speak of gdhededhá Claide…with two meanings. If you know something, you have a duty to the Crown to…"

"What have the Lachlans done for me?" Níkóá spat defensively. He did feel marginally guilty for not being straightforward with the Queen, for not revealing what little he knew, but he had reason to fear for his safety, and he had done his best to give them clues without endangering himself. "I gave them what I knew…figured someone would decipher them eventually…"

"The Crown enabled your birth, allowed you to live." It was hard to argue the Crown's direct influence on the life of a common man, but there was no doubt that King Farrell could have had Níkóá's mother killed for her pregnancy, could have refused to support the child instead of acknowledging him with financial gifts and the token of that royal ring. It might not have been enough to afford the child an easy upbringing, but it was enough to be useful, and his anonymity had protected him from King Bowen…who could have put him to death had he learned of a child that could be viewed as an heir to the Enesfel throne.

These were facts of which Níkóá was aware. He sighed, ran his fingers through his wavy hair, and said, "I know duty…but I also know fear. I can pass amongst Teren…as one of them. To speak out…to risk slaughter as many others have done…" He shook his head. "I am a coward; I know…but what more could I do? I don't want to die. I wrote…what I know, but it would be my word against his…and a reading, by you, Healer MacLyr, or any other Elyri, would have revealed who I am…what I am…and I was not ready for that. Until a few months ago, I was in Elyriá studying. It was rumor, the horrific tales of what was happening to our people here…that brought me to Rhidam before the fire. I saved those I could…I served the Crown as executioner…it was not until recently, hearing gdhededhá Claide's lesson during a Gathering…that I realized there was something more I can do. I reached out to you to reveal myself…hoping for guidance…but when I heard his lesson…I knew…but I need the ring back…"

"For what purpose?" Kavan squatted before him, listening, reading details in his features, in his aura, to gain an understanding of the younger man that might give them both direction.

"To gain his trust. He wishes to displace the Queen…I suppose because she is a strong woman he cannot manipulate." Níkóá's grin was lopsided and anxious. "He does not know who I am…but I told him I could present him an heir of Lachlan blood. He wants proof, of course, that there is such a man. But I have not hinted that man is me. If he thinks he can manipulate me…or that he at least has an ally with similar goals who might be willing to stage a coup…I can gain his trust…and when I have more substantial proof about his intentions, I can turn him in…or kill him myself." Seeing the flicker of protest in Kavan's face, he grunted. "I have no compunctions about killing a man who deserves it, Lord Cliáth. We both know his day will come, at either the people's hands, the Crown's, k'Ádhá's, or mine. It matters not to me, as long as his reign of cruelty ends."

Ignoring Claide's future for the moment, not feeling that it was his place to decide such things, Kavan asked, "You say you know things…have evidence to speak. Tell me. What do you know?"

"It's all there…in the verses. I overheard three men come before him, telling him it was done as he bid…that the fire would purge Rhidam of its sin. The three were killed…right in front of him…the sole witnesses who knew of his involvement in the fire no longer a threat. But I know; I saw them die. Before that…after the fire but before those men's death…I knew of an effort…something to be sent to Clarys meant to cause k'gdhededhá Dórímyr's death. I did not know what it would be…although poison seemed the logical mechanism if one wanted to kill from far away…nor did I know who was to deliver it…"

"Did you send Lord Dugan?" He did not ask how Níkóá had known or found Caol. The man was Elyri, any Elyri who wanted that knowledge could have found it if they tried hard enough.

Níkóá nodded his head. "I regret it was a wasted effort. When I first heard of the threat, I meant to go to Clarys myself but could not gain audience. Then I thought that an emissary of the Queen, a Lachlan by marriage, would have a better chance of being heard, being listened to, by the gdhededhásur and I sent word to the Inquisitor. Afterward, the executions came. Later…at the Boar's Head…when the tavern was near empty…"

He pulled a long robe from the bedpost and pulled it around his shoulders before rising to tend to the dwindling fire. If he was to be awake, without the warmth of his blankets, he wanted a fire. "I was passing…thought to go in for a drink…but I heard the dedhá's voice and stopped at the corner of the building to listen, leaning there as if already drunk…" He poked at the fire, threw on another log, and watched the flames crackle higher.

"I don't know who she was. I did not see her face…only the back of her head when they came out…when she kissed his cheek and walked west…towards the quarter most undamaged by the fire. I don't think he noticed me, or else had no reason to think his confession was overheard."

Still squatting where he had been, his head turned to watch Níkóá at the hearth, Kavan murmured, "Confession?"

"I did not hear all of it…as I said. He said he wished there could have been another way…that he had not wanted to make a martyr out of k'gdhededhá Tythilius to get power out of the hands of those who favored Elyri…but he'd had no choice…it was done and he was satisfied with that." The redhead shivered. "I heard dedhá Khwílen speak of the man's torture and death…during his campaign against k'gdhededhá Dórímyr in Elyriá…for his failure to protect our people, protect the faithful outside of Elyriá…thus I knew of it…but I did not know…I could not believe what I heard…until Claide…"

Kavan nodded. "Claide has been the primary suspect since that day, but with no e…and the Crown does not desire to put him on trial if they cannot prove his guilt without an unsubstantiated Elyri reading."

The Crown had done much since that day, had endured many losses, all in the name of finding proof of Claide's guilt. Kavan stretched out his hand and asked, "May I?" A reading would not suffice as proof to the Queen's advisors or the rest of Rhidam, but it gave Kavan more to work with and might prove helpful. It might also add some morsel of proof to the Faithful in Clarys that he was not guilty of Dórímyr's death, that the blame lay with Claide.

Níkóá stared at the hand, uncertain at first what was being asked. A glimpse into the bard's eyes, however, melted his resistance and he dropped to his knees at Kavan's side to take the offered hand. He knew how to read and be read, but he was surprised at the speed and ease with which he felt Kavan's thoughts probe his. He watched the bard's eyes flutter closed with the intimacy of a lover, the touch of Kavan's hand on his, the caress of thoughts no less tender, and began to tremble uncontrollably. He had been read by bhydáni and gdhededhá, had read them in return in practice, but those experiences had not felt to him as intimate as this did now.

It took several moments for his vision to clear, for him to close his slack-jawed expression, after realizing that Kavan had ended the contact. Kavan's expression was veiled, unreadable, although Níkóá thought he saw traces of embarrassment in the man's green eyes. The bard got to his feet in a fluid motion and helped Níkóá to stand.

"Wait for me here. I believe there is a way we can work together…with the Crown…to bring Claide to bear for his crimes. I am due to meet with the Queen. Allow me to speak with her and I shall return to you as quickly as I may." He caught Níkóá's shoulders between his hands, another vaguely intimate gesture that made Níkóá feel as if he would swoon, and add, "Be strong and trust me."

Níkóá's head bobbed once, as he was unable to find his voice. He blinked, considering why he should work with the Crown, and when his eyes opened, the bard was nowhere to be seen.

❧Chapter 23❧

The Queen, despairing that Kavan was sidetracked by some emergency, somehow harmed in Alberni, or was delayed by not yet finding anything she could use from those words of convoluted imagery, rose from the throne with a sigh. She could not be angry with him, as she knew him to be a man of his word who would not break a promise without good reason, but his absence was yet another disappointment in a day filled with them. In the gathering darkness, the last of the torches at the far end of the Hall beginning to splutter, she listened to the night, trying to imagine Muir beside her the way he used to be, the way Owain claimed he was now. Imagination had never been her strong suit, and thus far, her efforts to believe it to be true had failed.

The effort did bring her quiet footfalls, however, and it was with relief that she turned to greet the man coming in from her left.

"I began to think you would not come tonight…as did Owain. He is looking for you."

"Owain?" Guilt fluttered through Kavan's stomach and up into his throat. He had spared his friend little of the time and support he deserved after the death of his son. Kavan should have gone to him sooner rather than force the prince to seek him out. He would do that tonight, once this matter was dealt with, as long as the man was still awake. Owain deserved that much.

"He is leaving court…to be with his family," she sighed. "It is understandable…they need him and he has suffered a great loss that needs time to mend…but it leaves me at a loss for a chamberlain. Then with your tardiness…"

Owain was leaving Rhidam? Kavan swallowed hard, hit by another upheaval in the fabric of his life that he was unprepared for. With the Gates, it was no major change, but there had been too many changes in the last year. What Kavan wanted was calm and stability. "My apologies; research took longer than expected…and I had to meet with someone to verify what I learned."

"Are they threats?" It did not surprise her that Kavan chose duty rather than the emotional avalanche left by Muir's death. She knew how much the bard adored her half-brother and could imagine the pain he must feel. Duty was easier to cope with, easier to control. Her father had done the same thing and she was learning why at last.

"No…thankfully. The words are confessions of sorts…of a witness who has overheard k'gdhededhá Claide on multiple occasions uttering damning evidence of his crimes…first about the fire, and later about his part in Jermyn's murder."

Diona's eyes grew wide. "Where is he? Bring him in! Let me hear what he knows and then we can arrest Claide and be done with this misery and madness…"

"My Queen." His sternness undercut Diona's excitement and made her look at him with forced stillness. "It would be his word against Claide's, even though I have read him to know that those words, his memories are not falsehoods. What we need is evidence, more of it, something that could be viewed at his trial as more than hearsay or Elyri reading."

In her frustrated efforts for justice, she cried, "How do we get that? We have sought evidence for more than a year and still…"

"I…" Kavan took a step back, both to find distance from what he felt could erupt into outrage at any moment, and to put distance between his thoughts and his feelings. Emotional entanglement was unwanted. "He has a…" His lips pursed. "There might be a way…if you are willing to trust my judgment."

"You know I trust you."

"Allow me to bring him to you tomorrow. Meet him, but do not question him about Claide, and appoint him your chamberlain."

"Cham…? You wish me to appoint a stranger to such a…?"

"Not exactly a stranger; you have met him before…the executioner you chose for the last group of Coryllien prisoners. He is capable of the duties required, and one who can, and will, bring Claide to us if we are patient."

"We have been more than patient, Kavan," she scoffed.

But the tension on her face faded a little with the revelation of the man's identity. She had not learned his name when he offered his services, but she knew his mother was Elyri and knew he had argued a convincing case for allowing an Elyri executioner to kill those offenders. He had seemed respectable and courteous when they met, if secretive with his identity, and educated enough to be sharp-witted. If Kavan had spoken with him, approved of his person and ability, then perhaps the suggestion was not as far-fetched as it seemed.

Kavan caught her hands, touching her of his own accord for the first time since she had violated his trust well over a year before. The gesture silenced her. Trembling, she looked into his face, surrendering to anything he would ask.

"No one else must know of this arrangement…except for Princess Asta if you deem it fitting…not even Espen. My friend…" It oddly did not feel displaced to call Níkóa that though they had just met. "He is on the verge of gaining Claide's trust. If Claide believes he has someone within the keep who can benefit him, this appointment will, in time, bear his guilt to you."

"Appointing a relative stranger will be questioned…"

"He is no stranger to me." That would not be enough, would raise the suspicions of the anti-Elyri factions Kavan was endeavoring to appease with his absence from Rhidam. "Some will recognize his face after the execution I am told. My recommendation to your court should be enough to allay their fears or concerns about his qualifications or trustworthiness. To others…he may still need an alibi. Who brought him to your attention before?"

"Flannery."

"Then speak to the Chancellor and make arrangements to present his appointment as having come through Flannery. As long as everyone reports the same story, it will work…when Claide gets word of the appointment."

She nodded, glancing at their still-joined hands. Kavan was not a man to lie, but he did understand the political need for subterfuge. As it had been the Chancellor who brought the redhead to her as a potential executioner after the men met somewhere in Rhidam, such a tale of the Chancellor's recommendation would be more of an exaggeration of facts than a lie. Most people would not inquire about his qualifications. If he proved capable, his appointment would prove itself. It could work.

"Asta will be with Gaelán…probably asleep…but I will speak with her about this in the morning, and meet with Flannery as well before you arrive with this fellow. I will have them present to greet him…and we shall see if he is as you claim him to be. I hope this works, Kavan. There has been too much bloodshed. Claide has to be stopped. This has to end."

He withdrew his hands with an awkward expression and dropped them to his sides. "Agreed. I will return to him…tell him to come in the morning…then we shall make this plan work to Enesfel's benefit. Take heart, Diona. This shall be over soon."

Particularly, he thought as he bowed and departed, if Caol dealt successfully with Anri Heward.

❧*❧

The news of Prince Muir's death hit Caol harder than expected, resulting in a daylong binge of drink in the filthy cubby he had procured as a temporary residence. He had chosen this location because it was within visual distance of the náós, where he could keep his eyes on Claide until some trace of Heward surfaced. If Heward had any connection to the k'gdhededhá, there was a chance he would come here, and if he did not, at least spying on Claide gave Caol a way to kill time. He had recruited six Association members to join his undercover endeavor, to pretend to support the Coryllien's cause, and he had hopes of another two to four more. Men whose trade and livelihood were adversely affected by the devastating hit commerce in Enesfel had taken since the violence began, men whose businesses needed foreigners and clients with money to thrive. As long as Heward did not demand murder or torture as a show of support, these men, like Caol, were willing to do almost anything else, particularly if it meant and an end to the deprivation of Enesfel.

But all the recruits in the world would not bring back the prince. Caol had watched Muir grow up alongside his son. The prince had helped save his son's life, had tried to save his brother's, even though Arlan had never fully accepted him. Muir had proven to be noble and compassionate, the best of Lachlan qualities. Qualities demanded of the king he could have been…if only Arlan had been his father. Caol liked Owain well enough too, the man's previous years as king and Caol's attempt to kill him…and their love of the same woman…having leveled their hostility into cooperation over the years. Muir's parentage had stopped mattering to Caol sooner than it had for most. Now the Prince was dead…at Heward's hand.

Heward was going to pay for that single death more than any other…and Caol intended his suffering to be slow and painful.

᠅*᠅

Níkóá was still in the spot where Kavan had left him, eyes closed as though asleep or listening to something Kavan could not hear. He opened them when the door creaked and smiled in relief to see the bard return. Kavan wondered if the man had doubted him…or how long he would have remained waiting for Kavan to come back.

"I waited…as you asked."

"You did." Kavan motioned to the chairs before the fire and waited as the redhead joined him. "I have an answer…a plan…that I believe will benefit everyone…if you are willing…"

Níkóá nodded and waited for him to continue.

"You intend to gain k'gdhededhá Claide's trust?"

"Yes…that is the general direction of it. I have not thought far beyond that step…"

"Could you convince him that he has an ally, a way inside the castle in the hopes of supplanting the Queen from within?"

"You mean introduce myself as a Lachlan to the Queen?"

"I am not yet certain that is the wisest course…it might be best if no one knows the truth. The chamberlain is forced to resign, to tend emergency family matters, and I have convinced the Queen that you are capable of carrying out those duties."

Níkóá blinked. "Me? Chamberlain?"

"After what you've written…what you have done thus far…I believe you capable. You are a stranger to them, it is true…but if Chancellor McGranis recommends you…without anyone knowing you are a Lachlan…"

"I barely know…"

Kavan pressed on with explaining his plan, ignoring Níkóá's self-deprecation. "The Chancellor will vouch for you…and the two of you will have the opportunity to become better acquainted. The Queen knows you as the executioner…the author of the verses…and that you have access to Claide…which no one but she, myself, and Princess Asta will know…the princess as acting Inquisitor in her father's stead."

Again, Níkóá blinked in surprise and Kavan continued.

"You can, in turn, inform Claide of your identity if you wish…reveal your appointment as chamberlain at the chancellor's suggestion and the fact that your identity is hidden from the Queen. He will likely expect you to provide inside information, but between you, the princess, the chancellor, and the Queen, you should be able to manipulate what he knows…"

"And in turn, entrap him." Excited now, his nervous edge bleeding from apprehension into anticipation, Níkóá leaned his elbows on his knees to be closer to Kavan without moving his chair and encroaching on the man's personal space. "If you think this a wise decision…I can make this work and will endeavor to meet with Claide tomorrow if I…"

"After you meet with the Queen in the morning. I will take you to her, make introductions, as early as possible, offer whatever I may to the endeavor…but my own business keeps me away from Rhidam for now. This undertaking will be primarily in Princess Asta's hands. I trust you can work together…and that you will, in turn, ultimately be welcomed into the Lachlan family…if you choose."

"You think…do you believe…?"

"You may never be eligible for the throne…your mixed blood would be a dangerous thing to many…but you are a Lachlan by birth, if not by name. The Queen understands matters of illegitimacy. You would be neither the first…nor the last. Serving as chamberlain will benefit you, the kingdom, and the Crown I believe. If you need time to think, I shall return in the morn at the eighth…"

Níkóá shook his head. "I need no time. Ensnaring k'gdhededhá Claide is my one wish, and your plan seems sound…if the Queen can accept my lack of courtly experience. I will be ready when you come…and will send a message to Claide that I should like to meet with him in the evening. He knows where."

Kavan rose, relieved, although one troublesome detail came to mind that he had not considered before. "Very good. I will introduce you to Lord MacLyr as well…for he, more than anyone, might recognize your father in you…and will most certainly detect Elyri in your blood. Giving him that knowledge will prevent him from asking questions of the wrong people at inappropriate times. I believe," he gave a small, melancholy smile, "he will be pleased to meet you."

"I would be pleased to meet him as well, for I have heard nearly as much of him as I have of you."

Though surprised by that, Kavan nodded. "Sleep, friend. Daylight will come soon."

And their dangerous cat and mouse game would begin.

☙*☙

Prince Owain muttered in his sleep, half-aware that the surface beneath him was not his soft, warm bed, half-aware that there was a hand on his head, gently stroking his hair.

"Gabrielle…?"

No one else had ever stroked his hair or shown him such gentle affection. His mother had been a hard woman of de Corrmick stock, interested in nothing more than political advancement and personal security, a woman with no affection for anyone though she had, in her way, loved her son with fierce devotion. Nursemaids, nannies, and tutors had been nothing more than employees of the Lachlan or de Corrmick houses, not there to provide kindness or affection as Kavan did with his young wards when he took charge of their upbringing and education. In Owain's world, such people were there solely to provide the minimum service expected. Owain had not realized what he was missing, what his life could have been like, until he came to Rhidam and watched Kavan with the children, had seen what a difference loving guidance could make in a child's life. He was thankful his eldest son had been given that opportunity and had grown to be a man that any would be proud to call son.

But the fingers in his hair were not Gabrielle's; he knew her touch, and as he came nearer to waking, he knew it was not her. More gentle, in a way, but also more masculine, and that realization forced his eyes open. He was on the floor in the oratory, where he had knelt before the altar in prayer, begging k'Ádhá for some contact with his son. He must have fallen asleep and crumpled to the floor without waking. Kavan sat on the step beside him, and it was the bard's fingers that offered comfort of a sort no one else could give. It should not be any different, Owain thought, from comfort offered by family or other friends, but he could not deny that it was. Kavan's touch was unique, and tonight it brought tears to the prince's eyes.

"I am sorry I did not come sooner," Kavan murmured. "I should have stayed before...should have been here for you..."

Owain reached up and lazily dragged his hand down the side of Kavan's face without considering the bard's normal avoidance of physical contact. Kavan was still toying with his blonde hair and the prince interpreted that as permission. He was happy Kavan did not flinch from his touch. "Duty beckoned...and you came back when you could. Did you find anything useful?"

Not certain how much knowledge the Queen wanted Owain to have, now that he was due to leave the court, Kavan replied, "The poems were no threats but rather a relaying of information about k'gdhededhá Claide. She intends to discuss the matter with Asta in the morning, to contact the author...and, hopefully, gain more substantial proof against Claide then has been gathered thus far."

"Good. I wish them success." If Kavan knew more, the prince did not push to learn it. Soon his life would revolve around more personal matters; he would not be at the center of Enesfel's political controversy and intrigue any longer unless Kjell needed him to be. There was no need to know anything else, although he would miss palace life in Rhidam.

Kavan murmured, "She said you were resigning…" as if he had been reading the prince's thoughts.

With the physical contact between them, it was likely Kavan had read him, which made Owain withdraw his hand from the bard's face and stiffly rise to his feet. Kavan's hand fell away as well, and Owain breathed with both relief and regret. It was better, he thought, that Kavan did not know his deeper thoughts. That would likely embarrass them both…if Kavan did not know those thoughts already.

"I am needed on Káliel. Gabrielle will not admit it, but until Clianthe recovers, there is too much for Gabrielle to do alone. And I have missed too much of Piran's youth." Not as much as he had missed of Prince Muir's, but Kavan understood that parental longing for a child more fully than he had before.

"And Kjell?"

Owain frowned and shrugged. "I will send him word…make other arrangements for contact with him. It cannot be helped."

"No," came the solemn agreement. "It cannot."

Any hope Owain had fostered that Kavan would refute that need evaporated with those words. Owain sighed. "I wish…"

"I will come to you as often as I may," Kavan promised, the man's quivering pout touching his heart and revealing his wish where words failed him. Though Owain's hair was still blonde, the color was fading as silver gradually grew in to replace the golden strands. Around his eyes and mouth, the skin had begun to sag, crease, and wrinkle. Older than Kavan by a year, Owain's Teren mortality was creeping over him and soon, or at least sooner than the bard would like, Kavan would lose him too.

The thought unexpectedly compelled him to pull Owain into an embrace. "I...I...I shall miss him...miss knowing he is there..." he mumbled, his voice on the edge of breaking, speaking of Muir an easier thing than speaking of what lay ahead when Owain was lost to him. He was here to offer comfort, not seek it, he silently scolded himself. But the words were said and he could not take them back, nor did he want to. Perhaps Owain would feel less alone in his grief for hearing them.

The prince choked on emotion brought to the surface by Kavan's admission, Kavan's pain, as much as by his own, and he clung to the Elyri, his face buried in the silver-white hair. "I know..." he said with a sniffle. "Knowing that...I think...will make it easier...when tomorrow passes...and the day after...and the weeks and months and years beyond...with him not here to share it with...you and I will remember him together..."

The silence in the dark room, punctuated by a distant tolling of náós bells, was displaced when Kavan drew back far enough to look Owain in the eye. "Easier?"

"You were there for him...and I find it...comforting...to know he will be remembered even after I cannot...when most of those who knew him pass. As long as he is remembered, remembered well, he will not truly be gone...nor will I...and I thank you for that gift."

The bard bobbed his head but any words he might have said were quickly dammed up behind the wall he was endeavoring to erect, the wall that would, he hoped, keep his emotions in check. When Owain wiped his red eyes and stifled a yawn, Kavan rose and pulled the prince with him. "Come, my lord."

Owain did not resist, even when he saw that Kavan was pulling him towards the room the prince called his when he was in Rhidam. "I waited..." he mumbled. "I wanted to..."

"I am here, Owain." He steered him towards the bed, pushed the man gently down, and helped him pull off his boots then cover him with a blanket. The candles set earlier that evening were nearly extinguished, smoky stubs in cast iron holders on the oaken bedside table. Kavan blew the one out nearest Owain and pulled a nearby stool closer to the bed, intending to remain there in vigil throughout the night, offering his friend his presence to help him sleep. Owain caught his wrist, however, and Kavan stared into his face. Through that touch, and in the man's sad blue eyes, Kavan could see the things Owain wanted to say, wanted to ask, but did not dare.

For a brief moment, a war waged within Kavan, desire to accommodate his friend's needs clashing with Kavan's awkward discomfort. He did not allow Owain to see or sense that turmoil, however, and when the war was won, Kavan circled the bed and sat on it after blowing out the second candle. The prince rolled to face him, wrapped one arm around Kavan's legs, and buried his face against the clothed hip. He did not expect Kavan to remain until morning, but he did desire the bard to remain until he slept. Tonight he needed someone beside him, needed not to be alone, and Kavan was the best person to fill the void that gnawed at his soul from the moment the news of Muir's death had come.

It was a need Kavan understood perfectly.

He was consumed with nervous energy by the time he left the one place he had never expected to leave, to enter another he never thought to be able to see as anything other than a brief visitor. Making it to the executioner's block in front of the castle gates was the nearest Níkóá had ever believed he would come to the Lachlan halls, despite his dreams and the knowledge of who his father was. The late-night clandestine meeting that had won him the executioner's ax for that single day had been strictly between him, the Queen, and the Chancellor and he did not expect anyone except those two to recognize him today. Their curious stares as he entered the castle grounds made him anxious, but following in the White Bard's wake kept anyone from asking questions about who he was and why he was there.

Most of the Queen's advisors and staff were not born during King Farrell's brief reign, had been young children, or had lived somewhere far away from Rhidam. Ártur, as Kavan expected, recognized the man trailing behind him and did his best to feign ignorance despite the wide-eyed disbelief he showed in the initial moment of meeting. Prince Owain, whom Kavan realized almost too late would see the likeness between this man and the one Lachlan who had treated him kindly as a boy and young man, stared too but kept his verbal questions to himself.

Kavan drew the resigning chamberlain aside, as the Queen and Asta took Níkóá on a tour, laying the groundwork between them for the plan they would put into action as soon as he resided in the castle full time. Níkóá did not know why Kavan did not accompany them, did not know that Owain was one of the few who could identify him. By the time they rejoined prince and bard, the blond chamberlain eagerly offered his own, more extensive tour, under the guise of teaching him as much of the castle's runnings as he could in the days he had left in Rhidam. Owain's primary interest, however, was sharing what details he could recall of the sort of man Farrell Lachlan had been with the man who had never known his father.

Having someone within the walls and the family who would, Kavan assured him, offer protection and support should he need it, was reassuring, although the knowledge that he might need that protection and support when, if, the Queen learned his true identity, made Níkóá cautious with his words. The Queen who was legally a distant cousin, accepted him at Kavan's insistence and endorsement and insisted he be given ample time with Chancellor McGranis to develop a plausible backstory and history for how they knew one another. He was introduced to advisor after advisor, courtiers, nobles, and soldiers, some who undoubtedly would have their hearts set on the position of chamberlain if they had known it would soon be vacated. But Níkóá quickly realized that few knew Prince Owain was leaving or knew that his introduction was intended to instate him into a position of power in the Lachlan court. Before he left the castle, the Queen instructed him to return the following day at noon when the formal announcement would be made.

Níkóá was still not certain he was suited for this job, but Kavan assured him that, for however long the ruse was necessary, however long Prince Owain had to be away, his position would be secure and he would be trained and treated accordingly by everyone who mattered. Níkóá hoped the deception would work, for he had no desire to end up with his head on the same chopping block on which he had recently deprived many Corylliens of their heads in the name of the Crown and those butchered for their race.

To avoid being followed or seen by anyone who might later turn against him, Níkóá had spent an hour wandering Rhidam's cold, darkening streets, darting in and out of shops, waiting for the hour when he was to meet k'gdhededhá Claide. He intentionally delayed his entrance into the tavern until he knew the man had been there an uncomfortably long period, and then rubbed his cheeks until they were red, splashed water on them from a melted pool of snow, pulled his clothing askew, and came in with feigned gasps for breath as if he had been running. When he passed into the room, he made a show of tidying himself, slicking back his unruly hair and straightening his clothes before sauntering to the table where Claide waited, scowling.

"Some things can't be helped…my lord's plans are coming together and it is his bidding I hearken to."

"Plans?" The scowl lines on the bald man's pinched face deepened. "Who is this lord to command such obedience?"

Though he wanted to smirk, Níkóá instead donned an expression of offended pride as he drew the royal ring from the pouch within his tunic and held it forth in his palm. "He was given this by his father…King Farrell Lachlan…on the day he was born."

Claide reached for the ring but the hand holding it withdrew before it could be touched or taken. "King? A prince?" His steel-blue eyes widened a little with wonder and delight.

He had not known Farrell Lachlan, but public perception of the preceding spate of Lachlan monarchs held that Farrell was one of the more popular kings, a man who demanded little of his subjects, expected less, offended few, angered almost none. Everyone knew of his numerous affairs amongst the nobility and the poor alike, men and women, anyone who caught his eye. Followed as he had been by the oppressive and reviled King Bowen, it would surprise no one that any children Farrell had fathered would have stayed hidden in fear for their lives. For an illegitimate prince to step forward would be neither a shock nor a surprise. If presented properly as having a lack of faith in the new Queen's suitability for the throne, carefully exposed to gather supporters, dethroning the troublesome woman would be a relatively easy prospect. This prince, it seemed to Claide, had the ultimate goal of reaching the throne as well.

"Connections gained me an audience with the Queen today. Come tomorrow we will know if I shall be greeted in a position at court that might afford my lord eyes and ears within the keep…and in turn for your support, eyes and ears for you as well."

Eyebrow cocked, Claide leaned back on his bench, resting against the wall with his arms folded over his chest as he stared at the stranger across from him. Without touching him, Níkóá could not read his thoughts, and the k'gdhededhá was schooled enough at keeping his expression blank that Níkóá could not guess what might be on his mind. He was concerned that the k'gdhededhá might detect his duplicity, or might, at the mention of King Farrell, recognize him for the very lord of whom he spoke, but in the end, the man's blankness of feature was replaced by a faint smile and a glimmer in his eyes that Níkóá read as both promising and sinister.

"You will be able to meet me there, should you wish it, if I am appointed chamberlain…"

"Chamberlain?" Hope spiked in Claide's voice. "What of Prince Lachlan?" He knew that the prince, once a king with ties to Neth, was one of those who openly adored the White Bard, the Healer MacLyr, and every other Elyri in the Crown's employment. Few Elyri remained in the keep any longer, but the number of those who supported their return was too high for Claide, thus replacing even one of them with an ally was an opportunity not to miss.

"I do not know. I have heard he is leaving for personal reasons…the death of his son perhaps." Níkóá knew little about that death, had only heard mention of it within the castle as Prince Muir's burial had been swift and unannounced to the public. He shrugged. "The Queen wishes someone with fresh perspective, I am told, someone who is not of the court or one of her father's counselors, and I am told my recommendation is a welcome one. I can serve as translator, am schooled in numbers and currency exchange, and have done my share of business abroad. I go at noon tomorrow and will learn my destiny then."

"You will report to me at once if you succeed in…"

Níkóá shook his head. "I will report to my lord first…then to you, as he permits…"

"I demand to meet him face to face…"

"No one makes demands of my…"

Claide hissed, catching Níkóá's wrist, "He is no one…"

Níkóá dropped his gaze to stare icily at the hand on him and then back up with narrowed eyes. "He is of Lachlan blood. That is a claim you cannot make."

"I am k'gdhededhá…"

"He is a prince." A tendril of energy ripped through his body into the offending hand causing Claide to pull away without realizing why with an expression of apology. There was a long uncomfortable pause between them, both men assessing the other, but the older man finally grunted and relaxed.

"I will wait…for now," Claide huffed impatiently, rubbing his hand on his sleeve as if to wipe the imagined sensation away.

"For now, that is all he asks. You will have word tomorrow, provided I am given leave…and we shall make further plans."

"We shall indeed." Despite the secrecy with which this prince kept apart, Claide had little doubts about his existence. The ring could be a hoax, a false item of no worth; Claide had not met any king before Arlan to have seen such a ring and knew of no artwork with Farrell wearing it. Yet he felt certain this prince was real, and that he sought a way into the noble life he had been denied, into the family, and ultimately onto the throne. Together, he and Claide could work to make that happen.

Níkóá did not watch him depart though he followed the man's path with every sense he possessed to be certain the bald man was not waiting to stab him in the back to take the ring and did not stop to speak with anyone inside, or immediately outside, the tavern. If looks were shared between the k'gdhededhá and anyone else, Níkóá did not see it, but he felt no change in the demeanors of Claide or any of the other patrons present as the evening waned. He would wait them out and leave through the rear door as the owner permitted in case the prelate had arranged for someone to confront him, someone who could steal his evidence or kill him. Thanks to an Elyri trick of power, k'gdhededhá Claide trusted and believed in him. Níkóá did not need any trick or any use of power to know that Claide, on the other hand, could be neither trusted nor believed. The man was a killer and Níkóá was determined to prove it.

ᛒ∙Chapter 24∙ᛒ

K avan's return to Clarys was met with the news from
Hwensen that all but two potential candidates had arrived,
and those two were expected at any hour. With time running
short and his future in the Faith and in Elyriá balanced precariously
upon his success in finding the true cause, and guilty party, behind
k'gdhededhá Dórímyr's death, Kavan felt the frantic need to speak
with the three men he had yet to confront. Two were father and son,
both of whom, in the bard's eyes, had ample reason and cause to
wish the former prelate dead…or at least removed from their lives.

gdhededhá Ylár was rarely far from gdhededhá Tumm and
Kavan expected to find the men together, although he had been told
about the argument between them, an argument both Hwensen and
Khwílen had been unable to learn details of. Whatever was at its
core, the pair was still seen together. The wheeled chair required
pushing and the ancient man, who had lost the use of his legs in an
accident long ago, could not care for himself efficiently without aid.
Ylár had been, for the majority of his adult life, the older man's
caretaker. In public, at least, their relationship remained unchanged.

In private, however, according to the serving and cleaning staff,
there was less contact between them, and Kavan wanted to know
why, wanted to know if there was any connection to the history he

had uncovered and the k'gdhededhá's death. He could not help but speculate that one of them knew something damning about the other, a secret that would save Kavan's connection to the Faith, his ability to remain in Elyriá, and would put the future of the Faith's leadership on a right and respectable path.

Though Kavan preferred to speak with each one alone, he was running out of time. The k'phóredhet, serving as Faith leadership until the election was held, was already discussing beginning the proceedings without the remaining candidates present. Since it was the k'phóredhet who accused Kavan of heresy in order to hunt him for Dórímyr's death, Kavan did not rule out the possibility that they would vote in that direction merely to run out his time, his chances, of learning the truth. The possibility that they were trying to cover up the truth seemed a valid and concerning one. The Kyne was doing what she could to keep them on course, to pressure them to follow historical protocol, but the Faith did not need to follow her edicts in this matter. If they chose to ignore her requests, the initial question and answer period of the election could begin at any hour on any day.

Speaking to the pair of men was an immediate necessity. Kavan prayed as he approached them that they would not summon the guards and have him apprehended for this intrusion.

He hesitated on the balcony, adjusted his clothes, and pushed the partially open door wide enough to allow him to enter. Arriving this way, interrupting the pair at this hour, was a risk he felt he had no choice but to take.

Seated at the small table sharing a sparse pre-dawn meal in tense silence, Ylár lurched to his feet at the bard's uninvited appearance in the room, announced by the sound of the wind grabbing the door and banging it against the frame. He grabbed the bread knife from the table and waved it at Kavan with a measure of bravado that did not match the look in his eyes.

"Stay where you are," he hissed, voice relaying more uncertainty than fear or anger. He may not have known Kavan was accused of murder, but he did know the bard was accused of heresy, and as Kavan had not knocked at their door but rather come in through the open balcony entrance, Ylár's fearful reaction was understandable. Kavan did as he was asked, studying both men as Tumm gave him a cold stare before returning to eating with a wave of his skeletal hand.

"Put it down. If Lord Cliáth wanted to harm us, I suspect he would have without letting us see him." He pressed a berry to his lips, hesitated, and then added, "You do not belong here, harper. Go and I will not alert the guard," before devouring the morsel.

Tumm's recognition was no surprise. After having played many previous festivals in Clarys, being in the Kyne's residence on multiple occasions, most in positions of influence and wealth in the capital city knew the White Bard on sight. The rest knew him by reputation and description. He bowed to the man he wagered to be nearly as old as Tíbhyan, showing respect for his age, but made no move to depart as commanded. "I intend no harm, gdhededhá…as you say. I come under Kyne Mórne's bidding…"

"Then why not use the door?" The mention of the Kyne's favor brought relaxation to Ylár's posture and a lowering of his defensiveness, but his question was still terse and valid.

Kavan looked at him without blinking, prepared to reply, but Tumm spoke first. "And risk arrest for his heresies? He's smarter than that." The old voice was brittle and snide.

"I am no heretic, my lord," Kavan protested, regretting his impulsive defensiveness at once.

"I know the allegations. Such charges are never given lightly…"

"I could name several historical cases that refute that," Kavan refuted. "Charges of heresy are an expedient guarantee of silence."

"You need to be silenced?" Tumm snorted.

Having listened to the exchange and watched the bard's expression and posture throughout, Ylár muttered beneath his breath, "I think he has knowledge that someone does not want him to have...or share," as Kavan simultaneously protested, "I have never strayed from the Faith."

Again, Tumm snorted. "That is for the k'phóredhet to determine, not you or me."

"And you believe the k'phóredhet will be fair in judgment?" asked Ylár of the man seated with him. He had lived with these people, in these halls, nearly all of his life. He already knew the answer to that question.

The two men shared passionate glances of annoyance, one defensive the other in challenge, before looking away from each other, Tumm back at his breakfast as if nothing had changed and Ylár sympathetically at their uninvited guest. His assessment towards Kavan had shifted, and the bard made note of it.

"Is that why you are here, Lord Cliáth? To address the charges?"

Appreciating Ylár's cooler head and willingness to hear him, Kavan bowed. "No. I am not guilty and trust the gdhededhásur to make the appropriate ruling on that when the day comes. I am here seeking a murderer."

"Murderer?" On the other side of the table, Tumm's grey features paled and the hand on its way to his mouth with a bit of bread lowered shakily. The younger man fumbled for the table edge behind him to steady himself as he continued, "One of us is accused? Of k'gdhededhá Dórímyr's...?"

His mention of the prelate's name indicated already-present suspicion about the abrupt illness and death the Tribunal claimed. Or perhaps it was a hint that Ylár knew something of the man's passing that he should not. "I pray not; Kyne will be grieved to hear it...as will I." Kavan meant no reference to the man's relationship with the Kyne's granddaughter, but Ylár could not hide his flushed cheeks.

The bard continued quickly to keep the situation calm, relieved to know by Ylár's words that there was at least one man in Clarys who did not immediately accuse him of murder. "But someone with means, motive, and access to his rooms, his meals, his routine, saw to it that k'gdhededhá Dórímyr was systematically poisoned..."

"We were told..."

"He passed of fever," grunted Tumm without raising his eyes. "Your information is..."

"He passed weeks before his death was announced, I assure you, the night I was accused of heresy and murder by the k'phóredhet."

"There has been no mention of murder." Ylár did not want to believe it, but Kavan could feel that there had been doubt in him about the matter for some time, the suspicion that this accusation might be an honest one supported the doubts already plaguing him.

"I was with him when he passed...I had come to discuss the situation of leadership of the Faith in Rhidam. There were five sources of poison in his room, perhaps more. Three are being investigated in Rhidam as we speak."

"Rhidam...but how...?" Ylár began.

"k'gdhededhá Dórímyr was in Rhidam hours before..."

Tumm's eyes narrowed but he continued to eat. "Lies. He has never..."

"Ask Queen Diona...or gdhededhá Tusánt...or others in Hes á Redh. Ask hundreds of Faithful in Rhidam. Ask Hwensen. They will not lie. Or read me if you wish. I have nothing to hide. He visited briefly...a matter of hours, no longer...and received gifts from parishioners now sought for inquiry. The other sources are here...in Clarys...and I intend to find them."

"You will find no murderers here." Tumm pushed from the table, finished eating or having heard enough of this unpleasant discussion, and forced his weak arms to propel him from the room with a long, scathing stare of accusation at Kavan before he was out of sight. Ylár sighed and collapsed into his chair, fidgeting with the lip of his cup.

"This is a horror, if true, and I have no reason to doubt you, not if Kyne has charged you with the inquiry. But the night you say, the night you were charged, I swear on my faith I was here with him."

"And he would swear the same…?"

Ylár fumbled now with his finger cloth, seeking some means to calm himself. "Perhaps not…although such words would be a lie."

Kavan chose not to probe and instead said, "The poisoning was extended…had been going on for weeks, possibly months or longer…in his food, something in his fire, perhaps on the wood he burned or something added when his hearth was cleaned. Hwensen is questioning staff but has been unsuccessful in learning anything. Whoever did this had motive. It was not a crime committed purely for spite or madness…and I can think of little better motive than a shared Zythánite history."

The bald head popped up. "You know?"

"I have been to Bhórdh. I know enough."

Expression contorted by anxiety, Ylár mumbled, "Only recently did I learn the truth about my parentage, about the lies I was told; he should have…"

"But you understand why he could not…why no one could ever know, not even you?"

"Oh, yes. I have made great study of the saints and heretics, their beliefs, lives, and fates. I am a historian as much as gdhededhá, and it has taken exploring my own history in preparation for nomination to learn the truth, the history…of Tumm and Dórímyr. You believe someone else knew…and killed him for it?"

"Until this moment, I knew of but one other who knew about their history. If anyone else knows…I have not yet uncovered them."

"Tumm is a liar...but I do not think him a killer." He saw the flicker of uncertainty in Kavan's eyes as the bard looked away, and demanded, "What do you know?"

Kavan shook his head, refusing to share what was not his history to reveal. "It is not my place to tell his story...but if you know the history of the Zythánites, you know what they are capable of."

Kavan doubted now, upon further consideration, that the old man would have resorted to poison to be rid of Dórímyr if that was his intent and desire...not if he could kill in the preferred Zythánite manner without bloodying his hands. What Kavan did know was that any poisoning done at Tumm's request if he was responsible, had been done with someone else's hands. He was not physically capable, and now that Kavan was speaking to Ylár face to face, he did not believe this man was guilty. "Ask him, if you will..."

"I shall...and I shall do my best to uncover any Zythánites in Clarys...or any who might know of them and wish to eradicate them. There will be no witch hunt...but if a man is guilty of murder, he will be punished accordingly."

"gdhededhá." Kavan caught his wrist impulsively in the hopes of stilling the man's agitation. "Discretion, please. If you speak of murder openly...that knowledge has not left the k'phóredhet's chambers...except for a select few I have spoken with in Enesfel...and Hwensen and the Kyne...do not discredit them, or yourself, with discussions of facts you should not yet know."

Ylár began to speak, to disagree, but then bobbed his head. The bard's advice was sound, though it would not, in his zeal to learn the truth about his father, be easy advice to follow. He studied the hand that touched him, not considering that it was a touch that could know his heart in an instant, and asked, "What will you do?"

"I do not know. There is another I have not yet spoken with...but I admit reluctance for further confrontation."

"Tumm will not speak with you. He has little patience with heretics." The words were spat as though the hypocrisy of them left a bitter taste in Ylár's mouth. "There are others?"

"One more…who is much the same, I suspect…"

"Lláhy." Kavan did not need to speak the man's name for Ylár to know it. He lived and worked with every gdhededhá in Hes Dhágdhuán and knew them well. "I do not believe he would do such a thing…but until recently I would not have believed Tumm to be a Zythánite…and my father…either. A knock on the door, a servant requesting entry, brought both men to their feet. "One moment," Ylár called. To Kavan, as he steered the bard back to the balcony door, he said quietly, "There is a woman…I do not know her…but Hwensen does. Find her…she may tell you what you need to know."

Kavan's eyes narrowed but he had no time to ask questions or to consider this new trail in full before Ylár closed the doors and the drapes and summoned the servant into the room. Kavan chose flight instead of remaining in the open and risking discovery. It was cold and cloudy…and nothing would be accomplished by standing where he was. There was a storm brewing, hours from the Elyriá coast, and it would soon envelop Clarys with its late winter fury. Kavan had to find Hwensen…and unleash a storm of his own.

◈*◈

It had taken Princess Asta weeks, with the help of Fen Geli, Matus, and Wace Elotti, to trace the bottle of wine Kavan had brought to her, the one containing a poison that had made its way into k'gdhededhá Dórímyr's hands and may have contributed to his death. The winery that produced this vintage was a small one near Kilmacud, a region abundant with vineyards selling to every corner of the Sovereignties. It was a kingdom-wide practice that records were kept by each winery as to where barrels or crates of bottles were sold, even single bottles were recorded for taxation purposes.

By starting at the producing winery, Asta's resources learned where the sales of this recorded vintage had gone, who had bought crates of individual bottles, and each of those names was followed, each individual questioned. One of the twelve crates had ended up in Levonne, at a merchant's shop, and per Enesfel law, the buyers of each of the twelve bottles were reported back to the vineyard.

Though a tedious task that the Crown often considered abolishing, it enabled the buyers to be tracked, one by one, found and thoroughly questioned by a representative of the Crown. When there were but four more to speak with, most already having consumed their purchase or being able to present the unopened bottle from storage, the acting Inquisitor began to despair that this search would be yet another dead end.

It was a surprise, therefore, when the chamberlain-in-training came with a summons to the stateroom, where four soldiers and a smugly grinning Fen surrounded a meek-looking fellow with muddy brown hair and sunken cheeks who nervously wrung his cap in his scarred and stained hands when she entered the room. His doublet, silk shirt, pressed black trousers and worn but polished shoes exhibited signs of age and wear, not a nobleman or lord, but no peasant either. Likely a merchant, and judging by the scores on his fingers and knuckles, either white with age or red with newness, was involved in a trade that required rough work with his hands.

"I am sorry. I came soon as I heard, soon as I learned, soon as he said…" He glanced timidly at Fen, "I meant no harm to…"

One of the soldiers elbowed him in the ribs, making him cough and splutter, cutting him off.

"No…allow him to speak," the princess scolded. Whatever harm the man had or had not meant, whatever he had come to confess, she would hear him. "What say you, sir…what harm do you speak of?"

"I have heard tell of wine…a Fildanyo vintage given to k'gdhededhá Dórímyr by gdhededhá Tusánt…a gift…poisoned…and

I fear it may have been mine." His wringing hands shook more violently and then clenched hard around his twisted cap.

Níkóá, who remained in the room, watched the faint flicker of emotion play across the young woman's face as she studied the little man. A female inquisitor was unheard of, and this woman was barely more than a child. But the Queen was assured of her abilities, trusted her, and Lord Cliáth spoke highly of her, thus the redhead kept his misgivings to himself.

When she sat, her booted feet crossed before her in what struck Níkóá as a masculine pose, it was with a calm, almost disinterested expression on her face. "What makes you believe thus?" she asked. "You sought to poison...?"

"Not I, your majesty," he exclaimed, surging forward to fall at her feet. Asta drew her legs back rather than allow him to kiss her boots. "I bought the wine, it is true. I intended to give it to k'gdhededhá Claide upon his appointment, as he was a friend of my father's, who passed away this past year...my father would have wanted him to have it. But when I could not find the bottle, I discovered my daughter had sent it to dedhá Tusánt. I scolded her...told her that Elyri do not drink wine...and she was quite upset to learn this, was frantic to get it back as I recall...but to no avail..."

"Bring her to me; I must speak with her." Few fathers would lay the blame for their own crimes on a child, but it would require speaking with the woman to verify or disprove his claim.

The man lowered his gaze, still on his knees, and nervously resumed wringing his cap. "Your majesty, I cannot, for I do not know..." Though he did not see the princess' quirked eyebrow, he continued, "She was lost in the fires, your majesty...trapped when our shop collapsed. We could not find her body. Perhaps she fled...I do not know. I know no more than I have told you...save that perhaps her betrothed could offer information I do not have."

"His name?"

"Mikel Wistern…he is a blacksmith…his family hails from the hamlet of Rolstecher, where his father works still…"

"I know the man," one soldier said out of turn. "His father has done work for my father, repairing his plow."

There had been a previous meeting between Claide and a blacksmith from Rolstecher; Asta recalled hearing of it months ago during one of Claide's suspicious absences from Rhidam. She did not think this connection to a poisoned bottle of wine was a coincidence. "Then bring him to me at once…his father as well. I want words with both…in private." Her expression, part playful, part sneering, part serious business, faded quickly to neutral before the man at her feet could see it. "You, sir, will remain here, in protective custody, until we determine the veracity of your tale. If your daughter is found to be alive and in your home…or if we discover any part of your story is a lie, I will personally give the Queen your head."

She did not have the authority to make that decree, but the mousy man did not know that. The trembling of his hands consumed his entire body as he squawked, "I swear, my lady! I speak the truth. I love dedhá Tusánt…he gave me such hope when my wife…and then my father…passed. I would never wish him ill…would never give him wine…let alone wine tainted with…"

"We shall see. Guards, take him below but see to his comforts. Mr. Geli, well done. Let us hope you and Mr. Elotti can bring me more good news."

The princess believed the little man's tale, believed him to be as innocent as he claimed, but she was not going to risk either him speaking to the blacksmith in warning, or risk anyone finding him and killing him before she had the opportunity to prove his story. She would not make the mistake King Hagan had made…and it might result in promising news for the Queen.

❧＊❧

Kavan stared at the other man in disbelief, a man he had believed he knew well enough, a man he thought trustworthy. From the start, Hwensen seemed on his side, doing everything the bard needed, helping in any way he could to root out the murderer, as long as it would not directly put his life or his position in Clarys in jeopardy. Yet this one tidbit of fact, this one secret, could make the difference in their success…and Hwensen had kept it from him.

"I swore an oath," he explained, both frustrated and apologetic. "No one knows…no one but the two of them…and me…"

"And gdhededhá Ylár…and possibly Tumm…"

"Yes…" Hwensen sighed reluctantly. "So it seems. But I didn't know that. I spoke of it to no one; if he did, if he shared his secret…well, it was not my business! He made me swear silence."

"His death absolves you of that."

"Does it?" The other man lurched around to stare at Kavan. "Does an oath before k'Ádhá end because of the other party's death? There is still one being protected by it…"

Kavan did not know what this woman could reveal than he did not already know, but speaking to her was necessary as the storm blew through Clarys, bringing one of the final entrants into the city with it. He had not, after Ylár's mention of a woman, known if she would be connected to Dórímyr or to Lláhy, and what her connection would be, but Hwensen knew. Knew and had kept the information silent. "I want to meet her…I must. At once. Perhaps she is the…"

"You cannot…" Hwensen shook his head vehemently. "She would not…"

"She is not the first courtesan to a k'gdhededhá…nor will she be the last…"

"It does not matter…she cannot reveal secrets to you…"

"She can…and she will."

More exasperated than before, the former aide threw his hands into the air and cried, "The plague took her, my lord! The dead cannot give you what you seek."

Kavan stilled. To Hwensen's eyes, he did not blink, nor did he appear to breathe as he stared. He did not blame the bard for feeling betrayed as potentially critical information had been kept from him, but beyond the oath he had sworn, Hwensen had not thought it necessary to bring up a relationship with a woman long dead. There was nothing, in his eyes, to be gained from besmirching a man's name over a short-lived, singular affair or defaming the dead.

"As odd as it seems…" Hwensen finally said in defeat when Kavan failed to react or show a response, "he was my friend. She is gone…he is gone…what more is there to say on it?"

"Her name."

Hwensen shook his head.

"Her name, Hwensen." Even if a name was all he could have, if it closed a link to the murder that needed closure, it had to be spoken.

"I cannot…"

"Hwensen."

The other man blinked. In his chest, he felt his heart stop, his lungs squeeze for air as the bard's eyes narrowed. It was nothing the bard was doing, no physical act or touch of power that caused these things. Rather they were a reaction of fear, brought on by the suddenly cold burning smolder in Kavan's eyes, a look that suggested he would take what he needed if hindered, despite his desire not to resort to that offensive action. Kavan was a man backed against a wall, his life, his future, his faith at stake, a man with little to lose should he force something as simple as a name from one he had begun to consider a friend. It was that desperation, the perceived perception of betrayal Kavan felt, the understanding that Dórímyr had planted that desperation there…and the acknowledgment that a name might save Elyriá from having the Faith placed under the leadership of a murderer, that finally pushed Hwensen to reply.

He would trust Kavan to be discreet. And the bard was probably right. What harm could there be since both parties were dead?

"Hágae Rínes…but I swear to you, Kavan, that is all I know." He considered himself Dórímyr's friend, after a fashion, but not enough of a friend to have many details of the man's private life. More than most, perhaps, but not by much. He had known of his comings and goings, had known when the woman came to Dórímyr's chambers, and it took no great stretch of imagination to know what was happening between them, but anything beyond that was speculation. He had not investigated her, knew nothing of her family or her occupation, knew nothing about how she and Dórímyr had met. Hwensen had not felt it important to ask, and as the two had stopped seeing each other some twenty or more years before the Great Plague, it had not seemed important to know more of her afterward.

Kavan grunted, his stance relaxing though his expression did not change. "It will have to do." He hoped that what he could learn from the name would be enough to help him catch a killer. But it was too late tonight, and his agitation was too high as his time dribbled ever faster away. He needed prayer, he needed music. He needed home.

He stalked from the room onto the balcony.

"Lord Cliáth…where are you going?"

"Home."

He said no more, but that one word was enough. As he took to the sky, Hwensen dropped to his knees in prayer, seeking guidance and forgiveness. If his secrecy had hindered the investigation, he owed Kavan something, some form of aid and restitution. But what could he give that would be equal to a secret kept that might cost the bard so much more than the weight of a single name?

❧Chapter 25❧

light took Kavan partway home, but it was difficult through the gale the easterly storm brought with it, and the stinging hail pelting his wings and back did not help. The first Gate he located beyond Clarys' borders served to hasten his journey and brought him, cold and wet, into the Bhryell náós where gdhededhá Bhílári was awake, fidgeting as he paced from one side of the altar steps to the other, leading a group of twenty-five men and women in discussion and prayer. Many were faces Kavan recognized, the young people who had survived the attack in Rhidam and a collection of their friends, and even, the bard realized when he saw the familiar figure rise to greet him, his cousin Bhen.

"aendhá..." Bhen approached, removing his leather cloak as he did so, and dropped it around Kavan's trembling shoulders.

"Thank you..." Kavan accepted the warmth of the cloak and the arm around him as Bhen steered him into the midst of the group. "My apologies for..."

Bhílári shook his head and sat on Kavan's other side as the bard was brought to the bench where Bhen had been. "No need for that, my lord. You are welcome here...you are among friends."

One by one, Kavan studied those looking at him, for the first time in his life facing a collection of Bhryell citizens who did not hate or fear him, who did not reject him or hold him apart. It was peculiar that these younger men and women could offer the acceptance the majority of Kavan's peers and elders would not. Perhaps because they did not know him, perhaps they based their opinions on the rejection of legend, rumor, and myth, or perhaps their acceptance came with Bhen's influence. Kavan nodded his thanks and blinked away the unexpected tears that rimmed his eyes, before finding his voice.

"Tomorrow…or perhaps in a day or two after…the election should begin…" he murmured.

"You have found nothing?" Bhen paused but it seemed that everyone in the room already knew what they referred to. He could not gauge their thoughts on the issue; there were too many for him to easily sort through in his frustrated state, but he was sure that not one among them believed he was guilty of the crimes of murder or heresy. That brought a welcome surge of strength and reassurance.

"Nothing…except a list of the innocent…"

"That's somethingx56 BV…but you should not be here, aendhá."

"Should not…?"

A young woman in the group spoke, her pale blonde hair pulled away from her round face and round eyes, giving her a particularly child-like innocence. "There are ecclesiastical guardsmen here…they are looking for you and refuse to leave."

Kavan glanced at the gdhededhá with wary eyes, already rising to his feet.

"It is true," Bhílári sighed. "Different men than before. They said they had been told you would come here…we told them we have not seen you when they came through the k'rylag…but I fear they are about the streets of Bhryell seeking you. You are safe for now but…"

"My family…"

Bhen's hand around his kept him from immediate flight. "I sent a warning to Wortham...to aene and aendhá...to aene Syl...they will be prepared if...when...the k'phóredhet knocked..."

Prepared did not mean safe. He had told only one person he was coming here tonight, but surely Hwensen had not sent the k'phóredhet. No one in Bhryell had seen Kavan recently; what danger could anyone be in? They could truthfully claim that Kavan was not in Bhryell.

Only now, Kavan groaned, he was.

As if feeding on his fears, loud voices drew nearer outside and then boots began to tramp on the wooden steps and portico at the náós primary entrance, boots stomping off mud and rain before coming into the holy halls. Bhen pulled Kavan's arm, although this time, it was to yank him into the Purification chamber before the soldiers could enter. They could not see beyond the closed panels, but they could hear others with the soldiers, other footsteps and voices, most articulating displeasure and indignation at something the soldiers had done.

"What is this outrage?" Bhílári snapped, those with him having encircled to protect him. "When did the Faith resort to the arrest of innocent...?"

"Any hiding a heretic is guilty..."

"You searched the house, the grounds!" The incensed tone belonged to Wortham and it took all of Bhen's strength to hold Kavan back. "You saw for yourself that he was not..."

"But he has been...and will be again..."

"Someday, yes...it is his home. Of course he..."

"No longer. I confiscate it in the name of..."

gdhededhá Bhílári forsook the security of his followers and pushed in front of the commanding soldier. "You have no right," he barked. "There is no law, no precedent to allow...no cause..."

The vexed soldier, flustered at being called out, grunted, "I have my orders…"

"What orders? From whom?"

A baby began to cry.

"From the k'phóredhet…to do whatever is necessary to bring the heretic to justice…"

The young man spared the slaughter in Rhidam cried, "He is accused…not convicted! This is sedition!"

"With no law permitting the confiscation of property, or the detainment of kin…and the k'phóredhet has no authority to create such laws…you cannot…" began Bhílári.

Each word spoken, the sound of his son's cry, the uncomfortable indifference of the guards and the outrage and support of the growing crowd accumulating in the room, pricked through Kavan's core like icy daggers. He had few choices and much he needed to do. In desperation, he clasped both of Bhen's hands hard and forced his cousin to look at him. If he could not return to Clarys to investigate Dórímyr's mistress, someone else had to…someone who could pass Clarys' streets without fear of arrest.

'I cannot leave them…' Bhen began to silently protest to the commands inside his head.

'You must. I will see to the family…but if you step out there, you too will be accused, and I need this done if I wish any chance of freedom. Go. Now. And return what you learn to me…'

'How?'

'I will find a way. Trust me.'

Despite Bhen's reluctance, he accepted the vital charge, initiating the k'rylag as Kavan asked and soon the bard was alone in the enclosed chamber. He knew what he had to do, but was afraid to do it. Afraid for his family, for his life…for his future in the Faith.

"Stay away, gdhededhá," said the soldier who seemed to be in charge, "or we shall…"

Kavan was tempted to step into the room bathed in light, project some image other than his own into the minds of those present to prevent them from recognizing him. He was confident in that skill and in his ability to manipulate the minds of the soldiers into releasing the family members they held. But there were people in the outer room who trusted him, people, he was learning, who supported him and did not think him a monster. He had to consider them too, their welfare and what they might think, if he wished to retain their admiration and respect.

"Shall what?"

"Lord Cliáth!" someone exclaimed.

The soldiers turned, curved-bladed polearms poised to block him from his family, or perhaps, he mused, to protect themselves. What did they think he was? What did they believe he was capable of?

What did they see when they saw him?

Behind them, he saw not only Wortham, Zelenka, the nursemaid and two children, but his aunt and uncle as well. He was relieved to see that Syl, Ártur, and their children, as well as Sámel and the remainder of his family, were not amongst those here. If he remembered the date correctly, Sámel would be in Clarys, or on his way to make sales in the upcoming holiday festivities. And perhaps, Kavan hoped, Ártur's known employment by the Enesfel Crown had spared him and his family, for arresting any of them, detaining him from royal duty, would result in conflict between Enesfel and Elyriá, bringing their activities to the Kyne's attention, something the k'phóredhet would want to avoid.

Upon seeing him, Wortham surged forward but was blocked by the clatter of wooden and metal poles. Kavan shook his head, bid Wortham to relent with a glance, and then looked at the captain of the guard, refusing to look at the boys lest he belay his fear to them.

Sóbhán likely sensed it anyhow.

"Put down the weapons," Kavan murmured. "They are not needed."

The captain grunted. "Why should we…?"

"Look around you. We are in a holy place. This is no place for weapons." He gestured around the room with one hand. "There should be no bloodshed here. No one wants that."

"Then you will come with us."

Kavan wished, at that moment, that he had the scroll of pardon provided by the Kyne for just such situations. But he had become slack in carrying it, trusting the luck that had thus far kept him safe. He regretted that laxness now, although as he looked at the soldiers he doubted that writ would have done him any good. Hands kept where the others could see them, he said, "I shall if you release my family…all of them…now…and swear on k'Ádhá's name that neither they, nor anyone in Bhryell, will be further troubled."

"Do not do this, my lord!" gdhededhá Bhílári knew what was at stake better than most, for Kavan and for Elyriá, should he accept arrest by the men who had come for him. At his words, it seemed that many others in the room reached the same understanding, as many began to chant his name in low voices, demanding his release, proclaiming his innocence. His uncle said nothing, but stood with arms folded, glaring at his nephew with a look Kavan did not take the time to discern. Heart heavy and full, never believing he would see a day when any of Bhryell's citizens would not only welcome him and make him their own, but also stand up for him, Kavan shook his head, and raised one hand to bring silence down over the room.

"Please." He took a step towards the captain after a shared look with Wortham. "Release them. Swear it and I will accompany you."

Frowning, the captain weighed his options. Confiscating a house and arresting an entire family, blood or otherwise, for the sake of finding one man, he knew to be excessive. The threat had accomplished its purpose, drawing the bard out, thus there was no need to detain anyone else any longer. But it was setting a dangerous precedent if it came to be a tactic used by the Faith throughout Elyriá to control and manipulate people and he was likely to draw a reprimand for it, despite its positive results. It would be difficult to explain to the Kyne when he returned to Clarys with the bard's entire family...a family whose sole crime was an association with the White Bard. He could also see that, should he try to take them, the villagers would turn on him and his men, and blood would be spilled in a Gathering Hall, a blasphemous act he wanted no part of.

Eye to eye, he stared at the pale man, not pale but white as the snow on the mountaintops around Bhryell. He, like many in Elyriá, had heard the stories, rumors, gossip, and mythology about the bard and had no idea which stories were true and which were fabricated exaggerations. The man did not look as dangerous as the k'phóredhet proclaimed, and if he performed miracles as many claimed, it made little sense that the Faith elders would wish to arrest him as a heretic. What heretic would be permitted miracles from the divine? But it was also rumored that he could do great and powerful things few other Elyri could do, and if that were true, those miracles might not be miracles at all, but tricks meant to deceive. He was a soldier; it was not his place to second-guess the wisdom of those in power.

He decided, therefore, to do his duty and leave questions of power and faith and miracles and heresy to those trained to recognize the differences between such things. With a gesture to his men, he grunted, "Release them."

The crowd around Bhílári quickly drew Kavan's family into their midst to protect them should the soldiers change their minds. Wortham, however, resisted the pull of those hands and held his ground. "If you take him, you take..."

"No...Wortham," Kavan begged gently. "See to the boys."

Wortham's face was dark with irritation; Kavan wanted to soothe it away but he could not reach his friend. Wortham was a soldier, not a babysitter, despite his disability and age. He was not accustomed, after their journey of the year before, to taking a passive role in Kavan's life. But he was also a wise man, wise enough to relent to Kavan's wishes despite his annoyance. He would find some other way to help. He would do as Kavan asked but he would not be idle.

When Kavan accepted without protest the rush of men who encircled him and grasped his arms, gdhededhá Bhílári drew back his shoulders with uncustomary defiance. "We will not accept this, Kavan. We will see you freed. We will see your work is completed."

The captain, hand on Kavan's elbow, growled, "What work?".

His men were escorting the bard out of the náós, heading towards the lómesté building, the sole place in Bhryell with the capacity to hold someone should an arrest be made. Use of the two cells was rare, sometimes used to detain individuals who had been fighting or someone accused of theft or some smaller crime while the truth was investigated. The cells had been used to detain a number of unruly children in the past until their parents could come for them. They had held no heretics in Bhryell's history, no murderers. In the years Kavan had lived here they had not been used, and to his surprise and dismay, he was the one to make use of one of them.

The captain did not await an answer, following his men instead to be certain the bard did not escape. He was taking no chances that Kavan might avoid the trial the k'phóredhet had planned.

Not knowing where Bhen had gone, but trusting that Kavan had sent him somewhere safe, Bhílári, his face pale and hands trembling as the adrenaline began to leech from his body, said, "Tomorrow. Tomorrow I will go to Clarys. I will change this."

"I can come with you, gdhededhá, if I am needed" said the outspoken young man beside him.

"As will I," Wortham huffed.

"And I."

"Dháná," growled Tám at his wife's unexpected volunteering.

"We must do something! They will…"

"He will get what he deserves."

"I will see to it that he does," the woman said with atypical defiance that caught her husband off guard. It was obvious that husband and wife had different ideas of what Kavan deserved.

❧*❦

The messenger, a Nethite Asta deduced from his gold hoop earring and fur-lined cloak and boots, brought his message to her rather than to the Queen. The choice was even more peculiar when she noted the de Corrmick emblem on the case protecting the contents from weather and curiosity. She waited until alone to open it and break the sealed scroll to hastily read the news. She read it again with shock, although at heart the message did not surprise her.

After all, it had seemed likely, even if Neth was not the instigator of the anti-Elyri violence in Enesfel, that King Merkar would find a way to influence the situation, some way to aggravate the kingdom that had stripped Neth of a third of her territory in the last war. Neth was best at being a thorn in the sides of both Cordash and Enesfel.

Should she tell the Queen? There was little use in sending men, soldiers, spies, or emissaries to Glevum. By the time they reached Neth's capital, Heward would likely no longer be there, having instead returned to Rhidam to cause more trouble. He was probably already on his way. Asta needed to get this news to her father however so that he could prepare himself for Heward's return.

But hiding the news from her cousin was not an option. She would not retain the Queen's trust if she kept secrets, and Asta was not haughty enough to think she had the experience to have all of the answers. Perhaps Diona would have ideas that Asta had not already considered. Perhaps together they could create a trap that might ensnare Heward and bring the Coryllien mastermind to justice.

⬥Chapter 26⬥

Having been in Clarys many times over the years, coming with his kin to sell harps or seek new commissions or patrons or simply to attend one festival or another because he enjoyed the art, the music, the theatrical spectacles, and the food, the sole difficulty Bhen had in reaching the cemetery was the sea-blown natural elements that tore at his clothing and his hair. He was grateful Kavan had returned his cloak, for it kept him from being soaked through in the first few minutes of his trek across the city. Venturing between awnings and alley overhangs, dashing across streets dark with storm-doused lamps, Bhen began a tedious night of searching one headstone after another for the name Kavan had given him. With a handlight to illuminate his way, his cloak held closed at his throat by his free hand, and an attempt to regulate his body temperature the way Tíbhyan was teaching him, Bhen was thankful that the storm kept everyone else indoors. No one saw the tiny light bobbing between grave markers. No one saw the lone figure creeping through the burial yard in the middle of the night.

It would certainly have raised questions if they had.

As was common in many Elyri cemeteries, the dead were clustered together by the time of their passing, making the task of locating individuals a little simpler. The search was further simplified by plague victims having been interred at the far side of the plot as if to contain the contagion that had killed them. While there were few deaths by old age, a city the size of Clarys meant there had been many plague deaths, the number of dead on any given day occasionally high enough to require mass graves to contain them. There was no way of knowing whether the woman Kavan sought might have been buried amongst the masses or in her own plot, but Kavan believed she would have a private marker, and thus Bhen searched with that in mind.

It was dawn, hints of light clawing through thinning storm clouds, when he found what Kavan hoped for, and Bhen committed the few facts on the marker to memory. The dates, the odd symbol beneath her name, the single other name on the stone, none of it meant anything to Bhen when he left the cemetery and sought a tavern or inn open at this early hour at which he might be able to find warmth and a fire to dry himself.

Worried for his family, for Kavan, though told not to return too early in the morning, not to return until he had followed each lead to its end, Bhen sat near the fire, ignoring the chill in his bones and praying that what he had found would be enough for Kavan, enough to free him. He did not see how it could, but he would follow that last name to wherever it led, find everything he could before returning with his information, and trust that Kavan would be safe and know what to do with whatever he found. Bhen had few doubts about what action he would take if the man, and the rest of his kin, were harmed during his absence.

"Alty."

Caol felt his skin crawl as a stranger, someone whose voice he did not recognize, called him by a name few would use. This was not one of his recruits. Knowing most of Rhidam's Association members at least in passing, he was certain without getting closer that this was not one of them. He could not place the accent; there was a trace of Cordashian in the low, nasal voice, a trace of Cíbhóló influence, and something else Caol was not familiar with. It made him curious, but not curious enough to face the approaching man or give up the warm apple brandy cupped between his hands.

He did, however, remain vigilant to avoid any attempt on his life, should the stranger make one.

"Depends."

"On what?" The stranger waved to the barkeep and signaled for the same drink Caol had. For some reason, it made Caol frown.

"Who's asking," was his reply, casually shifting his body to the left to put space between them.

"Anri."

It took effort not to face the man or say something inappropriate that might get him killed. It took even greater effort not to pull his knife and kill the man there at the bar. The name might have been a coincidence; Anri was a common enough name, particularly in the northwestern corners of Enesfel across the border into Cordash. But what other Anri would know the name Alty, might recognize him, might be looking for him?

He stole a glance sideways and caught the face in profile as the man stared into his cup, or perhaps at the hand on the counter and what lay beneath it. Though his nose had a hawkish, beaklike shape, there was nothing else remarkable about his profile. The nose, however, was proof enough. He had seen the images Kavan had shared, those that Ártur had drawn, a man's face full-on and in profile, and he had no doubts that the shudder that ran down his spine was a result of standing elbow to elbow with one of the primary sources of Enesfel's heartache.

The man who had, in all likelihood, taken Prince Muir's life.

The stranger, shorter than Caol expected, older as well if the glimpse of grey at his temples and the back of his neck were any indicators, seemed not to notice the shudders or Caol's stolen glance. He slid the parchment beneath his hand across the bar towards Caol and said, "Tonight," before emptying his glass and swaggering out of the tavern into the first traces of daylight.

Caol shuddered again and put his hand over the page. "Tonight then," he murmured at the tail end of an inhaled breath. It was too soon to kill him perhaps, but Caol was a step closer to that moment, and sorely tempted to take the next opportunity that presented itself.

❧*❧

Kavan did not sleep, nor did his captors as they watched over him, expecting an escape attempt or some sort of mysterious, possibly deadly, action from the man behind the bars. Had he chosen to, Kavan knew he could slip past them without notice, but if the k'phóredhet had already underhandedly sanctioned the harassment of his family, Kavan would not risk their lives or freedom or positions within the Faith by doing anything to draw further attention to them.

As long as the storm raged, it was unlikely the last candidate would reach Clarys, nor would the citizens of Clarys be likely to attend any period of questioning as they avoided the worst of the storm. Thus the sequester would not yet begin. Bhen should have time to find details that might provide answers, and the bard would decide what course of action he should take. Whatever his choice, this humiliating arrest had brought him to a conclusion that he had wrestled with since the insult of heresy was first hurled at him. Bhryell was home, safe for his family, and now seemingly turning to support him as well. But the charge of heresy was a serious one, and Kavan did not want to live beneath that shadow. Nor was Rhidam a safe place for the children to be, not while the likes of Anri Heward and k'gdhededhá Claide poisoned the people's minds. His family would have to settle elsewhere until the threats were passed.

There were two obvious choices, but he did not know which he would make.

He felt the warming air on his skin, telling him that morning had arrived, a morning free of storm clouds and falling snow. Though he could see daybreak on the southern face of the building where the sun peeped through narrow windows, the languid speed of pink and purple clouds told him that the worst of the storm was passing, or else they had reached a lull in the maelstrom. The worst of the east-traveling storm might be over Clarys but it would not last long, a thought more troubling than his predicament.

The lómesté door creaked open and Sámel's wife and two other young women entered with a covered tray, a basket, and a clay pitcher. The guards perked up at the smell of fresh bread, but the women did no more than glance at them as they approached the cell and gave their offerings to Kavan through the bars. The soldiers could not deny their captive food, and could not complain about the actions of a woman they had threatened the night before, but they frowned and muttered amongst themselves hungrily.

Someone else entered with fresh clothing, a grey robe, the color St. Kóráhm most often wore when he appeared, and then another came to offer the use of a battered, but usable, Cliáthan harp. Each time the door opened, Kavan could see a growing gathering of townsfolk outside, a crowd that stretched entirely around the building as he could see their shadowy shapes through the rough frosted glass windows. They were a peaceful assembly, none raising their voices to offer challenge or threat, and when bhydáni Tíbhyan arrived, escorted inside because it was too cold for him to remain in the wind on frail legs that barely permitted standing, Kavan understood that each of those people, whoever they were, however many were present, were there to support him

"Leave the door open," the ancient man ordered. Dutifully, the captain obeyed though he would have preferred to leave in place that barrier between them and the crowd outside. He had never arrested a man on a heresy charge before, had never, in truth, arrested any man, and he had never heard of such a public display of support except in the old stories of saints and holy men. He remained outwardly unruffled, but he could see in the faces of his men that they were beginning to feel as uncomfortable with this situation as he did.

"Bless you for coming, Tíbhyan," Kavan murmured when the man was near enough to clasp his hands. "You did not need to…"

"And be one of the few in Bhryell not to come?" the sage scoffed with a sharp look at the soldiers.

"There are so many?"

"The young ones…Bhen's age and younger…and I tell you a secret…" He leaned closer, his walking stick precariously supporting his poorly distributed weight. He did not whisper and made no effort to keep his words from being heard by the guards. "Even some of your peers…and your elders…have been swayed of late…although few will admit to it." He grinned and gestured to the harp. "It was the best we could do on short notice…we did not want to risk yours. Please…play for us. Show these men…the world…who you are."

Who he was. Kavan stared at his teacher, mentor, and friend for several moments as he pondered that question…who he was. He realized he did not feel like he knew the answer anymore. A teacher, a father…a politician and advisor. ágdháni and miracle worker. The descendant of a saint, distant kin of an evil man, a seeker of the truth, and a friend. But was he an innocent man?

At the core, at the center of his soul in the place he had first tapped into at the age of three, he was a musician. A harper, a singer, a composer…and none of those pastimes he had been able to enjoy or share, since leaving Rhidam several weeks ago. Who he was, was the White Bard of Bhryell. Who he was, was music.

With the harp in his hands, quickly tuned to his satisfaction, he gave the villagers of Bhryell a gift he had not shared with them in years...since he had been a much younger man. The gift of himself.

❧*❧

The Hes Dhágdhuán bells tolled a single loud peeling tone and then fell silent. Hwensen hung his head and wrung his hands. Kavan was nowhere to be found...and Hwensen did not dare to share what he had learned with anyone else. Was it news that could halt the elections? He could not say. Kavan might know, and thanks to Hwensen's foolishness, he had turned his back on the Faith, left a killer to go unpunished. Elyriá deserved what they got from this election, for she had turned against the one man who might be able to sway the course of history.

The period of questioning was foregone. The doors of Hes Dhágdhuán were locked and sealed. The curtains that shuttered the windows were closed to prevent any from seeing within. The sequester of the gdhededhá had begun without questioning or interference from the citizens of Bhryell. Kavan was out of time.

❧*❧

The three Elyri before her, none of whom had ever met the High Mother, were tongue-tied even though gdhededhá Bhílári, at least, had seen the woman in passing many times. Seeing her now, however, near enough to touch, was different than seeing her across a room crowded with gdhededhá and dignitaries. The young man who had come on Kavan's behalf, while not nervous in the woman's presence, was at a loss for what to say or how to act, never having learned the proper protocol for approaching the Kyne. And Dháná, despite being distant kin by marriage, had met no one of more significance in Elyriá than Bhílári; even her intentions to save the man she had raised as her child could not untangle her voice.

Wortham, however, the only Teren in the room, had no such difficulty. He knew protocol and etiquette, having begun his years of training and service to the Dilyns on Káliel and having served the Lachlans and Lord Cliáth for the majority of his life. But, etiquette be damned. The man he would lay down his life for before any other needed help, and if the Queen of Elyriá could not help, or would not, Wortham was prepared to resort to any form of violence necessary to set him free…no matter how Kavan might feel about such an act.

"Your Majesty," he said, bowing in respect but not hesitating, now that they were alone. "We have come on behalf of Kavan Cliáth…who is in dire need of your aid."

The woman looked from the dark-haired speaker to the one face in the room she vaguely recognized. Whether she knew him or not, she recognized the robes of office, and that was good enough. "gdhededhá? Is this true? Is Kavan in trouble?"

"Aye…it is," Bhílári squeaked. "The k'phóredhet has arrested him on the charge of…"

"Heresy…I know," she sighed.

"Kavan is no heretic!" When she turned a perplexed eye on him, Wortham gave another half-bow and muttered. "Captain Wortham Delamo, Your Majesty. He is my lord and friend; I have served him for decades. He is no heretic. I demand he be released at once."

"I have no authority over the Faith."

Dháná dropped to her knees at the Kyne's feet. "I beg you, kinswoman; whatever he is, whatever he may have said or done that is in question…he is no heretic. He is the purest man I know."

"Kinswoman?"

Head still bowed, Dháná replied, "Dháná MacLyr, Kyne, formerly Bhostári, formerly Bhíncári…"

Mórne smiled and pulled Dhána to her feet. "Welcome to Clarys, daughter, to my home." Their kinship was several generations removed, but the Kyne knew the name Bhostári.

"They tried to arrest us...they tried to take his home..." Wortham growled. "Can you help him? Will you?"

Had it been anyone else, any of her advisors, her usual petitioners, or even her close kin, Mórne would have little tolerance for such impudence. But what she heard in Wortham's voice, saw on his bearlike face, was a depth of devotion and love for the man he hoped to save that he could not control himself and she found she could not be angry with him. Few individuals gained that sort of devotion from another; she doubted she had such devotees.

"I wish I could, Captain." Frustration caused her to sigh and step away towards the decanters on the counter nearby. "I will address the matters of improper arrest and property confiscation with those who dared order such a thing. But I have shielded him from the tribunal as much as I am able. My influence stops at the náós doors, unless they choose to accept it...outside of matters of the laws governing our people. More and more of late the k'phóredhet does not wish to accept my council on matters concerning Kavan. And now they and the gdhededhá are sequestered..."

"They skipped the examination?" Bhílári's face blanched. "But there is a murderer amongst them still..."

"So Kavan believes. I do not know if it is true or..."

"You know he is guiltless..."

"Yes, Captain. Of course, I know he is. Kavan is too wise...too cautious...too shrewd...and too benevolent to wish death on a man...even if that man has made many threats against him over the years. As I said, however, I cannot gain access to the chamber except under the most extreme circumstances, and only those within can lift the arrest order. The best I can do is write a command letter for you to deliver to the arresting officers; perhaps that will be enough to sway them. I will do that at once so that you may return…and I pray k'Ádhá will grant him one of the miracles I have heard tell of, for I fear no one else can protect him."

Wortham's face darkened and his arms crossed over his chest as he muttered, "I can."

❧*❦

Bhen stepped into the náós he had known his entire life, not knowing what he expected to find after the long wet night and exhausting day he had spent scouring Clarys. He still felt cold, his hair was disheveled from his efforts to dry it with his fingertips, and his clothes were wet in some places, muddy in others. He was eager to be free of them. First, however, he had information to depart, although to whom he was not certain. gdhededhá Bhílári was not in the Gathering Hall or the thóres, and the other three gdhededhá who served with him had not seen him since early morning when it was said he, Dháná, Captain Delamo and the spokesman of the Elyri youth had gone to Clarys to petition the High Mother on Kavan's behalf. The good news that provided, however, was that Kavan was still in Bhryell, held in the lómesté awaiting an improvement in weather to travel by land to Clarys. That the soldiers had chosen not to use the Gates, where they might not be able to control the bard's input of power, meant they would have a long journey ahead, and none would want to make that journey on foot in foul weather. They would need horses, supplies, warm clothing…things Bhryell's citizens were reluctant to provide.

Outside the náós, the sun was sinking to the west, over the Llaethlágárá, quickly bringing darkness. There were stars above, no hint of clouds, and the ground, while muddy and damp in places, was dry enough that it was likely the soldiers would depart in the morning, even without Bhryell's aid. Bhen frowned, wondering if

there was any way he could prevent this from going any further as he
trudged towards the building where the bard was being held…

…a building surrounded by men and women Bhen knew,
standing, sitting, or dancing to the chiming of harp strings he could
hear from within the walls ahead. Many had traveling supplies with
them as if they were prepared to follow the soldiers, and Kavan, all
the way to Clarys to speak on the bard's behalf if they had to.

It was a sight Bhen looked forward to witnessing if the trip
became unavoidable. Perhaps he would join them.

No one held him back as he wheedled his way to the open door
and descended the short staircase into the lómesté where some of
Kavan's kin, including Ártur and Syl, were gathered along with
Tíbhyan and the guards, to listen to the bard play on one of the most
decrepit looking quarterscale harps Bhen had ever seen. But it was a
Cliáthan, and the visual inferiority of the instrument did not affect
the tonal quality of the notes Kavan played, nor did it prevent Kavan
from drawing beauty out of its strings. Bhen considered briefly
bringing a better harp but decided against interrupting what appeared
to have been going on long before his arrival.

Ártur was trying to engage the captain in negotiation for Kavan's
freedom on Queen Diona's behalf, and though the armed man's
expression was sympathetic, he repeatedly shook his head to the
healer's arguments. Wortham was nearest the cell as if attempting to
squeeze through the bars, with Bhyrhán Bhíncári beside him, while
Tíbhyan had been given a bench against the wall nearest the cell,
which he currently shared with Sóbhán. Propped against the wall
behind him and the cell bars to his right, the bhydáni rocked his head
side to side in time to the music with his eyes closed and one hand
wrapped around the boy's. Neither made any effort to hide music-
borne sentiment nor did anyone else.

For this was no mere music coming from the man poised cross-
legged on a stool in the confines of a cell. This was the story of a life,

told through the passion of music, a life that, for all of the valleys and peaks, was music itself. Bhen felt it as the charged air pricked his skin, raising the hair on his scalp, causing him to shiver. He could see it in the bliss and tears and anguish that rolled like storm waves across Wortham's face and in the green of Kavan's eyes when their gazes met. There was much Bhen wanted to say, news and regrets and oaths, but he dared not speak. This was not his time. This was Kavan's. A final testament, perhaps, before his fate was sealed.

That thought made Bhen weep, and by the time he reached Wortham's side, progress forward impeded by the bars between him and Kavan, every defense he had ever learned was down, his soul laid bare to his kinsmen for the reading, the cleansing, the charging. Such a man, he thought, hands wrapped around the metal bars as if he could break them, should not be held like this.

☙*❧

His Association recruits, plus an additional five men who had avoided the Coryllien purge, were scattered and hidden around the abandoned shop where Heward's message had specified they were to meet. Heward might know the recruits were there and might not come in because of it, but Caol had not been told to be there alone and he was not willing to blindly meet with a man he had every reason to distrust...and every reason to hate. Caol was not taking unnecessary risks this close to obtaining his objective.

Upon arrival, he slunk through every charred, dilapidated room in the place. He made his way up the collapsing, burned-out stairs to the second story and the attic, and ruled out any presence of a basement, assuring himself that he was alone except for his own people. He crouched, backed into a corner where he could see both entrances, the shattered and missing remains of a window, anywhere a threat might enter. He listened as he silently counted off each passing minute until a lone figure entered the building without exhibiting the slightest trace of fear. Once inside, the other man lowered the hood of his cloak, drew off his gloves, and headed directly towards the man in the shadows.

"You're good," he said after a glance around them. "Cautious, thorough, discreet…efficient. Not the buffoon Layton was…"

Caol snorted, instinct telling him that he had been watched the entire time and that Heward knew about the men hidden around them. He did not think Layton had been that bad as a leader, given the sort of men he had to work with.

Heward, however, did not mention the others. "He told you, didn't he? That I would be in touch?"

"Yes."

Heward nodded approvingly." "Good…then he wasn't all bad. You realize there is no other viable replacement for him? Foolish errors and misfortune have cut our numbers…but we can rebuild, can't we?" His stare was one of a man not expecting a verbal answer but rather that of a man who expected Caol to do precisely what he said. It was an order, not a question. "Despite the setbacks, there are many in Enesfel who believe as we do…you can find them?"

"I've got more than a dozen," Caol muttered with a shrug, hoping to sound indignant at the suggestion that he might be incapable of something like recruiting new members.

"Indeed? Good." Smiling, Heward toyed with the gloves in his soft hands. Not a man, judged Caol, to have ever done much physical labor beyond riding a horse. If he was a nobleman, why was he so difficult to track down?

Heward turned his back to Caol, took a single step away, hesitating before pacing two steps left, four steps to the right, as if seeking something, and then stepped back to where he had been standing. A test, Caol guessed, to see if he would attack. Any trained, hired, assassin could have used those moments to strike without hesitation. But Caol believed Heward was waiting for such an attack, waiting to see what sort of man Caol was…if he could be trusted. Caol hoped, by not twitching or sidestepping away, instead waiting for Heward to continue, that he had proven trustworthy enough.

"There is a warehouse northeast of the river, near the first on Tanner's Row."

"I know it." Caol knew that first tanner to be Association, knew the small warehouse was used in the drying and preparation of skins and leather. It was a foul-smelling place, as tanneries were, but it would be empty now as the structure was damaged in the fire and the man had taken his business elsewhere for the time being. Curious as to the tanner's connection to Heward and the Corylliens, or if there was one, as that would again raise questions about the reliability of the Association as his informants, Caol made a mental note to seek out the man in the morning and ask questions.

"Bring those you can there tomorrow eve. Same hour. I would like to see what quality of man you can bring…gauge what we might accomplish next. Before that foolish attempt on the castle…"

"That was not my doing," Caol pointed out defensively. "Nor was it Layton's."

"I know…but it does not matter. What's done is done. We were close…so we begin again…and you will help me."

Watching Heward put his gloves back on, Caol mumbled, "I'll do what I can."

Heward smirked and added, "I am counting on it, Alty," before sauntering out of the building, his back once more to Caol. If he had believed he could have gotten the knife from his boot without notice, Caol would have thrown it, not caring for once about honor in the face of the Association. Caol had not been officially Association in years, nor did he intend to return to their rules of engagement. Not when the last time he had followed them had resulted in the death of King Arlan's eldest son and nearly in the death of his own.

He wondered, after Heward's shadow disappeared and he was satisfied that the man was long gone, if he could get his hand on one of the Coryllien daggers before his next meeting with Heward. That would be the ideal executioner's tool for this vile man.

❧*❧

The setting sun had pulled the temperatures down to freezing in the heart of Bhryell. Many of those outdoors built fires to warm themselves, while others gradually migrated into the lómesté for what warmth the small hearth and the press of other bodies could offer. Not many Elyri were trained to regulate their body's as Kavan could, and of those who could do it, fewer still chose to practice the skill. With the door and some of the windows open, the lómesté would have been little warmer than outdoors, but the heat of the multitude of bodies helped warm the room. As people pressed indoors, the efforts to maintain the hearth fire was abandoned as the soldiers could not get out of the building through the press of villagers to retrieve more wood. If they had tried, the captain was certain they would not have been able to get back inside.

The captain hoped that nightfall would mean the departure of the throng, but few chose to leave and the captain had neither the manpower nor the authority to force them out. How he could get the bard from the cell to travel towards Clarys come morning was a problem he had yet to solve. Kavan could command them to go home, and perhaps they would listen, but the bard had not surrendered the harp, or the music, since he had started playing that morning. Expecting the man's fingers to grow weary or sore, the captain wearily relaxed into the beauty of the current melody as he attempted to design a plan for departure.

As soon as the villagers slept, perhaps. Or while they ate. He could resort to extortion, but as outnumbered as he and his men were, his threats would be hollow and unable to be enforced. There was no guarantee that Kavan would cooperate to disperse his followers to make the captain's job easier.

If he was in the bard's place, the captain knew he would be disinclined to do so.

The dark-haired boy who kept vigil with the bhydáni had aided in lighting fresh candles and the crowd in the building was thicker than before. Even if they eventually slept, getting Kavan out of the cell unnoticed and sneaking past them would be impossible. And Kavan showed no sign of laying down the harp to sleep.

The captain muttered, crossed his arms, and relieved the two men posted to duty at the cell's door earlier in the day. Someone should eat and rest since the captain could not. Neither went far, as there was nowhere for them to go. The men reluctantly set aside their hunger and turned instead to listening to the music their prisoner provided, as enraptured by it as everyone else. The captain stubbornly refused to give the music his full attention, to allow himself to enjoy it. Someone had to remain clearheaded and something in that music seemed to muddle the focus of everyone who heard it. If he thought he could do it without starting a riot, the captain would have demanded the bard be silent.

Back to the cell, choosing not to look at the bard, the captain kept watch with his arms folded over his chest, his thoughts centered on the problem of tomorrow's departure. He had the writ from Kyne, brought earlier by Captain Delamo and the others, but the conflicting request left him more determined to hold to his orders and leave the clash of power to those who directed him and the High Mother. He was a simple man. He did not want to be caught in a dispute between the Faith leaders and the Kyne, though he realized inevitably that was where he already was.

Minutes later, he lifted his head and blinked. Had he fallen asleep, he wondered, aware of an unexpected change in the air, in the mood around him. Someone else was in the lómesté, someone with a commanding presence. He craned his neck to see beyond the crowd towards the open door, but he could see nothing unusual, no parting of the crowd or a coming together as if someone had pushed their way through. Frowning, he noted that the focus on Kavan had shifted, the expressions in the room having changed in subtle ways. He frowned, aware of something behind him that made his shoulders tickle and tense, and slowly he turned, his sword drawn.

The bard still soothed the harp strings into a new melody that, to the captain, sounded like a prayer or supplication. The cell door was still closed and locked. None of those on the outside of the cell had shifted position, telling the captain that if he had slept, it had been no more than a single moment. Kavan's eyes were closed, his posture relaxed, his hands caressing as though without thought across the brass strings. Behind the bard, however, the solid form of a man in an identical grey robe stood with fire-scarred hands on Kavan's shoulders. A man with waves of auburn hair, who sported marks of a fire's bite up his neck as well. A man who stared at the captain with wistfulness and disappointment.

A man who, after years of service in the halls of Hes Dhágdhuán, the captain recognized.

"Kóráhm."

The captain's voice barely rose above the music, but everyone in the room heard him, and those who were not looking already looked at him now.

Kavan had felt the building of power, the pleasant increase of warmth that marked the arrival of the Saint. This was not the first time the Saint had come when he was in trouble, and his presence within the cell, within the music was welcome. Until the captain spoke the saint's name, however, Kavan was not aware that others in the room could see him. Why should they, when Kóráhm was not the sort to appear in such a way to so many. It had not been his way in the entire time Kavan had known him.

The captain of the guard genuflected, staring, feeling the rush of something tight within his chest. Emotions he had pushed away all day, brought to the fore by the music the bard continued to play, crashed over him. The two men glowed, not in his imagination but in full view of others for they saw it too…a pale silver shimmer as though they were illuminated by the moon on a starless night. He opened his mouth to offer greetings, to question how the Saint had come to be in that cell. Not by key, not by another man's hand. Not by any mortal means the captain could devise or understand.

But this was Saint Kóráhm…Heretic Kóráhm. This was a man centuries dead, appearing to the masses here in the insignificant town of Bhryell. This was one who showed favoritism to the man the captain had been sent to deliver for the sentencing of heresy. A man, he decided suddenly, who deserved better than excommunication. If a man was visited by a saint, one who, if he were a heretic, should not have been able to appear before them, did that not speak highly of Kavan's character?

This was no demon, no devil. Such things did not take human shape. Not in Elyri legend at least. Not according to the annals of the Faith by which the captain conducted his life and on whose precepts he had been commanded to serve and obey.

Head swimming, full of questions and no answers, heart full of heavy, unexpected emotion, the captain wiped tears from his cheeks, choked on his words, and sank to his knees.

&Chapter 27-&

"Y̲ou're…"

The surprised word was followed by the clatter of a metal tray and cup on a stone floor worn smooth by centuries of feet passing back and forth from the kitchen to the rest of the castle. The jangle was followed by a louder crash as two startled kitchen cats stalking the counter for abandoned morsels leaped to the floor, knocking over the mopping pail in the process. The blonde prince looked up from the meal he had scavenged to stare at the last person he expected to see in the castle kitchen at this ungodly hour.

Fetching his own food was not something the King was known for. If hungry, he sent someone to the kitchen to bring something to him no matter the hour. Nor was the normally heavy sleeper prone to insomnia.

Enough days had passed, Kjell hoped, that Merkar had gotten past his paranoia and was willing to accept his brother back from hiding. Kjell had been safe, skulking wraithlike from unused room to unused room, sneaking into the kitchen at night after the servants were allowed to eat, listening in secret passages to the conversations of staff, courtiers, and family alike to keep abreast of the atmosphere in Neth since Glucke's death. The purge of soldiers and advisors ended quickly with the death of Fraen. True to his word, Captain Stone found access to the King, spoke his evidence of Fraen's intent to usurp the throne based on items and documents found in the man's quarters. Maybe the proof found against Fraen had been factual. Maybe it had been planted. Whatever the case, it had done the trick. Outraged that Fraen's accusations had led to Kjell's disappearance, Merkar had the man thrown into the bear pit to be torn to shreds by the ravenous animal he kept there and the King doubled his efforts to find his brother.

Kjell could have come out of hiding sooner…but he wanted to be sure of his safety first.

There were whispers hinting at lingering suspicion in the King's mind about Kjell, rumor enough to keep the prince in the shadows. Often the King forgot such reports within days, his love of drink erasing from his mind matters he deemed trivial. But rumors of treason were prone to sticking, burrowing like a mole in his brain. With nothing more than the gossip of servants to judge by, however, Kjell could not be certain if the King honestly perceived him to be a threat or if the anecdote was speculation circulating amongst the bored staff based on some offhanded comment the Merkar had made. Tomorrow, at dawn, Kjell had intended to take the risk, to come out of hiding and confront his brother, playing the innocent fool yet again. He wagered if he emerged without being hunted and found, he would look less guilty and the accusations against him would be put to rest. He had not forgotten Glucke's connection to the man named Heward, nor had he forgotten that his brother might be involved as well, and he needed to send an update to Enesfel soon. He could not learn the truth if he continued to lurk in the shadows.

"Greetings, brother," the prince chirped, quickly adopting his happy-go-lucky voice and smile as he resumed devouring the morsels of bread, roast pork, and sliced apple he had found.

"Where have you been?"

"Been? Here." Blinking as he wiped his fingers on the grimy cloth he held, Kjell continued innocently, "Where else would I be?"

"Here where? We have been looking for you!"

"In my room…mostly." Not mostly, but he had been there, creeping in and out for fresh clothing, his dagger, sword, and grooming supplies.

"You haven't been to meals…"

The prince shrugged. "You were mad at me…everyone said you were…so I stayed away."

"Everyone?"

There was menace in the King's step forward. The prince felt it and for once took a sidestep backward, putting his dirty platter into the washbasin, avoiding the spilled mop water. He had never exhibited fear of Merkar, but having expressed fear at his brother's anger now, if the King did read his actions as fear, Kjell did not think a sidestep would be surprising. "Servants, soldiers…"

"Who?"

The King wanted names, people he could blame for not finding Kjell when he had ordered it done. As there was no way Kjell would condemn the innocent, knowing what sort of retaliation the King was likely to take against them, Kjell shrugged.

"I don't know. I was hiding…heard their voices…"

"Who?"

The King would not back down until he had a name; instead of taking another step back, which would have pinned him against the counter, Kjell grabbed at the first name that came to mind. "Fraen…"

"Fraen is dead," Merkar snorted glibly, the wave of his hand making him totter to the side, a sure sign, in addition to his bellicosity, that the King was intoxicated, as was frequently the case with no wars to fight and no uprisings or chaos in his kingdom to quell. Kjell imagined that the hours after Glucke's death were the first sober ones Merkar had experienced since the loss of southern Neth to Enesfel and the aftermath of reinforcing the kingdom.

"He is?"

"Who else?"

Kjell shook his head and this time held his ground. He was within striking distance, but still had the option of darting to the side rather than coming to blows with his older brother. The King, further agitated by Kjell's silence, leaned forward and hissed, "Tell me…or it will be you in the bear pit."

"I am not afraid of you."

"Tell me!"

It was the first time Kjell had stood up to his brother's belligerence, his narrowed blue eyes a mirror to Merkar's expression. Infuriated, as much by Kjell defiance as by his refusal to give the names he wanted, the King swung, perhaps out of anger or fear, aiming at the younger man's jaw. Kjell ducked sideways, dodging the blow. Unsteady from drink and unbalanced by the awkward swing, Merkar slipped in the spilled water and fell backward. Though the prince grabbed his wrist, the weight of the King's round physique and the precarious angles at which they stood caused Kjell's grip to fail. There were two cracks, one as the king's head struck the wooden preparation table in the center of the room and another as he crumpled heavily to the floor.

The castle kitchen staff, having heard the King's thundering demands in the kitchen, particularly the final words and bellow of anger, scurried in as the King hit the floor. Each of the four saw enough to believe that the prince had tried to prevent the fall, the King's wrist slipping out of Kjell's hand as the prince stumbled backward against the opposite counter when the King lost his footing. They looked at one another fearfully, concerned about who would be held responsible for the spilled water that would likely, ultimately, be blamed for the monarch's fall.

Kjell, quickly assessing the appearance of the situation, not knowing how much the servants had seen or heard or what they might confess during an inquest, fell to his knees at his brother's side with an outburst of tears, feeling for signs of life as he cried, "Someone fetch a physician!" It was too late for one, he knew. Blood pooled beneath the King's head and grey-blue eyes were already glazing over as breath eased from Merkar's lungs.

For once in his life, Prince Kjell was the safest he had ever been. For what might have been the first time in his family's long history, a de Corrmick king had not been murdered by another for the throne.

๛*๛

If Kóráhm was aware of the others in the room, if he knew they could see him, he did not acknowledge them, not even Wortham whom he had conversed with before. His hands never lifted from the bard's shoulders, and when his gaze left the man before him, it shifted to the captain of the guard. No words were spoken, not one man or woman within the lómesté hall made a sound as music continued to fill the crowded space and tumble through the open door into Bhryell's streets. There was a collectively held breath when the captain climbed to his feet and slowly, as if mesmerized or controlled by an external force, fumbled with the key to unlock the cell door. He entered and stood speechless in front of Kavan, his gaze shifting back and forth between the bard and the saint. Kavan did not raise his head or his gaze, only uttered a small sigh as one of the hands on his shoulders was placed on the captain's instead. A single touch, lasting only a moment, and Kóráhm was gone.

Kavan lifted his head to meet the captain's awestruck expression. "Please…rise…lásánai…you are free to leave…"

"My lord?" Kavan heard the words, knew what the man meant and why he said them, but he was afraid to believe them.

"No man thus blessed deserves the fate and sentence awaiting you if I take you to Clarys. You are no heretic, sir. I will swear that with my life. I will not damn my soul by delivering you to injustice. We were never here," he looked at each of his men scattered about the room. "You were never here…none of this…" He shook his head. It might be a lie, but better that blemish on his soul than the darker stain Kavan's mistreatment would be. "You are free."

The music ceased and the harp was set on the floor, leaning against the stool where he sat. "What is your name?" Kavan asked as he stiffly rose to his feet. Knowing the captain's name had not seemed important or necessary before.

"Raenár Magk."

"Captain Magk…I thank you." He took the man's hand firmly with gratitude and bowed. "I shall remember your name…and what you have done for me and my family."

"Likewise, my lord. I do not know what your path is…but if we meet again, if there is anything I might do for you…"

"I am here for you as well, Captain."

Tears glistened at the edges of Captain Magk's lashes but he bowed with a smile rather than letting them fall. It was a sentiment he did not expect to hear from a man he had tried to arrest, but it served to strengthen the captain's conviction in his choice of actions. A saint had vouched for Kavan Cliáth. Captain Magk had the only evidence of innocence he needed.

Heward, cloaked in brown, face hidden from the men gathered in the abandoned structure, circled them slowly, studying each from head to toe. What criteria he was judging them by, Caol could not guess. Height? Weight? Age? Some hint of Elyri in the blood or something else that might make them unsuitable for the duties he would give? Or was he seeking some quality that might result in a special assignment for one or all of them? Caol saw nothing about any of them that should disqualify them from the sort of criminal endeavors Heward might ask them to undertake, and none were particularly noteworthy individuals, but Caol did not have a good understanding of Heward and could not gauge what he was thinking.

There was someone else, a smaller figure, leaner and lighter, too short to be gdhededhá Claide, who remained by the door, arms crossed as though daring anyone to leave before Heward dismissed them. Caol believed it to be a woman without seeing features masked beneath a robe identical to Heward's in color and cut. That was the person on whom Caol focused, though without looking directly at them. That person was an unknown, and Caol did not like unknowns. He had heard Layton once speak of another, someone possibly further up the chain of Coryllien command, someone General Agis had once spoken of as well, a woman who inspired another Cíbhóló to murder innocent children and deliver their heads, limbs, and torsos to King Hagan. Caol wondered if this was that person, that same woman, but without seeing inside the hood, without seeing the person's hands, he could not even accurately judge their gender.

What he could judge was the level of discomfort he felt in that person's presence. It was unsettling enough to keep him as near to Heward as he was able to be to keep distance between them. He did not trust Heward, but he trusted the stranger even less.

Heward stopped to stare into the face of the lightly bearded red-haired man at the end of the line of recruits and Caol held his breath. He knew nothing about the man except that he had come highly recommended by his daughter…and had been the one to take him to Clarys when Ártur could not do so. There had been no time or opportunity to speak with the stranger before coming to this place but he had faith in his daughter's recommendation. As with before, Heward neither shook the man's hand nor asked questions or names, maintaining a wall of anonymity between himself and the recruits that Caol understood to be a wise precaution. Heward might be many things, but he was neither foolish nor stupid. He had remained alive and avoided capture this far by remaining anonymous. None of the recruits could claim to have seen him, save for Caol, and Heward could not claim to have any knowledge of these recruits should he be captured. But he believed Heward would slip up, sooner or later. He planned to be there when it happened, a risk he imagined Heward was aware of.

Anri ceased his perusal and returned to where Caol stood about halfway between them and the stranger in the doorway. "I will contact you soon with instructions. Do nothing before then...except gather more if you can. This war is not over yet."

It will be soon, Caol thought with a nod. Just not soon enough.

It was dawn before Kavan picked his way through the crowd gathered in his support and arrived at the front door of Tíbhyan's home. It was the old sage's presence on his arm, supported on the other side by Wortham and Bhen, that allowed them to pass through the throng with little hindrance, but Kavan felt obligated to repay these people who had given much of themselves on his behalf. Most were younger, not those who had treated him as an outcast while growing up. Some were contemporaries who had shunned him as a child, sometimes at the prodding of their elders, but, for some reason, were now beginning to view him differently. Some of his elders were beginning to display a change of heart as well, men and women who had deemed his talent cute and precocious or who had been afraid of his early presentation of Power.

The people of Bhryell offered a degree of acceptance, support, and respect, and having craved those things most of his life, Kavan cherished what the villagers had given him.

Not, he knew, that they were treating him as any other man, for he could imagine no one else in the community, save Bhílári and perhaps the bhydáni, they might band together to protect or revere. To be counted one of that small number instead of being viewed as an outcast was an acceptable change. Perhaps, in time, he would feel at home and welcome in the town of his birth.

Wortham and Bhen left Tíbhyan's porch and returned to the bard's home together. The crowd was thick outside the ancient teacher's door, with people expecting Kavan to come where they might see him, speak to him, convince him to play yet another song. After several minutes of private exchange with his teacher, Kavan, in the form of a white dove, flew from the old man's rear door and made it home to find Ártur, Syl, Bhyrhán, and his aunt, cousin Sámel and his wife, and Bhen's brother Aleski gathered there. He embraced each one, a genuine gesture the weary bard rarely made, and then he collapsed into his favorite chair with Dhóri on his chest, delighting in the opportunity to hold the infant he feared he would not see again.

By the time Wortham and Bhen arrived, the morning meal was served. Wortham waited to eat and instead fed his friend so that Kavan did not have to rise or put down the boy. No one spoke, other than to ask if Kavan wanted anything, until the meal was complete.

"We will watch, allow you to rest," Bhen said. The ecclesiastical captain might have freed him, but there was no guarantee that the soldiers under his command would follow his unconventional order despite what they had witnessed. There was no assurance that they would refuse to take Kavan back into custody now that the crowd was out of the way. Bhen and Wortham had discussed the matter on their way to the house. After many hours awake, the bard likely needed to sleep, and they were prepared to ensure he had the chance.

Kavan shook his head. "I have duties to tend," he sighed. Though he had been awake for many hours, the music and Kóráhm's touch had revitalized his body, mind, and spirit, and he was ready to act. He had gained the evidence Bhen found in Clarys from Bhen's thoughts when the younger man had entered the lómesté, and while those tidbits were small, it gave Kavan the key he believed he needed to prove one man's guilt and free himself of the claims of murder. It meant returning to Clarys, where he knew the sequester had begun without the usual adherence to protocol. He needed to have every detail proven and perfect before interrupting that locked session.

"You need to rest," scolded Ártur, though everyone heard in his tone that he did not expect his cousin to heed his advice.

"I must…and I will…later. This is not the time. But I need you to do something for me…all of you."

Clutching Kavan's hand, Wortham said, "Anything, my lord."

"I am free…but the threat is not yet past. Accusations still hang over me, and when I go to Clarys, there is no guarantee what the outcome will be, whether I will be permitted to leave or not. Captain Magk may have shown leniency and sympathy, but whoever comes to Bhryell next is less likely to show mercy, and I might not be here to protect you. The people of Bhryell might but I do not wish to place anyone in harm's way."

"They would not dare…" began Dháná.

"They arrested kin to draw me out once. Each time I return it is drawing a tighter net of danger around you. The less reason I give them to come to Bhryell, the safer you and the others will be."

"What do you suggest? Do we return to Rhidam? Go to Káliel?" Wortham could think of nowhere else viable for them to flee, and he did not doubt that flight was what Kavan was suggesting.

"St. Kóráhm's." Kavan had thought the matter through during his hours of captivity and performance. Káliel was his other choice, but the Saint's hands on him had swayed Kavan's decision. The chellé was beyond the reach of the Clarys bureaucrats and beyond the chaos that plagued Rhidam. Alberni was likely the most Elyri-tolerant city in Enesfel, outside of Elyriá and with Kavan's home nearby, and passages and Gates connecting them, St. Kóráhm's seemed the ideal place for Kavan's family to be. "Wortham, I appoint you master of the Alberni estate…and none there will know or question a child with you and Zelenka. For a time, it will not be obvious he is Elyri. There are men in the estate and the chellé hábhai to guard you…you know them…and you have my permission to train more. If necessary, St. Kóráhm's is a fortress. You will be safe."

Dháná, her face sad, reached for Kavan's knee. "Tám will never agree to go, and we have the business to consider. I cannot leave."

"Nor shall I," Sámel added. The business was his life and this was his home. The Cliáthan center of harp making and family had existed in Bhryell as far back as the village's history stretched and considering relocating to Enesfel was madness. For those closest to Kavan, being dubbed mad did not matter. Wortham would follow Kavan anywhere. Kavan understood why others would not.

"And I must stay," murmured Bhen. "There are children to mentor." He grinned at Sóbhán but there was also young Llucás to train in the family craft. "But I will serve as the link to Bhryell; I can do that much for you, aendhá."

Bhyrhán put down the empty glass he had been toying with. "Whatever is to come, Kavan, you will have people throughout Elyriá who support you."

"And in Rhidam," promised Ártur, his grim expression souring with the thought that Kavan might not return from Clarys, that he might never return to Rhidam, but he understood both reasons. For the healer and his family, life would continue as it was. He did not expect his wife to take the children to Alberni when there was no indicator that they would be any safer there, though perhaps, in time, he and Kavan could convince her otherwise.

It was disturbing that his cousin faced excommunication when, to his knowledge and point of view, Kavan was the most righteous, moral man he knew outside of the gdhededhá. What did that say of the leaders of his Faith if they could easily excise the best example they had of what it meant to live in Faith?

He nodded his head, however, and offered his silent support for whatever decision his cousin made. "You know I am here for you, sínréc. And I will see to it that Sóbhán is safe wherever he is." The boy would want to continue his education, and though there was ample opportunity in Alberni, it was not the same as being with those he was accustomed to.

Accepting their decisions and support, Kavan bowed his head. Tám's still negative view of him might be enough to protect the rest of the family. Syl, he hoped, would have the Lachlan's protection to shadow her and her children even here in Bhryell.

"Then it is decided. Wortham, ready your things. Ártur will take you to Alberni. I will join you there when I may." He did not have to ask his cousin to do this. The healer would comply out of love and respect. It would take Kavan several minutes to write a letter to the Darys and to the acting head of St. Kóráhm's explaining the situation and what he asked of them both. Each knew Wortham from his many trips with Kavan to Alberni and Wortham had long ago been shown the catacomb passages between the estate house and the chellé. No one else knew of it, and Kavan intended it to stay that way.

Kavan handed Dhóri to his nurse, who nodded her nervous agreement to the plan, and after embracing Sóbhán and murmuring private words into his ear, beckoned Wortham and Bhyrhán upstairs to where the single gate was hidden. No one else followed although he knew many wanted to. None chose to believe this was farewell, seeing it instead as another temporary parting of ways, except for Sóbhán who tried stoically not to let his composure disintegrate as Kavan left him one more time.

"My lord?" Wortham knew Kavan well enough to know there was something else on the bard's mind, some other duty he was about to bestow, and he was ready for anything asked of him.

"I want you to find Captain Magk before he leaves Bhryell…and extend the invitation to St. Kóráhm's."

Anything but that.

"But…" he stammered, blinking in surprise.

"Whether his men back him, whether he can convince his superiors that nothing happened in Bhryell, that I was never in custody or escaped despite his efforts, he is a man at a crossroads, a man who will never be comfortable returning to the life he once led. The captain…any of his men…who wish to avoid the potentially negative repercussion of their actions…are welcome in Alberni. There is room in St. Kóráhm's…and the chellé and estate can use more men at arms. He might not accept the offer, but please present my request to him."

The six soldiers had remained at the lómesté to provide crowd control, although they doubted it would be needed. It was either that or start at once for Clarys and what awaited them there. None were eager to take that step towards destiny either.

"Aye," Wortham scowled. "I will do as you ask." He might not agree, but if Kavan felt the Elyri captain was trustworthy, Wortham would not question the offer again.

"Tell Bhen to extend my gratitude to Tíbhyan…and let him know where I have gone…what is happening." The bhydáni, his oldest friend, deserved better than a secondhand farewell, but Kavan felt he could spare no more time. He had to get to Clarys. With the sequester in session, he dared not risk it being so short a vote that he had no time to expose a murderer in their ranks.

"I shall."

"Bhyrhán…are you returning home?"

The other bard shook his head. "I travel to Clarys with you. My grandmother cannot give support in a more public way, but on her behalf, I can. I will go before the Tribunal with you if need be."

Having passed into his bedroom, Kavan graced his kin with a faint smile before sitting at his desk to pen the documents Wortham would need. "I pray it does not come to that, Bhyrhán. Help Wortham so he and the others will be ready to leave soon."

"If it does come to it," promised Wortham from the doorway, "I will free you. You have my word and my sword on that, Kavan."

Bhyrhán bowed and added, "Mine as well."

Kavan did not doubt that both men, and many others with them, would do precisely that.

❧*❦

"Healer MacLyr is not here yet."

Hearing footsteps enter the oratory, where he had chosen to wait, Owain glanced over his shoulder at Níkóá, a man who was, in many ways, so nearly a replica of the late Farrell Lachlan that to Owain there was no mistaking him for anything other than the late monarch's son. Seeing him the first time had been disconcerting, and he and the healer, the two in the keep to have known Farrell personally, spent many hours since reminiscing about the man they remembered. Farrell had been special to Owain, the one Lachlan in that past life to show support, affection, or sympathy; it made it easy to transfer that affection onto this man who came to the House at Kavan's recommendation. That Níkóá carried Elyri blood was of no consequence to Owain. Farrell had reveled in beauty. He had not cared about race, nationality, or creed. If he desired someone, in his court, his life, his bed, he had them. The women and men he had sought after and courted had been numerous and diverse.

"Are you in need of medical care?" Níkóá did not appear hurt or unwell, but looks could be deceptive. He was unaware of any other reason the soon-to-be-chamberlain might seek the healer. "I believe Rouvyn is with Gaelán…"

Níkóá shook his head as he reached the bench where Owain sat hunched with his elbows on his knees. "I just came from there. I thought he might be here." He studied the oratory around them, marveling at the warmth and welcome he felt, unlike any other place of prayer and worship he had been in. There were stains like blood on the carved figure of Dhágdhuán, a realistic effect that made Níkóá shiver without knowing the story behind the stains. He felt certain there was one. "Rouvyn is seeking him…not me…"

Lurching to his feet, Owain squawked, "Has something happened to Gaelán?"

"No, no change." That was a story Níkóá had learned from Asta, and it grieved him to think that the anti-Elyri violence had come down to brother against brother. "You are waiting for him as well?"

Owain relaxed, relieved to hear that Gaelán was no worse, although, he like many others, daily hoped for good news about the young man. "I am to travel to Fiara today…to share my intentions with my staff. I will return this evening if anyone needs me."

Sensing disquiet in the other man, Níkóá sat and murmured, "Your position will be here…when you are ready to return to it."

"I know, and I thank you for that." In truth, he was not certain he would return to this duty, short-lived as it had been, as his desire to raise his son and care for his stepdaughter had taken priority after Muir's death, but he valued the reassurance. "You can do this. If you have questions, you know where to find me, or Bhríd, or Kavan."

"The offer is appreciated." Even if he was fortunate to see a swift end to the reign of horror in Rhidam, he knew there was no guarantee that Owain's daughter-in-law would see the same rapid recovery. With two infants in his care, he doubted Bhríd Cáner, whom he had not yet met, would return to this post either. If Níkóá proved capable, the position might be his as long as he chose to keep it. A man of travel, a man who had put down no familial roots after the death of his sister, he was afraid of how long that might be…and whether he would be able to endure staying in one place so long to serve…and whether his mixed blood would be a benefit or a curse.

❧*❧

Mikel Wistern proved an easy man to locate, being part of one of the most reputable blacksmith families in Enesfel. The soldier with familial knowledge visited Wistern's home with the Queen's request and Wistern, believing he would be offered a position in the royal stables, eagerly accepted the invitation. The filling of such a position would normally be presented by the chamberlain, but Wistern, a handsome young man in his prime, with money, status, and faith in his skill, did not see it the least bit unusual that he was brought instead before the youngest Lachlan princess. Unaware that his father had been arrested and interrogated, and unaware that Princess Asta had recently wed, he gave his brightest smile and, in a room with the soon-to-be-chamberlain as escort, eagerly answered her questions about his experience and skills.

"You are betrothed I am told?" Asta asked, careful to push a hint of dismay into her voice, playing along with his obvious interest.

"I was," he said, his voice colored by what she deemed to be a requisite twinge of sadness, though the emotion did not make it to his eyes. "But alas, she perished in the great fire,"

"I am sorry to hear that. Was she beautiful?"

"She was suitable for a wife," he replied flippantly, "obedient and pure in heart."

"Obedient to her father?"

He shrugged. "That's important, of course, any woman should be, but it's more important she be obedient to me, not," he added quickly, "that I don't appreciate spirit and intelligence."

"Obedience is an admiral quality," agreed the princess, although she suspected he was the sort who loved the challenge of breaking a woman of spirit to do his bidding. "Was she a bright girl then?"

Wistern laughed. "No, thinking on her own was hardly her strength." He held his glass out for more wine, expecting the redhead to fill it, not knowing he was the chamberlain and not a servant. "Fildanyo?" he asked without a thank you when his cup was full.

"You know it?" It was not Asta's preferred wine, but she had acquired a bottle from one of those previously questioned for a handsome sum for this meeting, in the hopes that Wistern would recognize it."

"Who would not? It is second only to the wines of Káliel."

"Or Levonne."

He frowned over the rim of the glass as if the bouquet had suddenly gone sour. "I will not drink that filth."

"Why?"

Disarmed by the innocence on her face, he replied, "I will not drink anything made by Elyri hands."

"Made by…oh, you mean Duke Cáner. I doubt his hands ever touched…"

"He poisons the flavor merely by walking the land where the grapes are grown."

Asta laughed lightly. "Nonsense. That is not possible…"

"That is what gdhededhá Tusánt said…that a man's touch cannot poison a product…but he will see soon enough." he spat. "The Fildanyo we sent should be proof of superiority."

"We?" Asta blinked with innocent confusion. "You sent him this same vintage? I thought Elyri do not drink wine…"

"Some do," Wistern assured her, reaching for the bottle to read the code on its side. "Only the weakest are harmed by drinking spirits…just like anyone else. k'gdhededhá Claide told me so when he suggested the idea. Yes…yes…this is the vintage Alis procured from her father. We needed the best. Nothing else would do."

Princess Asta rose, smoothing her skirt to mask the emotions Claide's name brought with it, and retrieved an empty bottle from the cabinet. Níkóá almost choked but managed to make the sound no more than a soft clearing of his throat. "This bottle, perhaps?" She uncorked it and handed it to him, holding it so that the aroma within was near his nose. His face crinkled in distaste and his hand trembled as he took it, his gaze shifted abruptly away from her to the bottle.

"I do not…"

"You do realize that your generous gift was given in turn to k'gdhededhá Dórímyr when he was in Rhidam…"

"I cannot say…" He tried to rise, but Níkóá pushed him back down into the chair with more strength than Wistern expected. He scowled at the man behind him, unable to shake free of the iron grip of the fingers dug into his shoulders.

"Are you aware your efforts to show gdhededhá Tusánt what poison is has contributed to the death of the Faith's patriarch?"

Despite a blooming of concern and accusation in his eyes, Wistern grunted, "Teren owe no allegiance to the Elyri church! If he's dead, it is dedhá Tusánt's error, not mine."

"Because he did not drink it?"

"Yes!"

The princess did not smile or allow any hint of triumph to show as she stared at Wistern, waiting for what would come next. His words were enough of a confession for her. He had known the wine was poisoned when he had given it as a gift. He had coerced his betrothed into acquiring the bottle, but which one of them had poisoned it, Asta did not yet know. Not that it mattered. The idea, the plan, the intention had been Wistern's. And Claide's While the anti-Elyri bias he expressed was not a crime, it had prompted his decision to poison Tusánt. Asta would present her findings to the Queen, leave it for her cousin to make the final determination of guilt and pronouncement of a sentence, but Asta had heard enough.

"Take him into custody, Lord Chamberlain," the princess said coolly, her expression of interest gone. Wistern paled, realizing who the redhead was. He also realized that he had condemned himself with both the intention of murder and an actual one…just as the man who had killed King Hagan had done. And he had implicated a man with great power, a man he respected, one he had no doubt would kill him for it, even if the Queen chose to let him live.

"Keep him away from others and allow no visitors; I want no opportunity for mishap. I will go to the Queen; meet me there when he is secure. I assure you, Mister Wistern, what punishment the Queen may assign will be nothing compared to what the Elyri High Council will place on your head."

Wistern, yanked to his feet, nearly crumbled to the floor as his knees buckled. Factual details of Elyri criminal punishment were rare as there were few crimes committed there or brought to public light outside of Elyriá. What most outsiders believed they knew of those punishments were tales filtered through the hatred birthed in Neth, rumors of twisted tortures of the mind beyond Teren imagination. Wistern, a believer in those unsubstantiated tales it appeared, was struck dumb in his fear. He uttered no more than a squeak as Níkóá dragged him out of the room to where the attending soldiers waited in the corridor.

Níkóá had done little, owed this capture more to the absent bounty hunter's efforts than anything he had done, but for the chamberlain, the capture of another anti-Elyri murderer, however small his part in the act had been, was an accomplishment to be proud of. How he would like to be there to see justice delivered.

ᆋ*ᆋ

The wheels of Nethite investigation into the death of King Merkar spun swiftly, as such things often did when people were relieved to be rid of a monarch both feared and hated by everyone who knew him…or who had been ruled by him. Prince Kjell was questioned repeatedly, both by the leaders of the military, a gaggle of royal advisors, and by the three physicians brought to court to examine the late King's body and consult on the evidence of the man's death. It was the first time any of the royal advisors had seen a hint of backbone and intelligence in the prince, and with his story collaborated by every witnessing servant who had come into the kitchen, there was no way Kjell could be legitimately accused of killing his brother. There were no physical marks on the King's body to suggest a fight or struggle, no cuts or bruises; there was nothing more than the head injuries his impact with the table and then the floor…and enough wine in his stomach to prove that he had been far from sober at the time of his death.

Many were surprised his drunkenness had not resulted in such an accident long before.

Prince Kjell took great pains to explain that Merkar had spilled the bucket in his stumbling about, a detail supported by the splash of dirty water on the King's legs, to keep blame from falling on the kitchen staff for anything more than failing to empty it. That loyalty to them would, he knew, be rewarded in kind, as his work over the years in currying favor amongst palace staff, royal advisors, military leaders, and even his brother's wife would be. Other de Corrmicks would have ordered another contender for the throne, no matter how young, to be slaughtered within hours of a regime change, but Kjell did not. His nephew, Hesl, not yet a year old, was no threat to him, not even old enough to have gained any support from those with hopes of manipulating the throne. Legally, the infant was king, and unless Prince Kjell contested his legitimacy and right to the throne, he would remain the heir without the ability to claim the throne until his fourteenth year. There might come a day when the child's mother, out of fear, denounced Merkar as his father, thus removing the likelihood of assassination. For the moment, as long as Kjell wished the boy no ill, both Hesl and Kjell were safe.

Legally, supported by written law and customary practice, by the late King's Final Testament and the support of both the infant's mother and Merkar's advisors, Prince Kjell was given the title of Prince Regent, the sole sovereign in Neth as the sun set over the kingdom. As he had intended from his earliest days, he would not take Neth's throne by murder. He anticipated the opportunity to prove to these men who thought to manipulate and control him just how wrong they had been in their perceptions.

He also intended to prove, in the years he had available on the Nethite throne, that life did not have to be lived the way Nethites had lived for centuries, that not every de Corrmick king had to be a tyrant. He felt the regency crown settled on his head and tested the weight of the de Corrmick ring on his finger. Until the day came when he was required to turn the throne over to the boy he intended to have a steady hand in guiding, a prince he would prepare to carry on the changes Kjell intended to implement, he would succeed where no other Nethite King ever had in bringing true peace. He repeated the oaths to the collection of lords around him...and smiled.

❧Chapter 28✼

K avan was unable to remain angry with Hwensen despite the
details the man had held back. It was difficult to undo a
lifetime of loyalties and habits, and when that lifetime
stretched over two hundred years, it was even harder to do. What
mattered was the information Hwensen had given him and the details
Bhen found that Kavan gleaned from his thoughts when separated by
bars and the crowd in Bhryell's lómesté. There were enough details,
small things that most would not notice unless they were looking for
them, that gave Kavan a new direction, bringing him back to this
room, seeking clues he had not noticed before, things he had missed
that might point to a murderer and his motives.

Bhyrhán accompanied Hwensen to confront the k'phóredhet,
petitioning them for an emergency interruption of the sequestered
gdhededhá. That Bhyrhán was there on behalf of the High Mother
was the best chance they had for admittance, short of the Kyne
approaching the k'phóredhet herself, but convincing the Tribunal that
they had compelling cause for the request without divulging their
reasons, with their evidence still thin, was not going to be easy. The
hope was that, by the time the two men succeeded, Kavan would
have the necessary proof.

But this room, this too clean, too tidy room, gave up no secrets easily. Nothing Kavan touched yielded usable clues save one...that the room's occupant rarely slept here. Where he did sleep, however, was something Kavan gradually pieced together as he left that room and returned to the dead man's chamber. The k'gdhededhá's apartment had remained unoccupied since the prelate's death, left untouched at the command of Kyne Mórne despite the Tribunal's wishes to the contrary. When the sequester ended and a new prelate was elected, the disposition of the contents of this room would no longer be under the Kyne's direction, but while Kavan investigated, the High Mother had forced the k'phóredhet to leave the room as it was the moment Dórímyr's body had been found.

Despite the Kyne's orders, others had been here, however, and Kavan noted the presence of each one. A chambermaid who had stripped the bedding and closed the windows against the foul winter weather. The discarded meal had been removed rather than leave it to rot in place. A member of the Tribunal had entered to do no more than make a cursory glance around the room, touching nothing but the corner of the table to leave no other detectable impression of his passing. Kavan had no doubts that others had come seeking evidence against the man they hoped to indict but none had touched anything except the door handle and the floor.

Tumm had been here, his hand on the latch revealed his passage although nothing within exposed his presence. Had he come to look, to mourn, to remember? Had someone been with him? Hwensen had been here too, returning a collection of borrowed books to the dead man's nightstand.

Evidence of the room's sole other visitor was found accidentally as Kavan searched for sources of poison he may have missed before. A hand on the nightstand for balance as he knelt to peer beneath the bed, revealed that additional touch, the single contact by this individual that Kavan had not noticed. Without a touch of his hand on the main door, or the balcony door, Kavan presumed that someone had let him in, someone with a key, someone who had witnessed the placement of a journal in the drawer Kavan had previously searched. Dórímyr's journal; there was no mistaking the accumulated presence of his touch from years of usage. And the handwriting within was the dead man's writing. Kavan had seen many examples of it in the past and he could feel the old man's hand moving across each page when his fingers brushed over them.

There was no time to read the entire journal, but Kavan made sure to read the last dozen pages, seeking clues as to the man's final state of mine, seeking some reason as to why the journal had been taken and returned. The contact reminded Kavan of something he had sensed the day of Dórímyr's death, something he had felt on the meal tray, but had written off as inconsequential at the time. The new clues Bhen had provided, however, the evidence it led Kavan to, were the last sort he expected to find.

Shaking his head in disbelief, Kavan put both the journal and the unexpected evidence into the pack he carried. A tickle of energy at the back of his skull alerted him to his cousin's contact, and though he did not want disruptions, he had promised to keep communication open. With his family in Enesfel, beyond the reach of the Clarys church but in the sphere of possible anti-Elyri danger, it was important to keep in contact. Until Sóbhán learned better control of his gifts, Kavan had no one in Alberni to keep him informed. He had to rely on his cousin to do it for him.

He expected no more than an update, the news that Wortham, Zelenka, Nuryé and the children were safely installed in Alberni. The wet-nurse was understandably frightened of relocation into the troubled Teren kingdom, but the proximity of other Elyri within the walls of St. Kóráhm's reassured her and she agreed to give the new living arrangements a try for the sake of baby Dhóri. It would take them time to get settled, and Kavan expected Wortham to have many questions to relay through Ártur at every opportunity.

The healer's news, however, regarded the arrest of the man who was the ultimate source of the poisoned wine that had fallen into k'gdhededhá Dórímyr's hands...a man who implicated Claide in a plot against Tusánt that had gone awry. Kavan begged Ártur to implore the Queen not to execute the man but to hold him until Kavan could question him and present him as evidence to the sequestered gdhededhá and the k'phóredhet. With two of the five sources identified and accounted for, and a third hinted at strongly enough that Kavan felt that, after the search of one more location, he would know it as well, there would surely be enough evidence of his innocence that the k'phóredhet would be forced to drop the charges of murder and keep a guilty man from assuming power.

❧ * ❧

"Me?" Níkóá glanced between the Healer, the Inquisitor, and the Queen, not anticipating the mission they placed before him. Although he had come into the castle under the guise of assuming the role of chamberlain, he had not expected to be entrusted with such responsibilities a few days into his not yet official tenure. He accepted the princess's request of infiltrating the Corylliens to aid her father, it was a position they both believed would gain him further trust from Claide, proving him to be anti-Elyri.

But he had not expected to be sent to Clarys with a prisoner, with the man whose gift of wine had contributed to k'gdhededhá Dórímyr's death.

"You were a witness to his confession...a man...an adult...and bearing Elyri blood. They are more likely to listen to you than to me." Princess Asta rolled her eyes to show her annoyance with not being taken seriously, but then she grinned. She had a year or more before some accepted her work and position in earnest, and by that time she hoped her father would have returned and reclaimed the position. She enjoyed the role of Inquisitor and hoped to rightfully fill it one day, but despite her successes, she realized there was a great deal more she could learn from her father before she undertook the duty officially.

And soon there would be a child to consider, a complication she had never bargained for and, because it bound her to Gaelán, she would not relinquish for all the world.

"Kavan asked for you and Elotti," the Queen added. "Elotti's not yet returned to Rhidam, and I cannot spare Lord MacLyr for this, not while he has other duties and responsibilities to tend to." His main duty, although she would not reveal it to anyone except her husband, was to remain close in case she experienced difficulties with her pregnancy. The healer's proximity was the precaution that kept her fears at bay. Gaelán needed Ártur too, if he unexpectedly awoke.

"You know the Gates...and Clarys, I am told. He will tell you when and where to meet him, you will deliver the prisoner, give testimony, and return as quickly as possible. You must be here when dedhá Claide calls. We can stall him, but he will expect to see you, and when you meet with him next, be it here or elsewhere, it is time to initiate our plans."

If it was time for Kavan to confront the Elyri Faith institution, then Diona had to do everything in her power to give him the evidence he needed and hope that the timing did not present difficulty to either of them. Removing Claide from office was sorely needed, and Kavan believed they were on the cusp of that goal.

"Yes, Your Majesty." Níkóá bowed. If Kavan had requested him specifically, he could not decline. How he might accomplish three duties at once he did not know, but he would do his best.

❧*❧

It was the name that led him here, a name on a burial marker that Bhen had found, a name connected to a past the late k'gdhededhá had attempted to bury upon his rise within the ranks of the Faithful to the top position of religious leadership. For the surname Rínes was an old one, one that stretched back to the founding of Bhórdh, the founding of Elyriá. Though Kavan had not caught on to the name when Hwensen had spoken it, Bhen's investigation and the time Kavan had spent in contemplation while pouring out his soul to Bhryell in song had locked those stray pieces of detail into place.

Despite his efforts, it seemed, as Kavan picked his way through the labyrinth of closely packed dwellings, Dórímyr had not completely broken with his Zythánite past. He might have helped to destroy the conclave he had been part of, might have helped destroy its leader and scatter what remained of the Zythánites, but it was here he had found her, where he had fallen in love deeply enough to be willing to sacrifice his vows of Faith to be with her. He could not easily bring her to the halls of Hes Dhágdhuán without great risk to them both, and thus he had often come here to her, which meant ongoing exposure to the contrary teachings of his past.

If, Kavan mused as he rubbed his finger over the mark above another doorway, Dórímyr had again been swayed by Zythánite beliefs, his war against Kavan's alleged heresy was a hypocritical lie.

He frowned at a group of children who passed, their curious stares piercing out from faces that were familiar despite his never having been in this place. He watched them until they were out of sight, pondering their familiarity before ducking into the building an old woman had directed him to. He doubted she knew the occupant was not here, or else she assumed that no one asking after him in this place would be a threat to one of their number. Few Elyri locked their homes, as unworried about theft and violence as they were, and few felt they had anything to hide from any who might come in. This hovel's owner was among them.

What Kavan found inside, however, was not the trappings of a Zythánite, but rather texts, holy symbols and relics, prayer mats and trinkets of Faith, the sort of things he would expect to find in the home of a missionary sent on the assignment of conversion. Had he been wrong about this man?

No.

He picked up a vial from the bedside table, one of many that smelled of maran seed oil. The entire room smelled of it, potentially aromatic if not for its overpowering strength. The maran fruit was a delicacy grown in southern Elyriá, in the vicinity of Bhórdh, and while it was a much sought after treat, often dried and coated with sugar, the pit and the oil derived from the pit had proven useful as both a purgative and, if undiluted and unrefined and taken in significant quantities, a poison. The aroma varied somewhat from that of the fruit, being slightly more acidic and pungent, but its taste, from what Kavan recalled from his studies, was near enough to that of the fruit that it would go unnoticed if sprinkled on other fruits…or sometimes used in sauces to marinade meat, lamb in particular.

Kavan stared at the vials, twelve in all, each with the same aroma, each empty save one, with a bowl and pestle beside them still sticky with the residue where the fruit pits were crushed for their oil. There had been maran fruit on the tray in Dórímyr's room, a single bite of it having been taken the morning Kavan had found the dying man. There had been lamb as well, but he thought nothing at that time of the deep orange sauce spread across the tender meat. Even when he had suspected the meal to be poisoned, maran had not been an obvious suspect. Nor had he derived any connection between Bhórdh, maran, and the deceased man…until now. He did not need to touch any but the vial he held to know that the contents had been administered to one man by a single individual in a fashion that no one, particularly Dórímyr, would suspect.

From the doorway, Kavan looked up and down the street. Midday, it should have been bright here, but the overhang of buildings crowded too close together blocked the sun. This was an ancient quarter of Clarys, this cluster of four or five short streets built at a time when the Elyri were new to the land and wary enough of their surroundings that they built too closely, shielding each home from the weather and the wilds by the proximity of the home next to it. The residents here were not poor but rather were those who chose to live on the fringes of accepted society or had been pushed there for any number of causes. People like the Zythánites, though Kavan was surprised to find them living near to Hes Dhágdhuán, the most dangerous sect in the hierarchy's eyes living right under their noses within less than a mile of the náós walls, unprosecuted, unpunished. This man had come here seeking one truth, Kavan was sure, and had stayed to convert them.

One of the children he had seen earlier passed him again, going back in the other direction. A brief meeting of gazes and Kavan knew why this man had stayed. He understood each reason, the reasons for the vials he had wrapped in cloth and put into his pack, the reasons for coming here, the reasons for staying…and the reasons why one man might want to kill another. Kavan might have felt sympathy if his life, his future, were not on the line, if he was not being blamed for another man's crime.

He had what he had come for. Pieces of the puzzle of k'gdhededhá Dórímyr's death. He would have to do without the rest. Come morning, one way or another, he would present his proof to the Tribunal and the gathered gdhededhásur. He would live with the cloud of suspicion and perceived guilt over his life no longer.

☙*❧

The instruction to take Mr. Wistern to Kavan in Clarys had come, the bard giving detailed instructions on where to meet and when, but providing few other details of what he had planned or what was to come. The lack of information troubled Níkóá less than it did the Queen, who fumed and fretted and tried to think of a way to send additional soldiers with her chamberlain to prevent Wistern's escape. Unlike most Elyri, however, Níkóá was an experienced swordsman and he was not against using his skills to keep control of the prisoner. His assurance of success was the reason the Queen backed down from her intent, the sole reason, that was, aside from the concern that the High Mother might misinterpret the Enesfel Queen's purpose for sending soldiers into her kingdom through the k'rylag, might think the act one of flagrant hostility.

With the sun sinking in the west, taking with it the atypically warm winter day, Níkóá chose to go, unbidden, to Hes á Redh. He desired to speak to gdhededhá Tusánt, to gain information about Clarys that he might need, a risky visit if Claide were to see him. As nearly chamberlain now, such a visit could be explained as an order from the Queen if necessary. He believed he could talk his way out of anything, and if he could not, he would fight his way out.

If Claide met his fate at the end of Níkóá's sword, the redhead was comfortable with that…and with any repercussions it carried.

The fire damaged roof was repaired at last, and with the broken windows still boarded over and most of the homeless squatters having returned to their homes, shops, or to the homes of friends and kin, it was possible for Gatherings to be held once more. Faithful were leaving the náós, an evening Gathering Níkóá had not anticipated, but he had experience with blending into crowds, passing through them unnoticed, and no one yet knew his face or his name, his pending position or his parentage. No one acknowledged him or spoke to him as he elbowed his way against the tide of departing Faithful to reach Tusánt.

But talk overheard revealed that Tusánt was not here, that he had been called to comfort the family of a dying parishioner, someone of note it seemed from the tones of respect voiced by the gossipers. Thoughtful, Níkóá sat on a bench to contemplate waiting or returning another time, noting that k'dedhá Claide wore robes that suggested he had been the one to speak the lesson this evening. He was engrossed in animated conversation with another man, someone wealthy gauging by his royal blue trousers, doublet, and cloak, the polished leather of his boots and the fur-lined gloves in his hands which flapped about as he gesticulated with agitation.

Níkóá avoided eye contact but dropped to his knees and pretended to pray. Though there was nothing particularly suspicious about the two, Níkóá's widening experience with the k'gdhededhá and the responsibilities he had undertaken or been given demanded that he at least determined the other man's identity and pass it on to Princess Asta for investigation. With his eyes closed, he could stretch the range of his hearing further than any Teren, an action Claide would be unable to detect or prove. Too far away for anyone else to hear their whispers, with his head bowed and eyes closed, there was no reason for Claide to accuse him of eavesdropping…unless he was paranoid enough to have something to hide.

"…are asking questions," the stranger hissed, Níkóá coming into the conversation mid-sentence and thus not hearing what the man was referring to.

"It will not be traced to you," assured the hawkish bald man.

"But it is in Elyri hands…"

"They will not seek retribution, I promise. I made certain that enough have handled it that you are but one of many donors. No one will suspect or believe your contribution predated any others…"

"Save yours," the stranger snorted darkly. "Heward said you've destroyed the…" He glared at a trio of men who passed close enough to bump his shoulder; he might have sworn at them but they offered a quick apology and Claide genuflected in blessing, sending them on their way believing none had overheard the secretive conversation.

Picking up where the unspoken word had left off, Claide nodded and said, "What remained could not be left to be discovered. It was burned long ago."

"What if we need it? Orec is difficult to…"

"If there is a need to poison anyone else, I will have no hand in it." The words were spat in distaste. "What's done is done; he is gone and we have ample cause and opportunity to break from the Clarys church. The Faithful will see it in time…as will the Crown. We do not need them; they are poisoning us with their…"

Claide stopped speaking, seeing, at last, the redhead of hair that hung in prayer many feet away. Though Níkóá could not see him and dared not raise his head lest his action appeared suspicious, he could feel the shift of the man's focus.

"All will be well, Lord Bostik; you are safe," he said offhandedly. "Go home to your family." Claide left him there, the conversation abruptly abandoned in favor of one with the man he believed would help put a cooperative Lachlan on Enesfel's throne.

Footsteps whispered through the emptying náós. Níkóá listened to their approach without raising his head. When they stopped, he continued his feigned prayers until the other man hissed.

"We should not meet here," Claide said beneath his breath, his voice no louder then it had been when in discussion with the Lord Bostik. Níkóá raised his head and opened his eyes, showing an appropriate degree of surprise at seeing Claide there.

"Can't a man come to pray?" he asked with a hint of indignation. "I heard the Elyri was not here tonight…I thought it the best time to pray without his annoying presence." The words disgusted him to say, but they pleased Claide, who barely hid his smile as he nodded.

"Prayer is good for a man's soul. Has there been news? You are to be appointed I have heard?"

"Officially in three days', when Chamberlain Lachlan leaves Rhidam. I am in training until then. There is much to learn, but the Queen seems to trust and like me, and that is the important thing."

"Indeed...yes...and your patron? Has he revealed his plan? Will he meet with me and...?"

"He is meeting with you now." Claide scowled in confusion and Níkóá offered his hand. "Legally Níkóá McCábhá, my mother's name, or Pharis, my step-father's, but in truth, Níkóá Lachlan...son of King Farrell."

"You? You are...?" Claide spluttered and stammered, lost for words, his tone verging on offended and angry.

Níkóá continued. "I could not reveal myself before. No one knows me in Rhidam, not even the Queen. I needed to remain anonymous." He grinned roguishly and shrugged. "Neither Healer MacLyr nor Chamberlain Lachlan have commented on a family resemblance...which I was concerned they might. It would be the sort of detail they would not keep hidden from Her Majesty if they suspected the truth. But they do not seem to suspect me. Now that I am inside, I will continue to gain her trust and then, perhaps, I will reveal the truth."

"She might decide you are a threat to the throne," the k'gdhededhá warned.

Still smirking, Níkóá shrugged. "Aren't I? To be fair, it's a concern, but I will prove myself honorable, valuable, and capable, and when the time is right, I will strike. It will take time to sway staff, to befriend soldiers and prominent lords, but it can be done."

"And you will rid the Lachlan house of the Elyri taint?" Claide spat, his ire now redirected from Níkóá to those he perceived as the enemy within the keep. "If you require assistance, connections for support, a means to be rid of them or sources to do it for you...I know people."

"People?"

"Influential people. People with resources...people who are experts in ridding one of troublesome individuals."

"If they are...why have you not been rid of them before?" He tried to sound wary, not as if he was fishing for details of past efforts.

"I assume you must have tried...an effort must have been made?"

Claide nodded. "It is difficult to achieve from without, though I have tried. With you inside, it can be accomplished more easily."

"With suspicion thrown on me..."

"No...never..." Claide fought to reassure him. "We will plan everything to the detail. You need but to act...to do as we instruct, and Enesfel will be purged of Elyri and given a strong king to rule us...one who is sympathetic to the requirements of the Faith."

"We?" Níkóá scowled. "You think I will take orders from..."

"No...that is not what I meant," Claide hastily corrected though he did not address who 'we' were. "I meant that my resources have experience, and taking advantage of that will guarantee success."

Though Níkóá grunted, he nodded as though accepting the unspoken apology. Every word the man said was filed away into memory for Kavan to retrieve. He hoped he would be lucky enough for an arrest to be made of Lord Bostik before morning, but first, he had to get away from the náós without raising suspicion.

"When the time comes, I will seek out your resources...but I must return to the castle. I asked leave to pray for a friend, but duty calls...and I do not desire to disappoint the Queen."

"Yes...of course...you do not." As if to draw attention from their conversation, Claide laid his hand on the kneeling man's head in blessing, smiled, and stepped away to allow him to rise. He did not get far before he looked back at the redhead with wonder.

A prince. A Lachlan prince...illegitimate but a prince nonetheless. He looked young, younger than he should, but good genetics would mean a long reign. With the right spin, and perhaps a handful of paid witnesses, he could make this prince legitimate with falsified wedding papers or some other form of background documentation to explain why he was hidden from the public.

Given King Bowen's wrathful rule, it would not be difficult to explain hiding a prince in the same way Prince Arlan had been hidden to keep him alive.

Together, they could take the throne from the Queen and rid the kingdom of Elyri, strengthening the Faith, in one efficient strike. That was even better news than the death of k'gdhededhá Dórímyr.

As an after-effect of the laying of hands, Níkóá heard those fading thoughts and shuddered. How many Elyri readers would it take, he wondered, to convince a panel of judges that Claide was, indeed, a man guilty of murder many times over?

❧*❧

Wortham marched about the estate house, going from room to room, investigating everything, every door, every window, every piece of furniture, anything that might pose or contain a threat to any member of the family. In his eyes, in his heart, he and his wife were not merely friends of the White Bard; they were family, bound by the children in Kavan's care whom he entrusted to Wortham during these difficult, trying days. He had been in this place before, could have made it from room to room blindfolded, and he trusted the Darys with his life. There was little need for a thorough inspection. But the children's lives were his to mind and Wortham felt better for the reassurance of knowing they would remain safe.

With the legalities in place, it was understood that he and Zelenka would live out their lives in the Alberni estate, or at least reside there for as long as Kavan chose to make Alberni his home, assuming Kavan gained his freedom in Clarys to join Wortham here. Nothing would change for Martin Darys and his family, they would continue to manage the estate, the grounds, and the city while Wortham's focus was on the children. Zelenka fell easily into helping the Darys with the upkeep of the home, as everyone understood that the Delamos were on equal footing with the Darys. This new arrangement presented no difficulties for anyone. Seeing to Lord Cliáth's needs was the priority, whether the bard lived here or not.

Captain Magk accepted Kavan's invitation to serve St. Kóráhm's as Captain at Arms and two of his men followed him there. From the earliest days of the chellé's construction, Kavan had seen to it that some were empowered to act as gate sentries, and later, when the anti-Elyri violence began to escalate and spread, more men were trained and brought to the chellé to keep the residents and treasures within safe. Kavan and Khwílen wanted the chellé to be peaceful, a place of learning and arts and religious contemplation, but the high number of Elyri residents in this foreign land prompted Kavan to offer them, and those seeking refuge from across the lands, a haven secure from the threat of death.

With both Wortham and Raenár to train those men already serving here, as well as any others they might recruit, Kavan believed St. Kóráhm's would be the safest place in the Sovereignties to raise his children. There was no possibility of excommunication here. Nuryé, her child, and Dhóri would spend most of their daylight hours in the chellé until Wortham deemed the estate adequately provisioned and safe, and as no one in Alberni knew of the child or its relationship to Kavan, it was likely, Wortham believed, the child would be seen his and Zelenka's…as Kavan suspected. It was a ruse the nurse readily agreed to when in public, to protect the boy until his father could join them, but within the privacy of the estate, Wortham and Zelenka would be no more than his guardians.

The thought of taking Kavan's child from him, even in name or in a place of affection, was something Wortham could not stomach. Only to protect the boy's life could he even consider putting on the appearance of it. Taking the child away from the bard would break Kavan's heart, and Wortham's in turn.

Sóbhán, still spending hours each week in Rhidam and Bhryell, was eager for the unexpected learning opportunities the chellé offered. The chellé also presented him with the opportunity to sing, which he took to with great enthusiasm. While giving no pressure or preference, Kavan hoped the young man, who had already shown great aptitude with wood carving, would follow the family trade, as it would appease his uncle to have another harpmaker in the household since Kavan had shown no interest or aptitude for it. Sóbhán was not blood kin, might have another name and separate family, but he currently expressed no interest in seeking that family or in leaving Kavan's conservatorship.

Satisfied that the house was the secure fortress they wished it to be, that the men performing military drills in the courtyard were trustworthy, Wortham intended to be certain the guards were oath-sworn to the lord first thing in the morning. He gathered everyone, his wife, Kavan's children, and the Darys' for dinner. Working together was important. He knew Kavan would be pleased by their solidarity whenever fate allowed him to join them.

⟡Chapter 29⟡

The door burst open, forced from the outside by three dozen heavily armored and armed Lachlan soldiers, and though the family's sentries fought at first, they quickly realized who they were fighting and, not wanting to fall to the Queen's wrath, their resistance was short-lived. Justice Corbin and Chamberlain Lachlan, eager to make one last arrest together before Owain left Rhidam, barked orders, leaving men to guard the escape routes as others charged up the stairs in search of the lord's private chambers.

Children screamed and began to cry, startled out of slumber by the chaos. Women shrieked and tried to find safety, not realizing who their attackers were and fearing they were doomed to abuse at the hands of brigands or those brutish Corylliens. Lord Bostik, caught in the act of bedding a servant, was yanked from the kitchen by one of the soldiers. He wiped his splotchy face, sweaty and red from exertion, and attempted to fix his trousers as he was dragged into the entrance hall while the Justice escorted his wife downstairs. Bostik attributed the horror on her face to what was happening around them and not his own disheveled, compromising appearance or that of the untidy, pretty girl pulled along with him.

"Lord Bostik," Prince Owain barked, "You are under arrest for treason and conspiracy…"

"Treason…?"

The man's wife began to wail.

⫷*⫸

Hwensen did not know what, if anything, Kavan's investigation had uncovered the day before, but the bard's passion when he requested a covert middle of the night meeting in this small, little-used náós on the edge of Clarys suggested those secrets had borne fruit. While he was happy to have offered something beneficial, Hwensen regretted that he had not shared his secrets sooner.

They might not be forced to face this pressing deadline now.

There was nothing to fear, he told himself, as he crossed the dark city alone. Clarys, like most of Elyriá, laid claim to the safest streets in the Five Sovereignties. When the majority of those who passed on the streets could detect another without seeing them, could identify another without sight…by their aura alone…and might be able to fight back, stop, or even kill with little more than a look, crime was a rare thing. But without knowing what to expect from Kavan, without understanding why this meeting place had been selected, Hwensen's imagination was getting the better of him.

When he arrived at St. Bhyrínt's, it was to find three men with Kavan, one of whom was a Bhíncári judging by his features and the emblem hanging about his neck. Warily, Hwensen stopped in the doorway. The other two were royal escorts, members of the Kyne's personal guard. Anxious tremors snaked into Hwensen's belly and his hand tightened on the latch. Body tensed for flight, he squeaked, "My lord?" Was he to be arrested for k'gdhededhá Dórímyr's death?

"Please, gdhededhá…close the door. Join us." Though Kavan's voice was edged with excitement, Hwensen heard no threat. He closed the door and came slowly forward, paying attention to the décor, the places someone might hide in ambush, and the four men to Kavan's left at the front of the room. The náós showed signs of frequent use, the worn carpeting, scuffed wooden benches, and power-charged air all evidence of an active place of worship. It did not share the opulence of Hes Dhágdhuán, which he felt it should as a place of worship in the capital city. It was, he quickly decided, the sort of place a man like Kavan would prefer.

As amiable as it was in its antiquity, however, Hwensen vowed to see that some sort of donation from the mother church was made towards its upkeep.

Kavan's handlight, the sole source of light in the room, flickered a little as a static pop of energy burst from within the Purification chamber, and then Hwensen understood. The bard required a k'rylag, and those scattered throughout Hes Dhágdhuán were inaccessible. Or rather, Hwensen mused as he watched three men emerge from the tiny chamber, Kavan would have been able to use any of them if he traveled alone, but trying to bring others through, or take others through, would mean the risk of arrest.

One young man, broad-shouldered and muscular, wore the armor and crest of the Lachlan guard. One was bound and drugged, it seemed, as he was conscious and leaning heavily on the third individual with his eyes rolled back and his limbs limp. The third was Elyri…or half-Elyri, judging by his red beard, and it was he who approached Kavan with a hand outstretched in greeting.

Reluctant to accept handshakes, since few people, even other Elyri, were able to shield their thoughts from him, Kavan eyed the hand, then the man offering it, before accepting the gesture. Níkóá was offering more than a greeting, and Kavan was curious to know what the redhead had to share.

ॐ*ॐ

Four more seizures, five men dragged before the Queen before sunlight crested the Llaethlágárá. She dared not risk Rhidam's judges trying this matter alone, as she was first tempted to do, for she could not risk k'gdhededhá Claide interrupting the proceedings to plead on their behalf, or risk him finding out the reasons behind these arrests. Claide was a smart man; he would hear of the night's raid soon enough and would deduce the likely reason as soon as he got word about the appropriations of men and property. But in the midnight hours, when a summons was sent to the gdhededhá of Hes á Redh, Claide had not been present, a fact that pleased the Queen and her court. The man could not claim to have been intentionally left out. According to Níkóá, evidence would be presented against Claide as well, and the Queen heavily favored not allowing the k'gdhededhá the opportunity to interfere.

The Great Hall was empty save for the Queen's advisors, the arresting officers and soldiers, the seven Rhidam judges, and Bhríd Cáner who was reluctantly convinced to come to the castle before Ártur departed Rhidam for the night. His wet nurse remained to one side of the room, in the shadows, tending his sleeping daughters. He might not have come, but because this matter involved the death of k'gdhededhá Dórímyr, and finding evidence to clear Kavan's name again, as well as the possibility of obtaining damning evidence against Claide at last, Diona knew Bhríd would feel it a compelling duty to read the prisoners, should the judges request or allow it.

Mostly unaware of the charges levied against them, Lord Bostik and the others were calm and quiet, tension on their faces but little obvious fear. Lord Bostik was the sole individual to have heard the word treason spoken aloud, but he seemed dubious abut the weight of the allegations against him. Claide had promised. He cast sidelong glances at the one man he knew, Kent Gottfrid, but he quickly looked away when Kent narrowed his eyes, a threat warning retaliation should Bostik reveal they knew one another. Bostik was the first to be brought forward, sworn in before the judges, and given the one warning the Queen felt willing to offer as Idal Gottfried was dragged into the room from the dungeon where he continued to be held.

"Should any of you lie to this court, and your lie is found out, your families shall be stripped of lands, titles, and any rights they hold. Tell the truth, without coercion, and they shall be spared the punishments you face."

❧*❧

"dedhá Hwensen. Lord Bhíncári." Níkóá extended his hand to them but hid the secrets he had shared with Kavan. He could not stay, as he needed to return to Rhidam to learn the verdicts of hearings that would, he felt confident in informing Kavan, provide evidence with which to clear the bard's name. Kavan, in silent agreement, would wait here near the k'rylag for as long as he dared.

"We have an hour before dawn...thirty minutes beyond that before the Tribunal and sequester resume session," Kavan informed him as the men greeted one another. "Will you be back by then?"

"I will, my lord," Níkóá swore. "One way or another."

❧*❧

"How do you know we can trust him?"

Caol looked at one of the men he had recruited, barely believing the man had asked that question. The five surviving members of Layton's team had been sent into the city on reconnaissance, to bring back word about what the Lachlan soldiers were seeking as they stomped through the dark streets. Believing they had been selected because their long-standing Coryllien allegiance made them more trustworthy than the recruits, the five had gone without questioning Caol's orders. It allowed him to speak to these men unimpeded.

"Of course he can't be trusted...he's a Coryllien..."

"The Coryllien," someone corrected.

"As long as he thinks we are Corylliens too, he can use us. If he decides differently, decides we can't be trusted..." Caol shrugged. These were Association men, men who understood risk and reward, used to a degree of both in their daily lives. There was some trust among them, the rules of the Association protecting each man's back, but as far as anyone knew, Heward was not Association. How far he could be trusted was unknown.

"Acquaint yourself with the storage house, the paths around it, escape routes, and those living nearby. If it's to be our usual meeting place, I want to know what we've got to work with when we're there. And if we need it, I want us to be able to scatter quickly."

Heads bobbed and the group broke, men departing one by one or in pairs or small groups, heading in different directions to misdirect anyone who could be watching. Caol did not believe they were being monitored, either by the Crown or by Heward, but he was not going to take the chance of being wrong. What troubled him, however, was the absence of the redhead his daughter had sent to him. He decided it was time to investigate the man on his own. He needed to know who that man was...and why his daughter thought he was worth risking their trust.

⮞*⮜

"My..." Kavan was more surprised than any of those with him by Diona's arrival in Clarys. No Lachlan monarch since King Innis had come here, none had made any gestures or efforts to create a dialogue with the Elyri High Mother since Innis, and Kavan had not expected Diona to undertake such a direction. Politically, however, it was a wise choice, one female ruler to another, an effort not to allow the strains of Faith and anti-Elyri violence in Enesfel to affect the political relations between the two kingdoms. That Diona had decided to come without his guidance pleased him. His efforts to school her were proving successful.

"Kavan." Her desire to embrace him remained unfulfilled since they were surrounded by others, but she did reach for his hand. "Níkóá has explained these four to you?"

Wistern, Lord Bostik, and the two youngest Gottfrid sons were in the custody of six Elyri guards. Wistern still had the look of a drunken man, though the effects of the agent he had been given were wearing off, and Lord Bostik was pale and trembling, with the appearance of a man about to be sick, his gaze darting between the others in the room. The youngest Gottfrid was ashen, terrified, while the elder showed no trace of emotion on his face or in his posture. None of them knew where they were, but they knew they were no longer in Rhidam.

The hand was not accepted, his reluctance for contact fueled by a sudden flash of memory, but he covered it by beckoning the others around them to come closer. "He did…and the timing is fortuitous."

"I wish we had Claide for you as well…but these shall have to do for the moment."

"It will be enough." Kavan had to believe that. "You know Lord Bhíncári…and this is gdhededhá Hwensen, former aide to k'gdhededhá Dórímyr. Gentlemen, I present Queen Diona Lachlan and my friend Níkóá."

Both Níkóá and the Queen noted the epithet. Few in Kavan's life earned the distinction of friend. Kavan might not know the redhead well, but he knew him well enough to trust him.

Bhyrhán's bow was well-practiced and elegant, his smile to the Queen bright and welcoming. Already nervous about the day ahead, the unexpected arrival of Enesfel's Queen did nothing to ease Hwensen's nerves and his awkward, stilted bow expressed his anxiety. Perhaps her position would strengthen their chances of entering the chamber, of being heard, but the members of the Tribunal were, he knew, a prickly bunch who preferred to believe they held ultimate power in the Sovereignties. Hwensen was wary of how they would react to having that power undermined by a foreign monarch...or anyone at all.

"Your Highness. Shall I escort you to the High...?"

"I was hoping she would speak with me before the Tribunal," Diona said with a glance at Kavan. "We...Elyriá and Enesfel...Elyri and Teren...have a stake in these issues. This reaches beyond the guilt or innocence of a single man and I intend the Tribunal to see that before this day is over."

"I..." Bhyrhán bowed. "She did not intend to attend, did not wish to interfere in affairs of Faith...but I will approach her with the news of your arrival and request. Perhaps she will be persuaded to change her mind."

"You must hurry," Hwensen reminded him. "They will be sharing breakfast soon and will convene shortly thereafter. The earlier we arrive, the more likely they will hear us."

"They will hear us." Kavan would force his way into the chamber and force them to listen if he had to. "But yes, Bhyrhán, go quickly. Meet us in the antechamber..."

"With or without the Kyne," urged Diona. If necessary, the attendance of a single member of the Kyne's family would have to be enough.

Kyne? Tribunal? Understanding those parting words, Lord Bostik was no longer the only prisoner to look as if they would lose what remained in their stomachs from last night's dinner.

≈*≈

Owain held his ground as the Justice took away the men arrested and tried during the night on conspiracy charges against gdhededhá Tusánt, against all Elyri, against the Faith, and against the Crown. The suspicions and evidence Níkóá had presented to Asta and the Queen proved enough to bring in not only those connected to the poisoning of k'gdhededhá Dórímyr but also, as it turned out, one of the men instrumental in the abduction of k'gdhededhá Tythilius. The fellow knew nothing about those who had tortured and killed him, knew nothing about who had ultimately arranged the abduction, but he was able to provide the names of others involved, one of whom he claimed was the leader of their efforts. If anyone knew where the ultimate order came from, knew who was responsible for the beloved man's death, it would certainly be him.

Rhidam and its surroundings were scoured for the additional men named by those already detained. A steady flow of prisoners was dragged into the castle as arrests were made. The judges were kept in the keep to allow for immediate trials, as well as to protect their lives until the manhunt was over. There was little doubt that Claide or someone else within the order of the Corylliens would target those judges if the chance arose.

Many of those arrested would hang, Owain had no doubt, and he shamelessly hoped he would be in Rhidam to witness their deaths. He would return from Káliel to see this through if he could. Following this purge of agitators and criminals to the end would be a satiating legacy to leave behind if it was to be the last thing he could do for Enesfel and the Lachlans before his family took precedence.

Before departing for Elyriá with the red-haired soon-to-be chamberlain and Lord Bostik, the Queen saw to it that every witness, her advisors, judges, and the attending guards present this night, were sworn to secrecy. Not a word of the arrests, the charges brought, or the testimony given against the accused, was to be spoken outside of the stateroom where the trials were being held. Come dawn, there would already be rumors, as the families of those arrested in such an unprecedented fashion spoke with neighbors and friends, with anyone who might sympathize with them for the arrests of their loved ones. No monarch in memory, not even King Bowen, had resorted to midnight arrests of citizens, and the Crown's delay in making a public statement would be viewed with suspicion. It might lead to a period of mistrust of the Queen, but that was a risk Diona was willing to take in favor of catching Claide off guard.

Despite oaths sworn to the Queen, however, gdhededhá Valgis left the castle and scurried across the city to the home of a wealthy widow on the northwest corner of Rhidam where the fire had not touched. Having the financial means to do so, she had chosen to relocate rather than rebuild her damaged home. The sky was beginning to brighten as dawn drew nigh, but Valgis did not care if he woke the woman or the man she housed. This was news of a sort he believed the k'gdhededhá would want to hear immediately.

"What?" The widow let him in, knowing him to be an associate of Claide's; the man Valgis sought was found in the kitchen devouring a plate of breakfast.

"There have been arrests, Your Grace…"

"Arrests?" Claide asked around his mouthful of food, not sounding concerned.

"A Mister Jons, Mister Petin, and Mister Selis…"

"Who?" Those names meant nothing to Claide.

Valgis continued. "Kent Gottfrid. Lord Bostik."

Claide choked and stared. "Arrests on what grounds?"

Valgis cleared his throat. "That Lord Bostik supplied the means, the poison, used to kill k'gdhededhá Dórímyr. He confessed to it…"

"Did he mention me?" The hawkish man was up off bench seat, staring wildly about while trying to remain focused on Valgis. How likely was it that Valgis had been followed? That soldiers were seeking him now? "Did the Elyri interrogate him?"

"No, your grace. To either. He gave no names, and the judges satisfied themselves with his answers without the Elyri's help."

"And the Gottfrids? What of them? Did they speak of me?"

"No. The younger confessed to the most violent crimes…grave robbing…murder…"

Knowing what murders the three men had been involved in, Claide waved his hand and cut Valgis off. There was no guarantee, Claide knew, that the Elyri would not be later employed by the Crown to seek details from the men not given during trial, but he was relieved that none had implicated him so far.

"Good; we must care for Lord Bostik's kin while he is in custody and send a missive of regret and sympathies to Earl Gottfrid."

There were precautions to take today, plans to make and execute, but he felt secure knowing he had not been named. He might not be able to talk his way out of accusations with the Queen, once his name was brought forth, as he had been able to do with her brother. The Queen was neither gullible nor unduly trusting, and she was prone to believing anything her Elyri advisors claimed. She would need proof of wrongdoing; even if those men gave up his name, Claide was confident there was no proof to be had.

An Elyri reading would not, in his opinion, be proof enough to condemn him.

He did not ask what the others were accused of, charged with, or held for, thus Valgis did not speak further. He had no reason to suspect Claide's involvement with k'gdhededhá Tythilius' death or any plots against Tusánt. Both men had their share of enemies for their pro-Elyri positions, and Claide was too busy to dirty his hands that way. If he did not ask about the three, Valgis assumed their arrests were no matter of concern.

☙Chapter 30❧

The dour faces of the thirteen-member ecclesiastical tribunal stared at the collection of people who filed from the antechamber into the domed gallery where the sequestered gdhededhá met. The twenty-six members of the secular lómesté were brought in as well, at the High Mother's insistence, once the arrival of Queen Diona of Enesfel was announced. The gdhededhá and the k'lómesté had no inkling of why they were called together, why both councils were convened, why Enesfel's Queen was in Clarys, but they could see that the k'phóredhet, Kavan, and some of those who entered with him were aware of what this unusual convention of men and women entailed. An obvious trial of the four men under guard, something involving Enesfel and Elyriá, but nothing else was apparent, and Kavan wanted to keep it that way. The less the guilty suspected, the better.

Faced with scowls, long expressions of boredom, and furrowed indignant brows, it was clear that none were pleased with the interruption to their routine by this highly irregular situation, but as the gdhededhá had foregone the customary questioning period before the sequester, the k'phóredhet chose to permit it, particularly as they agreed that the matter of k'gdhededhá Dórímyr's death should be put behind them. As many still believed this death to have been due to illness, the hint of something darker, of murder covered up by their trusted members, made for considerable discomfort.

The ecclesiastical tribunal members were chosen from the rank of the gdhededhá from across the kingdom and replaced every twenty-five years unless ailment, death, or some other reason required an appointment sooner. As with the k'lómesté, there was no limit to the number of appointments an individual could serve, except that none could hold consecutive terms. There were no age or gender requirements. Votes were cast by every náós across Elyriá, choices made from the list of candidates willing to take the governing duties, much the same as elections were carried out for the k'lómesté. Members of the k'lómesté were given a stipend for living expenses and were supplied housing during their years of service, while the members of the k'phóredhet were supported and housed by the donations to the Faith. The short service tenure and modest pay were meant to discourage career politicians, but invariably those who served tended to cycle through service multiple times, particularly within the k'phóredhet, creating an elite pool of individuals who felt entitled, privileged and superior.

The Kyne or the k'gdhededhá could remove an individual from appointment should they prove unfit for the duties required, but within the walls of Hes Dhágdhuán, in the k'phóredhet, that rarely happened. People liked familiar faces around them, particularly ones with known views and policies, ones they could manipulate or sway to their causes or who already supported them.

The nine men and four women of the k'phóredhet were faces Kavan had seen in Hes Dhágdhuán over the years of traveling to and from Clarys. These were the tense faces of individuals who were aware that any surfacing scandal could affect their chances of re-election. The murder they had hidden was on the verge of exposure; once it was revealed, how they chose to deal with it would be crucial.

"Kyne." gdhededhá Éllés, speaker for the Tribunal, bowed respectfully to the Elyri matriarch before turning to the woman beside her. He had never met a Lachlan but had been told that Enesfel's Queen would attend, thus he felt confident this was her. He bowed to her as well and added, "Your Majesty. Truthfully…there is no need for both of you…for this…" he gestured around the room. "We can hear evidence without…"

"We shall hear it as well, gdhededhá," the High Mother said with a fine balance of terseness and warmth in her voice and on her face. "Matters of Faith and diplomacy have grown grave in the relations between Enesfel and Elyriá, between Teren and Elyri. They have been ill dealt with, and I mean to reassure Queen Diona that we are a people of greater integrity than words and talk. I do not intend to interfere, only to see that justice is done."

"Likewise," Diona promised.

"If there is any indication of misconduct," the Kyne continued, "be warned that I will not hesitate to act in the best interest of our peoples and our kingdoms."

Éllés fidgeted and shuffled his feet, looking less dignified than he intended. "We understand, Kyne," he said to the echo rustling in the seats and the murmured breaths of the Tribunal behind him.

"What is this about?" asked one of the gdhededhá who looked particularly perturbed. Other rumblings circled the room from those who likewise wanted to know why such a peculiar group had come here when there was an election to attend.

The High Mother lifted her hand for silence. "This is about murder…the cover-up of death, the failure to seek the guilty, and false accusations placed upon a man accused without proof or trial." The rumblings increased, carrying the burden of shock and dismay, as she turned to the men beside her. "Lord Cliáth has my permission to speak and proceed with this inquiry and no one…" her gaze traveled slowly around the room, "will silence him."

Kavan swallowed the tightness in his throat. This was not a place he had ever imagined he would be. He was not an arbiter, not a judicial representative. He was not a public speaker despite a lifetime of public performance. Outsiders rarely stood in this room, rarely stood before these people except when accused, and few besides the Kyne ever spoke before a joint council. Stern, hostile, confused eyes followed his movements as he stepped forward and he was tempted to turn back and accept the Faith's damnation.

Relenting, however, was not an option. His fate was not inevitable. He could do this. Too much was at stake.

He approached the podium in the center of the room and placed his hands on it, head bowed as if in prayer, allowing himself a calm moment before speaking. Often a speaker would place notes there, or a book from which they would quote but Kavan had neither. He knew what he needed to reveal, and with k'Ádhá's help, he would find the words as the need arose. He turned slowly to make eye contact with each person, wishing Wortham was with him, and then faced the k'phóredhet, the people who held his future, and Elyriá's, in their hands with a swallowed, anxious sigh.

"Within the last year," he began, "two great men of Faith, both the head of the Faith in Enesfel and the head of Faith in Elyriá have been murdered."

"Murdered?" squawked someone over the murmurings erupting throughout the room.

"k'gdhededhá Dórímyr died of fever at the turn of the year," chimed someone else.

"You were led to believe it, Elyriá likewise," Kavan corrected. "But murder it was; I know, for I was there at the time of his death."

The smug expressions of many on the Tribunal's faces, men and women who expected Kavan to be hailed as a murderer without evidence, turned quickly to concern as others in the room questioned this revelation in troubled whispers. How could this be? Why were they only now learning of murder? Why the secrecy? Who might desire to murder the patriarch of the Faith?

How did this connect to k'gdhededhá Tythilius' death?

Though Kavan could have condemned the Tribunal's decisions to keep the news hidden, he spoke instead in their defense. "There was no choice but to hide the truth in the hopes that the cause, and the killer, could be determined quickly. But finding both proved more difficult than expected."

"A man was murdered. How difficult could it be?" Lláhy groused.

Kluín glared at the Tribunal. "Did you not read him? The room? That would have revealed..."

"There was no need," gdhededhá Éllés huffed. "Lord Cliáth was found with the body. The animosity between them is well known."

"Lord Cliáth is no murderer. If you knew him half as well as I..." Diona started, her fists clenched at her side.

"Your pardon, Your Majesty...but you are not capable of reading a man's heart or..."

"Nor," snapped Kluín, "apparently, are you, since you did not, but made assumptions based on what you saw and on rumored past grievances."

Kavan straightened his shoulders and cleared his throat, breaking the impending argument of which he would have been the subject. "Two men were murdered, my lords...and here before us are two of those responsible for the torture and execution of one of them."

The soldiers steered the Gottfrid brothers forward, though neither was eager to move.

"They have been tried before Queen Diona and a panel of judges in Rhidam. One has confessed willingly and both have been found guilty of numerous crimes against the Crown, including grave robbing, harboring and funding criminals, conspiracy, murder, and treason, in addition to the abduction, torture, and execution of k'gdhededhá Tythilius. They are presented here for your reading, should you wish it, so that you may know for yourselves the depth of corruption within the Faith leadership in Enesfel."

He did not reveal that other accomplices were being sought and arrested, and did not mention that Claide was the one who had planned for, hired for, and paid for the abduction and execution. Those details the people in this room could learn for themselves should they choose to read the brothers, as Kavan hoped they would.

Considering the implications, however, that their resistance to interfere in the election that placed Claide in charge of the Teren Faithful, Kavan did not expect anyone to face that ugly reality.

No one came forward, as expected, none of those listening spoke a word about Jermyn's fate, although the sick, dismayed faces of many told Kavan that his unspoken accusations had struck home. If any of them had acted on behalf of the k'gdhededhá, conditions in both kingdoms might be significantly different.

When no one spoke or acted, the guards dragged the Gottfrids back into their places in line and Kavan continued.

"As I have said, k'gdhededhá Dórímyr was poisoned; I was with him at the moment of his passing…poisoned from four different sources." Again the looks and vocalizations of surprise circled, a more audible response than the death of Jermyn had elicited. He did not make mention yet of the fifth source, for he was not prepared to tip his hand to the murderer in the room.

"Before any declaration could be publicly made, it was necessary to determine which of the sources caused his death or was the catalyst that pushed him over. The task was then to determine where those sources originated…and who was behind each. With the k'phóredhet's consent, I ask leave to present the uncovered evidence. You are encouraged to read any of us and any object I present."

"That will not be…" began gdhededhá Éllés.

gdhededhá Lláhy snorted, "We should be able to take you at your word, Lord Cliáth."

"Aye, we should…" agreed Khwílen smugly. He was, perhaps, the only one in the collection of council members and gdhededhá who did take the bard at his word.

Not expecting that response from the Tribunal, or from Khwílen, Kavan bowed his head to each of the speakers before continuing. "Bring Mr. Wistern forward."

The blacksmith dragged his feet, his reluctance to face this large gathering of Elyri and to admit his actions obvious in his posture and face. The Gottfrids had not had to speak. Connected to Dórímyr's death, however, Wistern knew he would not be as lucky. The High Mother's personal guards pulled him to the podium and Kavan, removing the wine bottle from the pack at his feet, presented it for everyone to see.

"Mr. Wistern…do you recognize this bottle?"

"The vintage…the name…aye…but so many look the same beyond that…"

"That may be true." Hwensen and Níkóá had placed a small table near the podium and Kavan set the bottle on it. "It is also true, is it not, that you delivered such a vintage and brand…this bottle, in fact, to gdhededhá Tusánt as a gift?"

"I…I'd…" Wistern stammered and turned his head towards his Queen and sighed. His fate was already decided. He did not regret his choice, his actions, for he held no love for either the man he had hoped to poison or the one who had been. His family's fate, however, was on his shoulders; if he wanted his parents and siblings to be safe, to be able to continue their trade without stigma, he knew what he needed to do. He might hate the Elyri, but he loved his family. "Elyri can drink wine; I've heard it. It's true. He was supposed to drink it…he was supposed to die! He was not supposed to give it away."

"He?"

"dedhá Tusánt."

"gdhededhá Dórímyr would never…" protested one of the women on the Tribunal.

A glance at Hwensen prompted the man to draw back his shoulders and nervously say, "He did, on occasion; Fildanyo was often his wine of choice. There is a collection of bottles in his room."

Tumm nodded after a sidelong glance from Hwensen before saying, "It is true." Knowing that those two men had known Dórímyr the best, that Tumm had known him longer than anyone else present, their acknowledgment and agreement on the claim made it easier for the Tribunal to accept.

"No one searched his…?" began Kluín.

"It was wine…" Éllés protested.

"Wine alone could have killed him," one of the gdhededhá muttered. "If he chose to…he knew drinking is forbidden…"

"Not forbidden," corrected gdhededhá Syán with what sounded to Kavan like an amused chuckle. With his hand on his brother's arm to allow Bhín to hear what was being said, he added, "There are no tenants forbidding alcohol…only common practice to save lives. It is consumed with more regularity than you think."

"Wine which was poisoned, meant to kill another but consumed by Dórímyr instead," Kavan began again.

"Then he has killed…" began Syán.

"A Teren has killed our…" shouted another Tribunal member.

Quick to control that sentiment before it took root and erupted into a blossom of chaos, Kavan spoke as the soldiers drew Wistern away. "No, he did not. The wine did not kill him. As you can see, this bottle, while opened and then resealed, has little missing. The k'gdhededhá poured a single glass and consumed no more than a sip or two with his breakfast, hardly enough to cause the abrupt death he suffered."

"Then who…?"

From the bag, Kavan produced a two-inch-thick stick of kindling, about eight inches long, which he had taken from the hearth in Dórímyr's room. "Diwi was sprinkled on the wood in his fire pit; Diwi, as some of you know, is often used as incense. It would mask the scent of anything else burning. Oleander was found upon his hearth, amidst the logs for his fire. I do not know how he procured Diwi...it originates far south of Hatu and is only obtainable through Hatuish trade routes and merchants, but oleander such as this," he lay the branch on the table, "is grown in abundance in southern Elyriá...and within many courts and halls in Clarys. Many find the aroma appealing when burned, but I am assured by several healers that the smoke can be quite toxic. A single burning would not have killed him...but numerous exposures, over time, would allow the poison to accumulate in his lungs, in his blood, lessening his ability to breathe a little at a time...which would explain the shortness of breath he suffered for the last few years."

Hwensen, wide-eyed, stared at Kavan, his face colorless with shock and fear. "Then he would have been...I did not know...will I..." He had often been sent to fetch wood for the prelate's fire, and the staff knew to have a bundle set aside for him. Hwensen had also spent a considerable amount of time exposed to that smoke, though not nearly as much as Dórímyr had.

Kavan could not answer that speculative question for he was no healer. He heard no difficulty in Hwensen's breath and doubted the aide had endured enough exposure to the concentrated smoke.

"I think not," he finally said, believing as he spoke that Hwensen would take his words as truth.

Éllés continued to scowl. "How would either have ended up in his firewood?" He had no knowledge of the wood's toxicity, but he interpreted Hwensen's distress to be genuine.

"He requested it of the staff many times over the last five years," mumbled Hwensen.

"He must not have known…" someone scoffed.

Kavan interrupted by drawing Dórímyr's journal from the pack, opening it to one of the final entries, and laid it open to the marked page on the table. He could feel three men tense to his right but did not turn to look, not wanting to draw attention to them or cause others to presume some guilt where there was none. "He knew."

What he had read in that journal, combined with some of the imagery Dórímyr had tried to force into Kavan's head in his dying moments made sense. The prelate might have requested oleander because he enjoyed its burning aroma, but he was fully aware of its eventual side-effects.

Those two words brought stunned silence over the chamber. Within the canon of the Faith, the taking of one's own life was as discouraged as murder, it being a waste of the gift of existence k'Ádhá had given, an act of taking divine will into one's own hands. But within the heart of the Faith, there was a deep dilemma that most never spoke of and even fewer gave lingering thought to.

If an Elyri did not succumb to injury or disease, they would, at a certain age, a day and time that no one could anticipate or plan for, be compelled to leave his or her life and possessions and walk away. Into the forests, into the mountains, into the wildland nearest to where they lived, or into the sea; they would go…and not return. None knew where they went, whether they died of normal causes alone amidst nature, whether beasts devoured their ancient bodies leaving not even bones to be found, or whether they went into some other place, some other land or unseen realm, like passing through a k'rylag to a continuation of life on some other level. If that were true, if there was no death for the majority of Elyri, then the afterlife pledged to all by Dhágdhuán, an afterlife in Ethenae with k'Ádhá, the saints and záphyr and those who had gone before, was a cruel promise never to be attained.

Many Elyri, particularly those who had served the Faith their entire lives, were unable to reconcile that disparity and more than one, over the centuries had been rumored to have taken their own life, some by ceasing to eat and drink on a pretext of holy fasting, others in more creative but equally secretive ways. It happened to some outside of the Faith leaders as well, any man or woman suffering a crisis of faith, and Kavan could admit to wondering more than once if that choice would ever present itself to him.

Though no one was willing to say it, no one wanted to speak of it, Kavan's assertion that the k'gdhededhá had a hand in his own demise was a strong possibility. The possibility made sense in accordance to what Dórímyr had shown him at the end, a man afraid of not dying, afraid of withering in the time he had left and not knowing what would come after.

Kavan continued, "Though oleander smoke weakened his lungs and would eventually kill him…and certainly contributed to the ease with which he succumbed, it was not the cause of death."

There was obvious frustration in the room.

"There was poison in his food…but it was something else…this gift…" The chest of trinkets, relics, coins, and jewels was added to the table and opened carefully by Níkóá's gloved hand to make the contents visible. "The instrument of his death is here," he indicated the sharp metal hooking flange, "tainted with Orec, the poison favored by Coryllien during the Persecution. When introduced into his already weakened body, when it reached his lungs, it resulted in almost immediate respiratory failure, as is its primary symptom. And this man," he pointed to Lord Bostik who was detained between Queen Diona and Níkóá, "is responsible for that poisoning."

"Not I, my lord!" Lord Bostik exclaimed despite his earlier confession to the Queen. "It is true I carved that box, long ago, to be a gift for k'dedhá Dórímyr when he first intended to visit Enesfel…"

"A gift you presented to k'gdhededhá Claide to deliver, correct?" Lord Bostik's head bobbed to Kavan's question. "When Dórímyr did not come, what was done with the chest?"

"It was delivered to others who added gifts as they wished..."

"To express love and support of the Faith?" Kavan prompted.

"To make it more enticing...appealing..."

"Bait. Was that your intention as well?"

Lord Bostik did not concede the accusation, nor did he deny it.

"When it came to you a second time, before you returned it to k'gdhededhá Claide, you added one more gift, did you not?"

"I...there was no reason to believe he would ever come for it...that he would ever..."

"But there was hope that he would. else you would not have made the effort...and there was a plan in place to deliver it if he did not come to Rhidam?"

Still uncertain how that information had fallen into the Queen's hands, but not wanting his family to bear the punishment of traitors to the Crown for his choices, there was no use in hiding the truth from Elyri who could take it whether he spoke a confession or not. Queen Diona already knew the truth, as did, it seemed, the White Bard. Perhaps others here already knew as well.

"He promised Dórímyr would receive it if I provided the Orec."

"He?"

He twitched uncomfortably, but muttered, "k'gdhededhá Claide."

The sounds in the gallery were just as uncomfortable.

"And you provided the Orec as requested?" Kavan asked quickly to cut off outbursts from others.

Lord Bostik lifted his chin. "I did," he claimed with his first hint of defiance. His gaze circled the room across the sea of Elyri faces judging him. "Not one of you cares about the Teren Faithful. You make rulings, demand tithes, send your rejects to preach to us." His sneer was mirrored by a nearly identical one on Wistern's.

"k'gdhededhá Claide is right. We neither want your involvement in our Faith nor need your biased, hypocritical teachings…"

"Biased?"

"Hypocritical?"

"Please." This was not the time for an ethical debate on the precepts of Faith, as much as Kavan wanted to participate in a discussion between the Tribunal, the Elyri gdhededhá and the Teren who struggled against them. Perhaps if the Faith leaders heard that faction's beliefs and feelings, they would understand the risks Elyri face outside of Elyriá and would begin to address the distance they kept between Clarys and Rhidam's leadership.

A gesture brought Níkóá to Kavan's side. He stood close, not touching, but Kavan could feel that he was actively, consciously or not, drawing both energy and moral strength from him. The bard almost frowned, not liking that sensation, and stubbornly pulled his power behind well-practiced walls where the redhead could not reach it. If he realized that source was gone, that he could draw no more, he did not show it, leading Kavan to conclude it was an unconscious thing on Níkóá's part. He would have to teach the man to control that ability if they were to continue as friends.

"k'gdhededhá Claide sanctioned and instructed the use of poison, with the intent to deliver it into Dórímyr's hands…which he did when Dórímyr visited Rhidam."

Again, it was Éllés who protested, "He has never been to Rhidam, I assure you…"

"And I assure you, gdhededhá," Queen Diona spoke solemnly without rising from her seat or raising her voice, "that he was there, for I spoke with him myself."

Hwensen nodded, his expression discomfited and grave. "It is true, gdhededhá. I did not know until after…but he went…"

"I do not understand why he chose that path, but what I saw in his final moments, when he touched me…" Kavan put his hand on his cheek where the prelate had left bloody fingerprints on his white skin. Every member of the Tribunal had seen those marks the day of Kavan's arrest and they knew what it meant when Kavan touched his face. They knew that was where the blood had been, though none had likewise touched the bard to read him or to gather any impressions Dórímyr had left in that touch. "But I believe he made the trip with the intention of understanding k'gdhededhá Claide…to learn about the violence in Enesfel…to provoke violence that would support a separation of the Faith into Teren and Elyri entities."

Some mutterings in the room suggested that separation of the Teren and Elyri Faithful was not a prospect debated only in Enesfel…or an idea held only by Dórímyr and Claide. It apparently had also taken root within the walls of Hes Dhágdhuán, a realization that left Kavan cold with dismay.

With a sigh, he said, "I believe he may, in fact, have hoped he would meet his death during that visit, as a martyr to the Faith…to initiate separation."

Murmurs, mutterings, and the sounds of outrage and shock. Rather than give himself, or them, time to ponder or react to that surge of emotion, Kavan continued. "It was during this visit to Rhidam that he received both the wine and the chest of relics, and it was within two days of his return to Clarys, that I found him dying in his room. He did not speak to k'ghededhá Claide, was told he was away…but gdhededhá Valgis made sure that both gifts were delivered before k'gdhededhá Dórímyr departed. Yet there is proof that k'gdhededhá Claide was at the náós during that visit and instead refused to see him…that he made sure the chest was poisoned and delivered…threatening both k'gdhededhá Dórímyr and anyone else who came in contact with its contents…which I presume would have been many as those among you with interest would have examined the contents and taken what you wished from it. Dórímyr cut himself on the flange, allowing the poison into his blood more easily than if he had ingested it, and its effect on his already compromised condition resulted in a swift and painful death. As I mentioned, this is not k'gdhededhá Claide's sole crime…"

"We are not here to hear…"

"We should, Éllés," Khwílen rose indignantly. "Had he…had any of us…involved ourselves at the onset…shown compassion and offered support when k'gdhededhá Tythilius was abducted and found dead, much of what has been would not have come to pass."

"There is no proof…"

"Read me." Eyes turned to Níkóá. "I am your proof. I have overheard Claide myself…heard speak of having the k'gdhededhá tortured and killed…of orchestrating the recent fire in Rhidam which later contributed to the death of several young Elyri volunteers…of arranging to poison k'gdhededhá Dórímyr. Or read the brothers. They will substantiate my claims." He knew less about the latter, but he hoped the gdhededhá would read him alone and make the same inferences Kavan had made. Reading the brothers, two Teren, an uncomfortable task for many of those here, would not be necessary if they read Níkóá first.

"If this is true, if he is guilty," sniffed one of the gdhededhá being considered for the prelate's position, a derisive sound that made Kavan clench his teeth, "why has he not been arrested and…?"

It was Ylár who spoke next, his slow, steady voice blanketing the high tensions in the room. "Because this is an ecclesiastical matter for the Faith. The Queen is right to bring this before us; we should reprimand our own, if it is as is claimed." Other voices in the room agreed, though no one seemed willing to come forward and test Níkóá's honesty. "Pray tell, Lord Cliáth, you did not speak of the third poisoning…of his food? Was it accidental? Inconsequential?"

The bard and gdhededhá stared long at one another. Ylár knew from their previous conversation that the bard, whatever the personal beliefs were that had brought on him the accusation of heresy, was acting not solely on his own behalf but on behalf of the Five Sovereignties and the Faith that bound most of them together. As a man of the Faith, a man who sought to avoid the trappings of political games. So far the contributors to the man's death had been from Enesfel or had been at the prelate's own hands, with no mention of an Elyri murderer amongst them.

If any Elyri was among the guilty, if any of them had even tried to cause the prelate's death, Ylár wanted to know, even if the attempted murderer was his father. The thought of a killer leading the Faithful, as had already been done for several hundred years, did not settle easily in his stomach, his heart, or his soul.

Kavan released the breath he held in a long, slow hiss. He had, to his satisfaction, already proven that he was not Dórímyr's killer, that the ultimate guilt lay in k'gdhededhá Claide's hands. What the Tribunal and the gdhededhásur chose to do with that evidence, how they chose to deal with Claide and the Teren Faith establishment was out of Kavan's hands. A small part of him argued that revealing another man's guilt was less important, but when that man might potentially step into the dead man's shoes, Kavan knew he could not afford to be silent. He was grateful Ylár had called him out on his delayed omission; he had less chance of giving in to that fearful voice that worried about how he would be perceived when he spoke next, how those who still held heresy over his head, would react.

"It was no accident. As with the oleander wood, this was a deliberate poisoning occurring over several days prior to his death.." One by one, he set the twelve vials on the table, each empty except for the last. "...by the one who is his son."

He looked squarely at Lláhy, who lurched to his feet in remonstration. "That is preposterous! I would never..." Others looked at Lláhy as well, the revelation of his lineage no longer a secret with those few words hanging in the air. "Lies...all of it..."

"You have been reaching out to your mother's people…sleeping amongst them…to draw them into the Faith," Kavan said gently, for he admired the work the other man had undertaken Lláhy could not be faulted for his parentage, only for fathering children himself if his peers wished to call him out for misconduct others among them also committed. Lláhy should, perhaps, be rewarded for the good he was seeking to do, but his other, less admirable actions, needed to be exposed and dealt with.

"I found these in the room where you reside when with them, at your bedside." He placed the other objects he had taken from that room next to the vials. "Maran seed oil. Maran, your father's favorite delicacy and a poison easily masked. Maran sauce on his breakfast lamb, two fruits on the tray…one partially eaten. Adding the oil to the fruit, into the sauce, would not be noticed…no one would have known. When you learned the truth…when you believed that anyone knowing the truth was a threat to you…you began to poison him."

"I could never…"

"It is here." Kavan pressed his hand to the journal. "He knew what you were doing, yet chose to…"

"He could not protect me! His hypocrisy will haunt me…damn me forever! He said the seat was mine…but he would not die! No one was supposed to know! You should not know what he was!"

"But I do."

"Know what?" demanded Éllés, as he and the Tribunal and every gdhededhá in the gallery became aware that there was some secret in Lláhy's past more damning than illegitimacy.

Kavan shook his head, refusing to go through that open door. "That is a matter best left to the privacy of the k'phóredhet and gdhededhá Lláhy." There was no need for the details of those reasons to be made public, as it would in turn serve to cast a shadow over Dórímyr's years of service, and Kavan would not be the one to do that. Nor would he implicate Tumm, and possibly Ylár. Dórímyr had his faults, but he had served from his heart as faithfully as any man could. Kavan, for all of his disputes with the man called Old Marble, could admit that. He doubted Dórímyr's Zythánite connections alone would have been enough to keep Lláhy out of the prelate's chair, but the attempt to murder his father certainly would...or should.

Heads dipped low, back and forth amongst the members of the Tribunal as they whispered and passed words through the touching of hands, seeking some resolution to the tangled net uncovered here. Some of it was too complicated for a collection of political individuals to reach a decision quickly, even if the decisions seemed obvious to outsiders. They did, however, appreciate that he sought to avoid the scandal he could easily have created.

Perhaps that spoke more highly of his character than they had given him credit for.

Finally, Éllés got to his feet, looking as if the movement pained him. "gdhededhá Ylár...gdhededhá Sen...you will read each object presented...each suspect brought before us, as well as Lord Cliáth...and you will present the findings to the k'phóredhet as soon as you finish. Kyne, if you will appoint someone to oversee the reading...to be certain that none of these items, or individuals, are mistreated, the rest of you may depart...except of course, Lord Cliáth and the accused."

Kavan bowed, accepting the ruling with both trepidation and eagerness. He did not know Tribunal member Sen, save that she was from a prosperous family in the farthest southern regions of Elyriá and that she had not spoken a single word during the proceedings or communicated any facial expression that might reveal her thoughts. He could not gauge Éllés' reasons for appointing her as a reader.

But he knew Ylár's reputation for steadfastness, honesty, and honor. Ylár would find the truth in each bit of evidence without fearing the outcome, which would, Kavan hoped, result in his acquittal. The capricious Tribunal could rule differently if they chose, however, and it was that fickleness, as he retreated to the antechamber with the two ruling women who had come in his support, that Kavan was afraid of. He should thank both the Kyne and the Queen, but he was too afraid to speak before the Tribunal's final judgment was made. It was best to keep his thoughts to himself.

⋟Chapter 31⋞

The first to be read, Níkóá had already been sent back to Rhidam on a previously arranged mission for Princess Asta and two of his own, the chance to take the news of this day to Caol and to meet again with k'gdhededhá Claide. He would have preferred to stay and hear the verdicts to be the one chosen to bring Claide to justice himself, but even Kavan had bid him go.

For the bard, it would be difficult enough to shoulder the Queen's emotions if the Tribunal voted against him. Kavan did not want anyone else to be present to hear it, particularly if Wortham or Prince Muir could not be.

Each witness, suspect, and evidentiary object was read, with great reluctance shown when it came time to read both of the Gottfrids and the intimidating bard who was rumored by both Teren and Elyri to be immensely powerful. Bhyrhán, chosen by the Queen and High Mother to oversee the proceedings, gathered the items and oversaw their removal from the chamber as the Kyne's soldiers escorted the four prisoners, now ashen-faced and faint of appearance, to a temporary holding area. Being the only Teren in a room full of potentially hostile Elyri had been more than any of the four could bear, and their fear made their thoughts easier for gdhededhá Sen and gdhededhá Ylár to sift through and read. The readings had been completed hours ago, gdhededhá Lláhy sent out of the room to wait with his peers, and still, the joint councils and the collection of candidates for the prelacy continued to debate.

Kyne Mórne and Queen Diona had excused themselves to speak privately, leaving Kavan with two guards, Lláhy, and Bhyrhán. It was preferable, for Kavan found he could breathe more easily with the women out of his proximity, although the daggerous glares Lláhy threw made Kavan's skin and senses raw with energy.

Come mid-afternoon, the members of the k'lómesté, save for the Speaker, departed, leaving the Faith leaders to conclude the much stickier business of applying centuries of Faith and practice to a set of new circumstances. Eventually, Hwensen was sent to summon the Queen and Kyne back, and as darkness wound around Clarys, Kavan and the others were brought from the antechamber to face the men and women who held their fates in their hands.

≈*≈

Claide did not hide his scowl as he watched the woman slink into the collecting shadows. He had met her once before, in a time before he had begun his bid for power and position in Enesfel's Faith. He knew she was connected somehow to Heward, someone he had also met only once a little over three years ago. Although he believed they were fighting the same war, on the same side, he did not believe they sought the same result.

He did not know if he could trust her. Though she bore traces of Cíbhóló descent, he did not think she was fully Teren. Nor did he know if he should believe her assertions that the redhead was not who he claimed to be. Yes, the man had successfully infiltrated the castle and gained appointment as chamberlain. A Lachlan by birth, perhaps. But how could a man from relative obscurity, a stranger, gain the Crown's ear so easily?

Lachlan or no, it was not good policy, in Claide's opinion, for the Crown to appoint a stranger as a key advisor. Not, he sneered, that he credited the Queen for being capable of sound policy.

Had he known that the redhead had served the Crown as the executioner of Corylliens at least once?

A man had to do what he had to do to gain power and influence, no matter how distasteful or against one's moral compass it might be. Claide understood that. The captured Corylliens had been destined to die for their foolish attack on the Queen; choosing an executioner had been necessary. For the redhead to undertake that gruesome responsibility was an ideal way of gaining the Queen's attention, and ridding her of enemies had been a step to gaining favor. If, as the foreign woman claimed, the redhead had joined the organization he had slighted in that execution, did not that prove that he wanted an end to the Elyri occupation of Enesfel as well?

Or perhaps, the woman asserted, he was working for the Crown and using his new Lachlan influence to bring about the destruction and downfall of everything Claide and others like him had struggled long and hard to create.

Considering himself a good judge of character, Claide left a message with the tavern keeper to pass to the redheaded prince the next time he came for a drink. There was a simple way to prove what side the man was on, and that was to put his loyalties to the test. That was exactly what Claide intended to do. In the meantime, he would tolerate the stomach full of nagging, gnawing doubt and hope that his instincts were better than the foreigner gave him credit for.

৯*৯

Caol did not like it. As the sun settled over the western rim of Rhidam's houses, he shared a drink with the redhead his daughter had referred to him. Níkóá had connections to Lord Cliáth, had provided the details of murder that were presented to the Elyri High Mother, the Elyri High Council, and the Tribunal that morning. It was good news, and the redhead's connection to the bard made him as trustworthy as any man could be. Caol accepted whatever part he was to play in the mission to end the Corylliens. He needed as much help as he could get.

As they talked over drinks, Caol received word that he and his recruits were to gather at the same storage house, this time not for inspection but for an assignment. The request seemed atypical for Heward, a man who had not been personally involved in Coryllien acts before but routinely left them for another beneath him, like Layton, to carry out. He had taken great effort to avoid entanglement with the group, protecting his identity from the Crown. The death of the majority of his followers might have prompted him to take direct control, however, as might a desire to see Alty in action. Or maybe this mission, whatever it would be, was of personal significance to him and he wanted to have his hand in seeing it completed.

Or perhaps, Caol thought grimly, he did not trust Alty's ability to lead, considered him untested and perhaps untrustworthy. Caol was determined to prove his merit if he could, but he had to be given a chance. He had to gain Heward's trust enough to be alone with him…this time to take his life.

Kavan looked at no one as he waited amidst the other men facing charges, although he stood with his head high and his shoulders drawn back, appearing neither meek nor afraid. He could feel the Queen's gaze, her heart hammering within her breast as she waited for a verdict against him once again. Too often, since her grave error that had sent him fleeing from Enesfel, had Kavan been accused of heinous crimes when he had done nothing more than his duty to the Lachlans, to Enesfel and Elyriá, to Teren and Elyri alike. Why it had fallen on his shoulders to purge the lands, the Faith, of the cancer of hatred, she could not guess, but she prayed this would be the last time Kavan had to face such trials, that he would know the same peace and chance to enjoy his family as any other man.

"Gentlemen, the facts have been heard, read, and weighed accordingly, the murders of k'gdhededhá Tythilius and Dórímyr dissected, the attempts on gdhededhá Tusánt and the crimes against Elyri given voice and ears." Éllés sounded weary, thin, and stretched, but to Kavan, he also sounded victorious, a coloring to his voice that made Kavan's raw nerves crawl with distaste. "The pros and cons of punishment, of action, of policy and history, have been given due consideration, and our decisions have been reached in conjunction with Kyne Mórne, Queen Diona, the k'lómesté, the k'phóredhet, and the congregation of candidates…the highest authorities in the land. In accordance with the vote, our rulings are as follows…"

Kavan's hands clenched as he held his breath and waited.

"Lord Bostik and Mr. Wistern. We jointly find you both to be guilty of murder and attempted murder of officials of the Faith. Lords Gottfrid, we find you both guilty of the abduction, torture, and murder of an official of the Faith. As citizens of Enesfel, however, we have no grounds, according to our precepts, on which to administer punishment for your crimes. It is therefore agreed that you shall be taken from this place in the custody of Queen Diona, who will see to your disposal as befits the laws of Enesfel for crimes of high treason. For have no doubt, gentlemen, attacks against the Faith such as you have undertaken are attacks against the ruling authorities of the lands, both in Elyriá and outside of it, and shall be treated as treason henceforth whenever such a ruling can be made."

There was no need to look at the four beside him for Kavan to know they had gone pale and cold. Since their own words and thoughts had condemned them, death had been the only possible outcome unless the Tribunal cleared them of charges. While there was relief that they would not be subjected to some gruesome Elyri torture before they were given over to an executioner, it was well known now that the Lachlan Queen would not be lenient and what fate she bestowed would be equally horrible to consider.

"Lord Cliáth." Éllés looked at the smooth wooden surface of the podium before him, either reading notes or collecting his thoughts or, Kavan thought as a wave of annoyance lapped at his feet, an effort to delay the inevitable. "The veracity of your many claims has been noted. And proven., For your efforts in seeking k'gdhededhá Dórímyr's murderer, for your perseverance and success in presenting our joint councils with all available evidence, for the honesty with which you have dealt with us…" He cleared his throat and wrinkled his nose. "Your name has been cleared of charges of murder and those seeking your arrest are recalled to Clarys. The remaining charge will be discussed at a later time."

The breath he had held gushed out in relief and Kavan closed his eyes as he bowed. "Thank you, gdhededhá, for your wisdom." One charge at least, he was clear of, but he knew, even if the Queen did not, that the other still hanging over him, one that the Tribunal was disinterested in addressing at this time, was equally troubling. With an election in the offing, it was reasonable that matters of heresy would be addressed by the man elected as k'gdhededhá after the more pressing matter of Lláhy's Zythánite ties and attempts to against his father were handled. This step, however, was enough for Kavan, and enough for Diona and the Kyne, whose satisfaction he could feel warming the evening air.

Regardless of his personal views on Kavan's religious opinions, Ylár respected him and believed him to be honest and sincere. He had read the bard and found no darkness within. The others did not have that luxury, would have to take Ylár's word for it. If he could, the scarred man would remain on Kavan's side through the judgment that would eventually come, whether he was elected as prelate or not.

"gdhededhá Lláhy." Éllés' tone grew grave and sad, and Kavan suspected, by the looks of many faces in the room, that Lláhy had been the favored candidate, the likely choice for the prelacy…but no longer. "For crimes against your blood, against the Father of our Faith, it is necessary to extend punishment to you as well."

Lláhy scowled and opened his mouth in his own defense, but something, perhaps the harsh glance from the old, chair-bound Tumm to his right, made him clamp it closed, his teeth gritted in frustration.

"Your years of service to the Faith and your outreach to those fallen outside of our center have not been overlooked, yet a crime as serious as yours cannot be dismissed. You have confessed in word and thought the intent to take a man's life to assume his position, and that is something we cannot ignore. It is decided that, from this moment forth, you will be exiled from Clarys, from Elyriá, for no less than fifty years, during which time you are charged with a pilgrimage throughout the Teren lands where you shall visit each shrine, each holy house, not as a gdhededhá but as a wayfarer. Should you return to Elyriá during that time, you shall be detained and sentenced to the same death you attempted to bestow on your father. When your pilgrimage is complete, you may appear before the k'phóredhet if you choose and petition to have your exile lifted, to be welcomed back into the bosom of the Faith. On that day it will be determined if you have served sufficient penance for your acts and whether you may resume the mantle of gdhededhá…but you shall never be permitted on the seat you covet.

The Teren scowled and Kavan could feel the same dissatisfaction from others, but such a ruling was typical of the way Elyri law dealt with those caught in a criminal act. A non-violent solution was typically sought, something appropriate to the individual sentenced and for the crime committed. For a man of Faith, being cut off from those he had served with in Clarys would be a significant blow, as would the loss of the status he had worked long and hard to gain. Being denied the office of k'gdhededhá was another. On top of that, there was no small risk in being exiled from Elyriá into Teren lands rife with hostility. Some of those shrines he must visit were deep within Neth, and getting to them would be no simple thing. Every day of his fifty-year sentence would be spent beneath the shadow of violence and death, allowing him to ponder the act of violence he had perpetrated on his father. It was a wise, suitable, acceptable punishment for an Elyri.

Lláhy refused to hang his head, refused to show regret or remorse, which might be interpreted as weakness, although Kavan could detect both emotions roiling beneath the man's skin. When he made no comment of either acceptance or protest, Éllés sighed and cleared his throat.

"These matters have brought to our attention an issue which has not been appropriately addressed, one which deserves discussion and a decision to assure peace between Elyriá and our Teren neighbors. As a figurehead within the Faith, k'gdhededhá Claide is subject to the laws and rulings of the leadership here in Clarys. We, however, are governed by secular law, of which Kyne Mórne is our head. By extension, this would bring Teren gdhededhá beneath Elyri law, when, in fact, they should be governed by the laws of the lands of their birth and servitude."

Kavan scowled.

"It has been decided, therefore, that in this matter, k'gdhededhá Claide's arrest and sentence shall be handled by the Lachlan Crown."

"He is a criminal against the Faith!" Khwílen exclaimed in protest. Claide's actions were more criminal, in his eyes, than Dórímyr's had been, and he meant to see both men's crimes brought to light and see that punishment be placed where belonged. Dórímyr might be dead, but he would not be well remembered if Khwílen had anything to say about it.

"He is Teren…the highest-ranking gdhededhá outside of Elyriá, fairly elected by…"

"I would not say fairly," muttered the Queen indignantly.

Éllés bristled at her interruption but did not scold her. "Until such a time as the matter is satisfactorily debated and a final decision wrought, the Teren Faithful act under their own authority, under the direction of the chosen head at Hes á Redh, and is subject to the laws and decisions of its…"

Again, Khwílen interrupted. "There is no Tribunal in the Teren Faith. Cut off from Clarys, there is no one above Claide, no one to defrock him, no one to balance…"

"Then one shall be elected…"

"Under whose direction and authority? His? A man who orchestrated and partook in the deaths of two prelates? You have seen what this man has wrought unchecked…the chaos he has caused both in Enesfel and Elyriá. We acknowledge his crimes against the Faith. We should see to his castigation for them." Ylár brought a steadiness back into what had been about to erupt into a bitter, feuding debate. "Agreement has been reached that he should be reprimanded and punished for his crimes…and yet there is no Tribunal in Rhidam, in Enesfel, to try him. Only in the most extreme cases is secular law applied over Faith law…"

Éllés barked, "Then this shall be deemed an extreme case…and his punishment placed in Lachlan jurisdiction. Clarys shall not impose itself upon Teren rule. The Teren Faithful will need to govern themselves…and under no circumstance are we to…"

It was Hwensen, the man with the most constant contact with one of the deceased, and the one who had endured the entire day's proceedings despite not being a part of any of the governing bodies, who spoke next. "Such is what k'gdhededhá Dórímyr espoused…and you see the results of his disinterest."

"He died because he went to Rhidam," protested someone in the back of the room.

"He died because of his apathy to the suffering of our people outside of Elyriá, his apathy towards the Faithful in other lands, and his refusal to protect k'gdhededhá Tythilius that has created..."

"gdhededhá Hwensen." Éllés' rebuke cut him short. "There shall be no further debate on this today. After the sequester, when a new k'gdhededhá is installed under oath, we shall entertain further discussion on this sensitive issue. Until then, the ruling of the k'phóredhet and k'lómesté stands. Queen Diona, the right of law and duty places the dispensation of arrest, trial, and punishment of k'gdhededhá Claide in your hands and we shall provide a writ dictating our ruling so that you may act as you choose."

Tension rippled across his shoulders as Kavan listened to the Tribunal's rulings. He barely believed what he heard. With the turmoil and upheaval in Enesfel, there was the possibility that a panel of judges would acquit a man capable of buying them, influencing them with favors or threats, or merely winning them with a plea for sympathy, particularly once the news circulated about this new rift between the Elyri and Teren Faith. The Tribunal might have initiated a deeper split between Elyri and Teren, something that even Kyne Mórne could see, but they, in religious blindness, either could not or did not care about that. Segregating Elyri from Teren seemed their primary concern, and to Kavan, that was the saddest, most dangerous position of all.

❧*❦

Most of his men, as well as Heward and his female partner, were already in the storage house when Caol and the redhead arrived. Men held torches and lanterns, a few held small weapons carried as they crept through the darkening streets, but none seemed edgy or out of place. A quick perusal of the room showed nothing amiss, but every sense Caol possessed told him that something was wrong, even when Heward said, "Alty…a word…" and motioned him to the far side of the room. Caol tried not to frown as he sent the redhead to join the others with a glance and followed Heward. The redhead bobbed his head once and obeyed.

☙*❧

Kavan spoke little as he bowed his head to the Queen's bidding. He made brief mental contact with both the court healer and the man due to be formally appointed chamberlain the following day. Níkóá was in no position to aid, but Ártur traveled swiftly to Rhidam, to Prince Espen and Prince Owain to call on them to assemble soldiers and meet the Queen, the bard, and their four prisoners in Hes á Redh. The Queen also desired that gdhededhá Tusánt be present, and every other gdhededhá in Rhidam, to hear the decree she was to make.

There would be no waiting until daybreak, no allowing Claide the chance to escape. She had the evidence she needed, the permission of the Elyri tribunal and Faith leadership, and her mind was made up, her path set. k'gdhededhá Claide would be taken into the Crown's custody tonight and held under arrest for as long as it took to build an irrefutable case against him. They had the chest used to kill Dórímyr, they had the testimony of several individual men, and they had Hwensen's and Bhyrhán's willingness to come to Rhidam and report, on behalf of the Tribunal, the sentence the Elyri Faith had passed. Perhaps when Claide was in custody, others would come forward to speak evidence as well. If not, the Queen would make do with the facts she had, enough to condemn him in her opinion, and if need be she would execute him without trial.

No matter the stain it might cast upon her reign, if she could bring peace to her people by ending one man's reign of violence and horror, she believed that stain would be worth it.

Once certain that the requested soldiers were in place, that Tusánt and the other gdhededhá were gathering as well, Kavan stepped into the Purification chamber and drew Diona and the four prisoners with him. He could control them, keep them from harming him or the Queen, and he wanted to do this in a single trip.

He did not expect to return to Clarys for a very long time.

≈*≈

It was likely to be the best opportunity he would get.

A great cracking sound shook the building as he stopped beside Heward, drawing everyone's attention to the thatched timber ceiling. The distraction was not entirely unexpected, however, by the man few had ever seen, for in Caol's turn towards the sound, Heward drew a long slender blade and drove it between Caol's ribs as the splintering beams above began to collapse on the men gathered in the middle of the room.

≈*≈

"What is this?" barked Claide in annoyance, his disheveled state suggesting a man roused from his bed, as most of the gdhededhá had been by Tusánt's summons. Finding a dozen armed soldiers including Justice Corbin, Chamberlain Lachlan, and Prince Espen, led by General Agis, he scowled. Unlike others, however, Claide had not been asleep but had rather tossed and turned as he fretted over the puzzle of the redhead holding the Lachlan key to peace. The redhead was not here; there was no sign of him amidst the gathering Claide found within the domain he controlled. Even Princess Asta, Chancellor McGranis, and Healer MacLyr were present, the Queen wanting none of her advisors left out of this momentous occasion.

When no immediate response came to his demand, he snapped, "I want an answer." At this late hour, there were few reasons for this particular set of individuals to gather here, and as he awaited a response, Claide began to gauge his options. There was no reason to believe they were here for him, but there was also no reason to believe they were not.

If they had come for him, how might he talk his way out of arrest?

The Purification chamber door opened. The Queen, the White Bard, and four prisoners Claide did not want to see, stepped into the Gathering Hall.

"I do not believe," Diona said coolly, "you have any right to make such a demand."

๑*๑

Níkóá sensed the ripple of power moments before the crackling came, moments before the structure's roofing beams, which created the floor for the level above, began to crash down around their heads. He threw out a blast of energy, scattering much, but not all, of the debris away from the men around him as he spun to glare at the source of that power surge. Instead of finding it, he saw two men, breast to breast, holding each other fast by the arm, by the tunic, with one hand, each bearing a look of shock and pain as they stared one another in the eye.

Heward's hand, clenched around his knife and pushed tight to Caol's chest, dripped red.

๑*๑

Claide assessed the situation in the span of a few heartbeats. With Lord Bostik and both Gottfrid brothers bound beside the Queen, at the mercy of the Elyri he hated more than any other, there was no doubt that his freedom and life were threatened. Words, he knew, would be of no use, not with Kavan there to rip into his mind and extract anything he wanted to, no matter how trivial. It took no more than that same span of heartbeats for Claide to make his choice.

He lurched sideways, grabbed the Queen by the throat, and pulled her against him.

With Prince Muir dead, removing the Queen would leave Enesfel's throne vacant. If this act could maneuver the anti-Elyri Prince Lachlan onto the throne, Claide would have accomplished his ultimate goal, even if he did not live to witness the results.

"Back away or I'll…"

❧*❧

Men disappeared beneath the rubble, cries of pain and shock echoed on the tail end of the roof's collapse, and a lone figure dashed for the door through the barrage of dust, flying pebbles, and splinters that plumed up as the larger chunks of debris hit the dusty floor. But Níkóá saw none of that, and only heard the anguish of pain and death on the fringes of his perceptions. From his wrist sheath, a small blade was thrown at Anri Heward…who was already stumbling backward with shock and outrage on his face, a blade protruding from between his ribs as well. Níkóá's knife whizzed harmlessly past Anri's head as Heward stared wide-eyed at Caol Dugan.

"That," Caol hissed, "is for Prince Muir."

❧*❧

What Kavan heard at that moment was not the inhaled breaths from everyone in the room, nor Diona's frightened squawk as she tried, unsuccessfully, to twist free of the grip crushing her windpipe. What he heard, with senses more profound than his ears, with a part of him that reached deeper into the unseen world, was the distress of two tiny heartbeats, innocent lives too young to know what was occurring or to fend for themselves. Lives that, though he could not say how, were destined to be important. Lives spreading into the future of Enesfel. Lives he had not been aware of before this moment. While the mother's life was no less important, it was the children's distress that caused Kavan to lash out without thinking, wrapping invisible fingers of power around the assailant's thundering heart and squeezing, drawing the power tighter, restricting the flow of blood and breath all at once.

๛*๙

Níkóá flew after the blade he had thrown, his net of power no longer sheltering the recruited Association men from any debris that had yet to fall. Crying "Lord Dugan!" with the taste of dust and blood in his mouth, he caught Caol before the man hit the floor.

Nearby, a spark of understanding, disdain, and begrudging respect lit, and then bled out of, Anri Heward's dying eyes.

"Is he…?"

๛*๙

Claide did not know the source of his sudden agony, the abrupt wrenching pain in his chest that caused him to release the Queen and stagger sideways to trip over the nearest kneeler and crash to his knees. He did not know, most did not, but Ártur recognized both the flare of power in the room, stronger than he had ever felt, and an uncharacteristic darkness growing in his cousin's green eyes. "Kavan," he cried, hoping the shout would be enough to break the focus of the man he could not physically reach.

๛*๙

"The Corylliens are defeated," Níkóá murmured, knowing it was what Caol wanted to hear, clutching his bloody hand with a strength he hoped would pass into the injured man as he knelt with him in his arms. He could heal small wounds, but something of this magnitude was beyond him. "You've done it, my lord. Enesfel is safe."

❧*❧

"Kavan!" the healer repeated as he caught the winded Queen and put his hand to her throat to ease her breathing. Espen knelt with him, while Owain rushed to Kavan's side, not knowing the cause of the healer's cry but determining that the bard needed help. Some of the soldiers surrounded Mr. Wistern, Lord Bostik, and the Gottfrid brothers while others surrounded the choking, fallen k'gdhededhá that none, not even his fellow Faithful, seemed prepared to assist. Kavan, still near the Purification chamber, failed to react.

❧*❧

Knowing no skills to staunch the flow of life, to prevent the man's lungs from filling with precious fluid, to give a man back his breath and life, Níkóá swallowed the panic and did what he could to ease the man's pain. Caol nodded his head at the new chamberlain's words, smiled, and with a whispered, "Tell Asta…" slipped beyond Níkóá's grasp. What he was left with, when Caol grew limp within his arms, was a silence punctuated by groaning, whimpering men in the darkness of the late winter's night and a cold, hard ball of regret in the pit of his stomach.

❧*❧

The constricting power hold on Claide's heart released. Kavan blinked, his cousin's voice ringing in his ears where he had not heard it moments before. He looked at Ártur, seeing him in the room for the first time, and then down at the unseeing man crumpled awkwardly against the bench and kneeler as if he had been pushed and held there. Having heard nothing but the heartbeats of children, seeing nothing but red, Kavan felt his fists unclench and recognized the unraveling pool of power he had harnessed and used seconds before.

He knew his body well. He recognized the indicators of great energy spent, and judging by the way gdhededhá Tusánt and Ártur gaped at him, it took little effort to guess what he had done. He had, without conscious thought, killed a man.

Again.

He trembled, his center filling with disgust and dismay. The taste of bitter bile, the tang of incense lingering in the air, the weight of damning guilt were all heavy enough to choke him. When Diona croaked, "Kavan?" in response to a look of panic she recognized too well, her hand stretched out to offer him comfort. He stared at it long enough for his pupils to dilate until there was no green to be seen, and then he balked, fleeing into the Purification Chamber, disappearing into the night.

❧Epilogue❧

I n the days that followed, Kavan's absence was keenly felt in Rhidam as the pieces scattered by one chaotic night were brought together and reassembled with painfully gaping omissions. Unaware of what had transpired in the sanctuary of Hes á Redh, Níkóá left the Association members, who were unharmed in the collapse, to dig their comrades free and see to the wounded and the dead, while he carried Caol and Heward back to the security of the mostly sleeping palace, where Physician Talis pronounced him dead after a required, but unnecessary, examination. The location of the puncture, the amount of blood staining the man's clothes and filling his lungs left no doubt that he was gone.

No sooner was that done when the Queen was carried into the castle in her husband's arms, followed by an anxious Ártur and the majority of her advisors. Seeing her father's bloody, still form, Princess Asta broke into choking, uncontrollable sobs, clinging to him the way any young girl would to the father she loved and who was now forever lost. Laid upon the Great Hall floor was Caol's crowning achievement. Anri Heward, the man who had resurrected and led the Corylliens to the torment and destruction of many lives and Enesfel's peace, was dead as well, Caol's blade still wedged between his ribs, thrust deep into the man's heart. The evidence he had collected and given to Onea Pantel was delivered to the Queen, along with the woman's deepest regrets, as soon as word reached her of Caol's death. That Caol had done his duty, struggled to the end of his life to succeed on behalf of the Lachlans he loved and served, was Asta's pride and comfort, but that night, the fullness of both great deeds could not penetrate her grief.

She would accept the full title of Inquisitor from her Queen-cousin in time, and with Matus, Marta, and Fen Geli at her disposal, she would uphold her father's ideals, everything he had ever stood for and believed. The Association, out of respect, would soon give her the same consideration and cooperation they had given her father, even to the point of crowning her an honorary member of the Association as Caol had been throughout much of his life.

From the rubble of the collapsed building, one female was uncovered, a woman matching the descriptions others had provided during the months of Coryllien terror, but she remained a woman without identity, for Ártur's attempts to read her revealed nothing, as if she were a body without a life, without memory, without a past. She carried Elyri blood, and Cíbhóló too, but she was something else as well, something that no one could trace, and Kavan could not be found to read her.

Later, during moments spent where she was buried, the bard would realize that the woman he had sensed through Tíbhyan, the woman who had supplied the weapon that had killed King Hagan, was not this woman. Their features were similar but they were not the same. That woman was still out there. This woman was little more than a shell, a substitute for the real source of deadly power.

Claide's body was not removed from Hes á Redh. Despite the Queen's desire to bury the man in an unmarked grave, for the people of Enesfel to believe he had simply disappeared without a trace, it was gdhededhá Tusánt who advised against it. The Crown may have despised him, with good reason, and may have known him to be a murderer and a criminal, but most of Enesfel did not. There had been no trial to prove his transgressions, and presenting their evidence after his death would likely appear to the Teren flock more as an effort to besmirch the dead than to prove his guilt. A writ would be distributed to every congregation in the land with the list of charges with which he would have been tried and convicted, but it would not happen until after he received the sort of burial a man of his station should receive. The decision was made not to speak of Clarys' condemnation of Claide and his actions.

Some would believe that writ, others would not. Healer MacLyr's medical pronouncement was reinforced by the reports of at least one Teren physician, indicating that the man had died of heart failure. It was a diagnosis not entirely accurate, but anyone examining Claide's body would discover damage to the heart and thus the diagnosis would stand. Others in Hes á Redh that night had witnessed his collapse, giving no proof of any cause to the contrary.

The Crown would remain innocent of his death in the eyes of the Faithful. The people of Enesfel would be satisfied and his reign of prejudice would slide silently into history.

Only three men who would know the truth. Two made vows to one another, in those days of Kavan's absence and the initial medical inquest, to never speak of what they knew, not to each other, nor to anyone else. The truth of it would be buried with Claide in a plot near Hes á Redh reserved for any gdhededhá who passed during their tenure. Knowing the man had faced execution for his crimes, neither felt guilty for the secret they kept.

gdhededhá Tusánt, on hearing the Tribunal's decision to defrock Claide and provisionally break the ties between the Elyri and Teren Faithful, tore his robes in dismay and vowed to do everything he could, until his dying breath, to facilitate reconciliation between the Faithful of all lands. The Elyri Faith establishment might have turned their back on him, on the Teren, but Tusánt refused to turn his back on the Faith he had dedicated his life to, refused to leave Enesfel and the people he served. His initial campaign to undo the path to secession Claide had steered them towards, his continued generosity to those still enduring hardship due to the Great Fire and the Coryllien violence, his hand in electing a Teren Tribunal to balance his power in the eyes of Teren across the Sovereignties, and his insistence on a proper burial for Claide despite the man's anti-Elyri stance, cemented Tusánt's election to k'gdhededhá in Claide's place, and he fought tirelessly for fairness and equality between races.

The citizens of Rhidam, in particular, loved him for it. The rest of Enesfel, and the world, would come in time.

gdhededhá Valgis, condemned for his duplicity, was stripped of his position in the Faith and denied the right to serve for the remainder of his life. Without a reading, there was little direct evidence to indicate he had known of Claide's crimes, but Valgis had chosen to ignore the meaning of every damning word the man had ever said, and he had assisted Claide in many of his crimes, whether he was aware of the position he played and the result of his actions or not. What knowledge he possessed, however, remained undiscovered as Diona would not have him read. Both Queen and k'gdhededhá Tusánt chose to forgo execution in Valgis' case in favor of the one punishment that would stay with him until the end of his days. For on his hand, the branded mark of defrocking and with no Elyri to heal it, the scarred mark would tell others what he had been...but was no more. To Tusánt, that was punishment enough.

It was not as easy to keep the lines of peace open between Rhidam and Clarys, despite the ongoing talks and work between Queen Diona and Kyne Mórne. No matter how many treaties the women agreed on and their continuing efforts to facilitate a cultural exchange between Houses, their spirit of cooperation did not extend to many of those behind the walls of Hes Dhágdhuán. With Lláhy's disqualification and exile, the congregation of gdhededhá elected the chair-bound Tumm, a man with views little different than the man he replaced, a man who shared a vision of the future with the currently sitting k'phóredhet that kept the separation between Teren and Elyri Faithful in place through an endless series of debates. Khwílen Kesábhá, dismayed, frustrated, and disillusioned by the seeming shortsightedness of those who were to guide the Faith, returned to his post at St. Kóráhm's in Alberni where such political shenanigans could not touch him. In his place, choosing to champion the cause of reunification, gdhededhá Kluín and Hwensen remained. Hwensen abdicated his position as aide to the k'gdhededhá in favor of serving with Kluín and working with him in their shared cause.

It was the two of them, and a handful of others who served in Hes Dhágdhuán, who stood on Kavan's behalf when Tumm, for reasons not even Ylár could verify, upheld and passed Kavan's excommunication from the Faith on grounds of heresy within days of his ascension to the post of prelate. Though it was a painful, stinging burden to bear, Kavan had known it was coming since St. Kóráhm's words in Kílyn. Ylár and Kluín believed the choice to be a reaction by the ancient man and the k'phóredhet to Kavan's having meddled in ecclesiastical affairs, leading to the exile of a prominent member…whom Tumm had supported as his best friend's son. It might also have been an effect of Kavan bringing clouds of doubt and question over the memory of the late k'gdhededhá Dórímyr. It might, Ylár knew, have also been based on Kavan's knowledge of Tumm's Zythánite connections, knowledge that could be dangerous to Tumm's position in Clarys. So long as the heresy charge stood, and Kavan was forbidden to enter Hes Dhágdhuán, any charges the bard made against Tumm, any accusations he might reveal, would be suspect. Viewing the heresy charge as unfair, both Kluín and Hwensen made a pact to challenge Tumm's ruling and reverse it.

The separation of the Elyri and Teren ecclesiastical entities, however, meant that k'gdhededhá Tusánt did not need to uphold

Clarys' ruling on Kavan's position within the Faith. When Kavan resurfaced, weeks after the deaths of Claide, Heward, and Caol, it was to settle into the Alberni estate, leaving behind Rhidam and Bhryell in favor of raising his son and adopted son, in peace. It was a self-imposed exile, in which he rarely left the confines of his estate, the chellé, or his city, penance for the life he had taken.

For despite the voices, his own, his friends, and the residents of St. Kóráhm's…who would justify his act as defense of the Queen and her unborn children, Kavan believed it had not been his place to administer punishment to the man who had caused the deaths of too many. Part of Kavan's reason for exile, however, was to reconcile the part of him that felt strongly that he had every right to do what he had done…and that he did not regret Claide's death at all.

The times he did choose to travel away from Alberni were to visit Owain, Gabrielle, and their family on Káliel. The prince followed through on his decision to leave the chamberlain position in Níkóá's hands, and the Queen, unaware still of Níkóá's lineage, welcomed him amongst her advisors. One day a week Kavan would greet Níkóá on the threshold of the Alberni estate to instruct him, along with Sóbhán, in the ways of Power. Sóbhán continued to learn from bhydáni Tíbhyan and to spend time in Rhidam under Ártur and Rouvyn's instruction, but Níkóá, a much older student, chose to go to Kavan alone for training.

Later still, after the birth of Muir's son, a child lost-witted Clianthe was unable to care for and sometimes lashed out at with violence, the boy was placed in Kavan's custody. In Kavan's care, he was away from harm, for both Owain and Gabrielle knew there was nowhere better, and no one better suited, for a child's upbringing, than in the care of the Elyri bard who had lovingly raised the child's father into a kind and honorable man.

Kavan took responsibility for Gaelán as well, when it was concluded that the young man would likely never awaken. It was a difficult decision for all, but in the end, Asta and Bhríd agreed that moving Gaelán to St. Kóráhm's would be for the best. The men and women of the chellé were plentiful, and someone was able to be with Gaelán at all times without any duties being left unattended. Kavan spent considerable time with him, and Bhríd and Asta came often, but not once did the apprentice healer stir.

This gave Kavan the responsibility for the care and rearing of four young people, and then a fifth when Nuryé's daughter was old enough to receive training as well. Then came a sixth and seventh when Zelenka honored Wortham with first one son, and then a second. With the running of the Alberni estate in the Darys' and Delamos' capable hands, Kavan spent his time doing the things he loved, learning, teaching, and making music. Shortly after Asta gave birth to Gaelan's daughter, and introduced her to her silent father for the first and only time, Gaelán, in the company of his father and Kavan, let go of the ties that bound him, to slip peacefully beyond the walls that trapped him in a half-life and into the waiting arms of Saint Kóráhm the Heretic.

In Bhryell, Elyriá, despite the edicts from Clarys, the villagers erected a statue, near the fountain built to commemorate the village founders, to the heretic from their heart. The White Bard of Bhryell.

The End

Character Index Book 5

Agis, General--The only Cíbhóló nomad to serve in the Enesfel military. King Hagan promotes him to Lord High General after Ternce Wyndham retires the post.

Aleski MacLyr--Ártur MacLyr's nephew, he is the eldest son of Sámel MacLyr.

Alyná Dubuais Cáner--infant daughter of Bhríd Cáner and Madalyn Dubuais-Cáner. Eldest twin.

Alis-- Wistern's fiancée who supplied the poisoned wine sent to Clarys with gdhededhá Dórímyr.

Ámállá--a long time leader of the Zythánite cult, charismatic and wily, she is believed to have been killed by some of her own postulants several hundred years ago.

Anri "Hugh" Heward--A Nethite suspected of involvement with the upsurge of anti-Elyri violence during the reigns of King Arlan and his son Hagan.

Arlan Trebor Lachlan--The youngest son of King Innis of Enesfel. He is the 25th king of Enesfel, responsible for peaceful relations with Hatu, increasing Enesfel's size via the war with Neth, and opening a dialogue with the islands of Káliel.

Ártur MacLyr--Elyri healer, employed by Kings Innis, Donal, Arlan, and Hagan Lachlan. He is married to Syl Cáner and is cousin to Kavan Cliáth.

Asta Deidre Dugan--The daughter of Princess Deidre Lachlan and Lord High Inquisitor Caol Dugan, she is being groomed to assume the position of High Inquisitor.

Avner--One of the five Káliel guards sent by Gabrielle Dilyn to serve Arlan in his quest for the Enesfel throne.

Balint Gabersdon, Sir--Once the youngest knight in Enesfel, he is the Duke of Nelori.

Belda--Diona Lachlan's personal maidservant.

Bhendhámyn MacLyr--The youngest son of Sámel MacLyr, nephew of Ártur MacLyr. He is a harp maker in the Cliáth tradition who agrees to apprentice Ártur's son Llucás.

Bhílári, gdhededhá--head clergy of Hes Índári, Bhryell, who witnessed many of Kavan's "miracles" and has known him since childhood.

Bhílycá, Málneag--A female Elyri healer who was canonized for her extreme piety and her generous care of the sick. She is particularly known for her work with those suffering from the Great Plague, which she contracted. It ultimately caused her death though she continued to care for the sick and dying up until she could no longer able. She became the patron of healers (particularly Elyri healers) and the terminally ill. After a number of childless women reported having conceived children after visiting her shrine, Bhílycá has also become the patron of women wanting children.

Bhín Króel, gdhededhá--a candidate for the k'gdhededhá seat in Clarys, born deaf. Twins with Syán.

Bhyrhán Bhíncári--One of many grandsons of Kyne Mórne Bhíncári, the High Mother. He has chosen the life of a minstrel, and plays the shawm. He is distantly related to Kavan Cliáth, whose mother's maiden name was Bhíncári.

Bhríd Cáner, Lord High Chamberlain--A distant cousin of the MacLyr's, employed by King Arlan Lachlan as his chancellor, he resumed the post of Chamberlain upon the death of Guthrie McHador. He is known as the best swordsman in the Five Sovereignties, and is the King's Champion.

Bhyrínt, Málneag--an Elyri saint

Bianca MacLyr Dugan--An orphaned Teren, adopted by Ártur and Syl MacLyr, she is married to Wilred Dugan.

Birl--a member of the Corylliens

Bostik, Lord--Lord of Dorshur, who owns a home in Rhidam where he frequently stays in his efforts to manipulate a position with the Crown.

Bowen Ellard Lachlan--The 3rd son of King Innis of Enesfel; he was the 22nd king of Enesfel. It is believed by some that he was the father of Owain Lachlan.

Caol Dugan, Lord High Inquisitor--Originally the son of a member of the Association, now part of the Lachlan court and family, since he married Princess Deidre Lachlan, King Arlan's sister. He has maintained the post of Lord High Inquisitor for his entire time in Rhidam.

Cátá MacLyr--She is the wife of Aleski MacLyr.

Chethá Llyárá MacLyr--The infant daughter of Ártur and Syl MacLyr.

Claide, gdhededhá--the Teren elected k'gdhededhá of Enesfel

Clianthe Dilyn Lachlan--The daughter of Gabrielle Dilyn she marries to Prince Muir Lachlan.

Darius Corbin, Lord High Justice--A soldier of the Lachlan ranks, who rose to the rank of Justice when Minos Cornell assumed the post of Chancellor after the death of Guthrie McHador.

Dawid Coryllien--A figure once thought of as mythical, whose name is connected with the death of many Elyri and many Teren during the historical period known as the Persecution. His name was given to the daggers connected with those murders. Very little is known about him in the Five Sovereignties.

Denyan--One of the five Káliel guards sent by Gabrielle Dilyn to serve Prince Arlan in his quest for the throne.

Dhábhiyhá Coryllien--The true birth name of the man who came to be known as Dawid Coryllien to the people in the Five Sovereignties.

Dháná MacLyr--The wife of Tám MacLyr, mother of Sámel and Ártur MacLyr, Kavan Cliáth's aunt.

Dhóri--Kavan's son with Orynn.

Diona Cordelia Lachlan--The only daughter of King Arlan Lachlan; heir apparent after the death of her father makes Hagan king.

Dórímyr, k'gdhededhá--The highest religious leader in the Faith of Elyriá.

Editt--woman hired as wet nurse for the Dubuais-Cáner twin girls.

Edhriá, málneag--An ancient saint

Edward Lindunn--The son of a wealthy Rhidam resident, whose mother was from Cordash. He was to serve in the Cordashian military, but instead returned to Rhidam and eagerly agreed to enter the priesthood while serving as a guard for Father Tusánt.

Éllés, gdhededhá--speaker for the k'phóredhet; leads the trial against Kavan over the death of k'gdhededhá Dórímyr.

Ensgil, gdhededhá--one of four Teren emissaries sent to Rhidam with instructions from Dórímyr for the Teren Faithful to elect their own k'gdhededhá

Espen Harcourt, Prince--The second son of King Geir of Hatu, he is the brother of King Noreis.

Farrell Rasmus Lachlan--The 2nd son of King Innis of Enesfel; he was the 21st king of Enesfel.

Fendel Geli--a traveling trader who has done business with the Dugan family in the past and meets the royal family through Kavan.

Flannery McGranis--The former squire of Bhríd Cáner who is elevated to the post of Chancellor upon the death of Minos Cornell.

Fraen, Captain--a Nethite Captain who sides with King Merkar after the death of General Glucke

Gabrielle Dilyn Lachlan--Prime Magistrate of Káliel, mother of Clianthe and Piran, she is the wife of Owain Lachlan.

Gaelán Ágdhrán Cáner--The youngest son of Bhríd Cáner and Madalyn Dubuais who has shown that he possesses the Elyri talent to heal despite being half-Teren.

Garrett, gdhededhá--The acting head of Saint Kóráhm's while Khwílen Kesábhá is in Elyriá attempting to gain ammunition to confront k'gdhededhá Dórímyr.

Glucke, General--Neth's leading General, with personal aspirations towards the Neth throne.

Hágae Rínes--former mistress of k'gdhededhá Dórímyr.

Hagan Guthrie Brennan Lachlan--The youngest child of Arlan Lachlan, he is the 26 king of Enesfel.

Hazen--A female dedhá serving in Dhágdhuán Church Rhidam during the reigns of Kings Arlan and Hagan Lachlan.

Hesl de Corrmick--infant son of King Merkar de Corrmick; too young to rule; his uncle Kjell rules as regent in his place.

Hwensen--k'gdhededhá Dórímyr's personal aide

Idal Gottfrid--The youngest son of Charles Gottfrid of Erleta. He and his brother Kent have purchased a modest home in Rhidam, which is currently under suspicion by the inquisitor and Princess Diona.

Janette Mereki--older half-sister of Níkóá Mereki

Johann Alty--Lord High Inquisitor Caol Dugan's assumed name when he infiltrates the Corylliens.

Jons, Mister--arrested on charges of treason at the end of the Great Purge.

Kátá MacLyr--She is the wife of Aleski MacLyr.

Kavan Kóráhm Cliáth--Last of the Cliáth's, only child of Rístyrd and Llyárá, cousin of Ártur MacLyr. He is an admired harper, possessor of the Sight, holder of great psionic capabilities. Known as the White Bard of Bhryell for his tremendous musical talent and unique physical appearance, he was employed by Arlan as his court bard until his flight from Rhidam to the lands south of Hatu. He is also the Duke of Alberni and the founder of Málneag Kóráhm's Abbey.

Kent Gottfrid--The middle son of Charles Gottfrid of Erleta. He and his brother Idal have purchased a modest home in Rhidam which is currently under suspicion by the inquisitor and Princess Diona.

Khwílen Kesábhá, gdhededhá--Once an aide to k'gdhededhá Dórímyr, he was selected as the abbot of Málneag Kóráhm's Abbey in Alberni due to his gifts of oratory, learning, and painting.

Kjell de Corrmick--The youngest son of Loris of Neth, he is the brother of King Merkar de Corrmick and is the current heir to the Neth throne.

Kluín, gdhededhá--a member of the Order of Saint Kóráhm, a candidate for the post of k'gdhededhá in Clarys.

Kóráhm di Curnydhá, Málneag--Elyri málneag for whom Kavan was named, also known as Kóráhm the Rón by many in Elyriá because of some controversial writings he made before the time of his martyrdom. Few of his books are available and he is not commonly discussed. Originally born in the town of Ergoth, he was the half-brother of Dawid Coryllien.

Layton--A member of the Corylliens from who Johan Alty takes instruction

Lláná—granddaughter of Kyne Mórne who has been involved with a gdhededhá and borne many children with him outside of marriage.

Lláhy, gdhededhá--youngest candidate for the seat of k'gdhededhá

Llucás Phaedr MacLyr--The oldest child of Ártur and Syl MacLyr.

Llyr--A mythical/historic figure believed to be a dedhá and a fighter, responsible for the creation of the chalice Kavan seeks in connection to the thur thol below the Rhidam keep.

Logros--One of the five Káliel guards sent by Gabrielle Dilyn to serve Arlan Lachlan in his bid for the throne of Enesfel.

Madalyn Dubuais Cáner, Duchess--The Duchess of Levonne, she is the only woman in Enesfel to have control of her own lands; she is married to Bhríd Cáner.

Marta--An Association member used as a contact by Caol and Asta Dugan.

Martin Dary--the master of the Alberni estate while Kavan is away.

Matus Gardieu--a farrier from Hatu, member of the Association, who serves as the 'face' of Inquisitor for Diona Lachlan while Asta Dugan is under age

Merkar Rousset de Corrmick--One of the sons of the late King Loris of Neth, he is currently the ruling Neth king.

Mikel Wistern--a blacksmith in Rhidam arrested on charges of murder in the death of k'gdhededhá Dórímyr.

Mórne, High Mother (Kyne)--The matriarchal ruler of Elyriá; she is head of the Elyri High Council.

Muir Innis Lachlan--The bastard son of Owain Lachlan and Brenna Weylin Lachlan, he was raised as Arlan Lachlan's son. Upon reaching adulthood he gave his land and title as Duke of Alberni to Kavan Cliáth and moved to Fiara with his father. He is now married to Clianthe Dilyn and lives on Káliel.

Myreth--A singer of extraordinary talent, he is a man of unknown mixed heritage who was raised in the cloister of Gorbesh.

Níkóá McCábhá--half Elyri illegitimate son of King Farrell Lachlan.

Ninette Dary--daughter-in-law of Martin Dary, helps run the Alberni estate.

Noreis Harcourt--The current King of Hatu, he is the elder brother of Prince Espen Harcourt.

Nuryé--Wetnurse and part-time caregiver to Dhóri

Onea Pantel--The woman who heads the Fiara branch of the Association.

Orynn--A member of all three known races (k'kairá, Elyri, and Teren) she was chosen by Kóráhm and her own people to make contact with Kavan and assist in his quest for healing, redemption, and the items needed to cleanse the thur thol below the Rhidam keep. She is known among the people in the barbarian territories as k'ílshwythnec, "she who sees," because of her tremendous knowledge of the past, present, and future.

Owain Ustes Lachlan--He was believed to be the 5th child of Innis, son of Ula de Corrmick of Neth; he was the 24th king of Enesfel. He is actually the only child of Guthrie McHador. He relinquished the throne to Arlan Lachlan and has lived in the Neth city of Fiara since then. He assumed the title of Duke of Fiara when the area of Neth south of Lake Curo seceded and became part of Enesfel. He is the father of Muir Innis and, later, after marriage to Gabrielle Dilyn of Kaliel, also fathered Piran Guthrie Lachlan.

Peter--A page in Queen Diona Lachlan's court

Petin, Mister--arrested on the charges of treason at the end of the Great Purge.

Phaedr Cáner--The brother of Bhríd and Syl Cáner, he joined Prince Arlan's forces and lost his sight, then his life, for that cause

Piran Guthrie Lachlan--The son of Owain Lachlan and Gabrielle Dilyn-Lachlan.

Qol--A member of the race known as the phae k'kairá who has been serving as k'gdhededhá in the cloister of Gorbesh, and acting as the keeper of the relics Kavan seeks.

Raenár, Magk, Captain--captain of the ecclesiastical guard in Clarys, sent to Bhryell to arrest Kavan on charges of heresy

Rankin, gdhededhá--A Teren dedhá in Dhágdhuán Church, Rhidam.

Renfrid Valdis--The current king of Cordash.

Rouvyn Talis--A Teren physician who traveled with Kavan many years ago during his search for the kidnapped Princes Bertram and Wilred. A native of Rhidam, he returned there when his services to Kavan were no longer needed, and has lived in the area since. He has remained on speaking terms with Justice Darius Corbin and becomes the Lachlans Teren court healer after the attack on Ártur MacLyr.

Sámel MacLyr--Ártur's older brother and Kavan's cousin. He is a harp maker in the Cliáth tradition, like his father.

Saul Peado--A Teren from Talladegah who came to Rhidam to serve in the Lachlan guard but is chosen by Princess Diona to act as Father Tusánt's guard while studying as a novice for the priesthood.

Selis, Mister--arrested on charges of treason at the end of the Great Purge

Sen, gdhededhá--a member of the k'phóredhet

Sóbhán--An orphaned Elyri boy who manages to survive the ravages in Rhidam; Kavan adopts him as his son, making him a Cliáth.

Stone, Captain--a captain in the Nethite army who helps save Prince Kjell's life.

Syán Króel, gdhededhá--a candidate for the position of k'gdhededhá, twin brother of Bhín, lost his eyesight as an infant.

Syl Cáner MacLyr--The wife of Ártur MacLyr, she is also a healer, and sister of Bhríd Cáner. She is the mother of Llucás and Chethá.

Sylyhá Dubuais, Cáner--infant daughter of Bhríd Cáner and Madalyn Dubuais-Cáner; younger twin

Tám MacLyr--The father of Ártur MacLyr, he is a harp maker in the Cliáth tradition, and uncle of Kavan Cliáth.

Tayte McHador Cáner--The eldest son of Bhríd Cáner and Madalyn Dubuais, he is the heir to the Levonne estate.

Tíbhyan--Elyri Bhydáni, who was Kavan's private tutor. He is the oldest man in Bhryell and one of the top 10 sages in Elyriá.

Tulda Dary--wife of Martin, assists in managing the Alberni estate.

Tumm, gdhededhá--the oldest candidate for the seat of k'gdhededhá, long-time acquaintance and friend of k'gdhededhá Dórímyr, is confined to a rolling chair due to his great age.

Tusánt, gdhededhá--The only Elyri dedhá serving in Rhidam.

Valesce--A resident of the Gorbesh cloister and personal aide to k'gdhededhá Qol.

Valgis, gdhededhá--A newly ordained Teren dedhá from Levonne, currently serving in Dhágdhuán Church, Rhidam.

Wace Elotti--A Cíbhóló nomad turned bounty hunter, heralded as the best in the Five Sovereignties. He has been pursuing Halstatt Tarmajien since the man escaped his Neth prison.

Waljan--One of the five Káliel guards sent by Gabrielle Dilyn to serve Prince Arlan in his quest for Enesfel's throne.

Wilred Douglas Dugan--The son of Caol Dugan and Deidre Lachlan, he is the acting Duke of Durham, husband of Bianca MacLyr, and father of Coriana Dugan.

Wortham Delamo, Captain--Captain of the five elite Káliel guards sent by Gabrielle Dilyn to serve Arlan. He is the closest of Kavan's friend and considers himself the bard's protector and servant.

Ylár, gdhededhá--a candidate for the position of k'gdhededhá, frequent caregiver for dedhá Tumm

Yorick Zarkosta, General--He had joined Arlan's quest for the throne, and has risen to the rank of General in his years of service since then. He acts as the Captain of the Lachlan house guard when not in a state of war.

Zelenka--A young woman from Gorbesh with whom Wortham Delamo falls in love and who travels with them when her mother dies.

Zythán--called saint by some, heretic by most, the founder of an ancient cult from the Elryi's earliest days in the land. It is unknown if he was Elyri, k'kairá, or something else. His followers believed in sacrifice and orgiastic celebrations and learned ways of killing with the Power to protect themselves. Most were killed centuries ago, but the cult occasionally resurfaces through Elyriá.

Elyri Phonetics

á--ä (as in m**o**p)
a--ă (as in c**a**t)
ae--ā (as in **a**ce)
ag--ä (as in m**o**p) (HE**)
ai--ī (as in **i**ce)
au--aù (as in **ou**t)
é--ŭ (as in b**u**t)
e--ĕ (as in b**e**t

i--ē (as in b**e**)
í--ĭ (as in s**i**t)
ó--ō (as in g**o**)
o--ŏ (as in m**o**p)
u--ū (as in bl**ue**)
y--ē (as in b**e**)
yh--y (as in **y**es)

b--b
bh--v
c--k
ch--ch
d--d
dh--j
gae--gwā
gdh--zh (as in vi**s**ion)
gh--g (as in go)
gk--k̲ as in loch (HE)
h--h
hw--w (breathy, as in whale)
k'--k
k--k

l--l
Ll--l
m--m
mh--m (slightly breathy)
n--n
ne--nyä
p--p
ph--f
r--r
s--sh
t--t
th--th (as in thistle)
z--z

•   **C** is always pronounced **K** but the letter **K** is most often used to designate this sound. **C** mainly appears at the beginning of some proper surnames and place names and occasionally in the center or at the end of a word. This is believed to be a carryover from the earliest days of the Elyri language, or to have been influenced by the Teren languages, but Elyri linguists and scholars have not yet determined its significance. However, in keeping with this unspoken, unexplained rule, no Elyri have first names, or middle names, starting with **C**.

- The combination **gk** (pronounced as in the German ich) occurs only at the end of words unless there is a verb suffix or plural suffix behind it, and only in those words of High Elyri origin.

- The letter combination **ag** occurs at the end of words of High Elyri origin. If the combination appears elsewhere in a word, it will either be as a product of two words having been combined or will be the result of a suffix having been added. Though some Standard Elyri words have retained their **ag** ending, most words carried into the standard will have the **ag** combination replaced with **á** when written, though they sound alike when spoken.

- The **H** sound only appears in High Elyri words and in some names carried over from ancient sources; Standard Elyri derivatives will normally drop the **h** from the original word but there are exceptions to the rule

- Double **L**'s are found at the beginnings of words, single **l**'s in the body or at the end. When words do have the double **L** in a location other than the beginning, it is always the result of two words being combined into one.

- In High Elyri, there were no naturally occurring **B, P,** or **ow** (as in cow) sounds. These did not get introduced until Elyri acquired their current religious faith. Even then, the sounds were not commonly used until the standard Trade tongue influenced everyday life. These sounds mainly appear in proper names or religious settings.

- The combination of the letter **ne** occurs almost exclusively at the end of a word and is always pronounced **nya**, regardless of where it occurs.

The **ee** sound at the beginning or end of a word is always represented with an **I**. In the center of words, it is represented by a **Y**. When the **ee** sound is represented in the center of a word by the letter **I,** it is a result of two words being combined into one. In some cases, as with the name Cliáth, the original words may no longer be known. The few exceptions where Standard or High Elyri words begin with a Y for the ee sound are believed to have originated as intentional

· There is no **S** sound in the Elyri language. S's are always pronounced **sh**.

· The letter **Z** appears only in the High Elyri or in words derived from the High Elyri or originated as misspellings in one of the Teren languages and were absorbed back into Elyri in the aberrant form.

Elyri Grammar

In most Elyri words, the stress falls on the second to last. Words where the stress falls on the final syllable (or on the first syllable in words with more than two syllables) are either names, the result of an Elyri translation of a Teren word, caused by the addition of a prefix or suffix, or the result of a word being truncated, having dropped the last syllable over time.

The **k'** at the beginning of a word signifies importance or singularity. It is applied to a word that can have a common meaning and a special meaning: k'tyne would be a favorite niece or female cousin, whereas tyne is simply a niece or female cousin. In the case of the phae k'kairá, when the Teren translated the term into "the Others" it is the **k'** that indicates the O to be capitalized; not just any others but the Others.

The Elyri written language does not have additional characters for capitalization. The first letters words may carry a dot beneath them to signify that the word is a proper name, a place, or a title, but first letters of sentences are not capitalized.

Sentence breaks are characterized by either a new line of text or by a symbol that looks similar to an s. This has resulted in many mistranslations from Elyri into other languages.

Nouns

Noun forms of verbs do not have gender. When these nouns are made plural they take the plural inclusive suffix sur.

The prefix **íl** added to a verb makes it into a noun; the word then means "one who" as in "ílDaeni"-one who instructs, i.e.: teacher.

Some nouns are formed by adding the prefix **ai** to a verb; the verb dhesá means touch, aidhesá also means touch but is a noun. Not all verbs can accept the **ai** prefix.

-thé: the standard plural suffix

Nouns ending in **I** are both singular and plural and do not take the -**thé** ending

Elyri monetary denominations are both singular and plural.

There are other exceptions to the singular/plural rule, most being words carried over from the High Elyri. High Elyri contains very few words that are NOT both plural and singular. Any exceptions to the rule are noted.

Some words have gender. A word ending in **ne** is feminine and a word ending in **dhá** is masculine. Both are made plural in the same way (with the **thé** ending). Some gender neutral words that have been altered from their original form may have either ending.

Some words in Standard, those referring to a group that includes both male and female individuals, require the -**sur** ending, creating the plural inclusive form of the word. The same ending exists in High Elyri.

Adjectives

There are few adjectives in the Elyri language. Instead of saying someone is beautiful, or wise, and Elyri would say they possess beauty or they possess wisdom.

To modify such qualities, an Elyri speaker would say:

bhykólé aelá shwyth: She possesses wisdom. Teren: She is wise.

ochbhykóle aelá shwyth: She possesses more wisdom. Teren: She is wiser.

utbhykólé aelá shwyth: She possesses the most wisdom. Teren: She is wisest.

naimbhykólé aelá shwyth: She possesses no wisdom. Teren: She is not wise; or She is a fool.

The few adjectives that do exist come through the High Elyri and are believed by most linguists to have their origins in some language other than the Elyri.

Verbs

When **ibh** modifies a verb (ie: is singing, is looking) it is attached as a suffix to the verb. In all other instances, it is a separate word (bhydáni ibh gaeth: He is bhydáni.)

When **im** modifies a verb (ie: was singing, was looking) it is attached as a suffix to the verb. In all other instances, it is a separate word (ílDaeni im gaeth: He was a teacher)

There is no "be" in the Elyri language. Whereas a Teren would say, "He will be singing" the Elyri would say "He will sing." Instead of "I will be there" it would be "I will come" or I will go"; instead of "I will be here" it would be "I will stay", "I will attend," or "I am here."

Rather than using verbs such as "strengthened" or "beautified", in Elyri they would say "given strength" or "given beauty"

Verb Tenses

(present) do, does	(past) (ár) did, have done	(present) (ibh) am, are, is doing	(past) (im) was, is, were doing	(future) (ád) will do, to do, be done
aelá	aelár	aelibh	aelim	aelád
ándás	ándásár	ándásibh	ándásim	ándásád
árá	árár	áráibh	áráim	árád
bhaeá	bhaeár	bhaeibh	bhaeim	bhaeád
bheken	bhekár	bhekibh	bhenim	bhekád
bhair	bhairár	bhairibh	bhairim	bhairád
bhólon	bhólár	bhólibh	bhólim	bhólád
chóne	chóneár	chóníbh	chónim	chónád
daeni	daenár	daenibh	daenim	daenád
dhesá	dhesár	dhesibh	dhesim	dhesád
dhys	dhysár	dhysibh	dhysim	dhysád
donai	donár	donaiibh	donim	donád
ghlaiph	ghlaiphár	ghlaiphibh	ghlaiphim	ghlaiphád
ghytae	ghytár	ghytibh	ghytim	ghytád
kelém	kelémár	kelémibh	kelémim	kelémád
mairós	mairár	mairibh	mairim	mairád
naeth	naethár	naethibh	naethim	naethád
yháth	yháthár	yháthibh	yháthim	yháthád
zene	zenár	zenibh	zenim	zenád
zólágk	zólágkár	zólágkibh	zólágkim	zólágkád

Verb/Noun Tenses

	noun form 1(íl)	noun 2(ai)
aelá	ílAelá (one who owns)	
ándás	ílAndás (one who honors)	aiándás
bhaeá	ílBhaeá (one who asks)	
bheken	ílBheken	
bhair	ílBhair (one who accepts)	aibhair (acceptance)
bhólon	ílBhólon (one who purifies)	
chóne	ílChóne (one who brings)	
daeni	ílDaeni (one who instructs)	
dhesá	ílDhesá (one who touches)	aidhesá
donai	ílDonai (one who endures)	aidonai
ghlaiph	ílGhlaiph (one who sleeps)	aiglaiph
ghytae	ílGhytae (one who threatens)	aighytae (threat)
kelém	ílKelém (one who passes)	
mairós	ílMairós (one who heals)	aimairós
naeth	ílNaeth (one who finds)	
zene	ílZene (one who gives)	
zólágk	ílZólágk (one who reveals)	

Verb Tenses (High Elyri)

(present)	(past)(-ár)	(future)(-es)
aelás	aelásár	aeles
bhánys	bhánár	bhánes
dytae	dytár	dytes
ghai	ghaiár	ghaies
síndóbhaene	síndóbhaenár	síndóbhaenes
zugdhu	zugdhuár	zugdhues
tyreth	tyrethár	tyrethes
pháló	phálóár	phálóes
scenyhur	scenyhár	scenhyures
elzen	elzenár	elzenes

Verb/Noun Tenses (High Elyri)

(noun 1) (bhe-)	(noun 2) (ae-)
bheaelás (one who owns)	aeaelás (possession)
bhehánys (one who makes music)	
bhedytae (one who obeys)	aedytae (obedience)
bheghai (one who does)	
bhesíndóbhaene (one who forgives)	aesíndóbhaene (forgiveness)
bhezugdhu (one who protects)	aezugdhu (protection)
bhetyreth (one who knows/scholar)	aetyreth (knowledge)
bhepháló (one who buries/gravedigger)	aepháló (grave)
bhescenyhur (one who names)	aescenyur (name)
bhelzen (one who gives)	aeelzen (gift)

Foreign Phrase Index

ELYRI WORDS

HE: High Elyri   SE: Standard Elyri
n--noun   v--verb   adj—adjective
adv--adverb   prn--pronoun   prp--preposition
pl--plural   sng--singular   psv—possessive
pl in--plural inclusive

á (ä) (prp)--HE/SE; and, also, together with, together
Ádhá (Ä-jä) (n)--HE/SE; god; k'Ádhá-supreme deity in the Elyri monotheistic religion
aegaenag (ā-GWĀ-nă) (n) (pl: aegaenagthé)--HE; bite, sting, cut, puncture
aegaent (ā-GWĀNT) (n) (pl: aegaentthé)--HE; poison
aelás (Ā-läsh) (v)--HE; Have (has), possess, own
aendhá (ĀN-jä) (n) (pl: aendáthé)--SE; A father's male relatives, including his father, grandfathers, uncles, brothers, and cousins.
aeturbhae (ā-tūr-VĀ) (n) (sng and pl)--HE betrayal
aeturgaeag (Ā-tūr-GWAY-ah) (adj)--HE; honey, sweet, syrup, sap
átaelás (ä-TĀ-läsh) (prn psv)--HE; mine, my
áti (Ä-tē) (prn)--HE; I, me, myself
bhemethag (MĔ-thä) (n) --HE; rage, anger, fury
bhemethán (vĕ-mĕ- THÄN) (n) (sng and pl)--HE; murderer, executioner
bhith (vēth) (v)--HE; ruin, destroy, knock down, is ruining, is destroying
bhíth (vĭth) (v)--HE; tear, cut, divide, is tearing, is dividing, is splitting
bhíthár (vē-THÄR) (v)--HE; has cut, has divided, has torn, has split was cut, was divided, was torn
bhithár (vĭ-THÄR) (v)--HE; ruined, knocked down, destroyed
bhol (vŏl) (adv)--HE; when, at the time
bhólibh (vō-LĒV) (v)--SE; was purifying, were purifying
Bhórdh (vōrj) (n)--(HE); oldest settlement in Elyria; small mining town that produces gold and silver.
bhydáni (vē-DÄN-ē) (n) (sng and pl)--HE; This is both a title and a social standing. It can be translated teacher, master, sage, or wise one, though it actually encompasses all of these meanings. The

title is given to those who, through their exceptional psionic capabilities, wisdom, and intelligence, have demonstrated their worth. Psionic ability is the key to the title, though great ability without wisdom and intelligence will not gain the title. With the title comes the privilege of teaching their knowledge to the children, particularly their psionic knowledge. Each city, town, or village will have at least one bhydáni. Either the bhydáni will ask another into their ranks, or, in the event that a location has no functioning bhydáni, the inhabitants will select someone to fill the position. In extremely rare cases, someone can become bhydáni by accident; they accept mentorship of someone and others begin to ask for the privilege of learning from them as well. By becoming an unofficial teacher, the individual has become bhydáni. A little less than 2/3 of all bhydáni are female.

bhydhá (VĚ-jä) (n) (pl: bhydháthé)--SE; Father.

chellé (CHĚL-ŭ) (n) (sng and pl)--HE; home, house, dwelling, residence; also frequently used to as the shortened form of chellé hábhai, or Seeking House, the residences of various religious orders.

chellé hábhai (CHĚL-ŭ hä-VĪ) (n) (sng and pl)--HE/SE; Seeking House, an abbey or place of religious instruction

Chellé Udhan (CHĚL-ŭ ū-JĂN) (n) (sng and pl)--HE/SE; House of the Watch, guard

chínzé (chĭn-ZŬ) (v)--HE; stand, stands, standing

chóbhael (cho VALE) (interjection) --HE; very good/very well/as you wish/as you say/alright

cógdhut (kō-ZHŪT) (n)--HE; wrath, fury, anger

dedhá (DĚ-jä) (n) (sng and pl)--SE; priest or monk; the term makes no distinction between the two. The shortened form came into use after the Teren came into the lands and adopted the Faith as their own.

dedhór (dĕ-JŌR) (n) (sng and pl)--HE; young goat

Dhágdhuán (JÄ-zhū-än) (n)--HE/OE; the Intercessor, considered to be the founder of the Faith because his death is said to make it possible for mortals to reach the divine,

dhedhoc (JĚ-däk) (n) (pl: dhedhocthé)--HE; earth, world, land, place

dhín (jĭn) (n) (pl: dhínthé)--SE; a chamber or small room

dhín bhólibh (jĭn- vō-LĚV) (n) (pl: dhín bhólibhthé)--SE; Purification Chamber; a place within the náós where the Faithful

confess their hearts to k'Ádhá and receive forgiveness and
blessings from the gdhededhá

ededhór (ĕ-dĕ-JŌR) (n) (sng and pl)--HE; goat
et (ĕt) (prp)--HE; a
ethán (ĕ-THÄN) (v)--HE; kill, murder
ethár (ĕ-THÄR) (n)--SE; rage, anger, fury
gaeth (gwāth) (prn)--HE/SE; he, him, himself
gdhededhá (zhĕ-DĚ-jä) (n) (sng and pl)--HE/SE; priest or faith
teacher or disciple; the term makes no distinction between them.
gdhededhásur (zhĕ-DĚ-jä-shūr) (n) (pl.in)--HE/SE; A group of faith
teachers/clergy of both sexes.
ghymae (gē-MĀ) (n) (sng and pl)--HE; air, sky
ghymag (gē-MÄ) (n) (pl: ghymagthé)--HE; robe, gown
hábhai (HÄ-vī) (v)--HE; look, search
haes (hāsh) (n) (pl: haesthé)--HE/SE; woman, female
hállys (hä-LĒSH) (v)--HE; believe, believes, have faith
hes (hĕsh) (n) (sng and pl)--HE; heart
hne (hnyä) (adj)--HE; beneath, under
hwonághk (hwän-äk) (n) (sng and pl)--HE; any Elyri who has never
received training in the ways of Elyri power. Generally, this term
is used in a derogatory manner since those who are untrained are
viewed as dangerous renegades, but the term is actually benign
and unassuming.
hys (hēsh) (n) (pl: hysthé)--HE/SE; man, male
ibh (ēv) (v)--HE/SE; Is, are, am; its translation is dependent upon the
rest of the sentence.
ílMairós (īl-MĪ-rōsh) (n) (sng and pl)--SE; healer, physician.
índári (ĭn-DÄ-rē) (n) (sng)--HE; peace
ith (ēth) (prn)--HE/SE; it
k'aendhá (k-ĀN-jä) (n) (pl: k'aendáthé)--SE; A favorite paternal
male relatives, including father, grandfathers, uncles, brothers,
and cousins.
k'gdhededhá (k zhĕ-DĚ-jä) (n) (sng and pl)--HE/SE; The Elyri
designation for the male individual who is elected as the head of
the Faith.
k'ílshwythnec (k īl-SHWĒTH-nyĕk) (n)--HE; She (who) sees;
Prophetess. The K indicates a particular individual. Any
prophetess would be ílshwythnec.
k'kairá (also **phae k'kairá**) (fä k KĪ-rä) (n) (sng and pl)--HE; The
name given to the race of beings who inhabited the territory of

the Five Sovereignties before the Elyri arrived. By the time the Elyri came, all that remained of the k'kairá (as they are sometimes called) were crumbling stone circles, mounds, huts, some of which bore written symbols upon them. Unlike most High Elyri words which end with the ah sound, this one does not end with the letter combination ag.

k'phóredhet (k phō-RĔJ-ĕt) (n)--SE; ecclesiastical tribunal of the Faith in Clarys; when the k'gdhededhá is indisposed or has passed, the Tribunal rules in his place. Often used for trials of a religious nature and used to discuss matters of Faith with the k'gdhededhá

k'rylag (k RĒ-lä) (n) (pl: k'rylagthé)--HE; Once Korahm chose the word rylag for his method of travel, k'rylag was carried over into standard Elyri and came to refer strictly to the Gates, not a standard gate.

k'stomaer (k shtō-MĀR) (n) (pl: k'stomaerthé)--HE; The Pyre Symbol/Dhágdhuán's Pyre

k'ykurích (k ē-KŪ-rĭch) (n)--HE/SE; Elyriá's only sanctioned form of execution; it's use is very rare.

keh (keh) (prp)--HE; on, upon

kóh (kō) (pre)--HE/SE; in, within, inside

Kyne (KĒ-nyä) (n) (sng and pl)--HE/SE; The High Mother, the Matriarchal ruler of Elyriá. It includes the translation "Mother ruler", "Mother protector", and "exalted mother". Since nearly all Elyri families can trace some familial link to the Bhíncári, the Kyne is both a figurative, and near literal, mother of all Elyri. This position is both hereditary and elected, chosen from among all of the women in the Bhíncári family.

Llaethlágárá (LĀTH-lä-gār-ä) (n)--HE; The mountains separating Elyriá from Neth and Enesfel.

lómesté (lō-MĔSH-tŭ) (n) (pl: lómestéthé)--HE/SE; translated in the Trade tongue as council, it is a unit of 5 to 9 elders and bhydáni that govern a single town or region; k'lómesté is the Elyri High Council in Clarys. All bhydáni in the region will be a member of the lómesté, but the lómesté need not consist solely of bhydáni.

mai (MĪ) (n) (pl: maithé)—HE/SE; child; used in the Standard as a term of endearment

maran (MĂR-ăn) (adj)--HE; (n)--SE; in High Elyri, the word meant any pungent, sour, biting fruit. After the discovery of the pulpy orange fruits in the region of Bhórdh, the word became associated strictly as the name of that fruit. A rare delicacy, the fruit can be eaten on its own, mixed with other things, or is often used as a main ingredient as a sauce for lamb and other meat. The oil of the pit is toxic to Elyri and Teren alike.

móh (mow) (v)--HE; help; assist

naim (nīm)--HE/SE; No; denial.

naiaehállys (nī-ā- HÄ-lēsh) (n)--HE; disbelief

náir (nä-ĒR) (prn)--HE/SE; nothing, none

náós (nä-ŌSH) (n) (sng and pl)--HE/SE; a place of worship, temple; also occasionally used to refer to the altar.

nec (nyäk) (adj)--HE; bitter

nyek (nē-ĔK) (n)--HE; treason

nyrráhn (NEER-ayn) (v) --HE; need, require

phae k'kairá (fā k KĪ-rä) (n) (sng and pl)--HE; The name given to the race of beings who inhabited the territory of the Five Sovereignties before the Elyri arrived. By the time the Elyri came, all that remained of the k'kairá (as they are sometimes called) were crumbling stone circles, mounds, huts, some of which bore written symbols upon them. Unlike most High Elyri words which end with the ah sound, this one does not end with the letter combination ag.

phain (fīn) (prp)--HE/SE; of

phyghóth (fē-GŌTH) (v)--HE; collapse, fall

phyróth (FĒ-rōth) (n) (pl: phyróthé)--HE; demon, evil spirit, devil

redh (rĕj) (n) (sng and pl)--HE grace, sometimes used as forgiveness in a religious sense

sai (shy) (interjective question)--HE; can I, may I

serbháló (shĕr-VÄ-lō) (n)--SE; A form of Elyri wine with almost no alcohol content, used only for the purposes of religious ceremony.

stómaeph (shtō-MĀF) (n) (adv)--HE; apathy, uncaring, unfeeling, without feeling

sun (shūn) (prp)--HE/SE; to/from

thórgae (thōr-GWĀ) (v)--HE; burn, is burning

thurgag (thūr-GÄ) (v)--HE; eat, consume, devour, eating

udhan (ū-JĂN) (n) (sng and pl)--HE; watch, guard

Udhár (ū-JÄR) (n)--HE; Old year, used to refer to the end of year Holy Feast day on the winter's solstice or any festival, party, or religious observation in honor of the passing from the old year to the new.

zaene (ZĀ-nyä) (adj)--HE; gray

záryph (zä-RĒF) (n) (sng and pl)--HE/SE; winged beings connected to the realm of the holy; angels

Translations

sai móh, bhydáni   May I help you, master?
naim, gdhededhá. áti nyrráhn náir   No, Father, I need nothing.

Original: **High Elyri Translation:**
Wrath burns   *cógdhut thórgae*
When the kid stands   *bhol chínzé íth ededhór*
Beneath the grey sky   *hne íth zaene ghymae*
Of a faithless heart   *phain et hes naiaehállys*

cógdhut thórgae (wrath burns) (can also be wrath consumes…if uses *thurgag*)

ededhór (when stands the young goat/when the kid stands) (kid could be *dedhá*)

hne íth zaene ghymae (beneath the grey sky) (could be robe if uses *ghymag*)

phain et hes naiaehállys (of a heart without faith) (could be man if uses *hys* or woman if *haes*)

2ⁿᵈ High Elyri Translation: **Alternative:**
cógdhut thurgag   *Wrath burns*
bhol chínzé íth dedhá   *when the priest stands*
hne íth zaene ghymag   *beneath the grey robe*
phain et hys naiaehállys   *of a man without faith*

Original   **High Elyri Translation:**
The kid's sting   *íth aegaenag íth ededhór aelás*
is bitter honey   *ibh nec aeturgaeag*
to a world torn   *sun et k'dhedoc*
by apathy's rage   *phain bhemethag aelás k'stomaeph*
it collapses upon him   *ith phyghóth keh gaeth*
consumes the burning grey sky *thurgag íth thórgae zaene ghymae*

íth aegaenag íth ededhór aelás (the sting the kid possesses) (can also
be the sting the young goat possesses or the poison the kid
possesses…if uses *aegaent* which is poison.) (kid could be
dedhá)

ibh nec aeturgaeag (is bitter honey) (if *nec=nyék* and
aeturgaeag=aeturbhae, the translation could be 'is treason(ous)
betrayal)

sun et k'dhedoc bhíthár (to a World divided/torn) (if *k'dhedoc*
becomes *k'dedhá*, and *bhíthár* becomes *bhithár* the translation
could be 'a priest destroyed'

phain methag aelás k'stómaeph (by rage possessing Apathy) (if
bhemethag is *bhemethán*, and *k'stómaeph* is *k'stómaer*, it could
be 'by the killer with the god symbol)

ith phyghóth keh gaeth (it collapse on him) (if *ith* is *íth*, *phyghóth* is
phyróth, and *keh* is *kóh*, it could read 'the demon with him')

thurgag íth thórgae zaene gymae (consumes the burning sky) (if
thurgag is *thórgae*, *thórgae* is *thurgag*, and *gymae* is *gymag* it
could read 'burns the devouring grey robe')

2nd High Elyri Translation:	Alternative:
Íth aegaent íth dedhá aelás	The poison the priest possesses
ibh nyek aeturbhae	is treasonous betrayal
sun et k'dedhá bhithár	a priest destroyed
phain bhemethán k'stómaer	by the killer with the symbol of god;
íth phyróth kóh	the demon with him
thórgae íth thurgag zaene gymag	burns the devouring grey robe

Pronunciation of Elyri Names

Aleski (ăl-ĔSH-kē)
Alyná (ă-LĒ-nä)
Ámállá (ä-MÄ-lä)
Ártur (är-TŪR)
Bhendhámyn (věn-JÄ-mēn)
Bhílári (vĭ-LÄR-ē)
Bhílycá (VĬL-lē-kä)
Bhín Króel (vĭn krō-ĔL)
Bhíncári (vĭn-CÄ-rē)
Bhríd (vrĭd)
Bhryell (bhrē-ĔL)
Bhyrhán (VĒR hän)
Bhyrínt (vēr-ĬNT)
Cáner (KÄ-nyär)
Chethá (CHĔ-thä)
Cíbhóló (kĭ-VŌ-lō)
Clarys (klär-ĒSH)
Cliáth (klē-ÄTH)
Dhágdhuán (JÄ-zhū-än)
Dháná (JÄ-nä)
Dhóri (JŌR-ē)
Dórímyr (DŌR-ĭ-mēr)
Éllés (ŭ-lŭsh)
Elyri (ě-LĒR-ē)
Elyriá (ě-LĒR-ē-ä)
Gaelán (GWÄ-län)
Hwensen (HWĔN-shěn)
Káliel (kä-LĒ-ěl)
Kavan (KĂ-văn) (in Elyri his
    name is spelt Kabhan)
Khwílen Kesábhá (KHWĬL-ěn
    kěsh-ä-vä)
Kílyn (kĭ-LĒN)
Kluín (KLŪ-ĭn)
Kóráhm di Curnydhá (KŌR-
    äm DĒ kūr-NĒ-jä)
Lláhy (LÄ-hē)
Lláná (LÄ-nä)

Llucás (LŪ käsh)
Llyr (lēr)
MacLyr (mäk-LĒR)
Mórne (MŌR-nyä)
Níkóá (nĭ-KŌ-ä)
Nuryé (NŌR-yŭ)
Raenár Magk (RÄ-när mäk)
Sámel (SHÄ-měl)
Sen (shěn)
Sóbhán (shō-VÄN)
Syán Króel (SHEE-ahn kroh-
    EHL)
Syl (shēl)
Sylyhá (shē-LĒ-hä)
Tám (täm)
Tíbhyan (TĬ-vē-ăn)
Tumm (tūm)
Tusánt (tū-SHÄNT)
Ylár (Ē-lär)
Zythán (ZĒ-thän)

The Five Sovereignties - City Legend

Enesfel	Cordash	Elyria
1-*Rhidam	1-*Aralt	1-Clarys
2-Alberni	2-Anzet	2- Ánásair
3-Bryn	3-Ediug	3-Bhastyán
4-Chantel	4-Eleva	4-Bhórdh
5-Dorshur	5-Jassett	5-Bhryell
6-Durham	6-Kakkoris	6-Cármycá
7-Erleta	7-Korr	7-Cylleá
8-Jardin	8-Liatti	8-Dhánthes
9-Kamin	9-Lindumn	9-Ibhórys
10-Kilmacud	10-Matina	10-Káská
11-Levonne	11-Pesek	11-Khwíncanon
12-Nelori	12-Sebring	12-Rísóri
13-Seres	13-Trallan	13-Sábhóne
14-Talladegah	14-Verbier	14-Sídhári
15-Tarsee	15-Vioe	15-Turyn
16-Theron	16-Vron	
17-Wexel	17-Wynett	

Hatu	Neth	Káliel
1-*Natrona	1-*Glevum	1-*Káliel
2-Avarrou	2-Fiara	2-Jaffe
3-Cran Ufa	3-Gorea	3-Mara Qin
4-Drisoge	4-Mawr	4-Pháne
5-Enda	5-Nogero	5-Shola
6-Fa Ruqi	6-Pravek	
7-Furr Katio	7-Ruidoso	
8-Kílyn	8-Venago	
9-Palil		
10-Wasilla		
11-Yd Haszafni		

The Five Sovereignties

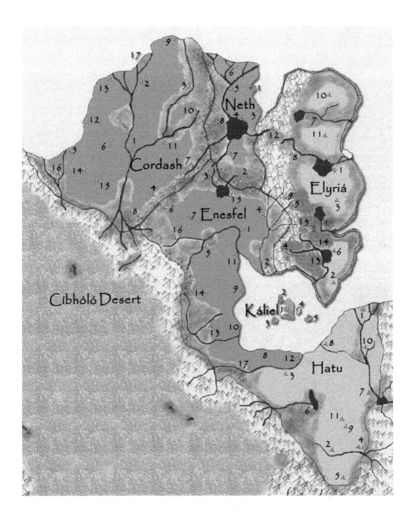

About the Author

With fantasy and sci-fi as her passions, Tamara has written multiple novels to date, including the first four books of the Kestrel Harper Saga, the first installment of The Scarecrow Trials, and the stand-alone novel Suspicion's Gate. Bleed the Earth is the second book in the Blood Wild Chronicles.

When not indulging in her love of words, Tamara relaxes in the company of her pack of Papillions, her horde of cats, and an ever-growing collection of films.

Learn more about Tamara's work at www.agdhani.com

White Pagan
Kestrel Harper Saga Book 6
(excerpt)

With no agenda or intention to his escape, the white kestrel had flown for hours across the vastness of sky until the first traces of dawn began to creep above the Llaethlágárá to the east. As was true so often of late, the sky had been clean of clouds, its blanket of stars spread in all directions, the pinpoints of light now snuffing out as daylight overtook each one and swallowed it. There was no surprise that his instincts brought him to the lakeside grove he had discovered as a child and had visited often throughout his life. It had been a long time since he had been here, responsibilities, duties, and his contentment in what he had been given gave him no cause to stray far from Alberni. But the quest to appease his troubled spirit this night invariably brought him here.

A figure lying in the shade of the trees, appearing to have crawled from the lake and collapsed, was invading his refuge, making him wary as he arrived with the intent of a swim and a short period of rest. He made several circles of the shrinking lake, seeking danger or a trap, but sensing none, he swooped down into the cover of parched forest. What emerged cautiously from it, however, was no kestrel, but a man who wore the same clothing as he had worn during the coronation feast the night before. No ghost, though some might think him such with his white skin and silver-white hair, he cautiously approached the twisted form. Piercing eyes quickly read the scene, the lack of trampled autumn grass that suggested she had neither wandered here nor been brought and deposited here by whoever her attackers had been.

No, he deduced as he knelt beside the woman dressed in a delicate gown of pale blue, what had brought her here had been a great surge of energy, maybe the very same surge he had experienced the night before which had drained him completely of power. There was strong residual energy throbbing in the ground beneath her, as though a Gate had opened and then closed again, though he knew there had never been a Gate in this clearing. When he reached for her, touching her arm to roll her towards him to learn if she lived, he gasped, his grasp tightening on her shoulder, and opened his mouth to take in the breath he now struggled for.

She was power. Raw, largely unfocused, virgin power underutilized, contained within a shell, behind a face, that he recognized though he had forgotten her until now.

They had never met, but once, long ago, the Sight had shown him a series of glimpses into this moment, a woman by his lake, a woman with the reddest of hair he had ever seen, a woman with Orynn's eyes though not Orynn. Kavan could not claim her to be distant kin to the woman he had loved, could not claim her to be his own unmet daughter for this woman, badly bruised and beaten as she was, was older than Dhóri by many years. Twice as old, perhaps.

Though her power lacked training and containment, he knew her to be Elyri.

Her shallow breathing felt warm upon his hand, making him shiver as he sought signs of life. There were dark splotches across her face, a split lip and abrasions upon her cheeks, a gash over her brow that left its red trail of blood down her skin to kiss her swollen eye. She needed medical attention, perhaps healing, but he was no healer. Of all of the gifts he had been blessed with, healing was not one of them, unless k'Ádhá granted a miracle. But he felt none of the familiar signs that tended to precipitate a miraculous event. Given the state of her injuries and the tears in her unfamiliar gown, he was afraid to move her, afraid he might cause more harm, but he could not leave her alone here while he sought help. His only option was the one he took. Reaching within himself and across the miles, he called to the one person he knew best whom he could rely upon for help. Contact made, request given, he pulled off his tunic, ripping it down the front so that it was big enough to cover her upper body and shoulders, he set about building a fire to stave off the morning chill and provide her warmth.

He would not leave her alone, no matter how uncomfortable she made him. He had forgotten those visions, had forgotten the feeling of panic experienced with those short bits of Sight, and yet now here she was, after so many years, someone he felt certain held the ability to turn his existence upside down. A woman this beautiful, this strong of power, could do nothing else.

.

CPSIA information can be obtained
at www.ICGtesting.com
Printed in the USA
BVHW060551300321
603656BV00001B/8